THE DIAMOND KING

THE
DIAMOND
KING

A Tale of Love, Hate, and Diamonds

V. KAHANY

diamond (*adámas,* Greek)—unbreakable

PLAYLIST

We Will Rock You—why mona
Residue—Benjamin Clementine
The End (Stripped with Strings)—JPOLND, Pan dö Baré, Chess Theory
Smoke And Mirrors—Gotye
A Dangerous Thing—AURORA
Bird On A Wire—Sarah Blasko
Fate (feat. Amber Mark)—John Legend, Amber Mark
Aventine—Agnes Obel
Howling at the Moon—D Fine Us, Vigz
Unholy (feat. Kim Petras) - Orchestral Version—Sam Smith, Kim Petras
Piano in the Sky—Winona Oak
Wash.—Bon Iver
Raven—Visiteur
I'm Numbers—Emily Wells
Witchcraft—Vian Izak, Juniper Vale
London—Benjamin Clementine
One—AG, MILCK
Train Wreck—James Arthur
Can't Help Falling In Love - DARK—Tommee Profitt, Brooke

Toxic—2WEI
Rescue—Lauren Daigle
It Never Went Away—Jon Batiste
I Love You, I Hate You—Little Simz

You can find the playlist on Spotify.

1

DRASKO

London, England, May 1892

The Great Bell in the center of London had just chimed three in the afternoon when Drasko Mawr walked out of an obscure building on the corner of 3rd and Blackberry Street.

His scarred face, as always, drew cowardly glances from passersby. His sharp gaze, dark with determination, made them shrivel into themselves.

Many had heard his name, but not many knew his face.

Soon, that would change.

Drasko took a deep drag off the cigarette that hung between his lips and squinted at the sky. A storm was coming.

How fitting.

After today, there would certainly be another scandal. But the game Drasko was involved in was more important. More important, perhaps, than anything he had achieved in his life. Considering that he was the wealthiest diamond miner in the world, that was no small thing.

Twenty of his men followed him, like an army. They were dressed in dark suits with crisp white collars.

Each was prepared for the worst.

Each carried a bag.

The late spring wind howled, tearing at the flaps of their jackets. The heavy dark clouds were about to bring a downpour. The wary passersby parted to let the men through as if they were responsible for the brewing storm.

A crack of thunder broke out through the heavy gray clouds above the city. But Drasko didn't flinch. He clenched his teeth as the building of interest loomed ahead.

Here it comes…

The letter in the inside pocket of his three-piece suit burned through the expensive fabric with a warning of the consequences if he didn't obey. The words echoed in *his* voice, the man long dead who had orchestrated this dangerous game that Drasko was yet to finish.

On May 28th, at precisely fifteen minutes after three in the afternoon, you are to walk into St. John's Church and present Charles Hatchet, the Earl of Weltingdon, with the document that is enclosed within this letter.

The words replayed in Drasko's mind over and over again, every step echoing with the instructions he must execute precisely. Or else…

He was used to these tasks, the simple sentences that affected his life every single time with the precision of a well-oiled machine. The dead man was about to change his life again, in a way Drasko had not seen coming. How could he?

The sight of the church's façade made Drasko flex his gloved hands in spiteful bitterness. Another crack of thunder split the gray sky, about to burst with rain.

He tossed the cigarette away and inhaled the muggy air deeply, his eyes narrowing below his black derby hat.

He was ready. He always was. Yet, one thought nagged at him—with all his wealth, these letters held power over him. Still.

You shall pay with your life.

Today's task made him steel his spine and grind his teeth with the never-fading hate for the man who had given him everything and yet, from his grave, still pulled the strings like a puppet master.

Who was Drasko to blame though? Years ago, he had sealed his fate with his own blood. And this game had to be completed. After all, this would reveal the decades-long secret of the world's rarest jewel—the Crimson Tear diamond.

Six tasks—those were the rules of the game. When it was all done, Drasko would be free to act and live as he pleased.

Yet *this* task was tricky. The bride—*that* little detail—marred it all.

The young woman in the church was undoubtedly part of the twisted game. Or a victim. Or collateral. Drasko already pitied her. And he hated himself for doing this to her.

But this was the legacy—years of work, two decades of twisted lies, lives buried and broken in the diamond-mining regions of India, others tarnished across the world, as if from a shockwave.

In moments like this, *his* words always came to Drasko's mind.

The path of a king is a solitary journey. Wealth is cruel. Love is poison. Compassion is a weakness. World power, however, is worth losing everything else, my boy.

Thunder cracked again above Drasko's head, and the first heavy drops of rain tapped against his hat.

Almost there.

He wove past the dozens of carriages and lackeys that crowded the building entrance. The doormen bowed, opening the doors for him and his men.

And in this last minute, his treacherous heart betrayed him with a heavy thud against his chest. Then a heavier one, threatening to break out of his ribcage. One had to look into the past to understand the present. And Drasko's was etched with losses.

The scent of flowers and burned candles wafted at Drasko from the dark gaping doorway. The scent of innocence about to be ruined. *She* was somewhere inside, and now she was part of the game.

She is yours..., the letter said.

Drasko's men exchanged knowing looks, their jaws setting tight as they opened their bags.

The church was ready for a celebration that Drasko and his men hadn't been invited to.

This wasn't an ordinary day.

Nor was this about to be an ordinary wedding.

Because no men came to a wedding with bags full of guns.

THE KINGS
AND
THE THIEF

The Port of London, England
Twenty years prior, 1872
Drasko, 9 years old

How does a street thief become a king?

On a dark night, in a dingy tavern in the Port of London, two gentlemen were finishing their drinks. The whisky worked its way smoothly into their blood, fueling their latest argument.

"I say, my good brother, a gentleman is not born but cultivated!" said Uriah, the older brother, thirty-five years of age. "There is no such nonsense as blue blood. Why, look where we are!"

The Mawr brothers, Uriah and Alfred, the owners of Mawr Diamond Industries, were better known across the world as the Diamond Kings. Despite their distant relation to French royalty and a fortune they'd amassed in diamond mining in India, the two brothers sat at Ol' Days, a dingy tavern close to the docks from which their ship, *Saint Catalina*, was about to sail off to India.

"See that?" Uriah pointed with his half-full glass at a boy around nine years of age, who was drinking ale at a lone table across the room. "Torn shoes, dirty clothes, thievish glances. He is searching for things to steal. I say he is from the slums but young enough to relearn."

"This must be a joke," responded Alfred, the younger brother, smoothing his mustache with two ringed fingers. He narrowed his eyes on the boy. "You do not truly suppose you can make him a gentleman. He shall never think like one. Nor shall he be like one. He looks like a little monster, truly."

At that, Uriah's gaze darkened.

Though brothers by blood, the two couldn't be more different.

Alfred was handsome and barely thirty years of age, with a flair for expensive things, good whisky, and gambling. He fancied horse races, loud parties, and attention. Reckless and careless with money, he was nevertheless the charming face of Mawr Diamond Industries.

Uriah was older and the true mastermind behind their successful enterprise. But fate hadn't been kind to his appearance. His face was marred with extensive scars from smallpox as a child. Called a "monster" behind his back when young, he'd heard the word too often, a word he'd made peace with.

But right now, he didn't like the sound of it coming from his brother's drunk mouth.

And the word, yet again, made his blood simmer with deeply engraved anger for his reckless brother.

"Don't you know the best fairy tales?" Uriah argued coldly, though bitterness burned him to the core. "A monster usually turns into a charming prince."

Alfred dismissed his words with a wave of his loose glove. "By God, Uriah, you have the silliest ideas. Whatever do you think can change him?" He lit a cigar and exhaled a cloud of smoke at his brother.

"Is that a bet?" Uriah pressed on, accustomed to proving himself right.

"You fancy sending him to a school? Oh, my!"

"I fancy taking him with us."

An amused chuckle escaped Alfred as Uriah retrieved a diamond-studded watch out of his pocket.

"The ship sails in two hours," Uriah said, checking the time.

He rose and walked toward the little fella, who stilled like a possum at the sight of the approaching lord.

The boy's name was Drasko, last name unknown. He was nine years of age—perhaps ten, or eight. The boy himself wasn't certain, nor did he care. What he did care for was that it was raining outside, and as he had no home, and the thieving business was quite poor at night, he needed a place to warm up, perhaps find a corner to sleep in for himself and his friend Zeph, who was also on thieving business at a nearby tavern.

Drasko's shabby patched-up coat was drenched with rain. Water squeaked through the holes of his boots. His trousers and shirt were too big for him—he had stolen the clothes from a drunk passed out on the street. His lucky day!

When a stranger walked up to his table, Drasko shrunk into himself.

He had already appraised the man's expensive suit from afar. But rich men never approached *him*. This was most positively bizarre.

"May I?" the man asked, pointing at the spare chair at the table, and took a seat.

Drasko looked over his shoulder, making sure the fancy lord was indeed addressing him. He looked like one of those lords with a title, the golden chain across his suit jacket thicker than any that Drasko had stolen before. His gloves were made of leather thinner than silk. Drasko knew—he had touched silk once.

"Do you like this?" The lord's eyes followed Drasko's glances at the chain. "Where I am going tonight, there is plenty of gold."

Drasko's ears perked up. "Where's that?"

The lord wiggled his head from side to side. "India."

"Inn-dee-ya," Drasko drawled. He didn't know where that was. "Far?"

"You have to sail on a ship."

Drasko had never been to *Inn-dee-ya* or on a ship.

"But there are better things than gold there," the lord said, his mysterious tone drawing Drasko in like those street magicians.

Drasko smiled and shook his head in disbelief. "There' nothing betta' than gold."

The man raised his eyebrows. "Oh, there is! *New* gold. Shiny. Light like pebbles," he said softer and even more mysteriously, then leaned on the table toward Drasko. "One pebble worth Buckingham Palace."

"Nah!" Drasko's face split into a grin that right away disappeared.

The man looked dangerous, his face dotted with scars, his eyes smiling cunningly—a man in charge, certainly. That gold chain dazzlingly reflected the candlelight.

"Whas' it called?" Drasko asked suspiciously.

The man's lips curled into a peculiar smile as he leaned forward even closer to him across the table and said a word that only Drasko heard. "Diamonds."

Drasko repeated it slowly, tasting the sinister syllables. "Die. Mons." He swallowed hard. "Soun' dangerous."

But he couldn't hide the awe that shone in his eyes brighter than gold nuggets.

The lord cocked a brow. "You don't take risks, you don't drink champagne, young man."

Young man?

No one had ever called Drasko that before. Nor had he ever drunk whatever stuff that rhymed with "pain." Everything that came out of the lord's mouth sounded dangerous but mysterious. There were no mysteries in the slums. And no gold. And no ships.

The lord's eyes were locked with Drasko's, just like that snake he had once seen at a street magic show. A *pie-thon*—a delicious name, really.

Drasko's belly suddenly howled with a loud need for food. He hadn't eaten in two days. But he'd forgotten all about it, for he knew right then and there that if he followed the strange lord, the future would bring more than food or gold. So much more!

"Are you hungry?" the lord inquired as if he were a devil reading Drasko's thoughts.

Drasko nodded timidly, forgetting about the *die-mons* and *some-pain*.

"My name is Uriah Mawr." The man offered his hand for a shake.

Drasko gawked in disbelief. Hesitantly, he wiped his dirty little hand on his soaked trousers and slipped it into the lord's gloved one. He'd touched silk once. Now he'd touched the finest leather. No one had ever looked twice at him, let alone shaken his hand. Until this lord.

"Drasko," he whispered, his little heart thudding loudly, then cleared his throat and, straightening his shoulders, said more confidently, "Drasko," and added, "Sir."

"Very well. Let us get some food in you," said the man. "And afterward, perhaps, you'd like to see my ship."

Drasko nodded absently, high on the thought of food and perhaps some warm place to sleep. He wished Zeph were with him.

He didn't know that he would board *Saint Catalina* that very night and sail across the giant oceans and past exotic lands. It would be six years before he would see the English shore again. But by then, he would be called a monster behind his back, and he would have lost the most important person in his life, the first of many.

Meanwhile, the younger Mawr brother smoked his cigar and observed the unfolding scene with great amusement.

"Madman," he muttered to his brother. "You will lose the bet and ruin the boy."

Little did he know that, twenty years later, the bet would ruin many lives, including his.

3

GRACE

Of course, she was happy!

Grace kept repeating it in her mind, pushing away an unsettling feeling deep down that didn't make sense.

This was the day of her freedom—marrying Charles, the honorable earl. She was going to be a lady. But most importantly, she would be free from her guardians. At twenty years of age, she was finally shaking off the chains that had held her captive for so many years.

"Eden?" she called softly for her maid.

She studied herself in the mirror, fixing her veil as she took in her simple but tasteful bridal gown, the lace covering her slender shoulders and arms, the too-pink blush and too-bright eyes. She had taken a sip of opium to calm herself, but now that she was about to walk out of the small suite in the church dedicated to dressing up, her nerves started tingling for reasons she didn't want to confront. She should be happy, but instead, unease scratched at her heart.

Grace wished Rivka was with her. But her best friend was hiding somewhere among the guests. After the events five years ago, Grace's guardians didn't let Rivka anywhere close to her. The two had been meeting in secret. But of all people, Rivka was the one Grace needed today. Perhaps the only one who cared.

Eden, the maid, smiled in the mirror, peeking from behind her. "You are beautiful, miss! His lordship will be mesmerized!"

"But where's Auntie? It is almost time."

Grace walked hurriedly to the door and swung it open, only to come face to face with Charles, scurrying by in the hallway.

"Oh, dear..." he mumbled with a shocked look on his face as he fixed his tie.

"Charles?" Grace winced at the sight of her groom with his hair slightly disheveled and a blush creeping up his cheeks. That familiar floral scent so out of place wafted off him. It wasn't hers or his, though she knew very well who it belonged to.

"It is..." *bad luck to see your groom before the ceremony.*

"Grace! Here you are," he mumbled, his Adam's apple bobbing as he swallowed hard.

The stomping of feet down the hall made their heads turn.

Grace frowned at the sight of the men following her aunt and uncle, who were her legal guardians.

Their faces were blank masks. Uncle sucked in his cheeks as he approached. "I'm afraid there is an important matter to discuss."

The four men in dark suits who accompanied them were strangers, out of place on a day like this. But only one immediately drew Grace's attention.

Him.

She felt a skip in her chest at the sight.

He was an intimidating man, though not a day older than thirty years of age. Grace had seen him before. It was impossible not to recognize those striking green eyes that had unnerved her the several times she had seen him at her concerts. And the scars. The four symmetrical lines across the right side of his face made his handsome features somewhat brutal.

He was taller than everyone, his shoulders wide. His expensive three-piece suit hugged his impressive body perfectly. His presence filled the hallway, making everyone else seem too small.

But his sharp gaze wasn't kind.

That gaze didn't bring good news.

That gaze was trouble.

Drasko Mawr, the Diamond King, the richest man in London —Grace remembered the newspaper headlines.

What was he doing here?

His face was expressionless, but those eyes—oh, they said so much that remained silent, none of it good.

Her insides twisted with a sudden instinct—*run*. Unable to look away from him, Grace found herself stumbling backward, tripping on the hem of her bridal gown, into the dressing room, her heart pounding loudly—thud, thud, thud.

"What is happening?" Charles's voice was slightly angry but unusually submissive as everyone crowded the room.

Something was so very wrong. No business was more important than the ceremony that was about to happen with a church full of waiting guests.

Without a word, the tall man reached inside his suit and produced papers.

Frozen in trepidation, Grace watched as one document was handed to Charles and another to her uncle. The other three men stood with their hands clasped in front of them.

The man in charge took off his derby hat, set it on the table, and, leaning back against it with casual slowness, pulled a cigarette out of his cigarette case.

"May I?" he asked, flicking his eyes at Grace, of all people.

He stood just a little away from Grace yet seemed giant. The musty scent of cologne and tobacco tickled her nostrils. Everything about him—his suit, the gold chain across his vest, the rings on his fingers—screamed wealth. Yet his skin was weathered from the sun, a tone darker than everyone's. His green gaze was so intense that it kept her hostage. His facial scars were so pronounced that they gave his handsome features a brutal edge.

She nodded absently.

The match he lit was like a splinter in his big hand. Its hissing made her flinch. Yet, she didn't utter a word. No one did, as if the mere presence of the man sucked the air out of the room.

"Oh, God," Charles exhaled loudly, clutching his hair while reading the document.

The stranger took a drag off his cigarette and exhaled leisurely in Charles's direction.

"Why now? Why today?" Charles's gaze snapped to the man.

"That was the agreement." His voice, low yet assertive, rumbled through every cell of Grace's body. "It could have been any day. Anything could have been the collateral. I merely follow the instructions." He handed the pen to Charles. "You do have a choice. Not signing the paper is one of them. In that case, my men and I shall leave. But as we all know, that will be a big loss on your part."

"What is he talking about?" Grace asked but was ignored.

With irritation, Charles snatched the pen out of the man's hand. "This is unspeakable. This wasn't... Ugh."

He signed angrily, then pushed the document to the man.

"Charles?" Grace repeated and was ignored, yet again.

Her uncle signed his paper, too, and handed it to the man, who folded it carefully and tucked it inside his jacket as the cigarette burned between his lips, smoke curling around his face.

Uncle finally met Grace's eyes. Aunt fidgeted with her fingers, averting hers.

"Dear," Uncle said to Grace, "I'm afraid your marriage to Charles is no longer possible."

If Grace wasn't so bewildered, she'd laugh. The words didn't make sense.

Charles moved first, walked up to her, and took her hands in his. "My love, I am so sorry, so awfully sorry for what is happening. I—"

"This is some sort of misunderstanding, is it not, Charles?"

Grace asked with a nervous chuckle, refusing to accept what he was saying.

"It is not. And there can be no other way. You are... You deserve better than me. And you don't deserve what is happening. But we cannot be married. Not now. Not ever."

He dropped her hands abruptly and nervously raked his fingers through his hair. "My apologies," he said and rushed out the door.

Loud sounds wafted in from the hallway—male voices, commanding and authoritative, a commotion, collective steps, screams.

But none of it shocked Grace as much as the sight of her fiancé disappearing into the hall.

Blood pounded in her ears. The room suddenly swirled around her. The ground roiled under her feet.

This cannot be.

"Uncle? Auntie?" She slowly turned to face her aunt. "What is going on?"

And there it was again, the familiar coldness in her guardians, the way they always were with her, controlling and apathetic as if she were a burden.

"I am afraid that certain circumstances have transpired within the last hour," Uncle said calmly, glancing at the tall stranger, who put out his cigarette and straightened up.

"What circumstances?" Grace asked, knowing she had never had a say in her own fate, except marrying Charles. *Look how that turned out.* "How can Charles walk out on me? What could this—"

Uncle's hand on her shoulder silenced her. "The circumstances are out of our hands but were agreed upon a long time ago."

"Agreed upon by whom?" Grace asked louder, unable to hide her despair.

"Child," he said coldly. "You are not marrying Charles today. Or ever. I am sorry. This was supposed to be a special day, but there are larger forces at play. And"—he cleared his throat as if with difficulty—"you are not getting married today. That's just it."

"But she is," a low deep voice corrected him. *His.*

The bizarre statement made Grace whip around to face him.

The stranger's eyes were on her again, that intense green gaze that made her knees buckle when he said, "She is marrying *me.*"

4

GRACE

Grace chuckled nervously as she stared at the man in disbelief.

"I apologize for not introducing myself," he said so casually it enraged her. He stepped closer and offered his hand. "Drasko Mawr."

She looked at his big, gloved hand—she would *not* shake it—then raised her eyes at him, trying to pin all her anger into her stare.

She wasn't striking some ridiculous deal. She wasn't selling herself like Charles had just done, or whatever had just happened.

This was nonsense, some sick joke. Grace wanted to fight. Or scream. Yet it wouldn't change a thing, she knew.

This was supposed to be her perfect day. *She* was supposed to be perfect. She was a piano prodigy, famous in London. She had been groomed by her guardians to be the epitome of perfection. She always followed the strict set of rules enforced by them. Even Charles—oh, her perfect Charles—had been introduced to her by her guardians. As if chosen. He was supposed to be her ticket to freedom. Yet, her guardians hadn't said a word when he walked out on her.

For the first time, Grace was witnessing her uncle and aunt comply with someone else's orders.

His.

It scared her, kept her frozen in place. But she wanted an explanation.

Lifting her chin in defiance, Grace shook her head at the stranger. "Is this some sort of joke?"

Keeping his intense eyes on her, he slowly withdrew his hand.

"I have funds," she said as confidently as she could, then slowly tugged her bridal veil off and carelessly dropped it on the floor. "I don't need to marry some diamond thug who barges in—"

"You do not," Uncle's voice cut in, "have funds," he added quieter.

Her mouth fell open in shock.

"I am afraid you don't have funds, dear," he said coldly.

"Impossible," she whispered, perplexed.

A lump in her throat made it hard to breathe. Tears stung her eyes. Any other time, be it a concert, a ball, or anywhere else in public, where her aunt and uncle watched her like hawks, she would put on her best face and smile.

Not today. Her marriage to Charles had been her only chance at freedom, and she had just lost it.

"If you do not agree to this deal," the stranger said, making her turn toward him, "you might end up on the street, Miss Grace."

The words twisted in her stomach.

How dare he?

"The truth is, you simply don't have a choice." The chill in his voice made shivers run down her spine. He took a step toward her as if approaching his prey. "If it is any consolation, neither do I. But this marriage has to happen."

A tiny sob shook her chest. Tears blurred her vision. She needed a sip of opium to calm down, fall asleep, wake up, and find this was all a bad dream. She contemplated pulling out the vial, tucked under her corset, and downing it all.

She tried to count in her mind—a trick she often used to calm herself in stressful moments.

She tried humming—her remedy for clearing her mind.

It usually helped. But there was no remedy for betrayal and defeat.

"This is a farce," Grace snapped, not realizing that tears had started rolling down her cheeks. "I cannot marry a stranger, not you, not anyone." She closed her eyes and took a deep breath.

The room was spinning around her, the whole world was, and so was her life. An eerie silence fell around her.

They all stared at her. *He*—coldly, without interest. His men —bored. Her guardians—indifferently.

"Traitors," she whispered, for the first time daring to speak her mind.

They were handing her off to a stranger. Oh, the joke! Grace didn't have relatives, nor did she have friends besides Rivka. Nowhere to go. Nowhere to run.

No funds.

Clutching the folds of her dress, she stood in a stupor, wanting to run to the London bridge and jump off.

He was the first one to move.

Slowly, the man bent down to pick up her veil from the floor. Grace flinched as he fixed the veil to her head as if she were a doll. He smoothed the translucent fabric, and when he muttered, "Perfect," she finally raised her teary eyes at him and met his gaze, so calm, unlike her.

A silent beat passed between them, and she thought she saw something else in those cold greens—a hesitation? Beautiful eyes, she had to admit, his face above her so close that she could see his scars, his clean-shaven jaw, his full lips, pressed tightly, *too* tightly for a man who seemingly didn't care. That cold stare was back again.

He was intimidating. No, no, petrifying! Larger than life! Taking charge of hers!

Just then, his lips curled into a smirk. "I detest this no less than you do, Miss Grace," he said. "Shall we?"

He didn't move, didn't point at the door and the hallway behind it, the hall full of guests waiting and the priest ready to seal this holy union.

Grace didn't ask what would happen afterward, where she would go, where *they* would go, her and her soon-to-be husband.

She was being sold, traded off for something more valuable, perhaps.

Wiping her wet cheeks with the back of her hand, she blinked and blinked, but the tears were still coming. She bravely lifted her chin and walked through the door.

After all, she had always been alone. She'd always known that happiness wasn't in her cards.

This? She would figure it out. She would talk sense into her guardians. She would hire a lawyer. She would make this disappear. She would *find* her goddamn funds.

But for now, she would play along. The priest might refuse the service. The guests would certainly raise hell. *You just wait!*

Grace stomped toward the main hall, not waiting for her uncle to lead her. If they wanted a spectacle, she would give them one and show everyone that this was simply—

She halted in shock when she stepped into the church hall.

The guests were gone…

The footsteps following her echoed through the desolate space, decorated with garlands and hundreds of lit candles. But the only ones in the hall were several dozen men in dark suits, watching her slowly step down the aisle. *His* men, she realized.

Her gaze frantically scanned the otherwise empty hall and stopped on the lone person at the back corner of the church.

Rivka…

The young woman stood in the shadows, like she was

supposed to, hiding from Grace's guardians. She had snuck in to witness Grace's happiest moment. Except now, her best friend was witnessing Grace's defeat.

Oh, Rivka…

Did Rivka know? She must have. Her "sight of the devil" was rumored about in many parts of London. Yet, she hadn't warned Grace of this disaster.

Tears burned Grace's eyes. She looked over her shoulder and saw *him*. Like a devil himself, his tall broad figure crowded the doorway, his cold gaze on her.

On shaky legs, Grace continued toward the altar.

Come what may be.

The old priest only nodded with an apologetic smile.

So, he is in on it.

"Are you all right, my child?" he asked.

No.

She felt a shift of air behind her. *He* stood next to her, like a monstrous shadow.

Drasko Mawr—the name she already despised, the man she already hated.

The priest read the official speech as Grace stood in stupor. Prompted, she faced the man she was about to marry. Her heart boomed as she met his icy green eyes.

He said the vows, his voice chillingly cold.

Her head dizzy, Grace repeated hers, not looking away from him.

He took her hand, took off her glove. Blinking down, Grace found a simple gold band around her finger. No diamond, though he was a diamond miner.

Would he want consummation? Not a chance! Children? She would not be used!

"You may now kiss your wife," the priest said.

Wife. Grace was a *wife*. To whom? To the stranger who stared at her with indifference, his much larger muscular body too close for her liking as he leaned over, his lips barely brushing her cheek in a kiss.

The brief touch made her chest tighten. A foreign scent hit her nostrils. Her lungs took it in, igniting a flood of familiar images in her mind. She liked the scent, but her mind screamed in rebellion. She was his, as per the law, and not a single person in this world could do anything about it.

"Welcome to your new life," he said coldly, adding, "wife."

Wife...

Absently, Grace brushed her trembling fingers over the wedding ring, the feeling so anticipated and now hateful. Her hand slid to the hem of her corset where the vial of opium was hidden.

The thought of spending a night with this stranger petrified her. She was Grace Sommerville, the prodigy pianist, one of the most celebrated musicians in London.

No, no, she would not give up this easily.

She thought of drinking the tincture herself. But no, she wasn't a coward. She'd agreed to this marriage, but that was it.

If this was some sick game, she would play along by *her* rules.

Tonight, she would rebel.

Tonight, she would drug this man and fake the consummation.

5

DRASKO

The carriage moved slowly through crowded Piccadilly. Too slow for Drasko's patience, though he didn't show it.

She sat right next to him. Grace Sommerville, the famous piano virtuoso, was now Mrs. Mawr.

Drasko didn't look at her, didn't move, didn't light a cigarette though he craved one, and a stiff drink as well.

The newspapers called Drasko the Diamond King, yet this brazen thing called him the diamond thug.

Fierce, he had to admit. But he hadn't expected anything different from her.

Drasko had a fucking wife, *her*, of all people. Incomprehensible, really, but nothing ever prepared him for the tasks of the dead man who had had his own plans in mind.

Drasko had a bad feeling about her. She absolutely could not become important, not to him, not in any foreseeable future. Because then history would repeat itself. It couldn't. Drasko was cursed, and she did not deserve to bear the consequences.

Yet here she was.

Two tasks had been accomplished. Now this third one.

Fuck Uriah Mawr.

If the man hadn't been dead, Drasko would have strangled him with his bare hands.

But then again, Drasko had agreed to this, hadn't he?

As per the bet with his brother, Uriah Mawr had taught Drasko everything he knew, made him a gentleman, slowly drawn him into his twisted games, and then got himself killed.

And yet, the dead man still executed his game from the grave. Drasko played along, curious about where it would lead.

Until Grace Sommerville had entered the picture. She was here, in the carriage, going to his house, to stay there... for good.

She was shivering, and he clenched his jaw at the fact that he felt bad for her. Only a short time ago, he had wished her to be ruined. Look at him now!

With a pang of irritation, he took off his suit jacket and slung it over her shoulders, carelessly and roughly as to not give away his gentleman-like intention.

She didn't say a word, kept staring out the window.

Spoiled.

She was a mere pawn in this game. Her role was yet to be determined. Drasko was puzzled as to why Uriah had chosen her. He couldn't have known what Miss Grace was, the self-conceited person who chased fame and wealth and, yes, surprise-surprise, an earl, the pathetic Charles Hatchet who was less of a man than a rag doll.

Drasko clasped his gloved hands, staring at the black leather and wishing he could rewind time, go back to the day he'd agreed to this, the day that had taken away his freedom that he would get back soon.

Very soon. Three more tasks to complete.

Six in total, and he would be free.

Her closeness was unbearable: that was now a fact. She was exquisite in her angry helplessness. Not a hair out of place, pristine and polished, graceful posture as if she were posing for a portrait. Her gloved hand rubbed her forearm through the fabrics, back and forth, like a meditation.

No tears anymore, though. *How strange.* Rather, her gaze was detached. There was something odd about how quickly she had submitted to this deal. But she was a vain creature, and she would act on this marriage. After all, she was a professional performer. *Exquisite*, as per the newspapers.

Simmering in angst, Drasko rubbed the ring on his thumb through the leather of his gloves until the carriage halted. The guards opened the massive gates to his home, and the carriage pulled up to the fountain.

The carriage door opened to let him out. He held his hand out to her. She didn't take it as she got out but studied the house, a newly built two-story mansion with an exotic greenhouse in the back.

Drasko didn't need all this opulence, but he had several such houses in London, one in France, and villas in India. And he certainly hadn't planned on a wife when he acquired the property several years ago.

Her face was pale, her cheeks puffy from dried tears. But she was still pretty. Half an hour married, and already he couldn't stop looking at her. He took in her delicate features, then moved to her lips, full and the prettiest shade of coral. He had seen her numerous times in the last few years. Now she was twenty, more beautiful than ever and *his*.

"Are you keeping me outside?" she asked, her chest shaking in a tiny snort as she caught him staring. Her eyebrows lifted. "Will you show your *wife*," it was impossible to miss the bitterness at the word, "where she will reside from now on?"

She was half an hour of tears and sobs out of the church but already demanding.

And Drasko was already enchanted. A beautiful woman, with hazel eyes, framed with thick black lashes that seemed to reach her brows. Not a sign of fear in them, just anger and nervousness. He saw the way she tried to project confidence yet flinched barely noticeably at his every movement—*barely*—but Drasko had learned to notice everything, read people like books.

She? She was pure talent wrapped in pretty looks, a newspaper headline, *The Virtuoso Pianist Who Continues to Stun London!*

Drasko enjoyed good music and despised self-conceited women. Yet every time he watched her play, she drew him in like some wicked spell.

The rain that was about to break out hours ago had cleared, the clouds still heavy, the wind still playful.

But Drasko felt hot, burned from the inside. Because *she* was standing at the steps of his house, and he wasn't certain how it truly made him feel.

"Welcome to your new home," he said.

He offered his elbow for her to hold on to, but she didn't spare him even a glance, only turned on her heel and walked toward the entrance.

Fine. He was fine. She would learn. She would understand that he didn't want this any more than she did.

Yet his chest tightened with regret at the sight of her—her slender figure, so small and vulnerable, the white dress, the hem of it muddied as it dragged on the ground, his black jacket like a mourning cape over her shoulders, her veil flapping in the wind.

She looked like a fallen angel. And he followed her to his own house, *their* house, a room adjoined his master bedroom already waiting for her.

The tingling of the tiger tattoo, Rakshasa, on his back made him shift his shoulders. That tattoo was the ghost of his past, haunting him in his present, talking to him like a live creature, especially in moments of tension.

And Rakshasa was chuckling.

Be quiet.

The dozen servants lined up at the entrance looked expectant as Grace confidently strode through the door.

Narayan, Drasko's chef, bowed. His bushy black mustache playfully wiggled over a cheerful white smile.

Samira, the head maid, pursed her lips and adjusted her *sari*.

His wife's eyes widened at the sight of the traditional Indian dresses, and Samira smiled at her new mistress and bowed with her hands pressed together to her chest as if in a prayer.

What in the devil was Samira happy about?

Drasko didn't have time for this marriage nonsense. He had a diamond empire to handle. When this wicked game was over, he would head back to India, and his wife would stay here, for years, doing whatever she chose to do. Two days ago, his life was perfectly on course, and now, now—

"My room?" His new wife's sweet voice irritated him like salt in a wound. She stood in the middle of the hall and defiantly stared at him.

Samira smiled broadly at her. "May I show you around, madam?" She turned to catch Drasko's eyes and mouthed in Hindi, "*Sundar.*" Beautiful. "*Raani jesi.*" Like a queen.

Drasko didn't need a queen.

The warning voice of the dead man echoed in his mind:

The path of a king is a solitary one.

6

DRASKO

Such was the brutal machine of wealth and power—it needed sacrifices. This was all part of a plan, a game orchestrated by a vicious heartless man who, for decades, had sold and traded people's lives like his diamonds.

Considering the strange day, Drasko had to remind himself of why he was here, with all this wealth, with *her*.

He was cordial at dinner, despite the fact that Grace Sommerville—*correction, Mrs. Mawr*—had changed into a different dress, a black one, like she was at a funeral.

She requested wine. Getting drunk was certainly a way to ease the tension. Her haughtiness was gone, and she asked questions about the house. Her voice was timid yet determined. Curious yet cold. It did not make sense and puzzled him.

"Your house is quite a masterpiece," she said.

It was. But he had asked Samira to pay special attention to arranging the new bedroom. Rose silk and plush carpets, fresh flowers and a floor-to-ceiling vanity mirror. There was a beautiful parlor with sensual paintings and lavender furniture. Despite his somber mood about what was happening, he hoped his wife was comfortable. Considering the circumstances and her naïveté about what was transpiring, she was doing quite well.

"Your maid gave me a tour," she said, taking slow sips of wine. "A library, bathing chambers, indoor plumbing, electricity, a greenhouse, an office, a library"—she glanced up at him—"all for you alone?"

He tried to make sense of her newly adopted polite attitude. "You and *me*, yes."

"I see. You have a music room"—she smiled into her wine glass—"with plenty of exotic instruments but no piano."

He did not respond, waiting for her to brag about her musical vocation and request a piano.

She did not.

"Perhaps, we should talk," she said after dinner.

Yes, they had to. And she was the first one to ask. Surprising, really, but even then, it didn't raise Drasko's suspicion.

"Whisky? Is that what you drink?" she asked too eagerly when they settled in the drawing room. When he nodded, she offered to pour him one.

She *was* learning. *Pretending*. But that was all right with Drasko. Except the intensity in her eyes was different from this afternoon. Her politeness wasn't genuine. Nor was her readiness to oblige.

"You don't need to serve me. I don't ask that of you," he said, noticing her quick smirk at the word "serve."

She stiffened as she passed him the drink—a minuscule movement that didn't escape him. Yet, he couldn't make sense of it.

"I assume that we shall work out what you expect of me," she said.

"And what you expect of me in return," he countered.

"I don't have expectations. But I would like privacy and freedom."

"Ambitious. So, you do have demands."

"Rules, I suppose. I did not ask for this. You, on the other hand, have a certain interest in this union, which puzzles me. I know who you are, or at least I have heard of you."

She took a brave sip of wine from her glass.

He took a gulp of whisky, amused by her sudden business-like manner.

"You have money, Mr. Mawr. You can afford to provide for me. And that wealth of yours—"

Wealth of yours—she certainly knew her way with words.

"—somehow depends on this union." She met his eyes and cocked her head. "Am I correct?"

Clever.

"My wealth comes from diamond mining in India." He took a sip of the whisky she brought him, then another, suddenly thirsty and surprisingly uneasy at being alone with her. "Surely, you've heard of it. But you are right, other things depend on this union, or the fact that it needed to happen."

"Oh?" She lit up with mild delight. "So, you need it on paper only? We are done, then?"

The words made his jaw tighten.

She was too quick, too arrogant, too confident, and he didn't like it a bit, considering she was his wife and now in his care.

"We are positively *not* done," he said with a smile. "The way I see it, you need it more than I, considering you don't have a penny to your name. Darling," he added just to throw oil into the fire.

A dangerous spark flickered in her eyes at the last word.

Darling... He liked the sound of it. She didn't. *Good.* Her eyes were even more beautiful with that haughty sparkle in them. He enjoyed seeing her unraveled, nervous, irritated. By God! Anything that knocked off the invisible crown she wore at her piano performances.

She rose abruptly and walked to the sideboard.

Drasko caught himself staring and peeled his gaze away from her, gulping the rest of the whisky in his glass.

"There," he heard her say, her footsteps approaching, and met her defiant gaze as she halted in front of him with that brazen smile again.

Mischief flickered in her eyes—*why?*—as she batted her impossibly long black eyelashes and—*interesting*—handed him another drink.

She clinked her glass against his. "Cheers!" Then she took a big gulp out of it and almost choked.

He chuckled, taking a generous swig of his drink, though the whisky tasted too bitter tonight.

"I have a suggestion," she said suddenly, too cheerfully, and turned her expectant gaze to him.

What Drasko didn't expect was his wife to take a seat next to him on the sofa.

Her perfume tickled his nose, the scent of hair powder so exquisite it filled his head. The room felt too hot.

Drasko loosened his tie. He was too tipsy. Only two drinks and he felt like he had drunk a bottle after a sleepless week. Something was wrong, and it wasn't the untimely feeling of languid pleasure spreading through his body at her nearness, though she had an effect on him, he admitted. Her eyes were too bright, like stars.

"What is the suggestion, may I ask?" he heard himself say, his voice unusually low.

"Regarding the marital duties," she said in a voice strangely distant.

"Despite this marriage being on paper only, the duties are part of the deal." He didn't necessarily intend to act on it but was curious about her reaction.

"I see." Her eyes flashed with defiance.

Oh, he wanted to yank her toward him and kiss her, those lips that would inevitably belong to him, one day, *someday*, if only to punish her for what she was and what she'd said to him once, though she probably didn't remember.

He shook his head, trying to get rid of the unusual haze in his head. He said something else and didn't understand the meaning of his own words, his mouth dry. Another gulp of whisky didn't help, so he chugged the rest and shook his head again to rid himself of the dizziness.

"I suggest we do it once," her distant voice said, "and get it over with. Surely, neither you nor I want to—"

Her voice trailed off—something about the consummation, about the heirs. But Drasko kept thinking about her sensual lips, her talented slender fingers, the way she cocked her head as if checking on him, how close she was, how much closer he wanted her.

The drink in his hand was empty. Two, he had had two, though he wasn't sure anymore. Time was too slow. He was drunk. No, not drunk—he was falling. Falling, falling, falling. And he knew that feeling, knew it wasn't whisky or his tiredness.

"Mr. Mawr?" She moved closer, too daring for their first evening together.

It didn't make sense. Neither did the room swimming before his eyes.

"Another drink?" she asked, sweetly but with a hint of surprising danger.

And then he sank into darkness.

THE BRIDE

Andhra Pradesh, India
Drasko, 9-10

And off to India!

It was a long three-month journey, but *Saint Catalina* sailed well and provided the Mawr brothers with lavish accommodations that included a library, a music room, a jewelry workshop, and multiple offices.

Drasko was adjusting nicely, occasionally stealing food from the ship kitchen, afraid he would not have enough. The little thief was given a wash, a haircut, and new clothes. He snuck around the ship like it was a new country to explore, tailed Uriah everywhere, asked questions, smiled politely, yet always kept a knife in his pocket.

It humored Uriah.

"I shall prove you wrong," Alfred, his brother, mused at dinner, observing the boy who had no manners and acted more like a stray dog.

"I shall let you do no such thing," Uriah countered confidently, right away showing the boy how to use utensils, if only to aggravate his brother.

You see, during this trip, there was the sweetest addition to their company—Dr. Lewis. More precisely, his pretty daughter, Clara, who was eighteen years of age.

Naturally, Uriah wouldn't let his brother win any bets or arguments. Even more so, when such conversations at dinners were held in the presence of Clara Lewis, the reason for Uriah's fast-beating heart.

"Carbon is black and unimpressive," Uriah would say proudly to his brother. "And yet, it morphs into the most beautiful stones on earth, diamonds."

This comparison, of course, was intended at Drasko, who did not care about beautiful things but marveled at the abundance of food.

Clara Lewis clasped her hands in delight at such words. And Uriah's heart fluttered at the sight of her.

Nothing tarnished his growing affection. Not the seasickness he'd gotten used to. Not the storm that damaged *Saint Catalina* in the Arabian Sea. Not the death of six crew members from typhus. Not even Clara's loud laughter at his brother's silly jokes. For when Uriah was alone with her, drinking coffee at dinner on the upper deck, with the romantic lantern light and the infinite ocean around them, her lovely voice made him swell with happiness.

"You are such an impressive man. Will you tell me more about your diamonds, Mr. Mawr?"

"Uriah," he corrected her every time, his heart howling at the moon when she blushed so sweetly.

Uriah could read the signs. Clara's loud laughter with Alfred was simply courteous admiration, whereas her blushes and stolen glances at Uriah were a sign that she was as wild for him as he was for her.

Of that, Uriah was certain. Rarely was he wrong.

She would be his, he decided on that trip, envisioning a happy family, their children loving their kind mother and admiring their ambitious father, following in his footsteps and growing their diamond empire.

When they reached the Indian shore, Uriah was set on revealing a secret that no person in the world besides his brother knew—the Crimson Tear.

They had harbored the secret for some time, the diamond the size of a walnut, the rarest shade of red. Neither the Princie Diamond, nor the Koh-i-Noor, nor any other compared to it. The Crimson Tear was worthy of a queen or—Clara Lewis, naturally.

"You cannot keep it for yourself!" Alfred angrily argued when Uriah shared the idea of turning the diamond into a pendant. *For Clara*, Uriah decided.

"I shall buy out your share," Uriah stated indifferently.

"You cannot. I do not agree." Alfred's lips curled in anger, eyes blazing. "We can auction the Crimson Tear off and make a fortune and an even bigger name for ourselves."

But Uriah knew that his queen would have the best of everything, including the rarest diamond in the world.

He spent sleepless nights contemplating the proper way to propose. He spent days, high on happiness, showing Clara his villa and the mansions of his top employees, then the vast river delta of Andhra Pradesh that gave birth to his fortune.

No promises were exchanged, but the smiles Uriah and Clara shared at dinners indicated one thing—she knew, her father knew, and he, Uriah, knew that in a matter of days, he would propose, and a new life would begin.

The evening he chose for the special occasion, he arranged for a lavish celebration. The partners from Hyderabad, the lapidary moguls of Golconda, the traders from Delhi—the guests arrived from everywhere.

Uriah put on his best suit, the cufflinks made of white diamonds, the gold chain across his suit studded with blue ones. The watch in his pocket, the custom piece made with 2500 melee diamonds, was checked every minute. He glowed like the biggest diamond himself. It was his time to shine. He would at last, after years of hard work, have it all.

The dinner took place in a luxury safari tent on a hill with a cliff that presented a breathtaking view of the Mawrs' vast lands, the rice fields and the wheat fields, and the river that gave birth to their wealth.

Dozens of lanterns hung off mango and banyan trees and illuminated the luscious green lawn. The musicians and servants wore colorful *sarees* and *dhoti kurtas*. The best whisky and sweetest wines were served. The most tender meats and richest curries spread a heavenly scent around. The moon shone brightly. The chai poured freely.

An elephant was brought for the guests' entertainment, though the only one who was impressed was little Drasko, who ripped his fancy English suit, trying to climb the majestic animal to the laughter of the guests.

During dinner, Clara didn't meet Uriah's eyes. Oh, she knew what he was about to do. His shy, sweet Clara was discreet. That was quite all right with him.

Uriah chose the right moment, cleared his throat, and tapped his silver spoon against his wine glass.

"I would like a minute of everyone's attention, please," he announced, his authoritative voice as always bringing everyone to full alert.

At that precise moment, Alfred stood up abruptly and raised his glass. "Yes! Ladies and gentlemen! We would like to make an announcement!"

Uriah's jaw tightened as he glared at his already tipsy brother beaming and smoothing his mustache in that careless arrogant way of his.

Uriah's eyes flashed with indignation when Alfred gestured to Clara Lewis. "Dear, will you please?"

And when she rose from her chair, Uriah felt a prickle of panic, a feeling so alien that he didn't quite register its meaning then. Not until Clara raised her smiling eyes at Alfred and blushed. Blushed! For him!

Alfred grinned drunkenly. His arrogant gaze swept across the guests but skipped Uriah as he said, "Miss Clara and I have something to share with you all. Joyful news, my friends. We have decided to get married!"

If someone had asked Uriah before what humiliation was, he would have given a dictionary definition, an example, perhaps, never having experienced it himself. Not even when mocked for his facial scars at a young age.

Heartbreak? He had had no notion of such a thing.

Hate? Oh, he was good friends with it.

But now, it was boiling in his veins, the bile of it rising up to his throat, cutting off his air, and making the world go dark. His blood pounded in his ears. His head roared. And his heart was breaking into a thousand pieces as the guests rose from their seats, offering best wishes and loud congratulations. They cheered, clinked their glasses, and hugged the lucky "lovebirds."

But Uriah kept his gaze on his stupid glass of wine, unable to take a sip, say anything, or make eye contact in fear of showing his shock.

His own brother had betrayed him, cowardly and disgracefully, and now laughed with everyone, *laughed*, Uriah knew, at *him*.

Uriah's mind roared. He clenched his teeth so hard they could crack. His gaze lowered, searching for something, a sign that he wasn't the only one who recognized this ultimate act of betrayal.

Until they stopped on little Drasko.

Two things left an imprint on Uriah that night. His brother's mocking laughter and Drasko's angry gaze.

That moment defined Uriah's life and his fast rise to power and madness.

That same moment determined Drasko's fate.

The little thief from London was the only one who didn't smile or cheer with the others, who didn't raise his glass as he sat by Uriah's side. So young, yet he already understood the cruel games that rich men played. His lips were pressed tightly together, his small hands balled into fists. His unusually green eyes blazed with indignation as he shared this moment with the man who had taken him off the streets and given him shelter.

This was the silent camaraderie of an impoverished child, who was given the chance of a lifetime, and a powerful lord, who had been knocked off his feet, if only for tonight.

Drasko lowered his gaze.

Uriah lifted his. He finally mustered the strength to look at his brother and said, "Congratulations."

His heart howled at the bright full moon, but this time, in searing pain. He decided that for the rest of his life, he would do everything to prove that no one, not a single living soul, would ever stand a chance at bringing him this low.

That very evening, he caught Clara alone, her gaze cowardly when it met his.

"Please, accept my congratulations," Uriah said coldly, wanting to do something atrocious and destroy her utterly.

If she hadn't responded, she would have been spared. But she cast her gaze down and said, "You must understand, Mr. Mawr..." *Understand?* "I would like to see my future child look at their father in admiration." He frowned, still not understanding. "And not... be scared..."

Scared?

Just then, for a second—a mere second that decided the future of that very child—her eyes flicked to Uriah's scars.

He had never loved anyone more. He had never loathed any person so much either.

But Clara Lewis was the proof that women were money hungry, they liked things shiny and perfect, and that was why they fancied diamonds.

For days, Uriah watched his brother and his fiancée and simmered with hate.

A month later, he attended their wedding and contemplated setting it on fire.

But Uriah wasn't a simple-minded brute. Oh, no. The best

revenge was drawn-out and etched with pain that wasn't physical.

Uriah got rid of the silly notion called love and the boring one called family. His hope for heirs had been crushed. But he had the boy he was intending to raise in his image. And he still had the Crimson Tear and knew what to do with it.

The Mawr brothers were called the Diamond Kings, but there was never room for two kings. Uriah would prove it.

And fate was already working in his favor.

Nine months later, Clara gave birth to a child and died shortly afterward. Her father soon succumbed to malaria.

While Alfred drowned his sorrows in a bottle, Uriah gloated.

A small victory? Perhaps. Though not by his own hands. One traitor was gone, leaving behind a baby girl who was the spitting image of *her*. The child bore her mother's eyes, and every time Uriah looked at her, hatred made his charred heart crack just a little more. Even more so when he noticed Drasko getting attached to the little creature.

This wasn't over, Uriah thought. No one would be spared. Neither would the spawn that reminded him of his single humiliating defeat.

"She shall be ruined, just like her mother," he promised himself. "I shall make sure of it."

8

DRASKO

Drasko hissed through his teeth as he opened his eyes, tried to rise, and groaned, falling back onto the sofa he was sprawled on.

Never in his life had he fallen asleep on a sofa.

The sharp pain was splitting his head into pieces. His tongue was thick.

The drawing room was quiet. The sun was blinding.

Drasko squinted around then noticed his trousers—they were lowered to his hips, the buttons undone.

What in the bloody hell...?

Grunting, Drasko sat up, bewildered. Mind dizzy, he felt like he did after being sick and taking too much... opium.

Frowning, he rubbed his face with both hands, shook his head, and buttoned up his trousers, focusing on the feeling down there.

Had he...? *No, not a chance.*

His new wife had been there last night, with her pretty face and full lips, her eyes too kind, considering what had transpired at the church.

He didn't... No, he absolutely couldn't... He'd never... Out of the question... Not to a woman and not remembering...

Yet the unbuttoned trousers were a mystery. *Fuck.*

He remembered her polite voice, "Mr. Mawr?" Her suspiciously sweet courteous, "Another drink?"

The sudden realization dawned on him.

Oh, the vixen!

The faint sweet voice in another room made his ears perk up. Laced with sunshine and the chirping spring birds outside, it seeped through the open doors of the dining room.

Drasko stood up abruptly, swayed for a second before he got a grip on himself, and stomped into the hallway.

Every step echoed with the memory of last night and the realization of what she'd tried to do. He would teach her a lesson! This nonsense would not stand!

Calm down, he told himself, slowing his pace as he walked into the dining room.

"Good morning, Mr. Mawr." Samira, the maid, smiled, her orange sari too bright for this morning and his clouded mind.

His glare made her smile go away.

He halted, his gaze pausing on his wife, her eyes on him, trepidation in them as she slowly rose from the table.

"Are you proud of yourself?" he rasped, not recognizing his voice and failing to keep the bitterness down.

She looked enchanting this morning, in a beige dress, her hair done up, so innocent, considering what she had pulled off last night.

She moved away from her chair to the other side of the long dining table separating them. A false smile flickered on her pretty coral lips. "I suppose you are talking about last night."

"Tell me what happened last night." Drasko took slow steps around the table.

He waited for her lies—surely, they were about to spill off those pretty lips.

Nervously, she swiped a strand of hair off her face and took a step away from him.

Little coward.

"I suppose we fulfilled a certain agreement," she said hesitantly.

A chuckle escaped him, though he was oh, so angry.

So, the mystery of the unbuttoned trousers was confirmed— his wife had tried to fake the consummation. Nothing much stunned Drasko these days, except, apparently, his newly acquired and very naive wife.

And he noticed a flicker of panic in her eyes as she started backing away, around the table.

His steps toward her quickened. "Agreement, huh?" he gritted out, his blood boiling.

"The consummation." She tried to smile but backed away like a thief. "Now that it is done and over with, we can keep our respectful distance—"

He lunged at her and covered the distance between them in seconds until her back was pressed against the wall and his hands went up against it on both sides of her head.

He lowered his face to hers to look into the eyes of the pretty liar.

"You are truly in over your head," he grunted.

"P-pardon me?"

Her startled eyes were too close, so were her lips that she licked nervously, a pretty mouth full of lies. Her chest rose and fell rapidly. She didn't fight, didn't protest. She bloody knew she was caught, and he liked her this way—haughty yet timid and closer than ever.

She opened her mouth to say something, but he cut her off with a soft, "Shhh. I will be the one talking right now. Your silly lie is one thing. You trying to poison me is a whole different matter."

"I don't know what you are—"

He wasn't sure what made him bring his hand to her face and drag his forefinger along her cheek—a movement that immediately shut her up and made her tremble.

She was guilty of—what was it?—domestic assault? The

thought was ridiculous but made him take her chin between his fingers.

Her sharp inhale was so delightfully precious.

There. Good.

His own fingertips burned at the contact with her soft skin, her pulse thrumming under them.

It wasn't their first touch, but the first one so charged with emotions.

His eyes dropped to her lips again. His thumb brushed along them, gently wiping away a tiny gasp that escaped her.

She was frightened, yes, so what had made her try such an unspeakable act the night before? She was haughty, yet what made her look so vulnerable when she faced him?

He felt her frail body against the weight of his own. He felt her jagged breaths, the tremor that ran through her. He smelled her morning freshness, the exquisite perfume and the flowery soap. Her closeness was maddening.

"Let us set certain things straight," he said, breathing through the tension in his body. "You shall never attempt to harm me again. If this marriage wasn't absolutely non-negotiable, I would have gladly let you go. You could have lived on the streets and played in taverns. I couldn't care less. But we are in this together now."

He tipped her chin, enjoying her submission. "Next. This marriage comes with the obvious."

He had just decided that, too, wanting to push her, to see how much she would accept.

"We *will* consummate it," he said, gloating at the indignation that flared up in her eyes again. "And you *will* give the only thing you are capable of giving this union—children. I suggest you start thinking about their names. If you are so scared about the one thing every married man and woman in marriage does in the bedroom, let me know. Perhaps, you'll need that vial of opium for yourself, after all. Or"—his lips curled in a smirk—"we can find a way to do it to both our liking."

Another glare came from her.

"Yesterday was a surprise for both of us," he continued. "I am not talking about your evening trick but the wedding." Her cheeks burned with a pretty rosy glint of shame. "Today, I would like to resume my business and expect to hear very little from you. Until we decide on the rules."

She didn't say a word.

Perhaps, because of that, his own hostility subsided. Perhaps because her gaze softened, so did his anger. And because of that, the situation acquired another overtone, intimate.

She was a stranger and yet his wife. He could touch her and do things to her. It was a bewildering thought, and it drove him insane, this very moment, in this very position, when he suddenly felt all of her, her gaze and breaths, her heartbeat and her femininity in that stupidly pretty beige dress of hers, the white ruffles matching the flower hairpins, her hair neatly pulled into a bun.

Fuck.

He had a wife—bought, forced, hostile like an angry cat, and very much off-limits, for now. For the first time in his life, Drasko couldn't *take* the woman he wanted, because she didn't want him back. It was a calamity, indeed.

Oh, and she was lovely. So perfect, flawless, and so very his.

For a moment, he forgot he wanted to despise her. She forgot she wanted to hate him. He saw it in her eyes, an indignant flicker that turned into surprise, her breath caught in her throat.

He forced himself to remove his hand from her face and pushed off the wall.

"Make yourself familiar with your new home," he said. "Have a great day."

He turned and started walking away, but couldn't help himself and added loudly, "Mrs. Mawr."

9

DRASKO

The journalists crowded the house gates as Drasko left in a hansom cab. Tripp, his Irish guard who had been with him for years, pushed his giant palms out to stop the invasive men from trying to get inside the partially open carriage.

"Mr. Mawr! Was your marriage to Grace Sommerville planned?"

"Was it a publicity stunt?"

"Are you friends with the earl?"

Drasko cursed under his breath. "We will have to ride in closed carriages from now on," he told Tripp with a heavy sigh as the carriage jerked into motion.

He didn't want this, didn't want Grace Sommerville—*correction*, Mawr—entangled into this game, but the dead man had a different plan.

The entrance to the Mawr Building on New Court Street was also crowded with the reporters that Tripp fought, trying to get Drasko inside.

"Unbelievable," Drasko snapped as the doormen ushered him inside, blocking anyone else from coming in.

Called a "stupendous pile" by *The Gazette* and monumental by the rest of the city, the Mawr Building had been erected only ten years prior. It was a ninety-foot tall, twelve-story commercial structure that housed exclusively the business of Mawr Diamond Industries. Behind it was a watch tower, added several years later, that rose even higher, forcing the outraged and envious Parliament to pass a Building Act that prohibited buildings over 100 feet tall.

But the Mawr Building towered above most, Drasko's office on the top floor.

The floor below his was the famous Mawr Wonders Room that showcased the entire range of diamond hues mined in India, rough diamonds of various sizes and purity, as well as other stones and, most importantly, the marvels of Golconda lapidary.

The building boasted the newest technologies, including the first hydraulic passenger elevator with automatic doors. It was completely electrified and incorporated an elaborate security system and underground vaults.

Drasko strode through the two-story marble entrance hall and took the elevator, still amazed by the latest innovation that had come from an American inventor.

He stepped out onto the brightly lit top floor where his assistant at the desk smiled broadly and motioned knowingly toward Drako's office.

"There he is! The talk of the day!" a familiar voice greeted him as Drasko opened his office door.

A pair of heavy boots were crossed at the ankles on his very desk.

Drasko smiled in relief at the sight of Elias Bayne, his best friend since childhood.

Leaning back in Drasko's giant leather chair, Elias raked his fingers through his shoulder-length dark hair as he held *The Gazette* before him and theatrically read out loud:

A Stolen Bride!
The Most Scandalous Wedding of the Year or How the Diamond King Acquired the Earl's Wife-To-Be!

Elias grinned, flashing his blinding smile in contrast with his tanned skin.

"Better yet!" He picked up another newspaper from a stack on the desk.

A Debt? A Gamble? A Business Deal?

Elias put the newspaper down and feigned shock. "Oh, my! Do tell!"

"When did you arrive in London?" Drasko asked with a smile, tossing his jacket onto the sofa and studying his friend.

A dashing captain and an orchid hunter, Elias was dressed in his sea uniform, his jacket off, his shirt carelessly unbuttoned.

"Just this morning." Elias scratched his several-day stubble. "And to what news!" He rose from the desk and went around it toward Drasko. "You could have waited for your best man, you know."

A prolonged hug followed.

Drasko closed his eyes, inhaling the familiar scent of sea and adventures and the freedom he had never quite had. There were three people he called family, and Elias was at the top of the list. He was the only one who knew of the wretched game and the letters.

"Fuck," Drasko exhaled in relief, still holding on to him.

"I hear you." Slowly, Elias let go, studying him with momentary worry in his eyes. "So, tell me!"

"You won't believe it," Drasko gritted out, raking his fingers through his hair.

Cigarettes were lit up and tea ordered.

"With cardamon," Elias requested the assistant. "You do keep my favorite in stock, I hope. Do you have Narayan's desserts? Oh, good. Bring those too. God, your office is one of my favorite places, I swear. So, tell me more about your new endeavor!"

They settled at the desk, and Drasko briefly filled him in, all the while studying him.

Elias's handmade jewelry around his neck and wrists, his salt-frizzed hair, his tan, the agility only acquired during adventures reminded Drasko of the times he had dreamed of seeing the entire world, every country there was. Elias belonged to the seas and exotic countries, not between the walls of this opulent office in the stone jungle of the city.

"The third letter from him, huh?" Elias mused, leisurely sprawled in the chair. "This game you agreed upon shall be a calamity."

She was a calamity, Drasko knew that much. "I am waiting to see what the next one is. Except it will have to do with the Crimson Tear. And it won't be good. Not when *she* is involved."

"Well, you should read what some of the less respectable newspapers wrote."

Drasko could only imagine.

Elias lightened up at the sight of the tray with Indian sweets that the assistant brought and right away stuffed his mouth with dried fruit and nuts wrapped in jaggery and rice flour.

"Well, I will tell you anyway!" he mumbled with his mouth full. "One printed that overused legend about the Crimson Tear diamond, saying how it has killed off every person who had it in their possession." Another pastry disappeared in his mouth. "It also alluded to the possibility that the said diamond was your wedding gift to your wife." Elias snorted.

Drasko sucked in his cheeks.

Elias shrugged. "Not a good joke, I understand."

He picked up a cigarette, lit it, and took a tasteful puff. He hadn't yet changed into an expensive suit, and that was how Drasko preferred his friend—being himself, in his captain's uniform that smelled of the sea, unshaven, suntanned, smoking, talking, eating, laughing, telling crazy stories and asking Drasko questions that could get any other person stabbed.

"Why not ignore the letters?" Elias mused. "Are you afraid that because of the deal years ago, Uriah would actually take the Mawr empire back? Destroy you? Kill you?"

Drasko thought it over, remembering what had happened after the second letter.

"I wouldn't be afraid to jeopardize Mawr Industries, despite what it cost me," Drasko reasoned. "I have enough of my own fortune, and *that* Uriah could never touch. But it is too late to stop now, you know that. He can end me, and he will. Despite being dead. There are people—a whole army, I am sure —who were paid well to execute his sick plans. The only thing…"

Drasko had to think it over.

"You were saying?" Elias prompted.

"Elias, I know you will call me a fool, but I am intrigued. So are you. This was a long time in the making. Nothing piques my curiosity more than science and *his* plan with this game that doesn't yet make sense."

Elias kept quiet, waiting for more.

"I didn't have anything to lose but Mawr Industries when I agreed. I was willing to lose it, because I knew I could always start fresh, elsewhere, doing about anything. By God, Elias, I wanted to! I cheered when I agreed, thinking I'd finally get my freedom when this is all over. Then entertained the thought of disobeying so I could go out on my own. Until…"

Elias nodded knowingly, then prompted, "Until?"

"Until *her*," Drasko admitted.

"Ah! There!" Elias stabbed the air with his forefinger. "At last you said it! Even more so now."

"Even more so now."

"Careful, my friend."

"About?"

Elias was one of the few who knew the decades of tragedies and what it had cost Drasko to get where he was.

"Her. Obviously." Elias took a drag off his cigarette. "I see where this is going."

"Which is?" Drasko raised a brow.

"In the same direction it has been going since you first saw her. I am not blind. Nor am I naive. I don't want to see you ruined, my friend."

"Uriah won't ruin me."

"If not Uriah, *she* will."

"She doesn't care."

"That's the problem. *You* care too much."

"Nonsense."

"She will make you reckless. She will turn your life upside down. She already has, I believe."

"We made a deal."

Loud laughter boomed through the room as Elias threw his head back in joyous amusement.

"The man of deals, ladies and gentlemen, Drasko Mawr!" He pointed his finger at Drasko. "Do you know what the difference is? She is not a businessman. She is a *wo-man*," he accentuated the syllables. "The one you have been obsessing over for a while."

"It is nothing."

"Oh? But when you stood in the church only yesterday, making that deal you speak of,"—Elias leaned over the desk and pressed his palm to Drasko's chest where his heart was. "Tuh-duh. Tuh-duh." He imitated his heartbeat, his brows furrowed in theatrical agony. "The cold heart of the powerful Drasko Mawr was beating, ohhh-sooo hard, was it not?" He playfully wiggled his eyebrows.

Drasko batted his hand away in irritation. "You are a fool." He pinched the bridge of his nose, trying to hide a smile.

"And when she gazed at you with her beautiful gray eyes," Elias carried on teasingly, "you were mesmerized, were you not?"

"They are hazel."

"You don't say?" Elias's eyes widened in mock intrigue. "What shade? Warmer? Colder? With specks of gold that make the invisible butterflies in your stomach flutter and your cock go hard at the thought of—"

Drasko picked up the newspaper and tossed it at Elias, who swatted it away with his hand and another burst of booming laughter.

Drasko sucked his teeth, lighting yet another cigarette. "You are so lucky I like you, Elias."

That was the truth. Elias would walk out soon, and Drasko would assume his so well-practiced indifferent expression. These days, Elias was the only person who ever saw Drasko with his defenses lowered.

Several years his senior, Elias was born in Borneo, had sailed to more countries than he could count, and had fought pirates in the Java Sea. Back in India, when they were adolescents, he'd joined Drasko for week-long hikes into the jungles and, one time, talked Drasko into making a fire and crouched around it for half the night, heating rough diamonds to see if they really combusted in the flames.

Those distant times had held fewer tragedies and more laughter. And this man was still by Drasko's side. So were Rupesh and Asha, but they lived in India, and their letters weren't enough to quench Drasko's thirst for the night-long conversations they used to have.

"Mrs. Mawr is lucky, not me," Elias said as his humorous eyes studied Drasko. "I simply curiously follow your adventures. *You* know what is happening with the letters. Your wife doesn't. She is only trying to make sense of it all."

"I know."

"Have you... Have you considered that this game Uriah planned for you is not about the Crimson Tear at all? Perhaps, not even about the auction. It is about you and her and Uriah's sickly habit of making others suffer. A sick test of sorts."

A nasty feeling started in Drasko's chest. "I have."

"You avoid my eyes, mate. Do you suppose she is in danger?"

"She cannot be. The only person Uriah would want to hurt is me. Uriah always played by the rules."

"I am not so sure."

"No, no, Elias. Please. Don't say that. She was a stranger until yesterday. She didn't deserve this."

Elias looked away, at the window. "I've missed you is all. I wish you well. And I am simply worried. I don't like this game. Not a bit. Nor do I like the fact that for the first time in your life, you are lying to yourself and hiding your feelings." He returned his gaze to his friend. "By God, Drasko, try to make her happy! This is the least you can do for the woman who did not want any part of this game."

"I know."

"You were so good to Yamuna."

"Don't…" Drasko threw a glare at him. "This is different."

"Absolutely! More so the reason for you to be patient."

"I am."

"You are. You are. You are. You keep telling yourself this. Fine! To hell with this grim business. A party at the Bayne house then!" With a broad smile, Elias rose from his chair. "Bring your wife, will you?"

"We don't want her to get used to being around much, do we?"

"So unlike you, Drasko," said Elias, approaching the door and swinging his jacket over his shoulder.

"What is?"

"Lying to yourself. There is only one way to win this deal with her."

"And?"

Elias's smile was growing slowly, unbearably slowly, testing Drasko's patience until Drasko rolled his eyes and Elias spoke.

"Why, make her fall in love with you, of course!" He winked and ducked out the door, avoiding being hit by the newspaper Drasko threw at him.

10

GRACE

"Unbelievable!" *True.*

"Preposterous!" *Sort of.*

"Unlawful!" *Is it?*

"Impossible!"

Grace ran out of words as she collapsed onto the divan in Rivka's drawing room.

"Not so impossible," said Rivka, stirring the steaming herb tea in a cup. "You are, after all, Mrs. Mawr now."

"Do remind me again!" Grace snapped.

The pinkish glow of the sun shone through the red curtains. The flat was in the back of the drug store Rivka worked in, helping her grandfather, though the store's reputation wasn't for its medicines but Rivka's "gifts." Its revenue was modest compared to the general donations of those who came asking for Rivka's help. Either for healing or advice. But mostly, hoping to solve their problems and heartaches. Rivka *saw* them all—the past, future, happy and tragic. Her "sight" was rumored to be the curse of the devil, but her gift helped many.

"It is all meant to be," Rivka said to Grace.

"You and your *amor fati!*" Grace exclaimed in annoyance, rose from the divan, and started pacing around the room.

"Nietzsche preached the love of fate. One does not have to love but simply has to accept the grand plan of the future."

"Grand all right," Grace muttered, discouraged.

Rebecca, or Rivka, as she preferred to be called by close fiends, was only four years older than Grace but so much wiser. As if her "sight" gave her some ancient wisdom into the meaning of life.

"Take this." Rivka passed her a cup of tea.

"No. You are giving me yet another potion to calm down. I am calm." Grace took the cup, nevertheless. "It's just... Do you see something?"

She cast her pleading eyes at smiling Rivka.

Black hair piled on top of her head, a dress with ethnic designs, and a cotton summer shawl over her shoulders, Rivka radiated the motherly care that often reassured Grace more than her words.

But not today.

"Tsk, of course, you won't," Grace muttered reproachfully. "You never tell me anything. Though you know. I *know* you know!"

Grace circled the room, taking in the so-familiar scent of herbs and medicine.

She had spent a lot of time here over the years and was used to the subtle smell of the incenses and old furniture. This room was dearer to her than the house she'd grown up in, wealthy but lonely, with its empty rooms and strict rules. Her parents had passed a long time ago and left quite a bit of money that was now gone. Her guardians had treated her like a pretty bird in a cage.

"What am I to do?" Grace asked again as Rivka lit an incense stick, and the warm smell of lavender spread across the room. "Will he hurt me?"

"He will not."

"Will he keep me locked up in the house?"

"Gracie..." Rivka creased her eyebrows in pity, knowing well what sort of punishments Grace had had to endure with the Sommervilles.

"Will he ruin me?" Grace asked with despair, searching her eyes. Rivka never said anything without "knowing."

"What do you mean by *ruin*?"

"Ah, you see? Already, you are sowing seeds of worry in me."

"I do not, Gracie. Perhaps, he will ruin your understanding of who you are and who you are meant to be. Or what he is."

Grace closed her eyes and whimpered in helplessness. This philosophical nonsense did not help much in calming her.

"Are you practicing for your performance at the marchioness's Summer Ball?" Rivka changed the topic.

"Distracting me, aren't you?" Grace feigned anger, though she could never be cross with her friend. She sighed, thinking about the performance. "I wrote to my guardians about my piano. They never responded. They did not bother writing back, Rivka! They never wanted me. No, no, I know it now."

She bit her lip to hold back tears and took a seat on the divan again.

"And do you know what the most awful thing is?" Grace lifted her eyes to her friend. "There is no piano in that house." *His* house. "He's been to my performances. But what if he hates music?"

Just like them...

Smiling, Rivka walked over and took a seat next to Grace. Her warm hand softly touched Grace's shoulder. "Then you ask him, my lovely. He is your husband."

"But how?" Grace asked almost in a whisper. "We pretend that this union is on paper only. And I tried to... Well, you know the story... Quite embarrassing. Wasn't so smart of me. And you want me to *ask* him for things after that?"

Rivka brushed her fingers along the ruffled neckline of Grace's dress, adjusting it. "Do not be so stubborn, my lovely.

Life is a compromise. Instead of resenting what comes your way, try to embrace it and learn. Make a deal."

"A deal..." Grace snorted. By God, even her friend now sounded like him.

Grace couldn't accept him, not yet, not until she knew what had transpired between him and Charles and what her part in this was.

This was a nightmare. Just like the nightmares she'd had since childhood. Just like the aches she'd had since she was little, though Rivka's healing rituals had made them much less frequent.

Now *he* haunted her, his mesmerizing green eyes and handsome expressionless face, his soft voice and brutal scars. The way he lifted a cigarette to his mouth, the way he flexed his big hands, his calm possessive gaze that made one feel that everything, including people, was his domain. The way that gaze bore into her as if he could read her every thought.

On paper, this man was her husband—the fact was truly bewildering.

What scared her was that he might turn out to be like her guardians, cold and distant. Or like some of the husbands she'd heard about, abusive and cruel. A monster? No, no, Grace did not deserve to spend more of her life in a cage.

She had thought of the episode in the dining room a dozen times, replaying it, repeating his words. He wasn't rough or violent. On the contrary, there was a gentle force in his movements and the way his hand held her chin in place.

She bit her lip at the memory.

It must have reflected on her face because Rivka's hand was on her shoulder again. "How are you feeling lately?"

She meant the pains, which came much rarer now. Years of healings, the potions and the prayers—they worked, just like Rivka had said.

Grace listened to her body—the throbbing under her ribs had

started again in the last couple of days, but there were more pressing issues to deal with.

"At a loss," Grace said instead and sadly smiled at the floor.

11

GRACE

After the failed drugging episode, Grace felt awful and embarrassed. Her husband, undoubtedly, resented her even more now. Why else had he been avoiding her for days? She saw him at breakfast once. She sat through four dinners by herself. She ran into him three more times during the day, into his courteous, "Are you adjusting?" that made her blood boil.

Adjusting to what exactly? His green eyes that unnerved her? His tiny smirks that provoked her? The house void of music?

She took long walks about the opulent mansion with its army of servants. The two floors were filled with art and antiques but not a single diamond or the wonders of Golconda everyone talked about.

So much for being the Diamond King.

She sent a letter to the marchioness about the piano performance at the Summer Ball in July. No response came. Her heart sank. She'd known that would happen. The newspaper headlines blasted her name with the most scandalous suggestions.

The Diamond King Snatches the Biggest Jewel Yet.
Will the New Mrs. Mawr Fall Under the Curse of the Crimson
Tear?

Most of them embarrassed her. The latter intrigued her.

She thought of Charles, but he seemed like another life and not hers. She felt bitter and humiliated but, oddly, not heartbroken.

And Grace brooded.

On day five, she finally decided to visit Rivka again, only to find out she was now to be escorted by a bodyguard.

"I am Nina," said the short slender Asian woman with a confident cold gaze. "I am at your service, ma'am."

Grace wanted to dispose of her, but that proved to be impossible.

"I don't need a chaperon," Grace complained to her husband's butler since her husband was never in sight.

"Ma'am, Miss Nina is not exactly a chaperon," the butler explained in a conspiratorial tone.

Nina might have looked small and ordinary, but in her past, he told Grace, there was growing up in the Far East, learning kung fu from Shaolin monks in Tibet, winning all-male underground fights in Shanghai, and serving in the private entourage of an opium trafficker out of Canton.

Grace observed Nina with renewed interest. The guards at the house, she noticed, bowed to Nina with utmost respect.

"And how would you fight if it came to it?" she asked one day, giving in to her curiosity.

"My skirt has a deep pleat, much like those bicycle suits for women," Nina explained. "And I wear bifurcated knee-length bloomers underneath. You mustn't worry, ma'am. I can run faster than a carriage if needed. And fighting—well, the skirt can fall off as easily as I can pull a gun out of it."

"A gun?"

Grace was speechless. And Nina was on strict orders to

follow Grace everywhere she went outside the house, usually without uttering a single word during the entire day.

Now Grace was walking with Rivka along Hyde Park, Nina following behind them at a short distance.

"Do you think he hired her to spy on me?" Grace asked Rivka.

She responded with enthusiastic laughter. "Why would he spy on you, Gracie?"

"I shall not hide," Grace said. "My husband shall have to accept you. You are my best friend, Rivka!"

Grace still hadn't summoned the courage to invite her to the house. Lovely Rivka—oh, Grace simply could not bear it if her husband, like her guardians, would not accept her friend.

Grace could not remember many happy moments from her childhood. She had grown up with maids who dressed her, fed her, and were the only ones in the house to talk to her. Her guardians were mere prison guards who enforced strict rules. Grace often wondered what she had done wrong. Why wasn't there anyone who cared for her, except Rivka?

"You are afraid, Gracie," Rivka said with a kind smile, always that smile as if there was no worry in the world. "But not of him, my lovely, no. You are scared that he will make you feel lonely just like your guardians always did."

"What if he locks me in for days, too? Punishes me?" Grace winced at her own words. "Why is it that never in my life did I have a say in what I truly wanted?"

"You wanted to be a pianist."

"And my vocation still depends on the men who dominate the craft. They won't let me perform with them on a big stage, will not allow me in an orchestra. Because I am… a woman. Gah! How awfully unfair!"

When she started playing the piano, only seven, so outstanding were her skills right from the start that the Sommervilles hired her the best tutor. Yet her upright piano wasn't the best one. When in three years, she outplayed the fifteen-year-old piano genius of London, the city took notice. Yet, Grace was only allowed to perform at selective events and under the careful supervision of her aunt.

Rumors spread about the female prodigy pianist. Grace was invited to play with the famous musicians. But she was a girl, and a girl had no place in the Royal orchestra or any grand philharmonic orchestras or on the big stages she so wanted to play on.

Her private life was a cage, too. Her guardians had money. Yet, Grace was never allowed any luxuries. At home, she was only permitted to play at certain hours. No suitors were ever allowed near her. No friends were ever welcome. Rivka was forbidden to ever set foot in the Sommervilles' house. The only time Grace could truly do what she wanted was when she composed her own music and wrote her songs. And that, usually, was when she was hiding in her room.

Until Charles, who, if only in words, offered a happy future. Finally, Grace would have her own family!

But that had gone up in smoke.

"I don't know what is happening in my life," Grace said solemnly, as always hoping for Rivka's reassuring words. "But come! Come to my house, Rivka, will you? Meet him. Tell me what you think. Perhaps he will like you. Oh, but that would be lovely!" That hope sent her heart beating wildly so abruptly that tears pooled in her eyes. "It would be, wouldn't it?" she added quieter, the hope already fading away like it always did.

Rivka smiled, her ebony eyes shining with kindness. She hadn't ever once shared her gift of "seeing" with Grace, not even in this, perhaps, the most important moment in Grace's life.

It scared Grace. *He* scared Grace. She didn't know him, nor could she explain how he'd made her feel every time they had briefly met in the past.

"Come visit, Rivka." Grace smiled through tears, her heart clenching at the words. "He might be away. He always is. He wouldn't care, I promise. And can you..." She bit her lower lip.

"Can you put on your best dress?" Right away, she felt ashamed of what she'd just asked, added too swiftly, "In case—"

"In case your new husband *is* at home and *is* like your guardians? Aw, Gracie..."

"I don't know what sort of man he is. But two things I cannot give up are my music and you."

Disheartened though determined to stay positive, Grace returned to her new house.

Full of exotic scents and lavish decorations from Asia, the mansion was like an exotic land with Persian carpets and thick drapes, elephant ornaments, colorful rugs, Indian pottery, and handmade throws. There were scandalous artworks with people performing God only knew what that made Grace blush. But she studied them in detail, thought about them at night, her husband's face occasionally replacing those of the men who performed obscene acts.

And it was so... lonely again. Perhaps even more so without her piano.

She stayed up late, listening to the sounds of her husband coming to the bedroom adjoining hers. In vain. And at breakfast, she would hear Samira's usual, "The master is gone. A little past dawn. He rises early, madam."

"Of course," Grace muttered. Maybe, like the night predators, he didn't sleep at all.

Until the morning she walked into the dining room and halted in surprise. Green eyes, assertive figure, indifferent gaze —her husband sat at the table drinking coffee and reading the newspaper.

"Good morning," he said coldly, his gaze sweeping over her dress.

Slowly, she took a seat at the table. "You weren't home last night," she said, suddenly nervous but somehow cheerful at the sight of him at home.

"I was not." His eyes followed her over the rim of his coffee cup as he took a sip.

"You didn't sleep at home."

"I did not."

"You own half of this city. You have other homes, I know that. Did you sleep in one of them?"

"I did not." He cocked his head as if waiting for more.

She ran out of questions that she could possibly ask without coming across as nosy.

Was there another woman? She shouldn't care. Yet she thought of Charles—the rumors about his paramour that she had ignored even after their engagement.

Grace felt a familiar sting in her heart.

After a prolonged silence, she raised her eyes, running right into his stare.

"Are you not talking to me? Avoiding me?" she asked with disappointment.

"What would you like to discuss? Another possible attempt at poisoning me?"

His face lacked expression, but his eyes, oh, his eyes burned through her like a hot poker that she felt in her very bones.

She huffed and cast her gaze to the table. "You said we needed to discuss the terms."

"Are you ready to give it your precious all?" The sarcasm in his voice was unmistakable. But why? He still hadn't told her why he needed to marry her. So, why the bitterness? Why the punishment?

She wouldn't take it. "The necessary minimum, I'd say," she replied bitterly.

"I see."

He rose without another word and left without a goodbye, leaving her alone with her disappointment.

Her heart stung, but right away, the usual response came—a melody started in her head. Her fingers played the chords on the tablecloth.

She heard a sound and raised her eyes to see Samira, her dark hair braided at the back, her bright blue sari decorated with pink flowers. The maid served her breakfast and poured her tea, while Grace watched her and felt an urge to write a song like that, for once happy, that matched Samira's broad smile, kind eyes, and vibrant dress. Most of her songs weren't that happy.

"Master said you are an amazing piano player," the maid said.

Grace forced her fingers to stop playing on the table. "He did?"

So, he mentioned her talent to others but didn't bother with a piano.

Very well.

Who was Grace to ask? She would stop by the Music Academy and reserve a piano room for practice.

What she wasn't all right with was not knowing a speck about her husband. And if he wasn't giving her the time of day, she would just have to find out for herself.

Naturally, from the newspapers.

So, in the afternoon, she ordered the carriage and headed to a library.

Morsington's Library was the newest archives collection sponsored by the Press Association. The large building on Sixth Street was comprised of multiple rooms crammed with shelves stacked with copies from the fifteen biggest newspapers, more than thirty smaller ones, and many other periodicals and journals.

For a fee, Grace had access to all of them.

But how would she find what she was looking for?

"I am afraid our budget is too small to have enough employees to catalog everything properly," the clerk explained. "But if you are after something that is frequently mentioned, a place or a person, we have reference cards for those. What sort of information do you need?"

"Mawr. Mawr Diamond Industries," Grace said, surprised at how important it sounded, the name that was now her own.

"Oh, that would be easy!" The clerk searched in the card catalog. "Ah, there it is." He pulled out a thick stack of cards. "Quite a handful! Mrs...?"

"Mawr," Grace said quietly, still getting used to her new name.

"Oh? I wish you perseverance, Mrs. Mawr. You have a lot to go through."

As she walked with her stack toward a row of shelves with the numbers he pointed at, she looked back to see the clerk peeking at her from behind his desk.

There was a lot, indeed, Grace realized as she found one newspaper after another among hundreds of them, leafing through the yellowed pages and reading the headlines.

The Gazette was the most reputable. She found some articles from 1879:

The Construction of the Mawr Building:
The Most Ambitious Architectural Design Yet.

Grace, of course, knew that one, had visited the building as a child when it was erected.

In one of the oldest issues of the *Tribune*, Grace found an illustration of the two Mawr brothers in India, an elephant behind them, trunks stacked up on both sides.

The Mawr Brothers Reveal Undreamed of Indian Splendors.

1855, the illustration said. That was before her husband was born.

There were articles about the Indian-English trade, about the Mawrs' scandal with the French royalty. One described the new steamship, the largest in Europe, commissioned by the Mawrs.

Then Grace stumbled upon an article from the *London Telegraph*:

Blood and Diamonds:
The Wollendorf Brothers.
Ambitions in South Africa and the New Rivals to the Diamond
Kings.

The *Weekly Courant* was less diplomatic:

Deadly Rivalry or Coincidence?

The articles described the death of Alfred Mawr. Some attributed it to the Wollendorfs. Others suspected Uriah Mawr. Several brought up the Crimson Tear legend.

And then Grace found another article with a photograph.

She held her breath, staring at the black-and-white photo of her husband, not even twenty years of age, in a suit and top hat.

On impulse, she stroked it with her fingertips.

"Hello, Mr. Mawr," she whispered, mesmerized for a second too long, then sucked in a breath as she read the headline:

Another Tragedy Rocks the Mawr Family.
Young Drasko Mawr Is Hailed the New Diamond King.

WHITE
SHAITAAN

Andhra Pradesh, India
Drasko, 10-14

Turning a street thief into a gentleman was no easy task. Not when one man wanted him to be a noble, the other one a savage.

A true bet, indeed.

Because of Clara's death and the passing of her father shortly after of malaria, the two brothers now shared the luxury home with a large indoor courtyard, rosewood pillars, and live plants throughout its many spacious rooms and corridors.

Drasko lived with them. So did Alfred's newborn daughter in the care of a maid.

Uriah's efforts in raising Drasko were fueled by his spite toward his brother. He got Drasko tutors in all subjects imaginable.

"Knowledge is a weapon," Uriah said, and by the time Drasko was thirteen, he spoke perfect English, was fluent in Hindi and French, could read and write in all three languages, and excelled in math.

Uriah took it upon himself to teach the boy the diamond trade, the gruesome work of the common laborers in the river delta as well as the intricate side of diamond importing. He brought Drasko to business meetings, introduced him to

Golconda's diamond traders, took him on a voyage across the Far East.

Drasko was ambitious. Perhaps, it was due to his survival instinct from the streets, which only pleased Uriah. None of the businesspeople, who saw young Drasko in a fancy English suit with immaculate table manners and so elegant at dancing, recognized him back at the Mawr mines, wearing the *kurta pajama*, often shirtless and barefoot, sitting with the locals near the riverbeds and rocky hills and eating rice, *sabzi*, and *dahl* with his fingers.

The workers loved him. Why, he was the only white lord who spent days in the dirt and mud with them, rain or shine, learning the underside of the mining business!

Drasko charmed the local girls and humbled the village elders. He made friends with Elias Bayne, another British boy his age, and sailed with him and his father to Borneo for a month. He learned how to shoot, carried a gun with him on business trips with Uriah, and once sorted out the Thuggees, who tried to rob them outside Golconda.

The only thing that reminded Drasko of England were bonfires, their pungent smell yanking him back in time to the cold winters and the meek fires they used to burn at night to stay warm on the streets. He didn't miss London but wondered what had become of his only friend, Zeph, a street thief just like him. He wished Zeph were here, for they could build an empire together!

And then there was Alfred Mawr, angry at life, who wanted to break something, whether a face or a person's life, indulging in drunkenness and women. He didn't like that Uriah had adopted the boy. Alfred had his daughter, but she was a girl, not an heir and with little prospect of continuing in his steps.

So, Alfred drank his bitterness away and ground his teeth at the sight of young Drasko growing into an inquisitive and extremely intelligent adolescent—the bet Alfred was slowly losing.

One day, when Drasko was fourteen and Uriah was away for business, Alfred took the boy to a faraway village, to a fighting match, a place that didn't like white men or tolerate weakness.

A small dusty field.

A stone fence with cemented glass shards on top.

A crowd of Thuggees, ruthless criminals known for very little compassion.

And Drasko against three boys, older than him, with scars, menacing scowls, and practiced fists.

Drasko was set up for failure. *Or worse,* Alfred hoped as he placed a bet with Siddharth, a man in charge of the local gang, then pushed Drasko toward his opponents.

"You think you can make it?" Alfred whispered to Drasko. "My brother turned you into a brat."

Bets were placed. Dozens gathered to witness a white boy be pummeled to death.

And Alfred would remember for the rest of his not-so-long life the spiteful stare Drasko gave him before he turned toward the three boys who leisurely circled him, ready to attack.

Drasko proved that night that he still had it in him—the survival instinct that had helped him on the streets of London as a child.

Incredibly, he fought like a true savage. Whether it was to protect the life he'd been promised or to prove that he wasn't a pampered foreigner who was given everything on a golden platter.

He saw the fight for what it was—a test. Three against one. Six fists against two smaller ones. And teeth, for Drasko used those too that night.

He was knocked down right away, then again, shock on his face at the sudden display of such violence. The onlookers spat chewed-up betel quid right at him, leaving red splatters on his skin mixed with his blood. Their laughter rang in Drasko's ears as he was beaten.

But nothing made him more furious than the smirk on Alfred's face.

So, Drasko kept rising from the ground, was kicked down, and rose again. He wiped the blood from under his nose with the back of his hand, and—the laughter quietened—angrily smiled back at the attackers, his own blood staining his teeth and dripping into his eyes, blurring his vision.

He roared then, charged at the opponents, threw vicious punches and kicks. When he started losing strength, his teeth bit into the men's flesh. When he couldn't bite anymore, he threw handfuls of dirt into their faces. When he was kicked senseless into the dirt, his weak hand found a stick on the ground, and he used it to stab at them, aiming for their faces. And when the three of them, beaten and finally giving up, crawled away, Drasko rose on all fours—all he could manage—wobbling, his face swollen with bruises, his body broken. Blood dripped from his face onto the dirt, but he raised his eyes at Alfred in triumph.

The crowd around went quiet, among them Alfred, cowardly trembling in shock.

Siddharth wiggled his head side to side, observing Drasko, and spat red quid at Alfred's feet.

"*Bahadur.*" *Brave*, it meant. "*Bahadur lekin paagal,*" he said. *Brave but crazy.* And his men nodded at young Drasko with respect.

Alfred only sucked his teeth, disappointment at his failed experiment sweeping across his gaze.

No one inquired about Drasko's broken nose and ribs, or the bruises all over his body.

Except Asha, who took care of Alfred's daughter. That night, Drasko, barely alive, made his way to her bungalow. She made him chai and gave him cold compresses.

Drasko grunted, trying to sip the warm liquid with his broken lips.

"Slowly, slowly," she muttered, tears in her eyes as she

exchanged glances with her husband, Rupesh, a supervisor of one of the worker teams.

Rupesh studied Drasko grimly, shook his head, and prayed all night at his *puja ghar*.

Alfred's daughter, only four years of age, crawled around Drasko with a naive smile that made his heart melt.

"They can't win," he whispered to her conspiratorially and smiled through pain.

The little one only grinned back and cooed as he tucked her under his arm.

This was the first fight of many. Until Drasko was old enough to know he didn't need to prove himself anymore. Until the word spread across the villages to stay away from the white *shaitaan*, the devil.

"He is like Rakshasa," some said.

A tiger terrorized the nearby villages. It attacked at night and had eaten many workers and a child. The mere sight of its giant paw prints on the ground by morning sent fear through the locals.

They called the tiger Rakshasa, like the evil god. Uncatchable, untraceable, and insatiable. And they compared Drasko to it.

"The path of a king is a solitary one," Uriah said. "Do not fret over others' insults. They are beneath you."

Drasko didn't care about being alone. But he despised the mockery and the envious rumors behind his back.

Rupesh had become his close friend by then. He didn't care about diamonds or where Drasko had come from or what reputation he had but watched him closely.

One day, Rupesh sat Drasko down in his house, in front of a *puja ghar*.

"Your anger rules your mind," he said, lighting the candles. "Learn to control it, before it starts ruling your heart."

"One's mind is a weapon," Drasko scoffed. "A true king is not concerned about the matters of his heart."

"Hmm. You do not have to be a king to be powerful," Rupesh said. "There are many roads to power. A great captain learns the sea and holds the helm during storms. A warrior dares to charge at death. A beast has the strength to fight it. A wise man knows how to tame his inner demons."

"Who has all of the above?" Drasko inquired, for Rupesh's wisdom was different from Uriah's.

"Oi, *bhaiya*, a god does."

"Can one be like a god?"

"*Haan-ji*," Rupesh agreed. "We all are."

"Why would one want to be a king if he can be a god?"

"Because kings are mortal."

"Exactly!"

"Exactly." Rupesh smiled. "Death is the only thing a god can't have. But who wants to be a god when all your loved ones die?"

In a few years, Drasko would get to know the dire meaning behind those words.

But as he grew older, he grew stronger, his fists tougher, and his mind sharper. Women couldn't stay away from Drasko. They always fancied things dark and devilish, especially with a dazzling smile and magnificent green eyes. Nothing was stopping them from pursuing Drasko's attention, much to the envy of the local men.

At last, Uriah caught a whiff of Alfred's wasteful attempts to bring Drasko down.

"Street dogs never lose fangs. They always keep their guard and aren't afraid to be alone," Drasko overheard Uriah say once.

To which Alfred answered, "A dog is still a dog, no matter how you dress it."

That was all Drasko was to the Mawrs—a bet.

He didn't care. He had his own plans. He *would* become a powerful man, and not for Uriah's sake of winning the bet. One day, Drasko promised himself, he would take Alfred's little daughter away from these cruel people, give her a new life, and surround her with those who would love her.

But for that, he needed to go back to London.

He didn't know yet that the two of them indeed would go to London one day, but only one would survive that trip.

13

GRACE

"Considering your circumstances," Grace mimicked mockingly out loud, "and the events that transpired in the last weeks, it would be best if you did not contact her ladyship anymore. Argh!" Grace angrily tossed her reticule on the floor of the carriage. "Can you imagine such rudeness? And from a titled person? Who does she think she is?"

Grace had just gotten rejected at the marchioness's house. And, of course, she vented to Nina, who followed her everywhere and now only nodded in silence.

That was Grace's life now—she would converse with her guards, the only people who had time to talk to her.

It was late afternoon when they returned to the mansion, and Grace ran straight into her husband in the hallway.

His bodyguard, Tripp, bowed to her. Her husband studied her with interest. His intense green gaze traveled down and up her dress as if she were there for his sole entertainment.

His shirt sleeves rolled up, his muscled forearms were on display, a leather bracelet around his wrist, no tie, the top shirt buttons undone. He was handsome and looked positively at ease, while Grace steeled her spine.

"Am I a prisoner now?" she blurted, which was the first thing that came to mind.

"Bad day, darling?"

God, did it irritate her that he was always so calm. And so gorgeous, she had to admit. And so magnetic that her body burned with unexplainable tension in his presence.

"Am I a prisoner?" she inquired with forced bitterness. "Do I have to be escorted everywhere?"

"I am merely making sure you are safe."

"Safe from whom?"

He was an important man, his giant red-haired guard following him at all times. Yet, Grace didn't need protection.

"From yourself," he said with the hint of a smile.

She wished she had something heavy in her hand to throw at him.

No, she couldn't.

Rivka would arrive soon, and Grace could not afford the wrath of her husband while she needed him to accept her friend.

Grace assumed a humble face, swallowed her pride, and silently recited a prayer before gathering the courage to speak on the topic.

"My friend is coming tonight." She recited another silent prayer at this announcement. "You do not have to be here for that. I assume—"

"I'll be delighted to."

Sarcasm? Very well, she would deal with that too. "There is no need for you—"

"I"—he took a step toward her, making her take a step back on reflex and cast her eyes down—"shall be here."

Defeated and now anxious, she went upstairs, changed into a lace dress, fixed her hair, and arranged for the tea, all the while listening to the sounds in the house. What was *he* doing?

"Mr. Mawr is in his office," Eden said knowingly.

Soon, the doorman announced the arrival of Miss Rebecca.

Grace darted downstairs. "Rivka! You are here!" She hurried

across the marble hall toward her friend. Her eyes fell upon Rivka's dress, and her chest tightened.

Rivka wore a bell-shaped red skirt, nipped at the waist, and a traditional red blouse over the corset. A matching hat crowned her luscious, braided hair with the veil that draped around her neck. Heavy long earrings adorned her ears. She looked magnificent but—

Oh, Lordy...

There came a flashback from years ago, Aunt and Uncle crunching up their noses at the sight of Rivka in her traditional dress.

"We do not want such individuals near you," they had told Grace. "You are a respectable young lady of the ton."

"Rivka, dear." Grace took her friend in her arms.

"Do not taunt me! I know! I know!" Rivka studied the exotic marble hallway. "Where is your husband?"

"Oh, he is busy—"

"Miss Rebecca!" His voice boomed through the hall, turning them around.

"Oh, dear..." Grace stiffened as she caught sight of the powerful build of her husband, who was striding toward them.

He flashed a smile at Rivka, while Grace studied his face, taken aback by the miracle—her husband was smiling broadly, which rendered his face in the most heart-warming way.

"It is a pleasure," he said, gracefully bowing and kissing Rivka's hand. "I have to admit that you are very special."

"How so?" Rivka smiled back.

"Well, you were my wife's only guest during the wedding, for one."

Grace flinched. How did he know?

"You are also the first guest since our wedding," he said. "I get a feeling people intentionally stay away from our house."

"Perhaps, they are waiting for an invitation." Rivka so openly studied Drasko that Grace held her breath.

"Perhaps," he echoed, grinning. "May I?" He offered his

elbow to Rivka and gracefully led her toward the drawing room, not paying any attention to Grace.

Confused, Grace followed. She had practiced what she would say in front of him, how she would introduce her friend, in the most wonderful words and with utmost respect to buy his good graces.

What she hadn't expected was for her husband to completely take over the entire meeting.

"Your dress is absolutely stunning," Grace heard Drasko compliment Rivka while Grace gave instructions to the maid to bring in tea and desserts.

"Romania? I haven't been, though I would love to visit one day," he said as they settled in the living room. "My own roots are a mystery, you see."

He asked Rivka about her work and inquired about her grandfather.

Grace had thought of a dozen topics to talk to Rivka about in his presence, but the two already seemed at ease with each other.

Completely dazed, Grace sat in silence and watched Rivka's kind smile, listened to her husband's stories, and didn't believe that life, for once, would be so kind to her. Her own friend at her house—a luxury she'd never had before!

Drasko was flawlessly gallant. Graceful when he asked Samira to bring an old manuscript from his library—a manuscript on Slavic shamanism that Rivka was delighted to borrow.

"Please, visit often, Miss Rebecca," Drasko said at some point, and Grace found herself biting back tears of gratitude.

He'd never been so graceful with her. He'd never looked so at ease as he did with Rivka. Grace had never seen him laugh so genuinely as he did when Rivka made a joke. His laughter traveled straight to Grace's heart. It was a low beautiful sound that left her stunned. Maybe, someday, she would learn to navigate this relationship. Someday, they could be at ease. It was a frightening thought, intriguing, and scratched at her pride.

Samira brought teas and pastries.

"I noticed some of your servants are from India," Rivka said. "Do you have an Indian cook as well, Mr. Mawr?"

"Naturally." Drasko nodded.

"Grace hasn't mentioned."

He shrugged. "We didn't get a chance to spend much time together. I am not sure my wife wants anything to do with who I am and where I come from."

The words stung Grace. "That is not true," she responded quietly, staring him down.

But he paid her no attention. "I love Indian cuisine, Miss Rebecca. If you perhaps feel like having a small tasting, I'd be happy to ask my cook."

Stunned, Grace looked at Rivka.

"Why, sure!" Rivka exclaimed with enthusiasm. "How exciting!"

He gave Samira orders in a different language, and Rivka raised her brows in surprise. "You speak Hindi, Mr. Mawr?"

He grinned. "Of course, I do. I grew up in India. As colonizers, we have only one chance to the Indians' hearts—by learning their culture."

So, he spoke Hindi. That was news, another thing Grace didn't know.

He caught her surprised gaze but right away turned his attention to Rivka, a triumphant smile on his lips.

Samira came back shortly with a tray that contained little jars and bowls and flatbreads and... no cutlery. She passed the moist napkins to Drasko and Rivka.

"To wash your hands, madam," she explained to Rivka.

"Oh!"

"It is called a *thali*, a personal tray," Drasko said. "And yes, we often eat with our hands."

A smell so wonderful enveloped the room that Grace at once felt the taste on her lips. She observed with a sense of envy as Drasko showed Rivka how to pick up the food from the tray, explained to her the sauces and the names, then picked up the tin bowl and scooped the content with the tips of his fingers and into his mouth.

Rivka did the same, laughing in delight. "Quite... peculiar, but I do like it, Mr. Mawr. Grace!" She turned to her. "Would you like to try?"

And at last, Drasko met Grace's eyes. "I requested that my kitchen staff only serve my wife English food. I don't think my wife is into new things."

How unfair that sounded! How much she resented him for this response! And she resented herself for wanting to join in yet holding back so as not to come across as too eager.

Samira brought exquisite desserts, then chai, milk tea with spices, and Grace finally gave in. She took a sip of chai, rich and flavorful on her tongue. Locking gazes with her husband, she picked up a piece of carrot *halwa* and betrayed herself, stifling a moan as she took the first bite, the sweet taste so delicious she wanted to close her eyes.

He watched her with a knowing smile.

"It's delicious," Grace said quietly.

"Absolutely!" Rivka exclaimed. "Mr. Mawr! You should let Gracie try new things!"

Drasko cocked a brow. "I didn't suspect that *Gracie*"—his eyes glinted with mischief at repeating her name—"was willing to try new things."

"Everyone needs time to adjust," Rivka said.

Drasko shifted his gaze to her. "You suppose, Miss Rebecca?"

"Absolutely! And time for acknowledgment, of course."

"Of what?"

"That what they thought they wanted is not always what they need."

"Oh, I have always found it the best truth."

"In fact, Mr. Mawr, you as a businessman know that new ventures sometimes might have a disheartening start but eventually become grand enterprises."

"Some do, indeed."

They chuckled like conspirators, but at once, a heavy weight lifted off Grace's chest as she realized her friend was welcome in his house. For the first time in her life, things were changing for the better. Because... of her husband.

Drasko took it upon himself to walk Rivka out and ordered his carriage to take her home.

"Madam!" Samira darted out of the house with a brown wooden box that she gave to Rivka. "Delicious desserts, Narayan just made them. Try, madam." She wiggled her head with a happy smile.

Rivka bade farewell to Drasko, then kissed Grace on the cheek and cupped her face.

What do you see, Rivka? Grace begged in her mind. *What is this man?*

Rivka's eyes glowed with kindness. "I shall see you soon," she said as they parted.

Grace walked back to the house, her husband at her side.

"You are good at making friends," she admitted when they walked inside.

He halted and turned to look at her. "I make allies." His smile was gone. "Friends? I have a few. But I rarely make new ones. You can't trust a person who doesn't accept where you come from and what you went through to get where you are."

Was he talking about her?

She remembered him laughing with Rivka, the way he kissed her hand when Rivka was leaving, and the coldness that shifted over his face as soon as he was alone with Grace.

She couldn't help but think about the article she had read in the archives.

A Predator or the Rightful Heir to the Mawr Empire?

14

GRACE

"Miss Grace! Oh, my Lord! Miss Grace!" Eden ran into Grace's room, panting, her cap askew. "There is a delivery for you, miss. Mr. Mawr is asking for you downstairs."

Grace frowned. "What sort of delivery?"

"Oh, ma'am. A piano!"

Grace's heart started humming, the tune so very happy, for the first time since her wedding day, that she darted out of the room at once.

A piano!

It was barely past noon. Surprisingly, her husband was at home. A smile flickered on her face, then grew bigger as she hurried down the grand stairs, then willed herself to slow down.

Not so eager.

But her heart didn't agree. It threatened to jump out of her chest as she stepped into the music room.

It was a wonderful, light-filled space with giant windows, parquet floors, exotic instruments lining up the perimeter, and colorful frescos on the ceiling.

Drasko and several of his men stood talking, their chatter dying out as they noticed her.

They parted to reveal a clavichord behind them.

"I got you what you wished for, wife," her husband said, the words so bitter she could hear the poison from a mile away.

Her eyes on the musical instrument, so small and lonely in the center of the room, Grace took a step toward it. Another step —her eyes roamed the old keyboard, several keys sunken. Another slow step—the hum in her chest turned into a false tune. One more—she noticed the scraped paint, the faded polish, the edges so beat up it looked a hundred years old.

The false tune in her head grew into screeching. This wasn't a gift but an insult.

Slowly, she turned to look at her husband. The beautiful bastard stood with his hands in his pockets, his head cocked, his shameless green eyes on her.

"You got me *this*?" her voice broke, her heart sinking.

"You get what you strive for, wife."

"This is garbage," she said.

"You are too quick to forget the conversation we had days ago. I will remind you. *The necessary minimum*, you said."

She remembered perfectly well what she had said.

He studied the old thing with feigned attentiveness. "I thought I'd do the same. After all, a marriage is a contract, is it not?" He turned his smirk to her.

She wanted to slap it off his face.

"I hope you enjoy it," he said.

No.

She would poison him again, certainly.

"I shall not touch it," she responded quietly. "Do you know who I am?"

"You know what they say? That the greatest musicians can play angelic music on the most devilish keys. Your talent, darling"—he walked up to the clavichord and tapped it with the tip of his shoe—"should shine through the broken keys and poorly tuned strings. After all, you seem to have been fond of used goods in the past."

She gasped. "How dare you? I shall not... this... this

garbage"—she nodded toward the instrument—"is an insult to my skills."

"Very well." He snapped his fingers.

In seconds, his men dragged the clavichord out of the room.

"Good," she said bitterly and walked out just to see it being hauled out of the mansion.

Her husband followed her, his leisurely assertive steps echoing behind her, a cunning smile on his face.

His men took the clavichord outside and set the old thing down in the middle of the green lawn, among the rose beds. One of them took a jar and sprinkled the liquid out of it onto the instrument.

"What—" Grace frowned, watching them from the front steps.

Another man struck a match and threw it at the clavichord.

"No!" Grace shouted.

But it was too late. A fire engulfed it.

She rushed toward it. "You can't do this!" she yelled at the men. "Put it out! It's an instrument!"

She covered her mouth with her hand, horrified at the sight of the flames among the rose beds.

The fire only grew higher, while the men watched, hands in their pockets.

"Aw, but it is garbage," a mocking voice came from behind her. Her husband strode toward her, lighting a cigarette. "It is not up to your standards, darling." He took a deep drag and flicked the match into the fire.

Tears welled up in her eyes. "If you intended to punish me, it is working."

"I am simply holding the negotiations. I've told you the deal is only—"

"As good as the parties fulfilling it," she cut in, her eyes on the clavichord, then on him, her heart weeping for the loss.

"Correct. This piano is the minimum effort. It is as good as your side of the bargain."

She balled her fists at her sides, fighting through the sting. "What do you want?" she gritted out.

He exhaled a cloud of smoke, then inspected the tip of his cigarette for some time, testing her patience.

"Three things from you." He raised his calm eyes at her. "Respect, marital duties, and heirs. At least until I have no interest in this arrangement, and I can let you go."

"Tyrant," she whispered but held his gaze.

"We can start with the first one on the list. No insults—that would be nice."

She lifted her chin in defiance. "I hate you."

He smiled coldly. "That'll change. They say the road from hate to love is a dark one. Only when you see the light ahead do you know you have arrived on the other side."

"How poetic. But wishful thinking."

"I need you to understand something." He stuck one of his hands in his pocket. "This marriage was arranged by someone else. The headlines already run all sorts of damaging accusations. It is my fault, not yours. I don't care about my reputation, but I need peace of mind. You *will* do your best to show respect and consideration. And I will do the same because we need to keep things civil between us and in public."

Finally, he was admitting the reason behind their marriage.

"The second agenda comes next. I do expect you to fulfill your wife's duties. And not the necessary minimum. I've changed my mind. I want it consistent." He cocked his brow at her. "Perhaps, we can agree on a schedule."

"A schedule?" she mocked.

"Yes. Business requires a plan. I promise to be a gentleman, and you shall learn to *please*—a concept perhaps foreign to you, but I heard you are a great student."

Bastard. "I shall hate every minute of it."

"Wishful thinking, darling," he said with a straight face. "You shall forget hating the moment you realize that my attention can be quite satisfying. When your little vain heart survives the storm, you might even ask for it again." His eyes twinkled with mischief.

Anger spiked inside her, betrayed by the blush creeping up her cheeks.

"Boy, is it hot here," he mocked her, as the clavichord was smoking like an old furnace. "As to the heirs? We can wait until you are ready. I am a patient man."

She wanted to call him names but couldn't find the words. She imagined what he would do if she suddenly vanished. Perhaps, she could stay with Rivka. Work in a drug store? Teach music?

Ah, that was the rub. Grace would have to say goodbye to her music career and the concerts and the stages and—

Music, yes.

All through the years with the guardians who never loved her, the friends she could never have around, her life carefully scheduled up to every hour of every day, Grace never had anything but her music.

No, no, she could not give it up.

And this man—her heart beat wildly as she stood her ground —could be a tyrant, indeed. Nothing she wasn't used to. But he could allow her to create. This house was an exotic cage, with its fountains and opulent furniture, Asian statues and a greenhouse with plumerias and mango trees and palms and wonderful flowers—but a cage, nevertheless.

What did Grace do when she had no escape? She played. And she sang. And she wrote her best pieces when she was at her worst. The best music was created by torment. There was no haunting beauty in peace.

So be it.

This was, indeed, a business deal.

"Very well," she said bravely, suddenly relieved at the decision. "Let's make a deal. In exchange, I can keep friendships with whoever I want. I go wherever I want. You shall not limit my freedom."

Her husband's head tilted just a little—a momentary surprise in his eyes, only a second of it that she caught and held on to with triumph.

A minuscule smirk tugged at his lips. "You have no notion of freedom. But whatever you think it is, have at it."

At the snap of his fingers, his men put out the fire.

Grace looked at the charred shape of the poor clavichord and swallowed the hurt and harsh words that begged to come out.

"This piano," he said right behind her, his voice surprisingly soft this time, without a hint of usual coldness, "was a used one and belonged to someone else. Perhaps, your supposed marriage to Charles wasn't what you truly needed."

For a brief second, Charles's face appeared before her, then the memory of the floral perfume on him on their wedding day, then him walking out on her.

She hated them, those visions. She resented the stranger who had forced her into this marriage and was probably right. Deep down inside, she knew he was, and she hated that too.

Only nine years older than her, he had sailed all around the world, lived in two countries, seen dozens more, helped build a diamond empire.

What did she have? Nothing, not even a family.

What had she done in her past? She had simply used the only thing she'd been lucky to have—her talent.

Was it worth surviving everything else?

Grace bit her lip, holding back tears. She was already starting to learn from him—everything was a business deal, and the answer to her question was simple. Yes. A thousand times yes. What else did she have left but her music?

His men were smoking and watching her. So were the maids peeking from behind the doorway and the windows.

Grace took a deep breath and summoned her courage. She walked up to her husband and looked him in the eyes.

He watched her in silence, the smoke from his cigarette curling in the air between them.

Grace nodded. "Business it is. Do I have to learn more about my husband from newspapers? Or will he spare me his attention from time to time? So that when we are in public and they ask me questions, I can answer"—she summoned all her bitterness—"with *respect*"—she faked a smile—"at least a few of them."

He cocked his head, that little motion she noticed when he was either curious or daring. "I suppose there is a lot to discuss."

"I agree," she said with determination. "I shall make this work, at least for the foreseeable future. If this is to work, there would be many rules. Before I was your wife, I was Grace Sommerville. My talent belongs to the people. I'd like you to respect that too. We cannot give up who we are, so we shall pretend to be who we are not. This will be perhaps the grandest performance of my life."

His lips pursed just a little to hide a smile. "I cannot wait. You have always been great at performing, Mrs. Mawr."

Anger flared inside her. Hurt twisted her heart. She broke their stare, turned on her heel, and walked away. Pacing herself, taming her hurt, she marched across the lawn toward the house and felt his eyes on her all the way to the door.

15

GRACE

"Dras-ko Mawr," Grace repeated slowly.

In her room, she sat at the desk and thought for the longest time about what exactly made her angry at her husband.

He didn't want her yet had to marry her. The wealthiest man in London had no choice—intriguing, to say the least. Perhaps, she was unjustly cross while he tried to navigate the new life he had been forced into just like her.

Her hopes and dreams only days ago were now engulfed in flames. Fate was strange. Cruel? Not yet. But *he* held it in his hands. And what had Grace done all her life in circumstances like this? Played by the rules and made sure everything was perfect.

Dras-ko, she mouthed again, rolling the syllables that tasted like whisky, heavy and sharp.

She had looked up his name in an encyclopedia. Of Slavic origin, Serbian or Montenegrin, perhaps. "Precious" it meant.

Unlikely.

But with bitterness, there came subtle acceptance. A tune played in her mind. She hummed. The lyrics started forming on their own, like they always did—places, feelings, senses. Some wrote diaries. Grace composed songs.

She took a pad out of a drawer and started writing. This was her talent. Music was her soul. Everything she'd ever loved or hated always trickled into her songs.

This time, she wrote about green eyes. The words, disjointed at first, slowly spilled onto the paper. The tune hummed in her head, a sad one, but hopeful. She *made* it hopeful, wanted it to be.

This marriage would work. She would make it work! At least until he decided to set her free, he'd said.

Her fingers started dancing on the smooth wooden surface of the desk, imitating the piano chords. Grace noted them down, and soon, she forgot herself. The chords formed into a sensual song. She rose from her seat and walked around the room, singing to herself. Her fingers flicked in the air as she mimicked the chords, her steps in rhythm with the invisible tempo.

She didn't know how much time had passed when she finally inspected her notes—songs and songs written about... *him*.

She dropped them as if they scalded her.

He did not deserve her songs!

She bit her lip and stood in silence by the window for some time, trying to calm her mind.

A frantic knock came at the door, and Eden burst into the room. "My lady! Oh, but you have to come downstairs at once!"

What now? "Is Mr. Mawr there?"

"Your husband? No."

Everyone was set on reminding her who he was to her.

"He left, ma'am. Business, he said. But there is a man asking for you. Several men, to be exact. And..." Eden's eyes glowed with a glee that only made Grace intrigued. "But come, ma'am! Please come!"

Samira stood outside the door, too, smiling, as always.

Loud noises came from downstairs—men's voices, harsh orders, the sound of something being dragged, someone's authoritative bark, "There! There! Oh, you be... Care-ful! By

God! It cost more than your life! *My* life, too! Right there! Perfect!"

What in the world?

Grace hurried down the stairs, into the music room, and halted in the doorway.

There, in the middle of the room, sat a full-size concert grand piano, its shape unmistakable under a beige cloth.

A grand piano for her? Broken? Crippled? Was that another lesson for her to learn?

Her heart painfully contracted in her chest—this must be another trick.

The workmen stepped aside, bowing to her.

A short elderly man with a cane and wearing glasses hurried toward her.

"I am Jacque Ormsby. I own Ormsby Pianos," he said, bowing with a broad white smile framed by a thick beard and bushy mustache. He reached for her. "Miss Grace Sommerville. Oh, Miss Grace! What an honor!"

She flinched at the sound of her former name.

His eyes widened in panicky realization. "Oh, pardon, pardon me, ma'am! Mrs. Mawr, of course! How foolish of me. Forgive me, forgive me." He bowed in apology and kissed her hand that she absently put into his, glancing curiously at the instrument. "We are not yet used to the change, Mrs. Mawr."

"We?"

"Well, yes, the admirers of your talent. We have delivered your order!" He hurried toward the covered instrument and paused with his hand on the cloth, smiling at her.

"My order?"

"Mr. Mawr ordered it for you. He did. And it is... Oh, but you shall be the judge! I present to you—"

His eyes glinted conspiratorially as he theatrically pulled the cloth up. The thin fabric flew upward and glided along the slick piano surface onto the floor.

Grace gasped. Her heart skipped a beat.

"It is a custom model by the talented American builder, Henry Steinway. Steinway & Sons," Mr. Ormsby announced proudly.

Grace walked as if in a dream toward the most beautiful grand piano she had ever seen.

"It is the classic but recently updated design of the concert grand. Rosewood, mother-of-pearl, and gold," Mr. Ormsby explained.

But Grace barely listened.

In awe, she walked around the grand piano, the light from the large windows beaming off the slick surface and the golden edges.

"For me?" she murmured in disbelief. She had never seen anything so beautiful. "Where did you get this beauty?"

She couldn't breathe. She was afraid to touch it. This was a masterpiece. And hers. She had never gotten a present like this.

"You see, Mrs. Mawr, Ormsby Pianos does not have such exquisite pieces in stock. Or even in England, I must say. This is the most expensive piece we have ever been commissioned. It took four months."

"How…" Tears pooled in Grace's eyes at the sight.

"Ah, but Mr. Mawr found out about it. He surely is persuasive, to say the least. He went to visit the customers who had ordered it. I don't know what he said or did. He is charming, of course. But—voila—they kindly agreed to sell it to him."

Unable to look away, Grace still didn't dare touch the instrument. She walked a circle around it like a sleepwalker.

"Mr. Mawr, oh, he is wonderful," the man said.

Wonderful? Something did not add up.

"When did my husband do all this?" Grace asked with a frown.

"Over a week ago, Mrs. Mawr."

"A week?" She gaped at the man in disbelief.

"Ten days, ma'am. Ten days. I have it marked on my calendar. It's a… Well, it was an event, let me tell you."

So, that was the day after the wedding, after she had poisoned him, when he used to spend nights elsewhere.

"Yes! I shall never forget!" Mr. Ormsby continued. "Mr. Mawr sent the telegram to the original customers, arranged the meeting, then traveled to Edinburg to talk to them and… Well, now it is here."

Smiling proudly, Mr. Ormsby stroked his beard.

Grace still couldn't believe it. All this before he brought the cheap clavichord.

A smile broke out on her lips. *Can't be.* She killed it with a pang of embarrassment and finally dared touch her present.

Her fingers tingled at the feeling of polished wood under them, luring her to sit down on the matching piano bench and try it out.

Mr. Ormsby motioned to his men, and one of them walked, almost on tiptoes, and propped the lid open.

With caution, Grace opened the fallboard, her hummingbird heartbeat putting her on edge. She brushed her fingers along the keys and finally hit the first chord.

Her heart answered.

Her entire body resonated with a sound she hadn't heard in days. And then her fingers briefly flew over the keys, playing the song she had just written upstairs. A song about *him*.

Mr. Ormsby stilled, slightly bowed, his eyes, full of admiration, on her hands.

She withdrew her hands abruptly.

Liar. Trickster. Manipulator.

She couldn't find the right words for her husband. He was playing games with her, and she knew it. She was like a mouse toyed with, and she understood it too.

But the sight of this most beautiful instrument made her eyes burn with tears. She was absolutely in love with it, wanted to be alone with it and make it sing under her fingertips.

"It is a superb piece," she said quietly through tears. "Thank you very much, Mr. Ormsby."

"My pleasure, my pleasure, ma'am. Mr. Mawr clearly cares a lot, despite—" His words cut off.

Grace smiled to herself. "Despite?" *Despite the dirty headlines.*

"Oh, nothing. My apologies, ma'am." Mr. Ormsby bowed apologetically. "This old man doesn't know what he is talking about. Your husband very much loves you."

She had to make an effort not to laugh in his face.

"Mr. Mawr said you use two pianos. One for performances, at the Academy, and an upright for practice. A true professional, he said."

"He said that?"

"He said George Steck, the American, was your favorite. Is that correct?"

She listened to him stunned. Where would her husband learn all that? How would he know? And most of all, why would he bother?

Oh, but this was a deal, she reminded herself. He wanted her to do her best.

Very well. A queen would've given herself to him for this instrument.

Grace trembled in anticipation, wanting to play the new instrument so badly but keeping her face straight in front of the man.

It was true, of course. It was much more practical to practice on an upright. But this—she stroked the edge of the grand piano —oh, this was just splendid!

Mr. Ormsby graciously motioned with his hand. "Mr. Mawr was so adamant about getting the best we had and hoped you'd love it. I have never met a man who was so dedicated to his wife's talent! So... Mrs. Mawr, where would you like the other one?"

At a loss, Grace shook her head in confusion as she met his eyes. "The other?"

"Yes! Mr. Mawr understands true craft. He insisted that you had to have the upright, too. For daily practice, he explained. So, where would you like my men to put the second one?"

16

DRASKO

How the Earl of Weltingdon Got Duped!
Or Is It a Trade-Off?

Elias theatrically read yet another headline as he and Drasko sat in the office of the Mawr Building.

"Please, don't," Drasko pleaded on an exhale, shaking his head in annoyance.

"Perhaps, if you talk to reporters and explain, these sleazy headlines will go away," Elias said, scanning the rest of the news. "It has been over two weeks, and the city is still buzzing about your wedding."

"Perhaps, if my wife didn't try so hard to show her resentment, we could indeed pull it off in public."

"Speaking on the topic, when are you going to introduce me to your wife? Or join us for dinner? My mother inquired about you. So did Uncle Sydney. You have some sort of deal with him, I heard."

"Elias, my wife doesn't leave the house much, doesn't care, would rather I didn't exist."

"You are exaggerating. Did you try to win her over?"

"Actively."

"Did it work?"

"Could I buy your friendship with money?"

"Absolutely not."

"You see? So, I am trying to buy her patience instead."

"Would you like to invite me over? I shall be the judge of your wife's character."

"Do *you* care?"

Elias rolled his eyes in annoyance. "When did I *not* care about what was happening with you?"

"This little incident will resolve itself eventually."

"Little incident?" Elias barked out a laugh. "You are married, mate!"

"And she doesn't want to have much to do with me. So, what is the point?"

"You are fooling yourself. I will go visit her, then."

"Suit yourself. Send my best regards."

Drasko blinked in annoyance, rose, and walked up to the window.

His gaze soared over the city below, its crowded streets and the buildings, rising higher every year. After centuries, at last, Europe was once again powered by knowledge more than titles. Science and technology were paving new paths for those who possessed unique skills and ideas. This was where Drasko was meant to end up after years overseas.

Yet he missed India, its nature, the simplicity of life. It was June, his favorite time of the year, the monsoon season with its rains and luscious greenery. He hadn't yet written to Rupesh with the marriage news. He should. The English newspapers were delivered to India with much delay. Yet, Rupesh had probably read about it already.

Drasko wished he were in India. There, he could get lost just about anywhere. Unlike London. It suffocated him, as did his fancy three-piece suit

And now he had *her*.

Drasko tried to spend as much time as possible away from

the house. He needed to avoid her. His initial anger gone, he understood that while he had agreed to this game with Uriah years ago, Grace had no knowledge of it. She was his wife against her will. So, he needed to tread carefully—break her in, tame her, show her what he was. If she still resented him, there was no way to force her to like him. He wasn't an animal. But, by God, he wanted to be! Every glimpse of her, every whiff of her perfume made him wish he were a brute so he could take her into his bedroom and snuff out that haughty gaze of hers with his caresses. She was a beautiful woman, yet untouchable. His, yet only on paper. Still, his heart burned with a hopeful "what if."

Something else bothered him.

For years, he had watched her from afar, at her concerts and social gatherings. Her interactions with her guardians were peculiar. He couldn't help noticing how stiff she was around them, how well-practiced her responses were, how often she flinched at the mere sound of their voices.

The Sommervilles were decent people, but somehow void of feelings. He had asked them about Grace's practicing routine, of course. He wanted her to have the best, even if it came with a bit of negotiation on his part.

But the Sommervilles had washed their hands of the entire deal as soon as they had gotten the settlement money as per the letters.

Odd, really.

But Drasko saw to it that Grace got her pianos. Prided himself as he remembered the way Samira talked about her new mistress.

"When the piano men left," she had said, "missus started playing. Oh, sir! She is an angel. Or a devil. I do not know how to put it or what gives her music so much power. The entire service staff of the house stood behind the music room door and listened to her play. Eden only smiled proudly. She heard it for years, you know. But Narayan closed his eyes as he swayed to the tune. Old Borga from the kitchen shed a tear. Missus is... Oh, she is... Sir, do make her happy! She is so lovely!"

Yes, she was. And she was his. With her elegant posture and skilled fingers and rosy lips and hazel eyes and the talent that conquered London and far beyond.

Except she hated him.

He needed to work more so he didn't have to hear her play the piano. He liked her music too much. It affected him too deeply. It stirred the memories from the past that needed to stay buried. It assaulted the fortress he had built around his heart— not to keep himself safe, no, but to protect others. Her, too. She could not get too close to him. Drasko knew what that would lead to.

And yet, he couldn't help himself.

Last night, he had listened to her play. From the hallway, like a thief in his own house, still like a statue, afraid to scare her off. The guards had perked up like they'd heard the most beautiful siren's song.

But as soon as Drasko had approached the door to the music room, she had stopped playing as if she knew he was there.

She was extraordinary, her sense of music exceptional. He felt every key, every chord tugging at the strings of his heart. And he couldn't have that—feeling vulnerable or not at his strongest.

He wasn't worried—yet—but was uneasy. The dead man kept him on his toes. Elias eased his days with his company. His Indian servants made him feel more at home. His men were loyal, for he paid them like royalty. Even the Metropolitan Police were paid by him—he never knew when he might need their help.

All his bases were covered.

Except her.

Grace was like the wind that blew over the high wall of his fortress. Like the groundwater that trickled through the stones. Like the scent that was carried through the air and got in his every pore.

They said that danger was tangible. Fools! The danger was an invisible force that possessed one's heart and mind a second before it was too late to act. You took the heart and mind of a man—and he was a prisoner.

Right now, Drasko was on a sure road to incarceration. He knew it, of course. In vain, he had tried to tell himself for years that she didn't matter. It was too late. She was now part of the game.

A knock at the door turned Drasko around.

"A visitor, sir," his assistant announced with a mysterious smile. "Mrs. Mawr."

Elias's eyes snapped at Drasko, who muttered, "Oh, hell," under his breath.

17

DRASKO

Elias jumped up from his seat, wiggling his eyebrows at Drasko. "Mrs. Mawr," he mouthed with an excited expression on his face. "Oh, my!"

Grace walked in like a queen—there were no other words to describe her lavish light-blue summer dress with golden trim, high necklace with ruffles, the tiny hat that rested sideways like an intricate flower on her dark hair, tied into a bun at the back of her head.

Despite the stale summer heat outside, Grace looked fresh and dazzling. Women, of course, had that talent of looking the best in the worst circumstances.

For a second, Drasko wondered if she had dressed up to impress him.

Wishful thinking, her voice echoed in his mind.

Their eyes met.

Grace smiled at him as she approached, no doubt aware of another person in the room.

"Husband darling," she said most endearingly with that hint of mockery only Drasko recognized.

"Wife dearest." He walked up to her and, unlike any other time, leaned over to give her a kiss on her cheek.

He needed to stay away from her, but his treacherous heart-beat thought otherwise, spiking at the innocent touch and the momentary shock in her eyes.

"What a surprise," he whispered before pulling away.

Now that he thought about it, they hadn't touched since the morning after the wedding, when he'd pinned her against the wall.

This time, there was no sharpness in her gaze. That was surely unusual.

"I told you I wanted to know more about what you do." She said with feigned cheerfulness, or perhaps genuine, Drasko couldn't quite tell yet. "When Muhammad does not go to the mountain, then the mountain goes to Muhammad."

She was definitely a stubborn pretty thing.

"Quite true," Elias said behind her, ignored until now, turning her around. "Mrs. Mawr!"

Drasko cleared his throat. "My friend, Elias Bayne."

"We have met before, Mr. Bayne," Grace said with a smile.

"Indeed!"

"At my performance at the Canterbury Music Hall."

"Correct."

"And at the charity function at the Shirleys."

"Oh!" Elias exchanged surprised glances with Drasko. "Great memory! I am a good friend of your husband's."

"My best friend," Drasko corrected.

Grace raised her eyebrows. "I didn't know my husband had friends."

Was she mocking him?

"One and only. A miracle, truly." Elias bowed with a broad smile. "Should I leave you two lovebirds alone?"

"No, no, no! Please!" Grace chuckled, strangely at ease with the words. "My husband is not into lovebirds' chatter. He is a busy man. Doesn't have much time for his wife. Do stay!"

Drasko held back a smile, amused by her acting skills. That was the thing he was finding out about Grace Sommerville—

correction, Mawr, he really needed to get used to that *Mrs. Mawr* thing—she had the most innocent and angelic expression, the epitome of humbleness. So, it was even more amusing to see her sarcastic remarks that she tried to pass off as genuine.

"I am an admirer of your talent," Elias said.

He gallantly led Grace to the desk and offered her a seat, all the while asking questions of all kinds. He intended to make friends with her, no doubt, and Drasko was looking forward to seeing how Elias's little enterprise went on.

The office sank into friendly chatter, Grace and Elias's eyes on each other as if Drasko didn't exist.

Drasko ordered tea and brandy and observed them, trying to catch her every movement, the elegant wave of her gloved hand, her graceful posture, the way her face glowed when she smiled.

"It is a pleasure to meet you again," Elias said, leaning on his armrest to talk to her as if he were about to tell her a secret. "You see, my friend seems to be too possessive of you. He simply will not bring you for dinner at the Baynes. He is afraid you will like his friends more than him."

Drasko sucked in his cheeks.

Grace burst out in laughter. "Mr. Bayne, may I tell you a secret?"

"Why, of course!"

She mimicked him by leaning over her armrest toward him. "My husband is not nearly as friendly with me as his friends or his guards."

Elias frowned, mischievous laughter in his eyes. "That is unfortunate. Perhaps, he is simply not very good at pleasing women."

Bastard.

Grace's laughter danced across the office, and Drasko swore to himself he would strangle his best friend.

"But!" Elias grinned. "Do not get discouraged by his perhaps generally hostile air. A man who eats with his hands and walks barefoot with his laborers in India cannot be too scary." Grace shot a surprised glance in his direction. "Are you familiar with Rakshasa?"

At that word, Drasko's blood turned cold. It wasn't up to Elias to tell her the story about his scars.

"Pardon me?" Grace asked.

Drasko gave him a warning glare.

"Never mind. There used to be a notorious tiger back in India where Mawr Diamond Industries operates. Since he was little, the locals called our Drasko by the tiger's name."

The memory flashed in Drasko's mind, sharp and bloody, making the tattoo on his back burn.

"Because of his green eyes?" Grace inquired with humor.

"That's a thought!" Elias nodded. "Women always notice his eyes. Perhaps, he will tell you the whole story one day."

Perhaps not.

"But my point, Mrs. Mawr," Elias continued in an overly cheerful and mischievous air that Grace was catching on to, "do you know what wild tigers do to their female mates?"

A pretty blush colored her cheeks as she cocked her head in endearing amusement. "Enlighten me, Mr. Bayne."

Fucking Elias. It was a Bayne thing—stirring trouble. All Elias's cousins, and Drasko knew a few, were notorious troublemakers.

"The female tiger bites the male to play," Elias explained, a smile never leaving his face. "But the *male* tiger bites the female… wait for it"—he raised his forefinger in the air—"to have a grip on her."

"A grip?"

"Yes. To have more control over her and make sure she doesn't swipe at him when she is angry. So, you see, it is an affectionate bite, more of a hold, self-preservation mechanism."

"I see, Mr. Bayne," Grace said playfully.

Drasko was about to burst out in laughter. Perhaps, there might come a time when he would tell his *dear wife* that what Elias had just described, in fact happened during tigers' mating.

"Our dear Drasko," Elias continued his little story, "is only trying to keep you from swiping at him or running away. A precaution. Don't mind him. He only looks scary when he is disarmed. And by a woman such as you! I am not a bit surprised."

A trill of laughter escaped Grace. The sound of it traveled through Drasko's skin and lodged itself in his chest.

Had he ever heard her laugh before today? No. He craved that sound again, the sight of her genuinely happy so uncommon.

But soon, Elias was leaving, kissing Grace's hand and inviting her for dinner with his family.

Grace pursed her lips for a second. "I am not sure my husband wants me around his friends."

"That is not true," Drasko interjected.

She didn't look at him, her eyes on Elias. "I am not sure he wants others to know I exist at all. If it were not for the newspaper headlines—"

"Nonsense," Drasko objected louder, his gaze burning into her though she ignored him.

Elias looked between the two of them. "I notice some sort of miscommunication going on. You see, Drasko is getting old. Yes, it's true."

Another trill of laughter fell off Grace's lips.

Drasko almost choked in surprise—he was twenty-nine and several years younger than Elias.

"Yes, yes." Elias nodded with theatrical graveness. "These days, he avoids company and declines social invitations. Perhaps you, being a young soul, could take matters into your own hands, Mrs. Mawr. Do come visit! I shall send a dinner invitation addressed to you, and if the old gizzard doesn't want to come, leave him at home."

Grace laughed again, that sweet trill so contagious, Drasko had to put a cigarette between his lips to distract himself.

And then his jaw dropped when she said, "Mr. Bayne, please call me Grace."

In an instant, Elias bowed. "Well, then it is only appropriate if you call me Elias. My best friend might kill me for such informality, but it is, oh, so worth it. It would be a dream come true to hear you play."

"You are always welcome in our house! Do come visit, Elias! It would be lovely!"

Elias raised his brows at Drasko in a silent, "I told you so."

But as soon as Elias walked out the door, Grace's cheerfulness was gone. It was so obvious she was nervous around Drasko. Her posture stiffened. He thought he caught a glimpse of panic in her eyes—was she afraid of him?

Drasko leaned back against his desk and stuck his hands in his pockets, studying her. "Tell me why you are really here."

18

DRASKO

So, the pianos did the trick.

Or, perhaps, an army of modistes that had come to their house to create lavish dresses for Grace. Or the unlimited funds Drasko had provided for her. Most women could be bought.

Yet, Grace's gaze wasn't bitter. *A miracle, truly.*

"I told you," she replied with a nervous smile. "I want to know more about you. The reporters downstairs asked me for comments."

Drasko raised his eyebrow in question.

Grace playfully swung the reticule in her hand, a gesture too forced, betraying her nervousness, as she took slow steps around his office, studying it.

"I told them that the engagement to the earl was my silly revenge on you. While, all along, you and I were madly in love." For the second time in the last ten minutes, Drasko almost choked in surprise. A little smirk curled her pretty lips as she met his eyes. "How is my performance?"

"Outstanding so far," he said with a sense of satisfaction, adding, "wife."

"So, will you tell me about what you do here? Or should I ask your assistant to give me a tour?" she asked again haughtily. "A random Londoner knows more about Mawr Diamond Industries than Drasko Mawr's *wife*. If you are busy, I understand. Perhaps, I shall ask the reporters."

Her stabs at him were so endearing. He easily saw through her forced confidence, her intentional bitterness, realizing it wasn't in her nature at all. For as soon as she forgot herself, genuine eagerness shone through her eyes. She was so lovely when she was herself.

"Very well." He pushed off his desk.

It would take weeks to show her the true scale of what Drasko's fortune encompassed. But he started with the Mawr Building.

"The elevator was constructed half a year ago by the American scientist," Drasko explained as they took a ride downstairs to the lower floors.

He tried to act nonchalant, but his wife's questions were on point, with genuine curiosity that killed off his bitterness. And as he started telling her about the company's history, he enjoyed giving her glimpses of what he was.

He showed her the stockrooms, introduced her to the managers, the people in charge of sales, all the while waiting for her to get bored.

She didn't.

"You are the goddess of music!" his employees complimented while Grace smiled politely.

"The Mawr Wonder Room," Drasko announced as he took her to the floor below his office where the masterpieces of lapidary and jewelry craftsmanship were displayed.

Etta Lauman was in charge of the collection and smiled graciously as she gave Grace the description of every art piece.

"I am such an admirer of your music!" she kept repeating, touching Grace's hand like she was holy.

"My favorite, I think," Grace said as she inspected the *Guardian of the Night*. The full-size raven was made out of obsidian pieces. Red diamonds for eyes. Blue diamonds for the threads in its beak. White diamonds created a glittering armor texture on its feathers.

Mine too, Drasko thought in surprise and studied his wife as she explored the collection and gasped in awe.

There were black diamonds with golden legs—spiders scattered on a piece of red marble.

A rose made out of emeralds and garnets, the diamonds sprinkling it with morning dew.

A chandelier, made of 120,000 melee diamonds.

Europa's Abductor was a bull's head with horns, diamonds of all hues decorating the skull.

Cupid's Spear, a Greek sculpture of Eros, had wings and bows made out of thousands of pink melee diamonds.

Manus Deae were a pair of women's gloves made out of colorless diamonds, and *Libidine* was a stunning woman's floor-length negligee made out of yellow ones. In Latin, *libidine* stood for lust.

Wonders of jewelry craftsmanship hadn't impressed Drasko in a long time. Yet he observed Grace with delight, catching her gleeful smile as she studied the pieces.

Several men walked in with heavy equipment.

"How timely!" Miss Etta exclaimed. "Mr. Mawr, this is John Figg, the photographer I was telling you about. He wants to take a photograph of you and the Mawr Wonder Room. Since Mrs. Mawr is here, it is only fitting that both of you pose."

And the two of them stood in front of the camera, Drasko half-a-step behind Grace. He couldn't help himself—he placed his palm on the small of her back. Her body went rigid right away, but she didn't move away, and his palm burned at the contact.

"There are several other things that you might like," Drasko said after the photos had been taken.

"What about the tower?" Grace inquired.

"It's connected to the building. One entrance at the ground floor. One from my office."

"Will you not show me?"

He shook his head—she was surely very inquisitive. "It is off limits."

"To whom?"

"Everyone but me."

Disappointment crossed her face. "Why?"

"It's my fortress of solitude. I like quiet places. I can hear myself then."

She nodded. "Interesting. I like music. I can hear myself better." Their eyes locked for a brief moment of understanding. "Very well, then! I'd like to see more! If you have time, that is."

They took a ride to the Grand Marquis.

For the first time, they were together in public, and he noticed the reporters following them at a distance.

For the first time, they walked together on the street, only a short distance from the carriage toward the Grand Marquis restaurant. He offered his arm to her, and, without hesitation, she curled her gloved hand around it, making his chest tighten with the unfamiliar warmth.

He wondered if she recognized the restaurant he owned.

"I remember this place," she said as they sat at the table.

He did not respond. It was unlikely she remembered the occasion that had once made him despise her so much and acquire this very establishment.

It had been mere weeks since their marriage. May had turned into June. And for the first time, the increasing heat and at times overbearing smells of the crowded city did not bother Drasko.

In fact, today, the summer felt charming, the colors of blooming trees unusually vibrant, the birds singing and the children's laughter on the streets intoxicating with their cheerfulness. Oddly, he enjoyed this spontaneous tour of the city that belonged to him but had never made home in his heart.

He took Grace to his small motor factory, where he introduced her to his mechanics. Most called them tinkerers. Drasko called them visionaries.

A large garage, or rather, hallway was loaded with strange

contraptions and monstrous metal mechanisms that one day, Drasko was certain, would be the future of the city.

"What is this?" Grace inquired in wonder.

"Brace yourself." Drasko nodded toward the mechanics, who started the motor of a carriage that didn't have a way to hook it to a horse.

"A vehicle powered by a gas engine," one of the men shouted over the blaring of the motor.

Soon, it was turned off, the garage filled with smoky fumes.

But Grace didn't scrunch up her nose, didn't open her hand fan, only studied the prototype of a motor car wide-eyed. "I've heard of those!"

The mechanics exchanged approving glances with Drasko.

"Yes," one of them said, encouraged by her enthusiasm. "Mr. Carl Benz has a pattern, but we intend to create our own. We had success with steam-powered prototypes. But we haven't established a proper way to run the gasoline-powered ones for longer periods and without such a terrible racket."

"How... extraordinary!" Grace marveled. "The future."

"The future with a terrible racket, ma'am."

She laughed. "But that is how it often starts. With a racket that turns into beautiful music."

Drasko's heart twisted at her words. On his back, Rakshasa grunted softly. Grace glanced at him from beneath her lashes and looked away too quickly, but the meaning of her words burned in the air between them.

And Drasko marveled at how her face glowed when she smiled, how everyone around her lit up in an instant when she laughed. Her laughter had the same effect as her music—heads turning toward her at the sound as if she were the sun that could warm with its shine.

A drug company on 7th Street, a gentleman's club and casino in Mayfair, a science center in Southwark—Grace only gazed at Drasko with fascination as he took her on the tour of his properties.

Whereas Mawr Diamond Industries was the Mawr brothers' accomplishment, Drasko was interested in industrial innovations and wanted to build a company of his own. He had always been fascinated with people and bright minds. Perhaps, it had stemmed from the opportunities the Mawr brothers had once given him. And so he was passing it on, investing his capital into everything profitable, but betting his money on everything that wasn't yet and seeking out brilliant minds that brought with them change.

Hundreds of Londoners, on foot, by bicycles, carriages, and trams, crowded the streets. London was changing rapidly. Technology was everywhere. Electricity wasn't a novelty anymore. In no time, the streets would see automobiles. What marvels! A new breed of businessmen was taking over England. And Drasko was planning on soon being at the front of it!

He swelled with pride under Grace's gaze as he showed her part of his fortune. He told her more as they rode through the crowded streets, got stuck in the dense traffic of carriages and drays, and he secretly cheered that he had more time with her.

She asked questions. He answered. Often, Drasko held back and let the more knowledgeable men who worked for him explain the businesses as they made stops across the city.

And he got lost in her. Her laughter grew happier. Her smiles were more frequent. Her gaze on him lingered longer.

Something extraordinary was occurring throughout the day —his wife was enjoying his company. This was by far the longest they'd been around each other. And when they arrived at the Port of London, their final destination, he felt disappointed that the day was drawing to an end.

The evening sun was low over the horizon when Drasko led Grace along the shipping docks. Her delicate gloved hand was once again wrapped around his arm—the gesture so simple yet more meaningful than anything that had passed between them yet. Her figure seemed so small and fragile next to his, her head reaching just to his chin.

He studied her face as they walked toward one of the piers, her gaze on the shimmering water of the Thames, reflecting the gold of the setting sun.

"Do you see those?" Drasko finally paused and pointed toward the barges with crates and containers. "They are going to be loaded onto that ship."

He pointed at the steamboat anchored in the bay. It was one of the fastest boats built in England. His. These days, it only took two weeks to get from London to Bombay.

Grace raised her eyes full of wonder at him. "And that is?"

"That's my ship, one of several used by Mawr Diamond Industries."

"Oh…" With her hand, she shielded her eyes from the setting sun, squinting at the ship in the distance while Drasko couldn't stop *feeling*, so acutely aware of her touch—her other hand was still wrapped around his forearm.

"It's magnificent," she whispered. "When is the next time you are going away?"

A momentary ache gripped his heart—perhaps, she was looking forward to being left alone.

"Not quite sure. There is a world's fair in Chicago in America next year. I intend to visit. Why do you ask?"

Silence hung in the air. Seagulls kaw-kawed in the salty sky.

Grace lowered her hand on top of her other one, both gently resting around his arm as she gazed at the ship in the distance.

The white of her gloves contrasted with his dark jacket. They were so different, Drasko thought at once. What would happen to them? Next year felt like a different life.

He wasn't sure why he asked quietly, "Would you like to go?"

He didn't turn to meet her eyes, wasn't sure he could. Her usual bitter response would come, he knew. He would bat it off with a joke. He was ready.

There came the longest minute of waiting, perhaps seconds that felt like an excruciating forever.

A fool. You are a damn fool, he told himself, regretting the question already.

He clenched his jaw, staring at the distance. That was stupid to ask. They'd agree to—

"Yes," she said almost in a whisper that felt louder than his booming heart.

THE
CRIMSON TEAR

Andhra Pradesh, India
Drasko, 14

They simply called her *choti*, a baby, a little one, motherless, unwanted by her father, but cherished by the servants.

Drasko called her little *jaan*, little life.

Alfred's daughter was five years old. Drasko was fourteen. And no human soul had ever loved him like she did.

He loved her back fiercely, with all his heart. He read her bedtime stories in Hindi and English. He brought her picture books, carved toy elephants and tigers out of wood, and fixed little diamonds into her bangles and anklets. He took her for walks in the wheat fields and told fantastical stories about Hindu gods.

She was his ray of sunshine, a girl with a "pure heart." One day, Drasko thought, she would be a diamond princess, he would make sure of it.

And one day, he caught a glimpse of the opportunity that would do just that.

Uriah called him one night to his office and locked the doors. Unlike the rest of the villa that smelled of charcoal, jasmine, and rose, the office smelled of leather and books.

"The London smell," Uriah used to say.

The candlelight was dim. The distant cries of the street *walas* seeped through the windows.

"I want to show you something," Uriah said.

He pushed aside the statue of Shiva, his favorite god of destruction, which hid the door to a walk-in vault. He disappeared inside and came out with a pouch.

"Come here, my boy."

This was the first and only time Drasko saw the Crimson Tear.

Uriah turned it in his fingers, exposing it to the lamplight.

The rarest shade of red, the color of blood, the size of a small plum, the brilliance mesmerized Drasko.

To a commoner, it would look like a regular gem. But Drasko knew the value of diamonds, the twelve base colors and many other hues, the cuts and clarity.

"This," said Uriah, his eyes flicking cunningly between the gem and Drasko, "is the rarest diamond in the world. It is worth a fortune."

Drasko had a business mind, so he simply asked, "Why not put it up for auction? In England or America?"

"Ah, that!" Uriah's eyes flickered with sinister glee. "All in good time. Yes, yes. I have plans. But they have to wait. And this"—despite Drasko being taller than him already, Uriah's bony hand gripped Drasko's shoulder—"will be our secret. You shall not tell a single soul."

Uriah's eyes narrowed on Drasko.

"Surely, Alfred knows," Drasko said.

Uriah only waved him off. "Yes, that. No matter. No one else, you understand?"

But who would Drasko tell?

Elias Bayne only came to visit twice a year. And when his best friend was gone, other foreigners didn't like Drasko. They called him *shaitaan* behind his back. Because his skin took up the sun faster, his hair was the darkest shade of black, his eyes were green, and his daring smile sparkly white.

But the night Drasko learned about the Crimson Tear, he was aching to share the secret with the one person he cared for the most.

And so he did.

That very night, he went to Asha and Rupesh's bungalow. Little *jaan* stayed with them that night.

Drasko picked up the little girl in his arms and asked her silly questions, amused by her clever responses. Her little fingers usually played with the bead necklace around her neck and the little bangles around her tiny wrists. But she creased her brows when they touched a small scar under his brow and the one on his jaw.

She was so precious in her tiny *salwar kameez*, the pajama-type pants and a long shirt, with her angel-soft wavy hair, her inquisitive eyes, and that smile, always that smile.

Drasko adored her. She wasn't yet marred by others' opinions of him, loving him for being next to her. She was too quick to forget things, little enough to be happy for no reason, dance to the songs in her head, and make friends with dogs.

And she was too little to understand what he was about to tell her. So, if he shared a secret, she would surely forget it.

He took her for a night walk to her favorite pond. A water buffalo often came there at night to drink. Pretty lotuses and water lilies glimmered in the moonlight.

Drasko picked her up in his arms and under the bright stars told her about the Crimson Tear. Told it like one of the fairy tales that she liked so much, in his best narrator's voice.

The legend made her tiny lips part in fascination and her big eyes widen in awe.

"One day, you will be a queen," he promised her. "You shall travel the world and to magical places. You shall have many dresses and many diamonds. The most handsome men will throw themselves at your feet. Perhaps a prince or a king who will love you and make you so very-very happy!"

"I want a knight," she said stubbornly, only five but already in love with fairy tales.

"You shall have anything you want. Even the Crimson Tear!"

"Why does the name sound so sad? I don't want tears."

Drasko laughed and tapped the tip of her nose with his forefinger. "Then so be it," he declared. "No tears for *jaanu*."

"No tears for *jaanu*!" she shouted happily to the stars, throwing her little arms in the air, then wrapped them around Drasko's neck.

They laughed into the starry night about the mysterious future. The future that, unbeknown to them, held so much pain.

Because one person, driven by sickly obsession, observed them from the shadows.

Uriah heard the words that were supposed to be a secret. He listened to their laughter that bore painful holes in his heart.

He was being betrayed, yet again. But this time, he would not let fate rule his life. He would take matters into his own hands and wipe the last traces of *her*, *her* spawn, off the face of the earth.

It would only be a matter of months...

20

GRACE

Grace stood at the door to a fancy house she had never been to, her heart pounding, but not for the reason it had so often in the past.

Nina waited by the carriage, in the shadows of the summer night.

Grace felt she was betraying her marital vows. This was unfitting for a married woman—to stand at the door of the man who had jilted her at the altar. But she wanted to look into his cowardly eyes, wanted an answer for why he had done it.

With a sudden fit of irritation, Grace fixed her hat and rang the bell.

"I am here to see his lordship," she told the doorman. "Mrs. Mawr is asking for him," she clarified, suddenly feeling a foot taller at the sound of her own name.

Once upon a time, she'd dreamed of being a lady, the wife of an earl. Well, now she was the wife of the Diamond King.

"Please, follow me." The doorman gestured for her to come in.

The place was much larger than Charles's former flat and decorated with expensive artwork. That familiar nauseating floral scent saturated the air, mixing with a heavy stench of wine.

"Gracie…"

The voice came from another doorway, Charles's slouching figure taking slow steps toward her.

A brief sensation jolted her heart, though she could not quite figure it out. It was nostalgic, like looking at an old rarity one was used to but sold it to someone else.

Charles seemed somehow small. *Compared to Drasko Mawr,* Grace thought briefly. She took in his uncombed hair, the crumpled shirt, the dark circles under his eyes. Everything once dear to her was oddly tainted with an alien sensation of disappointment.

"Does he know you are here?" were the first words, cold and wary, out of his mouth.

"No," Grace said, studying him. The flutter she used to get at the sight of him had vanished.

"Charles, dear, Tom said we have visit—" A woman rushed into the room, but her words cut off abruptly as she stopped in her tracks.

Meredith Sullivan, the opera singer. *Of course.* Grace knew her well, had been in the same company once or twice, the same company as Charles. The woman had attended their wedding.

The overbearing floral perfume hit Grace's nostrils.

So, this is true.

"Oh, Grace!" The woman flashed an insincere smile. "My apologies. I didn't know it was you. How… how nice to see you. You are married now…"

And not to Charles.

Now Grace understood what had bothered her on her wedding day, all the rumors about these two she had naively dismissed.

And here he was, a traitor, only weeks after the failed wedding and already with a paramour.

Grace looked at the man she'd thought she had loved and couldn't quite understand why. In fact, now that she thought of

Drasko Mawr, she saw clearly that Charles was a sheep compared to a wolf.

Embarrassment washed over her for having ever wanted this man.

Grace had far more respect for her unwanted husband than for these two. More admiration, yes. More curiosity, definitely. She thought about Drasko Mawr, the power that emanated from him, how it had made her feel walking next to him on the streets of London the other day—proud. Her heart started pounding at the mere thought of him, even now, while she was... betraying him.

"What brings you here, Grace?"

Charles's voice snapped her attention back to him.

Meredith scrutinized Grace's lavish dress. "Where is your important husband? Did he give you the biggest diamond yet?" She snorted. "Or is he saving them for his paramours?"

The words stung Grace. She didn't know about any women in Drasko's life. He could be just like Charles, having a woman on the side. The difference was that Drasko hadn't promised her anything, wasn't pretending to be in love with her like Charles once had. Look at him now!

Being in the same room with these two somehow marred her.

"I shouldn't have come," Grace said, turned on her heel, and walked out.

With relief, she inhaled the hot summer air outside, the smell of the blooming trees that erased the reek of Meredith's perfume.

Nina's shadow loomed by the carriage.

"We are leaving," Grace ordered as she walked hurriedly toward it, but her woman-guard stepped in front of her, blocking her way, and nodded up the street.

Another carriage stood a little up ahead, a tall broad-shouldered person next to it—Drasko.

Her knees buckled. "Traitor," she blurted at Nina.

"I had no part in this, ma'am," the woman-guard argued.

On shaky legs, Grace started walking toward her husband.

Was this the night he would punish her for her betrayal? Was this the night that would show his true character? That would give her a true sense of what some other women talked about, the "burdens" of marriage, the bruises and harsh words and occasional violence.

Shiver running down her spine, Grace approached and slowly came to a halt several feet away from him.

He flicked his cigarette away and stretched his hand to her. "Come here."

There was no anger in his voice, just the usual coldness. If it weren't too dark, Grace could have seen his eyes and perhaps been able to tell what was to come.

She hesitated.

"I am not angry, darling," he said, his hand still there for her. "Not quite yet. Don't be afraid."

But it terrified her, his calmness at what she had done.

She did not want Charles and had not an ounce of feelings left toward him. But—it was a revelation—she wanted to be with her husband, wanted to make this arrangement work, wanted to know he had the decency to stay away from other women.

One step, then another, her heart skipping a beat, she put her hand in his that closed gently around hers.

He led her to the open door of the carriage and helped her inside.

"Did you get your answers?" he asked as he took a seat next to her, filling the entire dim space with his presence.

Yes, her mind whispered. "No," she said, too ashamed to admit it.

"Wasn't that what you came here for?"

"I decided I already had my answers."

"And they are?"

"Not of any importance to you, I suppose."

Silence followed as the carriage started moving.

"We have made a deal, Grace," he said a tiny bit harsher.

"And we agreed that I can go wherever I want," she responded, hating her own weak defense.

"To a decent extent. I do not go to other women, do I? To prove my point and all?"

She turned to look at him. "I don't know that."

His green eyes met hers. One brow lifted in surprise. "Hmm. And you think I would?"

"I don't know that either."

"I would never do that. Because unlike you, I do value marital vows. Despite our peculiar circumstances."

She could think of no answer. Fighting through the sting, she stared down at her hands, hating herself for how right he was and how wrong she was about him.

"Forgive me," she said barely audibly, drowning in shame.

"Tell me something. Did you love him?"

That was why she'd come here, she now realized—not to get answers from Charles but to see if what she had once felt for him was true or just a silly infatuation.

Tears burned her eyes at the realization—her past feelings were a mirage.

"No," she said bravely.

"But you were looking forward to marrying him, unlike me. May I know why?"

"He was good-hearted."

"*That* he was not."

She huffed in frustration. She knew it now. "He was noble."

"Only in his title."

True. "Attentive."

"The clerks in department stores are attentive."

"Kind." She was running out of words and lies, for they definitely felt like lies now that she thought about Charles.

"A kind cheater."

The word stung her. "Will you stop?" she whispered, holding back a sob.

"They live together," he said quietly. "Since the day of our wedding. Perhaps, you understand now that all this was for the better."

She didn't answer, the remnants of the floral stench making her sick.

"What is it do you think makes a happy marriage?" he asked after some time.

That was an easy question. "Love," she declared bitterly, knowing she'd never loved Charles after all. "Friendship."

Her husband chuckled. "Love... Is that what you call it when your fiancé shags his paramour on your wedding day?"

She winced. A chill went through her. She didn't have time to process what he had said when he spoke again.

"What else goes into that precious list? Parties? Balls? Jewelry? Most of the married couples you know don't love each other. Nor are they *friends*. Wives are often trophies to men. Husbands are usually a necessity or a chore to women. You know what makes a marriage work?"

"Enlighten me," she said with bitterness, squeezing her hands on her lap to focus on the physical pain instead of her aching heart.

"Satisfaction, Grace. Give me time, and you will see that the day I married you I saved you from someone who would have made you truly unhappy. Our marriage might not sound like a fairytale or even a consensual match, but we agreed we shall make it work. With the conditions I provided. With the ones you asked for in return. And now I have more."

"Of course, you do."

"I told you I want heirs, perhaps two or three."

There it was—new rules. "Yes, we discussed that."

"I am a man, and I have certain needs. And I am—what was the word you used?—an *attentive* man."

She frowned, not understanding.

"I can make you very happy in bed."

Heat scorched her face at the words.

"And I will," he said. "So, we will kill two birds with one

stone. We will fulfill our marital duties and have children. Twice a month, we spend a night together."

She was acutely aware of her husband, of his words, the *two nights*, the idea of it suddenly setting her body on fire, much like those scandalous Hindu artworks around his house.

"I suppose I do not have a choice," she murmured just to say something.

His fingers tipped her chin, turning her face up so she looked at him.

That touch! The glow in his eyes! The way the air burned between them as their gazes stayed locked!

It mortified her, yet excited her. The thought that she, indeed, wanted to see what it was like to be a wife brought the deepest feeling—relief.

"You do, Grace. You are young and stubborn, but you do have a choice." His gaze softened. "People can be *forced* to do the most beautiful and the most atrocious things. Trust me, I know." She flinched at the words. "But your heart can never be forced. What it can do is accept what we have and what we *will* have, make peace with it instead of rebelling. Once you make peace with the agreement, it will be easier for you to tolerate me."

She didn't understand why she felt so weak and desperately wanted him to comfort her. Why she tried so hard to resent him, yet was relieved that he wasn't mocking her, moreover, that there wouldn't be any punishment.

His fingers still held her chin, the gesture so intimidating and possessive. She suddenly craved his closeness, wanted a kiss, yet there was no indication in his eyes that he wanted the same.

She let her lips curl into a smirk. "Is that what you have to tell yourself to be able to tolerate the wife you never wanted?"

21

GRACE

Her question stunned him. Grace saw him flinch, and his fingers let go of her chin.

The carriage pulled up at their house. The footman opened the door, and Drasko helped her out, never having said another word.

He didn't wait for her either, just strode toward the house, letting her follow him, Nina and Tripp walking behind her like prison guards.

Grace didn't understand his reaction, the way he had withdrawn into himself. She preferred his banter and clever jokes. Even mocking. Anything! But not the silent treatment, the sudden haunted look in his eyes.

Twice a month...

That was reasonable, though already she was nervous at the thought of being so close to him, in one bed. She needed to play the piano to clear her head. Yet, she was afraid to give away her emotions.

Grace had played for hundreds of people. Him? She felt vulnerable in his presence, as if he could see through her music, dissect the chords, read her emotions and thoughts. And what she thought about lately the most was him.

That was why she would stop playing when she sensed him behind the music room door. Why she couldn't sing when he was around. Why she would never let him read her lyrics, because he was making his way into them.

Grace went up to her room and walked circles around it for some time, trying to come to peace with what she had done today.

Perhaps, she needed to apologize. She had to, yes. She had hoped that Charles would be her chance out of the suffocating claws of her guardians. Turned out, she had been heading for another trap and was saved...

The realization made her eyes burn with tears.

"Where is my husband?" she asked her maid.

"In the grand bathing room, ma'am." Eden motioned toward the adjoining room. "Next to the master suite. He is taking a bath."

So, her husband took baths—that intimate detail created visuals in her head that were most scandalous.

Suddenly, an idea came to her. If they were to spend nights together, surely her husband wouldn't mind her talking to him while he... *Took a bath, yes.*

Grace dismissed the maid and knocked on the adjoining door.

No answer came.

She turned the handle to find the door unlocked.

Invading his privacy was a dare, if only with herself. Grace smiled despite her knees weakening with trepidation as she walked into his room.

She studied his dark bedroom, only lit with a sconce by his bed. Modest furniture, barely any. No carpet and a giant wardrobe, yet not a single personal item around, as if he didn't live there.

A strip of light sliced across the floor—the door to the bathing room was slightly ajar, the sound of splashing water spilling out.

Curious, Grace tiptoed toward it, halted at the door, and peeked through the thin gap.

The giant bathing room was cast in a warm glow. It glided off the lavish marble flooring, decorated sink basins, a toilet, and a bidet. The room was framed top to bottom with mirrors on two sides, and in the center of the room stood a giant marble-rimmed bathtub.

Steam rose above it.

Her husband lay facing away from her, his head resting on the rim. His arms hung on each side of the tub.

It was quiet. Grace had intended to barge in for a conversation. Yet, the scene seemed so intimate.

He brought both hands to his head and smoothed his hair.

She retreated into the shadows, but only a step, unable to take her eyes off him. She caught a peek of the leather bracelet around his wrist, a red thread, and metal rings on his fingers.

A loud splash startled her, spiking her heartbeat.

Her husband rose to his feet, his tall powerful figure towering above the bath. The candlelight flickered, making the shadows on his muscled body shiver.

Grace couldn't look away.

She'd never seen anything so majestic, so frightening, so sexual. Her husband stood in the bathtub, his back to her, his naked body on full display as he smoothed his wet hair in slow motions.

Grace couldn't breathe or move, paralyzed by the magnificent sight of him.

She had never seen a man of such physique. Where would she? Perhaps, in books, the Greek male sculptures or the drawings of the Spartans.

The candlelight flickered again, sending shadows rushing along his body, his muscles vivid and rippling in the light.

She held her breath at the sight of his back. A monster stared at her—a tiger, its fangs bared, a vicious expression on its face. The tiger had *his* green eyes.

A monster, just like in her dreams…

Except this monster belonged to *him*. As Drasko moved, so did the tiger. The longer Grace studied the ink, forgetting herself, the more she wanted to come over and touch it, run her fingers along the lines, down, down, down…

Her face caught on fire as she stared at her husband's buttocks.

He moved again, turning, so as to step out of the bathtub, and she took a step aside, into the shadows, away from the slice of light, then darted to her room, her heart poundIng.

Back in her room, she sat on the edge of her bed, unable to think of anything but her naked husband. The images of him were haunting, chasing her with a sweet longing that made her crave his nakedness again.

Two nights a month wouldn't be so bad, she reasoned. Heat gathered inside her at the thought. She would like his body close to hers, closer than ever before. She would like to play with that tiger, touch it. *Make it roar?*

Her cheeks heated at the silly fantasies.

And then a word came to mind, the one slipped by Elias the other day. The word that now sounded almost sinister.

Rakshasa.

RAKSHASA

Andhra Pradesh, India
Drasko, 14

Two things added fuel to Uriah's burning hatred.

One, he'd given the boy everything, and in his turn, the boy should have been Uriah's loyal servant for life, obeying his every command.

Two, Uriah couldn't stand another betrayal. As he spied on Drasko who held Alfred's little daughter in his arms and told her the secret that wasn't his to tell, despite the spawn's small brain in comprehending it, Uriah wanted to burn the two of them right there and then. The Crimson Tear secret did not belong to *her*!

Uriah retreated into the dark night with a clear plan in mind.

Rakshasa, the vicious tiger, legendary in the area, had long been roaming the villages by night, searching for prey. For years, the villagers had left offerings to Rakshasa in the jungle. For years, Rakshasa had come to feast, sneaky and unexpected, hence yet not captured. The arrangement worked out quite fine.

Well, not anymore.

Oh, Uriah knew just what he had to do. Every time men tied an offering to a tree in the forest, two men hired by him came afterward and stole it. Enough times done, and Rakshasa, by now entitled, angrily searched for its usual prey.

Hungry for weeks, it struck again. A mother with a baby from the village was eaten by the monster, only their bloodied clothes left behind.

A tragedy to their family. A shock to the terrified locals.

But Uriah gloated at the news. His plan was working. The next one would be an atrocious death, but righteously deserved by the spawn of a traitor.

And soon, it was time to bring in the killer.

It was a stuffy August night, darker than any before, when two of Uriah's men stole the sheep from the jungle, like they had done a number of times. They slaughtered the poor thing and painted a bloody trail from the jungle right to the village where Asha and Rupesh lived, who, as usual, had brought Alfred's daughter in for the night.

The slaughtered sheep was left by their house, blood soaking the grass, its presence unnoticed but the scent already luring the striped beast out of the woods.

There was one thing Uriah hadn't counted on—Drasko and the fate that always put him in Uriah's path.

That night, Drasko walked over to Asha and Rupesh's for *chai* and usual talks and the promised fairy tales for little *jaan*. He decided to stay the night and lay, as always, on a mattress on the veranda. The red tile was cool during the summer heat, and the occasional breeze swung the garments drying on the laundry ropes.

Drasko was half-asleep when a roar echoed through the village.

His eyes snapped open.

Another roar came closer, a distant scream making the hair on the back of his neck stand.

"If only you stay quiet," they said, "Rakshasa's fury will spare you. If you are inside, its hunger will feast on whatever it can find outside."

But little did Drasko know about the offering left behind the house, the blood smeared around, luring the beast, its hunger insatiable at the familiar scent.

Drasko wasn't afraid that night—he remembered clearly. Not for himself at least. But the sight of the monstrous shadow of the beast striding across the yard made his insides turn icy cold.

It wasn't the blood that made the beast angry but the humans who had dared take away their offering. And the only human Rakshasa sensed was Drasko.

Ready to spill blood, the beast lunged at the terrace, determined to avenge the broken offering cycle.

They named the tiger in honor of mythological demons. They named Drasko in honor of the evil tiger. The two were a match, for the tiger's hunger was as strong as Drasko's determination to keep little *jaan* safe. At fourteen, he already was as strong as a tiger himself. As fierce. And when the tiger roared at him, pausing at the steps, ready to attack, Drasko snarled and grabbed a sharp poker, determined to win.

The tiger swung its giant paw at him.

Drasko slammed the poker into the roaring tiger.

Enraged, it lunged at him, slashing Drasko with its monstrous claws.

Drasko got up and struck back.

The tiger roared and pawed again, razor-sharp claws slicing Drasko's skin.

Drasko roared in pain but struck back, his green eyes full of anger as they stared into the same green eyes of the tiger.

And then Rakshasa's eyes moved. The beast bared its fangs at someone behind Drasko—little *jaan* standing in the doorway.

She wore her little cotton *kurta*, her childish eyes angrily blazing at the monster who dared hurt her Drasko.

"Go! Awaaaay!" she shouted, throwing her diamond bangle at the beast.

With a roar, the tiger pounced at her.

For years afterward, Drasko would think of it as the single most terrifying moment of his life. It cut off his self-preservation instinct as he threw himself at the deadly beast in order to protect the only thing he loved.

His roars mixed with Rakshasa's. The searing pain from the razor-sharp fangs tearing through his flesh mixed with the fury with which he stabbed the tiger.

Until they were like one.

Until his white *kurta* was soaked with blood, its shredded pieces flapping like white flags among the striped fur of the beast.

Then everything went quiet.

Minutes later, the locals rushed through the gates toward the terrace, torches and guns in their hands, only to find the giant tiger who had terrorized them for years speared by a poker, dead on the floor, in a pool of blood.

Underneath his monstrous form lay Drasko. His body had been ripped by the steel claws. The side of his face was shredded. His blood laced with that of the beast, two shades of red pooling on the floor in a macabre marble pattern.

And next to them sat the little girl, her legs folded under her, her trembling fingers caressing Drasko's hair. Tears spilled down her cheeks as she begged for him to wake up.

23

GRACE

Grace slammed the giant mythology book shut with a puzzled, "Huh."

The library was cast into the afternoon sunlight, strangely bright after the dark stories she had just read.

So, Rakshasas were demonic creatures, the Asian myths said. There were many of them, malicious, monstrous, aggressive, and sexual. In Ramayana, one such demon kidnaped the main hero's wife.

How fitting.

Grace couldn't get the tiger out of her head all night. Or her husband. Or the image of his naked body, so glorious and alluring.

Two nights a month—she had already spent half a night wondering what it would be like. Perhaps, her husband was as cold in bed as he was in daily life. Or as brutal as the tattoo on his back.

And then Grace questioned Samira, who told her about the Rakshasas with hesitation, as if she were not allowed to talk about the legends.

He is not a demon, Grace argued with herself. But what was the meaning behind his tattoo?

A smile played on her lips as she remembered the powerful build of her husband. That Rakshasa was terrifying yet strikingly glorious on the back of its owner, its eyes green like emeralds—*his*.

A tune started humming in her head. She rushed into the music room. Right away, pen and paper found their way into her hands.

A minute later, she was rereading the words inspired by the myth. Her fingers touched the keys—the stunning grand piano that sounded even more enchanting than it looked.

And there they were—the low dangerous notes, morphing into aggressive ones, Rakshasa's story weaving into it. *He* was in her song again, the fact by now so common. And then a soft trill came—*her*. She was always there, in her songs about him.

Grace paused midway through the song, the smile falling off her lips. She'd been so preoccupied for weeks with her "accidental" husband that she'd made more songs of her own, disregarding practicing her performance pieces.

Julien, her instructor, had written to her several times. She had promised to resume the practice as soon as she was settled and *in my husband's good graces*, she had added bitterly.

I am absolutely thrilled to meet him, Julien had replied.

Oh, Julien…

Her husband might have accepted Rivka. But Julien, a man? That was a different story. She had never had the luxury of having friends or entertaining her own guests. This freedom was new, yet, she was sure it would come with exceptions.

Grace had gone to Harrods department store with Rivka, had spent a day walking through the Botanical Garden, had spent another day at a museum. And all she had gotten in the evening from her husband was, "Did you enjoy your day?" A cold smile. A too intrusive gaze.

Shaking off the thoughts about her husband, Grace took a deep breath and ran her fingers along the keys in C major scales. She carried on with the scales for some time, until her fingers were warm and pliable. She then opened the sheets for one of the concert pieces.

Focus.

She glanced at the music sheets only to align her mind with the piece she was starting.

"Danse Macabre" by Camille Saint-Saëns, transformed into a piano solo by talented Liszt.

A beautiful piece—she touched the keys softly, the D note, twelve times, calming like the strokes of midnight. Then a nervous trill followed—imitating the fluttering of her heart. Then the aggressive chords boomed—the tritone, *the Devil in music*, its dissonance instantly jerking her mind back to her wedding day.

And then her fingers raced over the keyboard with infuriating, urgent passion.

Grace attacked the instrument. It was always like this—her feelings against the piano keys.

Julien had once said, "An instrument is a lover. You give it your best and your worst. And if you want it to be yours, you'd better listen to how it responds."

Grace didn't know what it was like to have a lover.

The image of *him* and his Rakshasa tattoo flashed in her mind.

She faltered on the keys. Her hands paused in surprise—she had played this piece flawlessly many times.

Again, she commanded.

She resumed from the start of the last double bar line. Her fingers attacked the keys, in sync with her pounding heart, like a metronome that she forgot to use. They moved vigorously along the keyboard as the images flooded her mind, the lines of the Rakshasa's stripes, the fangs, the green eyes—

She faltered.

Again. Again. Again!

"Dammit!" She slammed the keys and threw her head back in frustration, staring at the ceiling frescoes.

Those were colorful and elaborate, but she had never paid attention to the details. Trying to clear her head, she studied the images, gods and goddesses, magical creatures and fantastical objects, intricate architecture and luscious gardens, flowers, animals, household scenarios, battle scenes, and—

Grace frowned as her eyes paused on a scene of multiple people entwined together. Naked?

Cannot be.

She rose from the piano bench, her neck craning as she stepped to the spot that gave her the best view of the fresco piece above her.

No, no, no. She was certainly imagining things.

She dragged the bench over and stepped on top of it to take a closer look at what was going on in the scene above her. And what was unfolding was truly scandalous.

She called for Samira.

"Samira, dear, tell me that is not what I think it is," Grace said as the two of them stood with their heads lifted to the ceiling.

"What are you asking, madam?"

"Are those people, a dozen of them or so…fornicating?"

"It is a scene from a scripture, madam."

Grace widened her eyes at the maid. "Scripture? What scripture describes this sort of thing?"

"Our art promotes fertility and the idea of procreation."

"But in the open like this? This is…" *Obscene,* she wanted to say, but could not take her eyes off the fresco.

Now that she studied it, the debauchery painted in the most vibrant colors and cheerful setting was unmistakable. Limbs and parts that were supposed to be clothed, legs open, bodies contorted, some upside down, standing on their heads, probing, fusing together.

"Vedas, the Hindu scriptures, promote the idea of creation and fertility, madam," Samira explained.

"Uh-huh."

"They find their way into Hindu art and everyday life. Did you know, madam, that many of our settlements and communities back home are built around temples? And because there is no other way to educate the poor about procreation and fertility, which is the essence of humankind, we use sensual images to promote the idea of a happy family?"

"Family," Grace echoed.

"Of course, madam. The union between two humans is sacred. It is divine. Your scripture preaches about sins and punishment. Eastern scriptures teach about liberation and achieving harmony."

"Harmony." Grace shook her head. The indecency unfolding above her seemed anything but.

"*Kama* in Sanskrit means pleasure, but also enjoyment. It is one of the goals of human life. Often, it is connected to children."

"But..." Grace tilted her head, focusing on a figure in the fresco that was bent over another, its mouth taking another man's member in—

Grace pointed to her own mouth. "You cannot make children like that."

Samira laughed, absolutely no shame in her cheerful trill. "There is more to a happy family than making children, madam. You have to be happy to make others happy."

"How... peculiar," Grace muttered and made a mental note to look for books on Hindu art in Drasko's library.

She walked about the house. It called to her—to be explored, to know what sort of man lived in it. A new house was always furnished with the future in mind but was, in reality, a reflection of the past. Habits, values, and memories found their way into every piece.

Drasko's house was a different world. Zebra rugs and masks of Hindu deities. Gods with savage faces and those with many hands. Tigers roared off the murals. An elephant tooted from a giant carpet on the wall in the summer room.

Grace's head spun at all the vibrant colors and scents, flowers and musk, woven together and gradually becoming her home.

She went outside to the greenhouse, a luscious garden with exotic plants. The parrots screeched as they flitted from branch to branch. A giant mango tree grew in the middle of it, reaching for the glass roof. And a sculpture of a majestic lion rested under its lower branches.

Rakshasa?

Its eyes sparkled with blue stones that reflected the sunlight.

Grace hadn't noticed them before and leaned in to take a closer look.

Diamonds?

"They are tanzanites, madam," the voice startled her.

Samira stood behind her with those kind smiling eyes, accentuated by the black eyeliner many Indian servants used.

"Kajal," Eden had explained to Grace one day, already more knowledgeable in their foreign culture than Grace. "They use it to ward off evil."

Grace smiled at Samira. "I thought those were blue diamonds."

The woman wiggled her head from side to side. "Master doesn't keep diamonds in the house."

"Why?"

Samira shrugged. "When you have many, they are like glass."

Grace went to the library, picked several books with Hindu art, and took them to her room, then spent the rest of the afternoon studying them, searching for naked bodies, the vulgar scenes that made her restless with curiosity.

Darkness fell outside when she decided to leave her room and halted at the top of the stairs—her husband was talking to his men in the hallway downstairs.

She hadn't heard him come home, was surprised he was at home at all. Her pulse quickened in cheerful anticipation. Perhaps, tonight, they could talk.

Loud footsteps came from downstairs, muffled voices, orders —he was leaving again with several of his guards.

Her body came alive at the sound of him, but her heart fell.

Another meeting? So late at night? A woman?

Was that why he hadn't touched her yet?

The thought stung her.

Grace stood on the stairwell and listened to the front door close, the house suddenly quiet again.

Frustration flooded her. In a moment, she made a decision.

She called for her maid. "Eden," she said in a hushed voice, "I need you to distract the doorman and Nina."

"How?" Eden blinked in confusion.

"Figure out how. Please, Eden. Now, hurry!"

Grace put on her hat, picked up her reticule, and waited on the stairwell as Eden loudly called Nina and the men to the kitchen, conjuring some silly lie that worked for a minute.

A minute was all Grace needed to slip out of the house.

She heard the clip-clop of the horses outside the gate. Her husband's convoy headed up the street. She rushed in that direction, her heart thudding like a drum, nerves on edge as she caught the first hansom cab and ordered the driver to follow.

Grace had never been so daring. Now? Now she was careless. This newly found freedom was alluring.

Her anxiety grew as she followed the carriages along the deserted streets. Soon, the men abandoned the horses and continued on foot.

Like a thief, she hurried after them, ducked into the shadows, jerked at every footstep behind her. The June night was pleasantly cool, yet she felt hot, her nerves on edge.

Perhaps, this was a bad idea.

Did she want to know he was seeing someone else? She didn't care, did she? But, oh, did hurt twist her heart at the thought. An unwanted husband, but a husband nevertheless, and he was hers.

So, Grace carried on in determination, in pursuit of the men who walked, in eerie silence, until they reached the river Thames.

Oh, Lordy.

They boarded small boats and pushed off into the foggy river. This wasn't a tourist pier, not the pleasure boats, not the ferries. Grace looked around—one small boat was left behind.

"I will pay you double," she said to the boater. "Follow!"

Petrified of the ride, uneasy about the fog, she stared into the distance, barely registering the boats ahead.

The night was thick. The summer smog was thicker. She ordered the boater to slow down when the boats ahead docked at a dingy pier. Only when men disembarked and the only sound was the lapping of the water against the hulls did she tell the boater to dock.

Darkness enveloped her. She shivered despite the summer night heat.

"Wait here," she ordered, stepping carefully out onto the wooden dock.

Her heart hammered in her chest. There was no light in sight, no lanterns, no signs of life.

And despite her orders, the boater stepped out of the boat right behind her.

A chill ran up her spine.

"I need you to wait in the boat," she repeated meekly.

He started approaching slowly. A step. Another one closer, his shadow moving into her.

What have I done? she thought in panic.

Just then a loud voice in the dark made her whip around.

"Thank you, Bard, I'll take it from here. Join the others."

She knew the voice so well!

The sound of a struck match hissed through the damp air. The sudden flame illuminated a face with deep shadowed scars, a cigarette jammed between his lips, the smoke curling in the air and dissipating into the darkness.

The familiar green eyes met hers.

Drasko held the match in front of him. Little fires flickered in his green eyes. That mischievous smirk of his made her heart skip a beat.

"Hello, wife."

24

GRACE

Everyone had disappeared into darkness. Gone, like ghosts.

Except him, taking slow steps toward her, his eyes on her as the shadows played on his face in the orange glow of the lit match.

Grace was caught...

The light from the match was fading. Drasko was right in front of her when the light flickered off.

Complete darkness settled in, save for the vague haze from across the river.

Yet, she felt him, saw the hissing red end of his cigarette as he took another drag.

A light suddenly came on, bright and intrusive. The gas lamp illuminated the space between her and her husband, his humorous gaze on her.

"Are you spying on me, darling?"

His voice, like that of a seductive serpent, curled around her heart, setting her on edge with panic etched with anticipation.

"You are easy to follow," she said, trying to sound brave.

He stepped closer and tipped her chin, that possessive gesture again as if she had misbehaved. A smile flickered on his lips.

"Darling, the moment you left the house, I was following *you.*"

And why was she not surprised? And why was she so acutely aware of his touch? Gentle and intimate, it was more assertive this time.

"I was planning on giving you a tour one day." He tipped his head toward the blackness ahead with absolutely no sign of anything being there. "But looks like you insist on taking matters into your own hands. Shall we?"

Grace nodded timidly, wrapped her hand around the arm he offered, and let him lead her away from the shore.

A faded light loomed ahead. Shadows shivered on the edges of it. But she felt safe by Drasko's side, despite the frightening darkness creeping to her toes.

Voices echoed ahead. Grace tripped on stones and wet gravel and felt Drasko press his arm closer to his body, tightening his hold on her hand.

"Animals?" she whispered at the distant sounds.

"My men."

"They are here?"

"Everywhere. By the docks. By the bridge. By the tunnels."

Tunnels?

She couldn't see a thing, save for several feet in front of them and that distant glow. But Drasko seemed to know the way by heart.

He whistled a three-pitched tune.

Like the Devil in music.

At once, the darkness in front of them shifted, unfolded into bright light as two men opened a heavy metal gate that obstructed an entrance into what looked like a cavern. They greeted him, then widened their surprised eyes at Grace and touched their caps. "Ma'am."

She stepped into a spacious cave, lit with lanterns. Stone towered on all sides and closed above her.

"A cave?" She stared around and above in amusement.

"A storage unit," Drasko explained, letting go of her and motioning to one of his men.

There were more guns around than men. Crates were stacked against the moist stone walls. Three men played cards at a wooden table by the wall, glancing at her and nodding in greeting. Their sleeves rolled up, suspenders over their shoulders, shirts half-unbuttoned, they looked like they were taking a break from work.

The gates behind Grace closed.

"What is this place?" she mused, looking around with fascination.

"One of our more discreet facilities," her husband explained. "This is our receiving room. Follow me."

She finally took him in.

Hatless, Drasko wasn't wearing a jacket or a vest either, let alone a tie, which revealed suspenders over a white shirt, dirty and damp with sweat. The shirt was unbuttoned at the neck, giving a glimpse of a gold necklace. His sleeves were rolled up. With a cigarette bobbing between his lips, he looked like a common worker. The glint of the rings on his fingers could make one think he was a gangster.

The Diamond King away from the public eye.

She was finally seeing the many shades of Drasko Mawr.

Her shoes sunk into the wet gravel as she followed him through a narrow stone arc.

The tunnel opened into another cave, bright with gas lamps, alive with men's chatter.

"This is our sorting room," Drasko explained.

"Sorting what?"

The chatter in the cave died out at once.

About a dozen men around the room gawked at her. Some of them shirtless, others in sleeveless shirts, dirtied, but with happy grins and cigars in their mouths. It smelled of ale and stale water and something achingly familiar—sandalwood, the scent that saturated many rooms in their house.

Grace studied the cave. Two long tables were located at the distant end of it. Several young boys, the youngest only eight or so, stood shirtless, only in their undergarments, and exchanged whispers, eyeing her with amused smiles.

"Gentlemen! Manners!" Drasko barked at them.

Gentlemen?

Only now did she notice that the tables in front of the boys were shiny with piles of glitter on top of them.

She frowned, not believing her eyes. "These are—"

"Diamonds, yes. Come." Drasko motioned for her to follow him.

Hundreds, perhaps, thousands of diamonds sat in simple piles on the table. Small boxes were arranged in a row. But of course, this shouldn't be a surprise. They said the Mawrs turned dirt into diamonds.

"There are five hues of diamonds here right now," her husband explained, hands in his pockets. "These gentlemen sort them by count and pack them into the small boxes, mark them, then put them in respective crates."

The word "gentlemen" didn't go with the sweaty half-naked grinning boys. Nor did the word "diamond" go with the careless piles of glitter on the table. Or the caverns with the water dripping off the slimy ceiling.

"Don't you sort them in… India?" Grace asked.

"The official import yes. These arrived this morning in dry fish."

"Pardon me?" Her mouth fell open.

The boys giggled. "And in tobacco," one of them said.

"Also, inside exotic flutes and bags of saffron, weaved into cotton and silks, hidden in sugar and salt, spice and tea," Drasko explained. "When crates with dried fruits are picked up in Morocco on the way to England, diamonds find their way into them, too."

Grace couldn't wrap her head around it. "Children? You employ children?"

She was taking the scene in, vaguely realizing that her husband was sharing something most people didn't know.

"They get paid. They get a place to live and food. That is more than most street children get out there. This job is safer than any factory one. And—"

"We get to go to school," one of the boys interrupted with a proud tilt of his chin.

"Correct." Drasko nodded. "What did you learn in school today, Benjamin?"

"That Mr. Brolentine has bad breath after eating oysters."

The other boys burst into laughter. But under Drasko's silent stare, the laughter died out in seconds.

"In-te-gers," Benjamin replied as if pronouncing a foreign word. Another boy nudged him with his elbow, and Benjamin glanced at Drasko from under his eyebrows and added, "Sir."

"Forgive them." Drasko led Grace away. "Their manners leave much to be desired. But they will learn. And when we have a society where children don't have to work, it will be a wonderful one."

"Why are they almost naked?"

"So they don't steal."

"And if they do?"

"If they get caught, they are back on the street. So they don't."

"And if they rat you out?" she mused.

Drasko's gaze sharpened. "They don't know where they are. They are blindfolded when they are brought and taken out of here. But they won't. They know this is a new life for them."

"Hmm. But I know where I am."

Oh… She shouldn't have said that. She didn't mean to.

A little smile tipped his lips. He cocked his head at her. "Considering you tried to poison me, living under the same roof as you puts me in more jeopardy than this."

There was something else in his gaze—trust. She understood now that this—these caverns and him slowly unveiling his life for her—was the most trustful move yet. And he was less bitter today, more open, more… caring?

Wishful thinking.

He led her to yet another archway that gaped like a monster's mouth.

"I didn't mean it that way," she apologized for being too clever.

He gently set his hand on her waist as they walked. "I know," he whispered into her ear and let go, leaving her heart pounding.

A man hurried up to them with a lantern and illuminated their way to yet another cave. A rail cart stood on the rails leading into a tunnel farther up.

"Why the caves?" Grace stared around confused. Water dripped off the ceilings. The pitch-black tunnel ahead wafted with coldness. "Your business is legal, is it not?"

"Robberies, ma'am," a voice said behind her.

One of the men had followed, dressed in trousers, suspenders over a sweat-soaked cream shirt, sleeves rolled up. A kind smile on his brutal face. An unlit cigarette bobbing off the corner of his mouth.

"Regardless of how good the security is, there are robberies, ma'am. We've had many. Right, boss?"

"Enemies, too," another man said, stepping from behind him. Old smudgy tattoos peeked from under his short sleeves. "You'd be surprised what those snakes, the Wollendorfs, can do." He spat on the ground.

Drasko nodded. "These grottos are owned by me, just like the strip of the city the tunnels lead to. They are protected day and night. We do have our traditional routes, secured vaults in banks and the Mawr Building. This"—he motioned around—"is a precaution."

"How many precautions do you have?" Grace asked, amused.

He leisurely studied her dress, taking his time to answer. "Perhaps, one day, you will find out."

She felt hot under his gaze and pursed her lips.

He flashed his brilliantly white smile at her, in beautiful contrast with his tanned skin. "Would you like to go farther?"

25

GRACE

"Hawkins!" Drasko called out. "Let us give the lady a ride."

One of the men hopped up to Grace and bowed charmingly. A grin split his face. He dusted off the box inside the rail cart and offered her his hand. "My lady?"

She glanced at her husband. He nodded. Despite the hesitation, she let the man help her into the dirty cart and sat on the box, feeling like a fancy peacock. She laughed in surprise when he shouted, "Departing!" and pushed the cart down the rails, the other man helping him.

Like the wind, they carried her down the tracks and paused in the middle of nowhere until the gas lamp was lit.

She found herself in yet another large cave, with stacks and stacks of storage trunks on each side.

Her husband helped her out.

The two men grinned and bowed theatrically. "The most notorious ride in London, ma'am."

She laughed with them, glancing at Drasko and his ghost of a smile.

"Something my men can do that I can't," he muttered.

"Which is?"

"Make my wife laugh."

She blushed as she adjusted her hat and skirt.

The men were already walking farther down the tunnel, the scent of tobacco saturating the air behind them. And Grace was suddenly too aware of being next to Drasko, alone, in a place guarded by dozens of men. A secret, really, and she was in on it.

"I want to show you something," Drasko said and walked over to a stack of storage trunks.

She took in the sight of him.

For the first time, she saw him not as the famous Drasko Mawr, with guards and carriages, people bowing and reporters gawking, the crowds parting to let him through and the noblemen cowering under his stern gaze—that was the Drasko Mawr that everyone knew.

This Drasko was different. Not the Diamond King but a humble man, among his workers, his hands dirty and his hair seductively tousled, the light of the gas lamps tinting his skin a golden shade and reflecting in his eyes.

Grace was still puzzled by the purpose of all this, the caves with thousands of diamonds hidden in them.

"Drasko," she called out as he inspected the markings on the trunks.

"Drasko," she said louder.

He unlatched the top trunk out of the stack, disregarding her.

"Drasko!" she insisted.

He turned around to look at her, a delightful boyish grin on his face. "Yes, darling?"

"What are you so happy about?" she scorned.

"I like the way you say my name."

She rolled her eyes, blushing a little. "But this is smuggling, is it not?" She motioned to the trunks.

His eyes swept over her figure, then returned to her face— this gesture had become his habit, which made Grace self-aware.

She pursed her lips, enjoying it, nevertheless. "Did you not hear my question?"

"I heard genuine concern. Or was it curiosity?"

He was impossible. "But these are *your* diamonds."

"Absolutely."

"You are smuggling your own diamonds? Into the country that easily allows you to bring them legally?"

"Correct."

She waited for the answer that didn't come. "Are you going to explain?"

"Come here." He beckoned her with two fingers, and she walked up, like an obedient wife.

His hands were on her waist again, turning her around until she faced the stack of trunks.

"Watch," he whispered in her ear, the sound of it sending tingles down her body.

He pushed the lid of the top trunk open, and she inhaled sharply, wanting to shield her eyes from the blinding glitter.

The trunk was lined with simple cotton cloth and held the treasures worth a fortune. A trunk full of tiny diamonds, hundreds, thousands!

They sparkled in the lamplight. Their glistening flickers danced on the stone walls of the cave.

"Oh…" Grace exhaled in astonishment.

The scent spread around, that of spices and foreign lands. And there were dozens of such trunks in the stack. This was Treasure Island!

Drasko gently took her hand, removed her lace glove, finger by finger, and then pushed her hand into the diamonds.

The texture of tiny pebbles prickled her skin while the diamonds exploded in myriads of glistening lights.

"We don't want to report everything that we bring into this country," Drasko said. "Not even half of it."

Grace tried to think of the right questions but was too distracted by the shimmering waves of diamonds, like sparkly water over her skin. Even more so by Drasko's hand still holding hers, guiding it, his fingers intertwining with hers in the sea of diamonds. His other hand was still on her waist, holding her in place.

"Why?" she asked.

"The Wollendorf Consortium, for one." He pulled her hand out, took a handful of diamonds, and poured them into her palm. "They are catching up and are the second biggest diamond mining company in the world. We mine forty times more than we sell, and they don't know that."

A tiny gasp of surprise left her.

His hand pushed hers into the diamonds again, both of them disappearing, his fingers caressing hers, so sensual it made her body hum.

She dared lift her face to look up at Drasko, meeting his eyes, like green diamonds, with specks of glittery reflections.

"Why don't we sell them all?" he guessed her question. "Because demand drives the prices." His fingers played with hers, deep in the diamonds. "Why don't we report them? Because we don't want anyone to know the true scale of our enterprise." He didn't stop touching her. "Moreover," he explained in a low husky voice, "if a diamond war broke out, and it would be bloody if it were to happen, we would have leverage by outselling the competition."

"You don't think your people pass on the information to your competition?"

"Clever girl." He smiled and glanced at her lips. "Perhaps. But no one knows how much we truly have."

"Except you."

"And a few others."

"But that is..." She didn't want to so openly admire him, yet there was no doubt in what she was about to say. "You are truly an extraordinary man."

"Did I receive a compliment from my wife?" He chuckled.

His face was only inches away from hers, a breath away, and she was *afraid* to breathe.

Something was happening. *At last,* she thought, then

blushed, shameful from this anticipation. But, no, no, she *wanted* this, *him*. This cave had brought them closer than ever before.

"They are all yours, Grace, if you want them," he said softly.

Not *darling*, but *Grace*—she'd noticed his change of words.

Darling was endearing, at times playful, but often bitter, sarcastic, and occasionally angry.

Grace was reserved for serious Drasko. *Grace* was for *sad* Drasko. *Grace* on his lips sounded intimate, and they hadn't had any intimate moments yet.

"Why do you suppose I want diamonds?" she asked, adding, "Drasko?"

His face inched closer. His hand in the diamonds left hers and reached her face, tipping her chin, his eyes locked with hers.

"What *do* you want, Grace? Tell me, and I will give it to you."

She didn't know what to say or what it was that he asked. She was afraid to ruin this moment—she had done that before. She hadn't yet learned to pick the right words around him.

"Anything but letting you go," he said even quieter, the words that scared her instantly. No, she didn't want that. She didn't know when her thoughts had changed, but she didn't want him to let her go.

She shook her head but didn't answer, hoping he would tell her what *he* wanted. One thing she knew for certain was that she wanted to know what his lips felt like on hers.

His warm breath ghosted over her face. "Would it be so bad if we found out that we both want the same thing?"

And he kissed her.

It was a chaste kiss, their lips pressing together. The slick metal of his rings grazed her cheek as he cupped it, the touch of his big hand unusually gentle.

She felt the minuscule tug of him pulling away—no, she wanted more!—and she stood on her tiptoes and pressed her lips to his, drawing him back into the kiss.

This kiss—oh, *this* kiss was different. The eagerness with which he came back for it. The gentle insistence of his lips. The sensual sweep of his tongue. The heatwave that ran through her as her tongue met his.

His arm around her tightened. The strokes of his tongue deepened in the ravishing invasion. This was a feeling unknown to her—being in the arms of a powerful man, the strength of his body so tangible that her own body grew weak.

Kissing had never felt so overwhelming. Her heart thrashed in her chest, wanting to leap out and join his. She was free-falling, felt weightless, and the only thing holding her on her feet was his arm around her waist.

She moaned embarrassingly loudly but was past caring. She prayed he didn't stop, drowned in the revelation of how amazing he felt, how gentle he was, his hand sliding to the nape of her neck and holding her tightly against him.

Giggles right behind them broke them apart.

She blinked, dazed from kissing, wanted to protest and pull him back toward her.

But Drasko's hands fell off her body. His gaze briefly met hers—a flicker of surprise from the intensity of what had just happened.

His gaze shifted to someone behind her. One step back, and the warmth of his body was gone.

"What did I tell you?" he reproached, annoyed.

Grace turned to see the boys, elbowing each other, peeking from behind the corner.

Fumbling, she brushed her skirt with her palms like she'd just done something scandalous.

The boys flashed brazen grins at her. "Would Missus have dinner with us?"

"No," Drasko answered. "Not today."

"Tsk." They hung their heads low and disappeared into the darkness of the connecting tunnel.

Baffled, Grace looked at Drasko. "You have dinner with them?"

"Occasionally, yes."

She waited for more. He didn't explain.

She finally stared him down, butterflies in her stomach as he finally met her eyes. "Will you start telling me more about yourself? Or do I have to spy?"

And that handsome boyish smile was back on his face. "Is that what you want, Grace? To know more about me?"

"Part of it, yes. But for that, you'd have to spend more time at home."

He cocked a brow, his eyes boring into her. "Is that what you want? Me at home?"

She held his gaze this time, nodded in confirmation, willed him to come closer and kiss her again.

"To learn more about me?" he baited her instead, that sneaky smile still on his lips and making her nervous.

"Part of it, yes."

"And the other part?"

His smile grew mischievous, but he stuck his hands in his pockets, turned around, and studied the cave as if letting her summon her courage.

Only now did she notice how damp from sweat his white shirt was on his back, clinging to his skin, the dark tattoo visible through it. *Rakshasa.*

"Tell me something." He turned around to face her again, his smile gone. "Does your music help you forget?"

"Forget what?" She licked her lips, disappointed at the change of topic.

"Anything. When you are sad, can it make you happy? When you are angry, can it make you kind? Does it help you erase painful memories?"

She shifted uneasily, thinking about her nightmares, about the years with her guardians. "Yes. We all have a weapon like this. Some work better than others."

"I don't have weapons, Grace. I would like to have your music." There was a question in his eyes as if he were making another deal. "This"—he nodded toward the open trunk of diamonds—"doesn't do it. It's a trading coin."

"But, all these diamonds, they can buy off so much pain. Others' futures. Children's education. You…" She wanted to bring his smile back. "You are not a king. You are a god, Drasko Mawr."

A sudden change in his expression made his gaze almost haunted. His face was often a rigid mask. But his eyes—she had studied him lately, determined to learn what he felt or thought—they revealed a lot of what he was trying to hide inside him.

And now the light in his marvelous greens was waning.

Sadness? Drasko Mawr was sad?

No, no, that wasn't it.

He blinked slowly, as if blinking away some distant memories, and there it was—her heart squeezed so hard at this revelation—Drasko Mawr was vulnerable.

But why?

Grace had wanted to please him yet had unknowingly pained him with her words. And she wanted to know what made this indestructible man lose his composure for even a second.

"A god…" he said bitterly, stepped back, and aimlessly looked around. "I don't want to be a god. There is one thing a god can't do that I would've given all these diamonds for."

"And that is?"

"Bring loved ones back from the dead."

JAAN

Andhra Pradesh, India
Drasko, 14

"Can't be! It simply can't be!"

Uriah paced around his office, his jaw clenched.

"The boy is doing all right," the doctor said, pinching the bridge of his nose. "He sustained many injuries. There is an infected wound on his leg. He will recover. But it is…"

He fell silent until Uriah stopped pacing and glared at him. "It is *what*?"

"It's his face I am worried about. The wounds will heal, of course. But the scars will be for life and very"—he sighed wearily and with pity—"very prominent. Unfortunately."

He was dismissed, and Uriah resumed his pacing around the office.

Alfred sat behind the giant wooden desk with his feet crossed on top of it, another drink in his hand. He chewed on the end of his mustache and observed his brother with unusual interest.

Uriah didn't feel sorry for the boy but was furious, nevertheless. At himself for the fact that the whole enterprise with Rakshasa hadn't worked out and had put Drasko out of work for weeks. And, more importantly, at that little monster, Alfred's daughter, who was still well and alive.

"Tsk-tsk-tsk, what have you done, brother?" Alfred's quiet words turned Uriah around in confusion.

His face bloated from whisky and sleepless nights, his cunning eyes locking with Uriah's, Alfred undoubtedly mocked him. Alfred couldn't possibly know Uriah's part in that. Yet Uriah hated that knowing gaze of his.

It was a failure! Even Alfred's liquored mind could sense it.

"I am taking the boy to London," Uriah stated, pouring himself a drink. "It's time for him to learn the Western side of the business."

"Planning on flashing your loyal dog around? With those scars? A monster?"

Uriah's own scars reddened with rage as he walked up to the desk and leaned over to stare his brother dead in the eyes.

"Yes, a monster. A pair of us," he hissed. "He and I. We will take over that pitiful hole called London. And if I ever hear anyone say that word again, I shall personally put the nails in their coffins and bury them."

He straightened, his malevolent smile at his brother widening, making Alfred look away in unease.

"That goes for you too," Uriah said, "brother," he added with a scowl, turned on his heel, and marched toward the door.

Abruptly, he came to a halt. "And I'm taking your daughter with us."

"Why?"

"*Why* do you care? She is a bad omen. I shall put her in private school or something."

He left then, "or something" lingering in his mind with a much more sinister plan.

He went to see Drasko. Alone in his room, the boy lay sedated on a bed, his torso wrapped in gauze and cloth, more gauze on his face, a compress on his forehead.

"An Egyptian mummy," Uriah muttered as he stepped closer and cocked his head, studying the boy. A smile curled his lips. *The pair of us.* Drasko was becoming just like him. *Good.*

Something shifted by his side, and Uriah's smile disappeared —*her* again.

Like Drasko's guardian angel, the little girl stood next to Uriah and gazed at the bed. Her long hair was loose, falling onto a white chemise. She looked like a little angel, only five years old but already so pretty.

A deliciously atrocious thought crossed Uriah's mind. Only thirteen years until her legal age, and he, Uriah, could—

No. That would indeed be revenge. But Uriah's hate at the sight of her trumped the twisted idea that had just bloomed in his head.

No. No. She had to go.

"It's a pity," he said as he studied sleeping Drasko. "He will look"—for the first time, Uriah savored the word and had a hard time concealing a smirk—"like a *monster*, don't you think?"

His eyes shifted to the little girl, who craned her neck to look up at him. He chuckled at the spite in her eyes and her little hands balled into fists.

She didn't respond, only walked up to Drasko and took his big, bruised hand in both her little ones.

Uriah turned on his heel and stomped away, grinding his teeth. Even looking like a monster, the boy was still loved.

Two weeks later, *Saint Catalina* sailed off the Indian shore, Uriah, Drasko, and Alfred's daughter on board among others.

Drasko was seasick and feverish for the first week of the travel. And when the bandages were taken off, he looked at himself in the mirror and winced at the disfigured face that stared back at him.

When little *jaan* knocked on his door, he tried to cover his face so he didn't scare her off.

"I don't want you to see me like this," he said.

But she sat next to him on the berth, took his hand in both of hers, and smiled. "You killed a beast. Like a knight."

He snorted.

"*I* am a monster." He gritted his teeth.

She furrowed her little brows then. "In fairytales, a monster turns into a prince."

He shook his head. "In fairytales, *jaanu*, in fairy tales," he replied, gritting his teeth.

Another week later, still at sea, she fell ill.

"Seasick," the doctor said.

"Some sort of infection in her stomach," that same doctor said another week later.

She turned for the worse. Her fever remained. She grew weaker by the day.

"A poisoning?" The doctor was at a loss.

"What is happening?" Drasko asked Uriah.

But Uriah only shrugged, his cold gaze on the horizon. "We shall see, we shall see."

Drasko's wounds were healing, though he still wasn't used to the scarred face staring back at him in the mirror. He spent all his time looking after little *jaan*. When she was too weak to walk, he carried her to the top deck and sat her down. The ocean winds would ruffle her long hair and make her cheeks rosy as she nestled in the crook of his arm. And he told her sea stories about grand adventures and a beautiful country called England and a splendid city called London.

"Is that where we are going?" she asked weakly. She never smiled anymore.

Drasko nodded, though he didn't remember London. An eerie feeling gathered inside him at the sight of her in pain.

When they finally reached the English shore, she got worse, delirious as they finally stepped onto English soil.

They settled in Uriah's London house, and Drasko was right away whisked to a business meeting, then another. When he didn't find little *jaan* at the house that very night, he asked Uriah.

"She is under the doctor's observation. She is not well," Uriah said, a menacing glint in his eyes.

And he kept Drasko occupied for days, as if distracting him.

"Do not worry about your scars," Uriah said when Drasko noticed the gaping stares at himself when they walked around London. "This city doesn't care about looks anymore. It cares about money."

The city was magnificent! Busses pulled by horses. Monstrous locomotives. Electricity everywhere! Photographs. Opulent buildings and the marvels of architecture Drasko did not remember from his childhood.

If only little *jaan* could see it!

"She is about to have surgery," Uriah said two days later when Drasko demanded to visit her.

"Surgery?" Dread crept inside him at the word, at the casual way Uriah said it. "I want to be there."

"And I"—Uriah snapped—"need you to do what we came here to do—business."

Diamonds, diamonds, diamonds.

Drasko got so used to the words that became a mere trade coin. And he wanted to disappear in the city that swallowed one whole, turned people into ants, and drowned with its permanent noise his own grim thoughts.

The next day, Uriah told Drasko the morbid news. "She passed..."

Drasko shook his head, not understanding.

Who?

"Alfred's daughter," Uriah said simply. "She had complications during the surgery. She passed."

It was the day the world went dark.

They simply called her *choti*, a little one.

Drasko simply called her *jaan*.

She was five years old. Drasko was fourteen. And no human had ever loved him like she did. Nor would there be anyone like her.

He broke down on the streets of London, broke into tears he couldn't control. For the first time in his life, he roared and wept, mourning the loss of the only person who mattered, who brought him joy every day and was now gone. And he was left a monster.

"It's your fault!" Drasko shouted at Uriah, blind with rage, his bowler hat on the ground, coat flapping in the wind, his facial scars wet with tears. "You never liked her! You did something, didn't you? Just like—"

Uriah's eyes flashed with malice. "Go on, boy?"

Drasko wanted to spit out the harsh words but swallowed his hate. "I want to see her body."

"No," Uriah snapped, his cold gaze unmoving. "She had a disease, some sort of virus. You shall not jeopardize your life or mine—"

"I have the right!"

"You don't have anything, you fool! And she was growing up to be another skirt who would—"

Drasko's punch came so fast that Uriah's knees buckled as he fell back against the carriage parked at the curb.

Drasko's strong hands fisted the front of his coat, eyes burning with madness an inch from his.

"Don't you dare talk about her like that," Drasko snarled into his face.

A monster, truly—Uriah only smirked in Drasko's face contorted in fury, his scars crimson from anger. The boy had grown up tall and muscled, much bigger than Uriah and fearless, though Uriah knew he would always have a way to control Drasko.

"Another slur against her," Drasko growled, "by God, I will rip your tongue out with my own fingers."

Amused, Uriah pushed him away. "So, the dog grew teeth." He fixed his vest and coat. "Has it ever crossed your mind that you'd be nothing without me? One of those"—he gestured at the beggar on the corner—"or worse. And look at you now. Wealthy." He nodded toward Drasko's coat. "Educated." He tapped his temple with his forefinger. "Smart."

"I paid you back with my work," Drasko gritted out.

"True."

"I made you a lot of money, with mining innovations and all. The deals with the Indians—"

"All true. Yet you still don't understand what power is. I have learned a lot in this life. And you are only a speck of what I am."

Drasko spat on the ground and picked up his hat. "And I regret I bear even a speck of a resemblance to you. I wish I was nothing like you. Goodbye, Uriah."

Drasko disappeared into the streets of London.

Days spent roaming the streets, marveling at the new world that was so different from India.

Nights spent in taverns, drinking himself into oblivion.

He went to the Port of London, then to the East End, searching for Zeph, his best friend, who would be unrecognizable, save for the bright burgundy birthmark above his right eyebrow.

No such luck. Zeph could be dead by now, the usual fate of homeless children.

Drasko got drunk for days, mourning little *jaan*'s death. He went to a dingy opium den, traded a diamond for the poison that made him forget, and got high.

Five days later, Uriah found him in a small tavern in Whitechapel.

"How did you find me?" drunk Drasko mused, secretly relieved to see the only person he knew in the city.

Uriah shrugged off his coat, took off his gloves, and, taking a seat next to Drasko, ordered a whisky.

"I have people," he said simply, checking his diamond pocket watch like he had more important business to attend. "I need you to come back to India with me."

Drasko had money now. He'd brought with him a pouch of diamonds, worth a small fortune that he'd earned. Perhaps he could start his own business.

"I know you can sell those diamonds and get rich quickly. How long would that last you?" Uriah asked, reading his mind.

Right now, Drasko wanted to drink himself to death. Right now, he despised Uriah more than ever.

But he had reasons to go back. He wanted to understand why Uriah's hate ran so deep. He wanted to have more connections. He wanted to "have people" just like Uriah did.

More importantly, Drasko knew there was much more to learn. Despite his black soul, Uriah was the smartest man Drasko had ever known. And now fourteen-year-old Drasko had an agenda—he wanted to learn everything he could about the business. He didn't want to be like this monster. One day, he wanted to be a whole different man, powerful enough to avenge little *jaan* and destroy Uriah.

A week later, they were at sea.

Three months later, Drasko was back in business.

Asha cried when she learned about the little girl's fate.

"The saddest thing in the world is a child's casket," Rupesh said grimly.

The most heartbreaking thing was not being able to say goodbye. So, Drasko grieved in silence.

By day, he threw himself into work with unseen-before dedication. By night, he learned the ways of grown men, with liquor and women and fights. And later, in his drunken dreams, he prayed for the soul of his little *jaan*.

It was a single event, the first of many, that taught him a simple truth. Despite the enormous wealth and the power it brought, what truly gave life meaning were human emotions. The happy moments, but even more so, the tragedies. The tragedies were what made men who they were.

"The more you acquire," Rupesh said one night, "the more you have to lose."

But if what you had was soulless, it didn't matter if you lost it at all.

Diamonds didn't have a soul. There were plenty. And Drasko wanted one—the Crimson Tear.

He didn't know that at the end, years later, when he found it, he would be on his knees, his heart breaking into pieces as he wished it had never existed at all.

27

DRASKO

Grace played. Drasko listened. She practiced. He listened. All the while being anywhere but in the same room with her. For as soon as he stepped into the music room, she stopped. If she caught the sound of him in the hallway, her music ceased.

It was a curse, day after day.

Drasko worked more from his home office, its doors always ajar so that he could hear her practice. He learned her repertoire. Samira became his spy as she inquired about the names of the musical pieces from Eden and reported back to Drasko.

Once in a while, Grace played something entirely different, some sensual tune he had never heard before.

"Missus composes her own songs and lyrics," Eden said proudly.

One such night, he walked into the music room while Grace was playing.

One glance at him, and she stopped and set her hands on her lap.

He took a seat on the sofa. "Will you play for me? I'd like to hear it."

It took her a minute to compose herself.

He watched her shoulders rise and fall, her fingers brushing against the piano keys as if she were deciding what to play.

She tried, then faltered. Tried again. Faltered. Blushed. Shook her head in frustration.

"I think I am a little tired," she said softly without meeting his eyes. "Forgive me."

His heart fell. She played for thousands, but not him.

"You should probably know," she said, staring down at her hands, "Julien will start coming here now and then."

"Julien?" He had never heard the name.

"Julien d'Auvergne, my instructor, yes." She finally raised her eyes at him. "He has been with me for years. If that's all right with you."

Drasko had wondered why he had not seen her instructor yet. Was she afraid to bring him here?

"It is," he answered and walked out of the music room.

He continued to listen from the shadows, a thief in his own house. And by day, he would walk into the empty music room and brush his fingers against the beautiful keys of the grand piano, the keys that *she* had touched every day, conjuring the beautiful sounds.

It was driving him to the brink of insanity. And so was the kiss they had shared in the tunnels.

The night at the caves was a genuine surprise. He had expected her to follow him—she was a curious young lady and determined to learn more about him, much to his delight.

What he hadn't expected was her staying in the tunnels for so long.

He was still trying to figure her out.

Grace was the epitome of perfection, from her perfectly done hair to every perfect detail in her dress to the perfect softness of her summer gloves and the perfect little bowties on her shoes. She moved with well-practiced perfection as if she would be punished if she wasn't more perfect than other young ladies.

Perfect, perfect, perfect, as if this flawed world wasn't meant for her.

Yet, her bedroom and dressing room were quite different. He had been there in her absence, the wonderful disarray so in contrast with what she looked like outside her room.

Scents. Dresses. Stockings. Flowers. Papers with lyrics and music sheets were on the bureau, on her bed, on her nightstand. Books were left open. Among many, one on Hindu mythology and another on Oriental art, a travel almanac and one on the history of gemstones.

Her room with open windows and fresh flowers was something he did not know Grace was—free-spirited.

He had learned that side of her in the tunnels. She hadn't grimaced at the dirt and dampness, hadn't scrunched up her nose, not once shied away from the helping hand of his men, despite them being dirty and sweaty. Drasko had observed her scrupulously the entire time, and not a second had been marred with even a momentary display of vanity or contempt. Grace had sat in the rail cart and ridden down the tunnel! It was as if the veil had been lifted and he had seen a different Grace.

And then came the kiss, the kiss that slowly, for days now, was destroying Drasko's sanity.

She was a delicacy. Her kiss was exquisite. *Perfect, too.*

Being next to her was becoming torture. What he wanted was to taste her lips again, hear her little moans when they kissed. He wanted her in his bed. And his patience was running out. His right hand would soon fail from the never-ending solo rides into the night. He was playing overtures, sonatas, fugues, like a bloody Paganini, with his cock in his hand instead of a violin. All the while thinking about his wife.

He wanted to find out more about her, what she liked. Tea? Reading? Sewing? Crocheting? Any such silly thing? He wanted to find out what she was like in bed. Women were quite easy to please if done right. What if she resented him? Resented sex? What a shame that would be. But then... He just needed to get that silly hostility out of her—by kissing or fucking. For Christ's sake, he was desperate to have her. And he was in desperate physical need to please his wife.

These ideas danced in his head with growing insistence every day.

He had never lacked women's attention. Women came and went. Drasko was careful about not forming attachments. Yamuna was occasionally on his mind, like a wilting flower, summoning a sad smile on his lips at the memories of what he had once had. Since her death, he had been careful with women. He had a curse, he was sure of it, and no one deserved to be punished for getting close to him.

Until Grace.

She was a curse too, following him for years. Yet, she did not deserve to pay the price. Hence, he needed to keep her at a distance. Two nights a month could work, yet he already knew he was lying to himself.

One afternoon, Drasko sat in his home office. The cigarette burned his lungs nicely. Whisky burned his throat even better. What occupied his mind was the usual—his wife.

His body stirred to life—a frequent occurrence lately when he thought of her.

Two nights a month.

There it was. A deal. The one Drasko was patiently waiting for. He just needed the right time and place to catch his wife off guard.

The thought had tortured him through many nights. And now it was unbearable, creating a "situation" in his trousers that he needed to urgently take care of.

A knock at the door straightened him up.

"Bloody Christ," he muttered, rubbing his face with both hands and exhaling heavily.

A woman—what do you know?—a woman was disrupting his peaceful existence.

"Come in!" he barked, irritated.

His butler walked in with a tray. "A letter for you, sir."

Drasko motioned for him to approach and tensed in unease when the letter landed on his desk.

Cream paper.

Brown seal.

A diamond in the center.

Letter number four was finally here.

The Mawr Auction is to happen in London at the Benham Auction House in one month. The crown jewel of the auction—the Crimson Tear diamond.

Drasko's blood cooled.

All right, nothing terribly surprising.

The auction had been discussed when Uriah was still alive. The display room in the Mawr Building had dozens of such pieces, and Drasko had vaults full of diamonds and a list of renowned jewelers who would create several extraordinary pieces at the snap of his fingers.

The project, the Marvels of Mawr diamonds, had been in the making for several years. With one little exception—now, the Crimson Tear, finally, came into play.

The game was in motion again. Even though Drasko still didn't have the bloody diamond.

Drasko went straight to the Benham Auction House and was lucky to run into Mr. Kleinstein, the director himself.

Any auction house across the world would be delighted to display Mawr masterpieces. Nothing had more influence in the city of London than the surname Mawr.

Peasants didn't bow to a king as much as Mr. Kleinstein bowed to Drasko as he cleared the auction house schedule and called a crew to get to work on the future event immediately.

Drasko's assistants were right away sent to over a dozen newspapers with a brief about the auction and a copy of the photograph taken only weeks ago—he and Grace in the Mawr Wonder Room.

He still didn't understand the purpose of the diamond game and didn't have the Crimson Tear. There would be a lesson—he knew Uriah too well. There would be a sacrifice and pain and choices to make. But what?

"You will pay with your own life," Uriah had said.

And Drasko could not come up with the reason why, if he had the Crimson Tear in his possession like Uriah had promised, displaying it at the auction would be out of the question.

That very evening, in his Mawr office, he opened the door that revealed a spiral staircase. He climbed the stairs until he was in a small round room at the top of the tower, with only a lantern and a mattress on the floor.

He'd spent so many nights here, alone, thinking and dreaming. He'd spent several nights here after his wedding, trying to come to terms with *her* in his life.

Drasko stepped outside, onto the railed observation deck, the wind right away wafting into his face and playing with his hair.

He loved being here, on top of the world. The city lay unprotected below, with its snake-like paths of wide avenues and train tracks, the city lights like fireflies. The factory smoke rose above them, the clouds hovering over the Thames. Vast and beautiful under the setting sun, the city noise was reduced to a muffled humming and the rambling of locomotives in the distance.

The dizzying height was splendid, as success always was. But one was often lonely when reaching it. Once at the very top, one was empty with the realization that the one thing that had kept one's heart racing on the way there was now gone.

It was called a dream.

Drasko had a different dream now. It had the sweet face of a piano virtuoso with hazel eyes and a pretty blush, soft coral lips and contagious laughter.

Gracie…

Drasko wished there would come a time when he could call her by the name reserved for her friends.

Her eyes often paused on him and flashed with a fleeting surprise as if she had just found out a secret about him. In moments such as those, a fleeting hope swept over him that perhaps, one day, when he told her all his secrets and what this strange game was, she would still find the strength to smile and the will to forgive him.

No, not much time had passed since he had forced her into this marriage. Since she had called him a tyrant. Since the day, years ago, he had made a promise yet to be delivered.

No, she could not possibly have feelings for him.

Yet, the hope was there, however brief though powerful only in a way a hope can be in a man who could buy anything in the world except one thing—affection.

Drasko kept lying to himself that the years of watching her play in public were a mere curiosity. He kept pretending that she was nothing, and—by God!—he made those precise words his mantra.

Even later that night, when he arrived home, he tried to ignore the way his heartbeat spiked when he walked in. Stepping into the hallway, right away, he listened for the sound of the piano. Or her voice. Or any indication that she was home and not hiding in her room.

It was late. Music came from behind the closed doors to the music room. Grace was playing, practicing a concerto, intricate and wild, so preoccupied that she did not hear him come home.

Being as quiet as he could, Drasko dismissed the servants, picked up a glass of whisky, and walked toward the music room.

The music ceased altogether, and he stilled in the shadows, holding his breath as if Grace could hear him.

Shortly, she resumed, but not her classical piece. She was playing something different entirely.

Drasko sat down on the floor by the doors, his back against

the wall. Whisky pleasantly burned his throat. Tiredness weighed down on his eyelids.

One month until the auction. And then what?

Grace was playing the grand piano, the beautiful instrument that was privileged to sing under her fingers. And she was magical.

He listened to the sensual tunes that trickled from the music room. He thought of her delicate hands. Thought of her laughter. Thought of her smile, a timid one and a different one, broad and happy, at ease, when she thought he wasn't looking.

The notes in her song changed, suddenly happy, then gradually grew into mournful again.

Elias was right, always had been, all that nonsense about the affections that Drasko had so stubbornly tried to deny.

Would there be a time when Grace would feel the same?

And then Drasko heard her voice, soft and sensual, like the sweetest wine—his wife was singing.

And his heart woke up.

Drasko closed his eyes and let the music seep into him. He pictured her at the piano. Her fingertips, conjuring the gentle notes, laced with sorrow and tenderness. Her hands so expert with the piano keys yet shy and hesitant when she touched him back then, in the tunnels.

It was all in her, the woman he now called his wife, but who was not and might never be truly his.

Every sound of the keys tugged stronger at his heart that was being gently ripped into pieces, petal by petal, like the wedding flowers that had cushioned the floor on their wedding day, the day fate had brought them together.

His body started humming along. As whisky burned his chest, memories of the past suddenly rushed to his head—love, hate, grief, all of them at once. Drasko wanted to be in the room with her, breathing her in and simply watching her play.

And then suddenly, he made out the words of her song, the words that made his chest tighten.

The words tiptoed into his heart, for a brief moment making him so weak that he wanted to rush in, sweep her into his arms, and not let go until he told her all his secrets, all his deep thoughts, most of them about her. Tell her that it didn't have to be a game. That what she sang about could be real. If only he told her the truth. If only she gave him a chance. If only that didn't jeopardize their future.

Her songs didn't have to be a fantasy. And the one she was singing right now could one day come true.

Her voice seeped into his soul, making him dream again— Grace was singing about love.

28

DRASKO

It was late afternoon, and Drasko was so preoccupied with his office at home that when he finally walked out into the hallway, he was surprised to hear the piano from the music room.

The music ceased abruptly.

"What is the matter, dear?" A man's voice in the music room echoed into the hall. "You sound like a debutante performing at a ball with her secret admirer in the crowd knocking the courage out of her."

The voice was young and pretentious, or perhaps Drasko was already prejudiced against the man who had spent years by Grace's side.

Drasko did not like men around Grace. Especially when they were allowed in the music room where she played, and played so brilliantly, while he wasn't welcome.

The rhythmic sound of the metronome was unusual, too, for Grace had never used it before.

Today was the first time Grace had invited her instructor to the house. *Sneaky*, Drasko thought, for he had told her he would be away for business all day.

Well, he'd lied.

He stood in the hallway for a minute before finally making up his mind and opening the door to the music room.

Julien d'Auvergne was a slender man in his thirties, just a bit older than Drasko. A dandy, he was dressed in creased dark trousers and pristinely tailored waistcoats over a starched yellow shirt with a brown silk puff necktie. His straw-colored hair was a curly whirlwind cascading onto his shoulders.

The man half-sat on the puffed sofa, his legs elegantly crossed. His blue eyes brightly widened at the sight of Drasko. He pushed off the sofa and rushed toward him with fierce determination.

"Mr. Mawr!" he exclaimed, taking Drasko's hand with both of his and shaking it enthusiastically.

Grace jumped up from her seat. "Julien, this is my husband."

"Mr. d'Auvergne." Drasko nodded to the man who studied him with admiration.

"Julien," the man said, not letting go of Drasko's hand. "Julien is quite fine. It is a pleasure to meet you, Mr. Mawr."

"Am I interrupting?"

"Not at all, not at all. It is wonderful that you are here!"

Indeed.

That was Drasko's precise intention. If his wife would not perform for him, her instructor, no doubt, would make her.

Drasko settled on the sofa facing the grand piano. He crossed one leg over the other and spread his arms on the back of the sofa.

Glancing at him in unease, Grace lowered herself back onto the piano bench.

They had agreed that she had her freedom as to what friendships to keep. Yet, she shrank into herself every time one of her friends was around.

It puzzled Drasko.

Julien stopped the metronome and leisurely took a seat on the sofa next to him.

"Mr. Mawr," Julien drawled, his blue eyes on Drasko, "I hope you do not mind Gracie playing at night. You see, the Sommervilles were strict about it, to say the least. But she loves practicing at strange hours of the day and night."

There it was again—*Gracie*. Who were these people calling her so endearingly? And the mention of the bloody Sommervilles in yet another uncomfortable context wasn't to Drasko's liking either.

"*Gracie*"—Drasko smiled at the name—"can play any time she wants. I *want* her to play."

"Wonderful! Mr. Mawr, you have a heart of gold. You see, the Sommervilles were so strict that Gracie used to sneak out of the house so she could join me—"

"Julien!" Grace snapped, panic sweeping across her face.

"Pardon me." Julien shrugged.

Drasko glanced at his wife. "Julien, please, continue. I am intrigued as to where my wife used to sneak to at night."

Julien gracefully flicked his wrist. "Oh, it is not like that, Mr. —"

"Mr. Mawr," Grace interrupted too swiftly, her panicked stare on Julien, "is not interested in what my life was like before."

"Mr. Mawr," Drasko cut in, "is very interested."

Julien cocked his head at her. "Your husband might be entertained."

"My husband"—she flinched—"doesn't need to know."

"Is that so?" Drasko let a smile out to play. He liked *my husband* on her lips.

He turned his attention to Julien, running right into his admiring gaze. *How peculiar.* Drasko knew that sort of stare, usually from women.

"Unfortunately, Julien, my wife will not play for me," Drasko said with intentional sadness.

"We shall change that! Right away!" Julien exclaimed enthusiastically, then added in a lower voice, "Though she is not herself today. By the way, the grand piano is outstanding, Mr. Mawr. What an exquisite wedding present!"

Wedding present? Drasko bit back a laugh.

Julien motioned to Grace. "Gracie, dear, would you play us something from your old repertoire? Albéniz, perhaps? Mr. Mawr, do you like his work?"

"I love his work."

Drasko flashed a daring grin at Grace. "Marcha Militar" by Albéniz was the piece she played that night, years ago, when they were first introduced at Canterbury Music Hall. The night she so rudely dismissed him. Something she probably didn't remember and he would never forget.

"Gracie, please!" Julien theatrically waved his hand in the air. "Indulge us!"

And what do you know? Grace took a deep inhale and obeyed.

Drasko studied his wife, her back perfectly straight, determination on her face as she started playing "Spring" by Vivaldi.

Pompous chords thumped through the room. The dry staccato lifted the corner of his mouth in a smile. *Stac-cato*—he had learned that word that was more appropriate for a gun name. Or her attitude when they married. *In spring.*

But then the softer higher-pitched trills came in, playful and sensual. Could that be the indication of how she felt these days?

He could have listened for an eternity if Julien hadn't motioned to the ceiling frescos.

"I do love those, by the way," he whispered.

Drasko knew exactly which ones.

"The explicit imagery—truly fantastic." Julien's eyes returned to Drasko's. "The East is so much more romantic and sensual than the rigid West, wouldn't you say?"

"Agreed." Drasko motioned upward. "I hope it creates an inspiring ambiance for my wife."

Julien broke out in laughter.

Grace faltered, eliciting a momentary surprised frown from Julien. But then Julien asked Drasko about India, and Drasko talked, intentionally quietly, so he could hear the music.

Soon, Grace seemed at ease, for the first time playing for him, perhaps, getting used to his voice. If he had to entertain the instructor to hear his wife play, he would talk until the next century. He would sit in this room until dawn, as long as he could watch the elegant dance of her fingers over the keys, effortless and sensual. The pinkish-gold glow of the piano in the soft lamplight was magical. Everything about her was when she did what she loved.

Grace finished the music piece and smiled at Julien's compliments, her cheeks flushed as her gaze met Drasko's.

He ordered brandy. At Grace's permission, cigarettes were lit. The playful tunes of Mozart's sonata followed as Grace resumed playing.

Time slowed. Drasko lost track of it, didn't care, wished the night would last forever, just the three of them. It might take a long time, or never—he tucked the hurtful thought away—for her to want to be alone with him. So, he would bring her friends around, he decided, make more friends, and give her something that the Sommervilles, he realized, had never given her—the feeling of being cared for.

And he wanted more of her music, that enchanting torrent of sounds, sweet sounds and those that tasted bitter, seductive ones and those that cut deep into his soul. She was music. It was in the imagined taste of her. In her shy smiles and endearing little frowns, depending on what she played. As well as the elegant swaying of her body like that of a flower in the wind.

"Tell me about her practice routine," Drasko inquired softly and let Julien talk just so that he could lose himself in her music.

It grew dark outside as they found themselves deep in a conversation interrupted by Grace, who stopped playing. "It's dinner time."

"Will you stay for dinner, Julien?" Drasko suggested and caught Grace's hopeful gaze at the instructor.

"Oh, that would be a pleasure!" Julien exclaimed.

The pleasure was all Drasko's.

He found it endearing how her resentment changed into eagerness she couldn't hide, the glow on her face and frequent smiles when she heard Julien and him joke.

What had the Sommervilles done to make her so desperate for friends yet so afraid to bring them around?

Julien told stories about the musical world. Drasko shared his. After dinner, they moved back to the music room, late into the evening but all of them eager to spend more time together.

Grace was at the piano again, brandy coloring her cheeks, her eyes sparkly. Drasko caught her glances at him from beneath her lashes, her pursed lips that tried to hide a smile, all those little bits and pieces of her that were making their way deeper into his soul.

He couldn't look away from his wife. Her music and voice were a warm fantasy, for as soon as she stopped playing, the dirty world pulsated back, reminding him of his past and his losses and more to come.

A sudden crash on the upper floor made Grace still in the middle of the music piece.

Drasko cocked his ears, listening to more sounds.

The doors flew open, and Tripp and Nina stormed into the room.

"Sir, we have a situation upstairs," Tripp announced, a gun in his hands. "A break-in. There are men in the house. They ran into one of the maids. Two of ours ran upstairs. There might be more intruders."

A gunshot echoed from upstairs.

Both Julien and Grace jumped up from their seats.

Drasko rose abruptly and stomped toward the sideboard, nodding to Tripp and Nina. "You are staying here and guarding the doors."

He reached behind the sideboard and pulled out a loaded revolver. There were many of them hidden throughout the house. There were plenty of thugs who thought that the house held treasures that would make them rich.

Never had they made it inside the house before.

Until now.

They will bleed.

Drasko checked the bullets, then met Grace's worried gaze.

"Drasko?" she called out to him in a shaky voice, and her eyes dropped to his cocked gun.

Was that worry on her face? *How sweet…*

"It will be all right," he said with a reassuring smile. "Play, darling. Play something fierce."

He winked at her and stomped out the door.

THE
WOLLENDORFS

Andhra Pradesh, India
Drasko, 20

The Wollendorf brothers, Franz and Heinrich, had noses like sniffer dogs. For diamonds, naturally. They owned the Wollendorf Consortium out of South Africa, the newly found diamond hub that was yielding more diamonds than India ever had. The Consortium had expanded with astonishing speed, and the Wollendorfs, the serpents of diamond mining, wanted it all, including the Mawrs' share of the business.

The Wollendorfs had already acquired the diamond-rich regions in Brazil, and, rumor had it, made a deal with the Russians.

Now they'd set their sights on India.

No one knew how and when, but the rumor about the Crimson Tear spread across the oceans. The King of Spain wanted to see it. The Queen of England had sent the Mawr brothers a letter. The jewelers exchanged theories. The richest lords and ladies in Europe sent inquiries. And the British *Gazette* did a front-page article about Mawr Diamond Industries, this time giving more attention to Drasko Mawr.

He used to be a homeless child, it said, *adopted by one of the Mawr brothers.*

Perhaps an illegitimate son, one of the European newspapers suggested. *The only heir to the fortune!*

A lot of those rumors came from Alfred's drunk blabbering during business trips and official events.

Uriah didn't care. He had planned on it.

And now the rumors brought the Wollendorfs to India.

"They are young and fearless. They think they can disregard the traditions and connections we have built for decades," Uriah told Drasko as they hosted the Wollendorfs. "Nothing is more important than decades of knowledge."

Drasko did not agree but was intrigued. Two days of the subtle game of business seduction, and they were yet to discuss what the Wollendorfs had come here for.

Uriah was in his forties now. His hair had a few grays, he had lost weight, and his gaze had acquired razor-sharpness.

Alfred, though the younger of the two, looked a decade older than his brother, heavier, bitterer, and permanently reeked of alcohol.

It was Drasko, everyone knew, who would be the successor to Mawr Diamond Industries. The older men in the business resented him. The wise ones foretold his brilliant future. The envious spread more rumors.

Naturally, the Wollendorfs were polite with the Mawr brothers and overly friendly with young Drasko, who, they hoped, would be easier to manipulate.

It was 1883. Drasko was twenty, more knowledgeable in the diamond business than the Mawr brothers had ever been, and Uriah let him take the reins, carefully guiding him and watching his every move.

Drasko had a woman now, Yamuna. He had a villa built just for the two of them and felt like his life finally had meaning.

"The diamond trade," Yamuna said to him once, "it's dangerous. It's cruel. It hardens your heart. And it will make you just like them."

Them, the Mawr brothers. After all, Drasko's legal last name was the same.

Elias Bayne, his dear friend, now sailed his own ship. He was visiting at the same time as the Wollendorfs.

"There is that air of superiority about them," he said, observing the Wollendorfs. "They are younger than the Mawr brothers. Hungrier. You watch them. They will try to destroy you."

The next day, Drasko learned what they had in mind.

"We offer to buy out your land," Franz Wollendorf said as the Wollendorfs and the Mawrs gathered in the office for the much-anticipated business discussion. "For a much larger sum than what it is worth, considering business predictions for the next decade and all. You can keep part of the shares. But with the potential of the resources, the Wollendorf Consortium will overrun Mawr Industries in no time. You understand. It's in your best interest."

Alfred's eyes lit up with a greedy shine as he turned toward his brother.

Uriah didn't respond, only checked the diamond watch in his hand.

Drasko observed everyone with the odd sense that a war was about to begin.

The Mawrs had expected a few proposals, including a merger that could—would have—made all of them more powerful than any such enterprise before. Such a merger would have let them buy out the Russians, explore Australia and other parts of Africa.

But the young Wollendorf brothers turned out to be greedy. Ambitious, too.

Drasko, the youngest of the men in the room, understood it all as the Wollendorfs talked. He saw through Alfred's greed and laziness. Tensed at Uriah's quietness that was an ominous sign. The proposal was an insult to the Mawrs on their own soil. Diplomatic but an insult, nevertheless.

Uriah stayed silent.

Drasko waited.

The Wollendorfs exchanged expectant looks.

The room was quiet as a cemetery until Alfred spoke. "That's a great proposal. And the capital—"

"Quiet!" Uriah shut him up in a clipped tone, then shifted his eyes to the Wollendorf brothers and said the five words that sealed the Mawrs' future, "You have overstayed your welcome."

That night, Drasko stood in the courtyard of the Mawr villa, leaning against a wooden column, and smoked. The scent of blooming flowers calmed him as the sound of the two brothers fighting echoed through the house and spilled into the courtyard.

"We can wash our hands of the business and never have to come back to India!" Alfred shouted.

"You are a fool and a drunk," came Uriah's clipped reply. "You want to throw away everything we have built."

"Who are you building this for? For your imaginary heirs? For your precious Drasko?" Drunken laughter followed.

"I shall buy you out," Uriah offered. "Take your money and run. Go soak your sorrows around the world."

"Better than rotting in this place. And no, brother. I am done with your game. Done swallowing your orders and my pride."

"Pride? What pride do you talk of? Humor me, Alfred."

"Done!" roared Alfred. "Everything! Always! Happens! As! You! Wish! I am done with you! And you know what? You are not getting my share. Noooooo. Oh, nooooo. I am selling my part of the company to the Wollendorfs. Yes! I have decided! My choice, not yours!"

An eerie feeling made the hair on the back of Drasko's neck stand up. Something had just been decided, but it wasn't up to Alfred.

Alfred stormed out, stomped through the courtyard, noticed Drasko smoking, and halted. His bloodshot eyes for once weren't spiteful but awfully sad.

"I know I lost the bet. Years ago," he said in a shaky voice, slowly approaching Drasko. "I know you know about that bet too, and I am glad for the way you turned out. Truly am. Despite the many wrongs I did to you."

Alfred nodded, drunkenly studying Drasko as if searching for his next thought.

"Me? I should never have married Clara. I should never have let him take my daughter. He is sick with an obsession for power. Infected with vanity. Riddled with loneliness. And he sees to it that everyone always ends up like him. Alone. Full of anger and hate. But if you want a life, Drasko"—Alfred suddenly walked up to him and halted, face-to-face, so close that Drasko could get drunk off the pungent stench of alcohol—"any life besides this desert of existence"—he motioned around— "then you need to run. Far far away. So far that no one can find you." His expression darkened. "Because if they do—*he* will too. And unlike anyone else, you, you..." His voice suddenly acquired a venomous bite. "He thinks you are his property. And Uriah never gives up what is his."

Alfred stumbled off.

A nasty feeling gathered in Drasko's chest. He left the house but didn't go home to Yamuna, who was so good at calming his storms. No, she didn't deserve yet another storm.

He went to see Elias, who didn't care for the diamond trade but cared for his best friend.

"Tell me, brother," Elias said as they sat on the veranda that overlooked the luscious gardens and the mango trees that obscured the starry skies. "Do you suppose a great man ever says, 'Stop' to himself? If he is at the very top and all? Does he look at his kingdom one day and say, 'I have enough'?"

Drasko didn't have an answer. He wasn't at the top, didn't have it all.

"I was thinking..." he finally said, taking a drag off a cigar and a sip of whisky.

Elias chuckled. "That's already a good sign."

Drasko smiled. For a while, he had felt a change in himself, brought by Yamuna. "Now that I have Yamuna, I wonder if I always thought wrong about the future."

"Elaborate?"

"I don't want to be like them." He meant the Mawrs and the Wollendorfs. This thought had nothing to do with Drasko's future ambitions but rather with the subtle sense of what the men represented—a constant battle for power, a rat race, vicious and blood-thirsty. "I want children and a home and a family and peace. But I don't want Yamuna to choose."

"Choose what?"

"Between prosperity and happiness."

Drasko thought of Uriah. Now that he understood Uriah's ruthless carelessness about the people who surrounded him, Drasko had a feeling that Uriah would never let him have what he truly wanted. Instead, Drasko would follow in his steps, lonely and hateful.

Alfred was right.

After hours of talking, when the night grew late, Elias patted Drasko on the shoulder and said, "You shall figure it out. Perhaps, you don't need to be a king. Perhaps, you don't need a kingdom at all. Why would you if you can have the whole world?"

Elias, the dashing and fearless captain who owned oceans, laughed then, the low warm sound of it briefly putting Drasko at ease. Unlike him, Elias came from a loving family, knew the value of love, whereas Drasko was only now finding out how important it was. Thanks to Yamuna.

"Something is about to happen," Drasko said grimly.

"You know what they say about Mawr Industries in the West? They say that Mawr Industries sells many hues of the best quality diamonds. But all of them are tarnished with blood."

Drasko nodded.

"Come away with me, brother," Elias asked. "Take Yamuna and come with me. Tomorrow. The day after. Anywhere. Just leave this place and him. You have to, mate. You need to break away from him."

That night, as Drasko walked home, his mind hazy, his heart heavy, he saw two figures in the distance. The figures headed for the cliff on the hill. The muffled voices sounded familiar, and Drasko wondered whether Uriah and Alfred had finally made peace.

The next day, he woke up to the maid's urgent knocking at the door.

"It's one of the masters," she said. "They found the body of Master Alfred, down below the cliff. He must've stumbled off the edge in the dark."

Drasko understood then what Uriah was. Despite his wealth and power, he lacked the only thing that wasn't dependent on either—affection. Uriah tried to control the ones closest to him in the hope of being the center of their universe. And when he failed, he tossed them out of his life, squished them mercilessly so as not to witness his own failure.

Clara Lewis. Dr. Lewis. Little *jaan*. Alfred Mawr.

Uriah had only one person left, the one reared to his liking, proving fate wrong—Drasko.

Run, the thought pounded in Drasko's mind. But he refused to.

He had never been afraid. Nor was he now. He also knew that Elias was wrong—Drasko would never be able to run far enough.

So, from now on, he had to watch his back.

30

GRACE

Gunshots boomed through the house as Grace tried to play, her heart in her stomach and her mind upstairs, with Drasko.

Julien sat on the sofa with a brandy in his hand, tense as a rod but not saying a word.

Nina and Tripp didn't flinch, guns in their hands as they guarded the door.

Grace stopped playing abruptly, and the echo of the music sank into the room's silence. The house was eerily quiet, too, but her heartbeat was wildly loud.

Please, come back, Grace prayed, realizing she was afraid to lose her husband.

The door opened, and Drasko walked in, sharp determination on his face.

"One down. Three ran," he said in a low voice to Tripp, tipping his head toward upstairs.

"Everyone is all right?" Nina tucked her gun into the folds of her skirt—a hidden holster that Grace had never noticed before.

"They are cleaning up, yes."

"Sir?" Nina pointed at Drasko's shoulder and the red seeping through the shirt fabric.

"Only a scratch."

A scratch…

Grace stood up, her knees weak with sudden relief, her eyes on Drasko's stained shirt.

"My guard will escort you home," Drasko said to Julien. "It's a precaution. I deeply apologize for what happened."

Julien only nodded, his prolonged gaze on Drasko as they shook hands.

"That was—"

"That never happened before," Grace cut him off with an apology as they walked toward the entrance doors, guarded with more men than ever before.

"Life is not fair," Julien said with sadness.

"What do you mean by that?"

Julien put on his suit jacket and picked up his fashionable cane and hat from the doorman, then turned to Grace.

"Ah, because you seem not to value your husband, Gracie. Whereas I, oh…" His eyes flashed toward the end of the hallway where Drasko and several of his men stood talking. "If he were mine, I would worship him—"

"Oh, God, stop!" Grace exclaimed with a coy smile.

Julien gone, she waited with the rest for the Metropolitan police. The hall was crowded with the servant staff and the guards. Drasko exchanged hushed murmurs with his men.

Grace studied him openly—his rolled-up sleeves, the wound on his shoulder, the way he blinked in irritation. There were little things, sounds and scents and gestures, that belonged only to him. The scratch of a match when he lit it. The crackling of the tobacco and his eyes narrowing just a bit as he took the first drag. The way his lips puckered just slightly on an exhale. The smoke curling around him from the burned end of the cigarette. The glint of the metal rings on his fingers. The way he slid his other hand into his pocket. The shift of his broad shoulders.

Across the hall, he caught Grace's gaze. She didn't avert her eyes, let them linger on him, knowing he was watching. She knew that his eyes were on her as she followed the cigarette to his lips, then studied his lips when they took a drag and curled into a knowing smile.

She wanted him to know she was watching, baiting him. Was that called seduction? She wouldn't know.

Many things intrigued her about him. Every new day was a revelation. He had guards but did not let them handle his jacket or his hat. He had unimaginable wealth yet worked with his men in the tunnels. He shook hands with the Lord Mayor of London and the men in Parliament yet was most humble with street children. He mined diamonds. Yet... There wasn't a single diamond in his house, his cufflinks of plain silver.

In less than an hour, the house was quiet again.

"There will be more guards now," Drasko informed her. "I am sorry. Please, rest."

In a minute, he was gone, and she was left with Eden.

That was it? He just left her on a night like this?

"Where is my husband?" Grace demanded sometime later, disappointed.

"In his room, ma'am. With Arjun, his servant."

"With a servant?"

"Arjun is taking care of his wound."

Grace huffed in disappointment. That was her duty, not a servant's, to take care of her husband, call the doctor perhaps, have him check the wound, do compresses or—

She halted at the door to his bedroom, listening to the muffled voices behind it.

She didn't bother checking what room the intruders had snuck into, what had been broken or taken. Drasko was behind the door in front of her, wounded, and her heart beat like mad at the thought that something could've happened to him.

She knocked.

"Come in," he called.

She took a deep breath and opened the door.

If the episode in the bathing room had left her yearning for more of him, the current scene in front of her was going to ruin her sleep.

Her husband sat on a tabouret, shirtless and barefoot, only in his trousers. The soft light from the sconces illuminated his strong body. It beamed off the golden chain around his neck, reflected on the rings still on his fingers, glided off the wide leather bracelet around his right wrist, highlighted the red thread next to it.

He looked so...primal.

She'd never seen him naked so close, the muscles so beautifully defined, and... scarred so viciously.

His torso was etched with scars, dozens of them, shallow and deep, across his entire front, several giant scarred lines, like ravines sewn shut. Four of them, like an imprint from monstrous claws.

Who did this to you, she wanted to ask, but he wouldn't tell her, she knew.

She forced herself to look at the fresh wound gaping on his shoulder, blood smudged around it.

"Did you need something, darling?" he asked, his voice sinking deep inside her.

She tore her gaze off his body and met his eyes, emerald, with mischievous specks of gold from the reflected light.

The servant stood with a cloth in his hand, his eyes on her as if waiting for a signal. A bowl of steaming hot water stood on a small table next to him, the smell of the antiseptic spreading in the air.

Grace took it all in, already unsettled at the sight of her husband half-naked.

"I shall do this," she said firmly.

The servant bowed a little. "Madam, I will take care of it. You should rest."

"Rest?"

"I have done this before."

Drasko was calmly watching her. His broad chest rose and

fell slowly. She caught sight of his nipples, then immediately looked away, blushing—there was no way of unseeing that now.

The servant said something in Hindi, but Drasko didn't take his eyes off her.

"Leave us." Grace nodded to the servant. "I will take care of it."

She waited for the man to leave, then picked up the cloth, soaked it in hot water, and took a deep breath before facing her husband—she'd have to be close to him half-naked, and she had no idea what she was doing.

His head cocked in that amused way of his.

"Is everything all right?" he asked gently.

He widened his legs, leaving nowhere for her to stand but between them, and she stepped in. His large hands rested on his thighs, metal rings sparkling dangerously, his face lifted toward hers. Even sitting down, he was almost the same height as her standing up, his face so close it made her dizzy.

Grace kept her eyes on the wound, brought the cloth to his shoulder, and started dabbing the drying blood.

The wound wasn't deep, thank God. She gently blotted it, noticing his muscles in her peripheral flexing just slightly.

She wouldn't look anywhere else. Absolutely not! Not up, not down where there was so much bare skin. Or where his hands brushed against her skirt.

"Why are you avoiding looking at me?" he asked, tilting his head to catch her gaze.

"I am not."

"But you are."

She paused and met his eyes.

They intimidated her, sent flutters through her heart, that treacherous thing that acted of its own volition lately. Especially in such close proximity, at the sight of his soft lips.

"Are you hot?" His voice was like a warm embrace. "Your cheeks are red."

His smile widened. He shifted, his nose almost touching her

chin, his gaze gliding down to her lips.

This was the reason she couldn't play in front of him. The reason she couldn't sing. Why she checked herself in the mirror every time she left her room. Why she blushed as she caught him looking at her.

And that kiss—it had erased everything she'd felt and thought about him before. It had ruined her peace. It had made her restless at night, wanting her husband in a way she'd never wanted any man even in her most wanton dreams.

Something had snapped in her after that kiss. The lies, the doubt, the usual bitterness were gone. She wanted more kisses, more attention, more of his time, more of him. She wanted it all.

"Who were those men?" she asked as she continued cleaning his wound.

"We will find out tomorrow."

"They hurt you."

"I hurt them too."

"You have guards. What are they for?"

"There are not enough."

She stopped and gave him a reproaching gaze.

"We will have more guards," he said. "At least until the auction."

A month from now, then.

That was another thing that intrigued Grace. The auction had been announced the other day, a grand event Europe had been waiting on for years. Yet she sensed it worried Drasko, but she wasn't sure why.

"You are a public person, you said so yourself." His voice distracted her, his warm breath grazing her neck as he talked, his eyes never leaving her face. "And now you are married to another public person. We need to be protected."

"My talent is nothing compared to the value of your wealth."

He placed his hand on hers, stopping her. His thumb stroked her skin, making her body hum in response.

This innocent touch was too much. The touch that unraveled

her. The touch that she dreamed about at night. But it hadn't led anywhere at all. Not yet...

"Most musicians play from the sheets," Drasko said, his gaze dropping to her fingers like they were a miracle. "Great ones play from the heart." He raised his eyes toward her again. "The biggest talent is making those who live through tragedies dwell on happy moments. Making those who shed too many tears smile. Making cold hearts beat so hard that they catch on fire. Taking away the vicious flames that torment others and cool their burning minds."

He leaned in just a fraction, moved his head just an inch, and his nose grazed her chin in a soft caress.

She held her breath.

"That's what you are, Grace—a heart-whisperer," he said.

He shifted, and his lips touched the side of her face in a butterfly kiss.

No one had ever talked to her like this. This man was weaving some magic around her, and it was getting harder to resist. She didn't want to. It wasn't a matter of feelings. No, no, no, she wasn't giving in to his charms, she was simply curious. She had been telling herself this for days. She was a woman, yes, married to a fascinating man and still clueless about what it was like to truly *be* with him.

Shame—that was what burned her when she heard occasional rumors about Drasko's former lovers while she didn't know what it was like to be a wife.

She trembled at his touch but didn't meet his eyes, continued cleaning the wound like it was the most important task.

Drasko shifted again and rested his hands on her waist.

"I wish you would play for me again, like you did today," he said softly.

His hands shifted to her hips, their weight burning her even through the fabric of her skirt.

"I will," she whispered.

"That will make me very happy."

"We all have something to make others happy."

He dropped his head and kissed her shoulder.

"What do *I* have, Grace?" he murmured against her skin.

She flinched, her entire body flaring up at his kiss.

"You..." She tried to bring her thoughts together. "You give people jobs. You make marvelous gems—"

"Not others—you." He dipped his head to catch her gaze, no trace of humor in his eyes anymore, only kindness, inquiring and expectant. "What do I have to make you happy? We might be in for a long ride. And I always make sure that people who matter to me are happy."

"The ones who matter..." she echoed.

He leaned over again. Another kiss on her neck. His hair brushed against her skin.

Her eyes fluttered closed, but she forced herself to focus.

"Yes," he breathed against her skin, then looked up to meet her gaze as if checking her reaction. "I'd like to make you happy, so you don't feel like this marriage is your worst misery."

"I do not... I don't think that." *Anymore.* "You got me pianos. They are—"

"Things, Grace, objects. That's not what I meant. Look at me." She did, surprised to see unusual softness in his eyes. "What will make you happy?"

They were treading on sensitive ground. Things between them were changing. She knew he didn't despise her the way she had first thought. And she... well, she couldn't lie to herself anymore, pretending that she resented him, while in fact, he had done more for her than anyone before, made her feel like he cared. Made her *feel*.

"Well." She took a little step back, letting his hands fall off her, then took the ointment and dabbed it on his wound, hoping it would distract him.

"I suppose, we all have hands that have special talents," she said, pursing her lips, immediately regretting the stupid words.

She finished with his wound and put away the ointment,

then wiped her hands on her skirt, not knowing what to do with them or herself.

He looked perplexed.

Was he truly that thick?

Despair took over her. How was it possible that she now needed to tell him that she wouldn't mind the *two nights a month*? Perhaps, one? Just one, to find out.

"My hands?" he mused.

"I suppose your hands would make me happy if you ever made good use of them," she blurted. Her face grew hot that very instant. "I should leave," she muttered and dashed toward the door, trying to hide her embarrassment.

She heard him move behind her as she struggled with the door handle and pulled the door open.

Too late.

He slammed it shut, whipped her around, and pinned her against the door, his weight on her.

"Darling, you cannot walk out after you just said that."

A whimper betrayed her as his lips met hers in a kiss.

31

GRACE

It was only the second time they had kissed, and already his lips felt familiar.

Her body surged toward his, though there was nowhere else to go, his arms holding her tightly against him. And when his lips left hers, Grace prayed they came back, or were elsewhere, as long as they were on her, because she had just flirted with him, asked to be with him, if only indirectly, and she wouldn't have the courage to say it out loud again or tell him she wanted this.

"My patience is running low." He placed a kiss on her jawline, his hot breath on her skin, then moved to her neck. "*Your* curiosity is too obvious. And by God, I wish I were a better man and could give you more time. But I'm not so patient, not with you, Grace. You are driving me completely insane."

Did he know how he made her feel? Unlike him, Grace didn't dare to tell him what she wanted.

"Stay tonight," he whispered.

His kisses felt hot, and so was his skin—so much skin, so bare, so soft over the hard taut muscles, so warm under her fingertips.

"Yes," she whispered back, right away trembling at the decision.

But his lips took hers in a kiss. A kiss that wasn't as patient as before.

Thoughts about this had haunted Grace for days. Would he like her body? Would he notice the scars on the inside of her forearm? Or the one under her ribs that was an ugly mark, from her childhood, made even uglier by the healing episode five years ago?

Grace wanted the lights off, wanted this to be quick, just to know what it was like, hoping he would not bring it up the next day.

These thoughts flickered in her mind but faded away as she lost herself in his kiss, his hands already undoing the buttons of her bodice.

"Take my trousers off," he ordered, undressing her as she tried to calm her breathing and hesitated. "Grace?" he repeated.

She did as she was told, aroused at being in charge of undressing him, pushing his trousers down his hips. She undid his undergarments next and tugged them down, releasing him from the fabric.

He kicked away his trousers and undergarments, all the while kissing her, and she prayed he didn't stop so she didn't have to look him in the eyes or down, especially down.

He was so confident and glorious, standing naked in front of her. She was still almost fully dressed and nervous, shrinking into herself in white-hot shame.

"May I?" In seconds, he expertly undid her corset, as if he had done it before, then moved to her skirt, undoing it and pushing it down her legs, letting it pool at her feet.

He studied her with a soft smile as he dropped her garments on the floor, one by one. The camisole was gone, leaving her naked down to her waist. The undergarments followed, leaving her in nothing but her stockings.

Shame scorched her. Her hands, rigid as iron rods, pressed to her sides as she tingled under his gaze. It slowly lingered on her nakedness, taking it in, pausing on the spots that she wanted to hide the most.

And then her husband kneeled before her.

He rolled one stocking down, his fingers intimately grazing her skin. He did the same to the other. His face was so close to her abdomen that she held her breath. That scar—that ugly mark—was right there, in front of him.

He stroked her hips as his gaze leisurely glided up and down her naked body, taking in every detail.

Then his eyes locked with hers. He leaned in and kissed her right thigh.

Her face caught on fire. Heat burned through her.

He did the same to the left one.

She felt her need seep out of her, squeezed her thighs together, and trembled as his kisses went higher, inward, along her inner thighs. She felt his soft lips inching closer to her junction, then his tongue licking her skin, taking a swipe between her legs, darting so shamelessly to her junction, then again, sneaking its way into her privates.

Shock washed over her.

She took a tiny step away from him.

"Shhh, darling," he calmed her, reading her thoughts. He trailed kisses up her abdomen, all the while caressing her hips. "There's no need to be nervous."

She didn't answer but let herself sink her fingers into his hair, let him touch her where he wanted. She wanted to pull back when he cupped her breast with his hand. Wanted to protest when he kissed it. But her body leaned into his touch, her need betraying her with the gasps she couldn't hold back.

Slowly, Drasko rose to his feet. His hands didn't stop caressing. His mouth didn't leave her skin. His touches were everywhere, soothing and making her forget herself.

"Have you ever been with a man?" he asked against her lips.

How dare you…?

"No," she said on an exhale.

He kissed her, insistently, so deeply it made her dizzy.

"Let me show you what a lover can do," he murmured.

She had desires—it was too late to deny it. Being so close to him had some wicked power over her. Her body burned for him. She thought of him as a ruthless man, taking what he wanted, and expected him to be rough. Yet his touch was shockingly tender, left her weak and yearning for more.

Drasko picked her up like she was a feather and brought her to his bed. He lay her down on the sheets, kissing, kissing, making her forget the logistics of what this would be like or what she was supposed to do.

She'd thought she'd be an offering. Instead, he offered himself.

She'd thought he would use her and take what he wanted. But he didn't seem to be in hurry, his hands and mouth slowly exploring her body.

His hand slid between her legs, cupping her, his fingers opening her up. *There, right there…*

She still tried to hold on to her modesty and covered his hand with hers, protecting what she thought belonged only to her.

He broke the kiss. "Grace, darling, let go of my hand," he said softly but with authority. "Let go."

She moved her hand off his, and his fingers resumed the strokes, circled her tender flesh, igniting the sensations that made her thighs fall apart wider, inviting more of his touches.

"Good," he whispered as she echoed with a whimper.

His mouth took hers in a kiss again. His tongue stroked hers. Heat pooled between her legs as he touched her.

"You are so ready," he murmured, settling between her legs. "Darling, look at me."

She opened her eyes and met his. He guided her hand to his waist, leaving it there. "We will do it slowly. It might hurt. If it is too much, you tell me."

She nodded timidly, taken aback by the concern in his voice.

She felt the pressure of him against her entrance, invasive and making her hold her breath. She closed her eyes, bracing for that pain she knew would come.

"No, no, no, eyes on me, darling." His voice brought her back.

He kissed her gently, calming her. And then he was pushing inside her.

Quick sharp pain tore through her like fire, but she didn't take her eyes off his as he searched her face for signs of how it felt. He gently lowered his forehead to hers and pushed inside her again. And the pain subsided, dissolved under his caring gaze and the unexplainable pleasure that started spreading inside her where he made her feel so full.

"Just breathe," he whispered and kissed the corner of her mouth as he slid deeper inside her. "There." He kissed her again. "There." He thrust inside her, filling her up, then stilled.

"How does it feel?" he asked and cupped her cheek.

She rolled her hips, adjusting, wanted to be brave for him, to show him she could do anything, could be like those scandalous women who made men feel so good.

"I am going to move again," he whispered.

And he did, gently thrust into her, this time the slight pain mixing with a physical craving for more of him.

"Ah," she whimpered in surprise, rolling her hips at him.

His hand was down there again, stroking her as he thrust inside her in slow rhythmic movements.

She tried to catch up with the spark of pleasure that was starting inside her. And then she caught it. With the friction of his thrusts. Under the stroke of his fingers.

His hand moved to cup the back of her head, holding her in place. He thrust into her deeply but gently, in rhythm with his tongue that invaded her mouth again, seeking out hers. His gold chain fell onto her chest, tickling her as he moved, his body so big and yet not heavy at all.

She didn't understand the way her own body reacted to his.

He was already weaving himself into her, slowly, like a sensual tune weaved into one's mind, the phantom of it echoing off one's lips for hours afterward. But the tunes were temporary, and Drasko was a constant. He was hard to ignore or resist, and every day, she found herself seeking out more of him.

Her body now did too—responding to him, so sensitive to every movement, to his bare skin against hers, the silky sheets under her back, the mattress under her toes that she dug into, riding that wave of pleasure.

Everything felt different, the scents and touches too sensual, her surroundings too vague, his lips everywhere on her, while the sensations in the spot where the two of them fused together saturated her body with a wild need that grew in giant waves.

The orgasm caught her by surprise, washed over her like the most wonderful bliss, tearing moans out of her. The feeling was powerful yet too short.

Drasko grunted into her neck as he carelessly kissed it and stopped moving.

Suddenly, Grace felt empty, void of that bliss that was quickly leaving her body. She wondered why it couldn't last longer, if it possibly could, and if they could do it again.

It felt so raw and somehow unclean, too physical but so much more erotic than what she had been led to believe. It had taken away her nervousness, like the effect of an opium tincture.

But now she was too aware of herself again, the way Drasko eased out of her. The silly books she read—they were too romantic. *This*, this felt like a dirty secret, delicious and improper at the same time. Right away, she wanted to tuck it away, hide her nakedness, run, so as not to meet his eyes.

Drasko kissed her cheek.

"Not what you expected, wife?" His smile touched her lips in a more possessive kiss.

He pulled back so he could meet her eyes. He stroked her cheek with the back of his fingers. That twinkle in his eyes, his gaze dropping to her lips, the way he said the word 'wife' felt almost… scandalous. The two of them naked, still wrapped in each other, felt outrageous.

He pushed away and lay on his back. Grace stilled, not knowing what to do.

Now that the euphoria was gone, Grace was shy again.

Would he taunt her?

Would he mention her moans?

She had moaned, hadn't she?

That very moment, his arm slid under her shoulders and pulled her into him. And she lay against him, rested her hand on his chest, afraid to say a word.

They lay like this for a while as she was acutely aware of both their naked bodies next to each other, her thigh on top of his, skin against skin, the sensation bewildering yet intimate.

His breathing grew even. She still didn't look at him, but at last, untangled herself from him and sat up, her back to him.

This was it. She needed to go and was praying he was asleep and wouldn't confront her.

He shifted behind her and sat up. His arm wrapped around her waist, making her hold her breath, and his body pressed against hers from behind.

"Running away?" His hot breath in her ear made her tingle with a promise of more.

His muscled forearm moved up her torso, pushing her breasts up, her nipples shamelessly perky.

He pressed a tender kiss on her shoulder. "It's perfectly fine to want more. You don't have to hide."

His fingers tilted her chin up so she had nowhere to look but him, his warm green gaze unraveling the memories of their lovemaking.

"Do you know what makes me unexplainably happy?" he asked. That she enjoyed it? "That I am and will be the only man to ever touch you and have you all to myself."

"Two nights per month, right?" she blurted out without thinking and right away felt like a stubborn child.

She shouldn't have said that and regretted, regretted right away her silly reminder.

"If you are afraid, Grace, you can leave. If you resent me, go. I won't stop you."

Disappointment pricked her. She didn't resent him. This was all too new, and her nervousness got the best of her.

"The night isn't over," he said. "We have five hours until dawn, and then with the first light, you can forget this ever happened. Though you will not."

His words started a brush fire inside her. Another feeling laced with her desire—curiosity.

"You… you can do it again?" she asked.

His body shook against hers in a low chuckle.

"What do you think?" He bucked his hips against her, his hardness pressing into her thigh.

His lips pressed against the sensitive skin behind her ear in a soft kiss, making her slick with need again.

"Did it hurt?" he murmured against her skin.

She let out a needy whimper, trembling with need at the way his fingers grazed her nipple. "Not much."

"Are you sore?"

A wave of hot shame washed over her. The words were so open and concerning, that she wanted to scoff and tell him it was none of his business.

"No," she lied, wondering what he would ask next.

"Then you tell me," he whispered, kissing her neck, sending pleasant shivers down her body, "how many times you can take me, and I will show you many ways I can do it. Come here."

He pulled her into his arms again.

32

DRASKO

He might just start hating mornings. To be exact, the particular time of the morning when Grace was leaving his bed.

The sun was not up yet. The morning haze was leaking through the half-open curtains, and his wife was fleeing his bed.

"I suppose, we are done," she blurted. "I... I am going to go..."

Drasko watched her as she fumbled with the sheet, clutching it around her body, trying to hide her nakedness. Her hair was a beautiful mess cascading across her shoulders. Her face flushed, lips swollen from hours of kissing, the lips that had kissed his shoulders and neck with mindless passion—she was now back to her modest self.

She'll learn.

He caught every bare inch of her as she hurried toward the door to her room. He listened to her quick steps behind it, the rustling of the clothes.

I suppose we are done.

That was a travesty, for sure.

Drasko flung himself onto his back and rubbed his face with both hands, grimacing in a frustrated, "Argh."

His cock was hard.

Rakshasa grunted happily but wanted more.

And his mind replayed the scenes from the last night. The way Grace felt under him, how she trembled under his insistent caresses, the shock in her gaze when he first entered her, her whimper when he penetrated her with careful thrusts, the little frown on her face when he touched her down there as if he'd invaded her privacy.

And invaded he had, several times, her face rendered in utmost surprise and angelic wonder when she came around his cock, again and again.

Lovemaking would do that to a person—strip away shame and shyness, make one's bodily sensations override one's mind.

And they had.

His body stirred at the memory of Grace's hands exploring him, only hours ago, venturing farther and farther down.

Oh, the look of surprise and shock on her face as he had let her touch him!

He had taken her three times last night.

Her "privacy" must certainly be a little sore today.

Drasko's "privacy" demanded more. So, he flung his sheet aside, wrapped his hand around his erection, and stroked himself to the thoughts of her naked.

Grace had a beautiful body, he thought later as he washed up and remembered her splayed naked on his bed, the lamp light painting her skin with a soft shade of honey.

The thought made him smile as he dressed, paying attention to every little detail. He stared at the rings on his fingers, remembering how they glistened against her silky skin as he caressed her breasts.

And he was getting hard again.

Dammit.

Two nights would not be enough. Not with the way he craved her. Not after he had heard her needy whimpers, how she absently murmured, "Yes," as she forgot herself, the way she moaned his name when he held her thighs open and rubbed his cock on her, teasing, until she asked for it.

He adjusted himself and took a deep breath, trying to tame his hardness.

About to leave his room, he looked at himself in the mirror.

What did Grace think of his scars?

He studied his but remembered hers—the jagged lines on the inside of her forearm. He now wondered if that was the reason for her long sleeves, even at home, in the heat of the summer. And there was a big one under her ribs. He wanted to know where it had come from, felt a pang of anger at what had caused it. It was too early to ask. His wife would avoid any conversations about their night together. And he cut off that silly proud smile that split his face.

He fixed his tie and—what do you know?—wondered whether Grace would notice the extra care with which he dressed today.

Oh, hell! He was concerned about his looks and what she would think!

Irritated, he tugged at his tie carelessly and strode out of his room. Then, walking down the hall, he fixed his tie again.

Sitting alone in the dining room, he stared at the clock on the wall for half an hour, waiting for Grace to come down for breakfast.

He was on his second cup of coffee when he heard the hurried clicking of her heels against the marble floor in the hallway. They slowed down as they approached the room, then halted behind the door.

He tensed when she stepped in. A peach-colored dress with a high neckline accentuated her dark hair. Long lace sleeves hid the scars he had kissed last night. Her lips looked swollen—his doing. Her face was flushed—it must've taken her a while to summon the courage to come downstairs.

Little coward.

Her smile was courteous, her glance at him too brief. "Good morning."

Samira hurried to pour tea for her.

Drasko draped his arm over his chair back and studied Grace, remembering what it had felt like to finally have her in his arms. He should have kept his mouth shut, but he couldn't help it.

"It would be better if you didn't leave my bed so soon this morning," he said. "I had urgent business for you to take care of."

The crimson of her face made him harden with want.

Samira bit back a smile.

"When would you like our second night?" he inquired, though he had promised himself he wouldn't tease her. "We can try something different." Grace turned scarlet and so wonderfully baffled. "Have you ever paid attention to the ceiling frescos in the music room?"

Even the tips of her ears turned bright red. She picked up her teacup, fumbled, and spilled a little.

Samira covered her mouth to hide her grin and hurried out of the dining room.

And Drasko studied his wife, her lovely summer dress, which hid the swell of her breasts that he'd kissed last night, her buttocks that fit perfectly in his big hands, her body that he'd had all to himself. One night and he was starting to lose his grip. He needed to think about the auction. But all he thought about were her creamy thighs wide open, all her charms on full display for him. He would give a fortune to take her upstairs right now and kiss her blush away.

A sharp knock sounded at the door, and Grace's face filled with relief as Tripp walked in.

"The team is assembled, sir."

As much as Drasko wished he could spend all morning enjoying his wife's blushing, there were pressing matters to attend to.

Sure enough—the sheer size of the team that gathered in his office was a sign that the times were changing.

The men from last night— *inside* his fucking house—weren't simple thieves.

Then who?

The Metropolitan Police were useless. The man who ended up shot and in the hospital wasn't yet talking.

The Wollendorfs' hounds, Drasko was sure, his jaw tightening and his fists itching just thinking about them.

Even the most powerful often resorted to dirty tricks when their power couldn't solve a problem. And Drasko had been a problem for them for a while. Especially with what had transpired when he had received the second letter.

Drasko studied the new men with anticipation. Several dozens of them, chosen carefully by Tripp, now stood in a line like an army of soldiers, dressed in expensive suits that hid unparalleled brutal skills.

"Gentlemen." Drasko nodded in greeting.

Most of them didn't come from the good parts of the city, but all of them were vouched for. And he had invited them here, to his house, to his office, because this was his business. These men would be in charge of his and Grace's safety. And the one thing Drasko had learned a long time ago was to treat the men who worked for him with respect and pay them generously. Whether they were the little boys sorting his diamonds in the caves, the kitchen staff cooking his food, the lawyers who handled his accounts, or the bankers who took care of his fortune—they all deserved the same respect, the poorer even more so, for their loyalty was unmatched.

Uriah Mawr had once had a lawyer who was selling Mawr information to the Wollendorfs. Uriah, of course, treated people as objects. And the lawyer... Well, the more wealth people had, Drasko had learned, the more they were willing to betray for a juicier piece. No one survived Uriah's wrath. Naturally, the lawyer was ruined.

That was why Drasko's guards were paid more than the clerks in his company's offices. That was why he dressed them well, kept them happy, knew their families, allowed them in his home, and never let himself disrespect them even with a single word.

That was Drasko's way.

Now, he walked the line, assessing the new recruits.

"Name?" He pointed at a short stocky man.

"Aaron Gelski, sir." The man nodded.

"Language?"

"Hebrew."

"Good." Drasko nodded and took a step toward another man with the same question. "Name?"

Thato, South African, spoke Dutch.

The next one was Italian. There was an Asian man. Another was German.

Drasko nodded in satisfaction. He needed someone German in case they were around the Wollendorfs, and Jewish if he wanted connections with the Yiddishers, and many others— Drasko wanted them all, and to hell with the wealthy who would soon spread the rumors that the Diamond King was hiring "undesirables" from all places on earth. The titled still called Drasko that behind his back. He knew it, didn't care about the occasional "gypsy" that Tripp reported now and then.

Drasko's guards carried guns and could fight like illegal underground fighters. Very soon, Drasko would know where they had come from, whether they had families, and would arrange their accommodation.

"How many children do you have? Do they go to school?" Drasko asked Aaron Gelski as they walked down narrow Poplar Street later that very day.

Drasko enjoyed talking to his men and learning about their backgrounds. One could learn from anyone and anything. And he never stopped learning.

He was having a chat with each of the new men one on one.

The rest followed as Tripp filled them in on the current course of events. Later, they would show the men the port docks and the warehouse where the official shipments came, then determine where each of the new men would be useful.

It was a fine afternoon, not too hot despite the growing summer heat. Poplar Street wasn't busy. It wasn't the safest area, but Drasko had a dozen men with him.

He was in the best of moods. The night with Grace was fresh on his mind. *Two nights a month.* Well, he might just use the second one tonight. And tomorrow—he'd just borrow from next month.

Drasko stifled a chuckle, imagining Grace's face when he would tell her just that. Nothing tamed women like gentle hands, deep kisses, and a skillful tongue—Drasko was yet to show her all he could do with it. His bedroom might just become the best place for their negotiations.

He felt himself growing hard.

Fucking hell.

He cleared his throat and asked Aaron to repeat his last comment when a loud whistle pierced the air.

It came from a shoe-cleaning boy ten feet away from them. Nothing unusual, but the whistle was followed by another one down the street. Then another.

Drasko slowed his steps.

Tripp walked up to him. "Boss?" Wary, he undid his holster and put his hand on the revolver, scanning the street and the buildings around them. "Boss, something is not right."

Drasko halted at once, studying the surroundings.

Everything seemed ordinary, save for the strange emptiness of the street. London streets never cleared out by day, unless on purpose and done under someone's orders.

His men approached and surrounded him, his backs to him, their eyes searching the area.

"Boss, I know that whistling," Tripp said, sucking his teeth. "The Bankees' street runners."

"The Bankee Syndicate?"

"That's their calling card, yes."

"What do the Bankees have to do with us?"

"Boss?" Tripp nodded around.

The few people on the street hurried inside the buildings. The street stalls and shopfronts took down their "open" signs. The window shutters closed.

Even though it was the middle of the afternoon, the street went quiet, the distant sound of the horses' clip-clops barely reaching it.

"Look." Tripp nodded toward the end of the street and pulled out his gun. "Weapons," he ordered, and a dozen guns came out.

Drasko narrowed his eyes at the end of the street.

There they were—whoever tried to rob or attack him last night, he was sure—the men at the end of the street were coming for him again.

Several dozen of them were walking in his direction. Measured steps. Hands on their holsters. Three followed on horseback, the horseshoes clacking against the cobblestone.

Another whistle came.

Shotgun barrels pushed out of the several windows on the upper floors and pointed down.

"Fuck," Tripp muttered. "This is an ambush. Boss, step back," he ordered, shielding Drasko as he faced the approaching group.

Drasko's heart thudded with a jolt of anticipation. He used to like danger and had been in so many fights that he'd learned to recognize that pleasant surge of energy that suddenly rushed through his veins.

He'd been in worse places and in worse times. This wouldn't be the end. Even the likes of the Wollendorfs couldn't get rid of him yet, not when they didn't know what would happen to the Mawr empire if they had or to the auction or the Crimson Tear that everyone, undoubtedly, was curious about.

Everything was a negotiation.

In moments of danger, the phantom of Rakshasa behind him was more tangible than ever, its low growl drumming along with his heartbeat, a silent cue to be ready to strike.

If worse came to worst, Drasko would rip someone's face out. *At least one, or two.*

But he wasn't willing to sacrifice his men for this silly harassment.

"Tripp, step aside," he ordered coldly.

His blood simmered with the need to fight as he shoved his hands in his pockets and stared at the approaching men.

33

DRASKO

The Bankee Syndicate was the biggest mafia outfit in England, operating for almost a century.

Seventy years ago, they were but a street gang, the Bankee Boys, out of St. Giles. Forty or so years ago, they had signed a truce with the Smethwicks, another local gang, then started running deals with the Sixty-Fivers from Manchester. Liquor, tobacco, guns, illegal imports—it wouldn't be an exaggeration to say that the Bankees ran South England.

And now they were in the diamond business.

It puzzled Drasko. He wanted to know what exactly they wanted. Yet, if needed, he was ready to fight.

He could use the razor hidden in the leather bracelet on his wrist—it had proven useful in the past. His arm pressed against his body, feeling for the concealed shoulder holster in his jacket. That was an option, too.

The question was—how far would the attackers go?

He narrowed his eyes at the approaching army.

No, they wouldn't dare hurt him. His men, though—it was his duty to protect them from unnecessary bloodshed. The Bankees wouldn't even blink at shooting all of them down, and now dozens of them pointed guns at Drasko's guards.

Drasko squinted at the sun, then at one of the windows, another shotgun barrel pointing down at him.

He thought of Grace. If something were to happen to him today, it would be a pity, for he would've liked to bed his wife a dozen more times, a hundred, thousands. He could make her happy for a lifetime. At least, in bed.

The thought about her was, as always, untimely.

Drasko sucked his teeth and moved his shoulders, feeling the sweat-damp shirt sticking to his back, Rakshasa uneasy and wanting to fight.

Slowly stepping forward, he reached inside his jacket and pulled out a cigarette. He lit it, his eyes staring from under his bowler hat at the Bankees who as slowly stepped toward him, only twenty or so feet away.

The man in the center, a step ahead of the rest, the one in charge of the gang, was smaller and shorter than Drasko, as were most men. If it were only Drasko and him, the man wouldn't stand a chance. Most men didn't.

Drasko flicked the match away and took a long drag off his cigarette, then cocked his head and studied the enemy from the bottom up.

The man's shoes were polished to a mirror shine. The three-piece suit was expensive. So was his derby hat and a crisp white shirt like he was going for a fucking dinner. A brooch shone in the center of the man's silk necktie. *A gangster and a man of fashion —what do you know?* A cocky smirk under a black mustache. A scar tugging at the corner of his lips—the mark of a dangerous profession. He'd come to cause harm.

A pair of tar-dark eyes, fearless and mocking, cut into Drasko as he approached, and—

Drasko stopped abruptly and huffed in surprise.

"Can't be," he muttered, his eyes searching the man's face.

The man and those following him stopped, too, arrogant smirks on their faces.

This was a standoff. Drasko's men behind him pointed their

guns in all directions. But the enemies were everywhere—all corners of the street, the open windows of all floors, the roofs. *An ambush, indeed.*

But Drasko was still coming to terms with what he was seeing.

His heart gave out a violent thud.

Fuck...

He gave the leader a backward nod. "You lost, little man?"

The man didn't move, but his eyes on Drasko flashed with anger.

"Boss," Tripp whispered in a warning.

Drasko took a step forward and halted to a stop again.

What are the odds?

His lips curled in a smile. "You little gypsy scumbag," he said louder.

"Boss?" Tripp warned louder.

The man in charge scowled. The Bankees glared at each other and cocked their guns, cursing under their breaths and ready to shoot.

So did Drasko's. But he lifted his hand in a sign to hold back and took another step toward the leader.

"You forgot where your little gypsy arse came from?"

Confusion swept across the leader's face.

"I'll fuckin' dust 'em, boss," the tall man next to the leader hissed and spat on the ground.

But the leader shut him up with the snap of his fingers, his eyes widening at Drasko.

"Ooooh..." The sound escaped him but was cut off abruptly as if from shock.

The burning cigarette forgotten between his fingers, Drasko only smiled, glancing again at the unmistakable birthmark right above the leader's right brow. "You lost, little Zephie?"

The leader's eyes bulged in shock as he took a step forward, then another, and cursed under his breath. He ducked his head, his eyes bulging in shock at Drasko.

A louder, "Aaaaaaaaa!" came from him. And then he reached Drasko in several wide strides and pulled him into a bear hug.

Confusion swept across the two lines of men. They exchanged bewildered glances and lowered their guns. The shotguns disappeared from the windows, replaced by the baffled faces of the Bankees.

If it weren't for that birthmark, Drasko would've never recognized the only friend he had once had in London, a street thief just like him, lost for years.

"Fuck! Me!" The leader pulled away and held Drasko's head between his palms, his wild eyes roaming his face and outfit. "Oh, my fucking lord and savior."

Grinning, Drasko took in the sight of his friend. "Long time no see, Zeph," he said softly.

At that moment, Zeph's violent agenda didn't matter. Neither did a battalion of armed goons by his side. What did were his eyes that, despite two decades, were so familiar, except for the tiny wrinkles around them. His dark hair was now longer, with an addition of the sideburns and mustache, but the same shade of raven black.

Drasko couldn't take his eyes off Zeph, examining every bit that was new atop the familiar sense of a strong bond, forged a long time ago.

"Bankees, huh?" Drasko nodded.

Zeph produced a mad laugh, then a surprised whistle, his gaze sweeping over Drasko's clothes. "Drasko-fucking-Mawr? That was *you* all this time?"

"Well, Drasko is not a common name." Drasko shrugged. "If your head wasn't filled with chicken shit, you would've thought of it. I've been searching for you for fucking years."

Drasko was brazen, too informal with a man who could still be his enemy despite once brotherly bond. Yet Drasko *felt* people, and years hadn't erased the memories of poverty and hunger the two of them had fought together in the slums.

At last, they let go of each other. Their eyes locked, stayed locked for the longest time, yanking them back in time, to the dingy streets of the slums that had raised them. Smiles chased each other.

Until Zeph lifted his derby hat and, exhaling loudly through his puffed lips, ruffled his hair, wildly looking around. "Fuck… Fuck… I mean… Drasko fucking *Mawr*?"

He whistled to someone and motioned with his head.

In an instant, the guns were tucked away. The tension dissipated with the wind.

"Zeph Brodia, huh?" Drasko lit another cigarette and offered one to Zeph. "You didn't have a surname last time I saw you."

They started walking, the street suddenly filling up with people and carriages, the shop shutters opening.

"Ha! Neither did you," Zeph answered with amusement, puffing out smoke as the two of them studied each other with broad smiles, walking shoulder to shoulder. "But that was two decades ago. I am a man of stature, mate."

"Was that the stature that punched you in the face?" Drasko nodded at Zeph's scar that ran across the side of his mouth.

"Something like that. And you?" Zeph nodded to Drasko's scars. "Got yours in a battle with diamond gods?"

They both laughed.

They walked along the now suddenly busy street, the crowds quite thick, the carriages and trams passing by like they'd been there all along.

"*The* Mawr, huh? Fuck. Me…" Zeph studied Drasko in awe. "I had no clue. Didn't even cross my mind. I mean… If I knew, I would have come asking for a job."

Drasko snorted. "Looks like you can clear a street with your current one."

"I can clear a city, if needed." Zeph nodded proudly, his thumbs tucked under his belt, the cigarette bobbing in the corner of his mouth.

Their men followed, an army of them dispersed at a distance.

Drasko and Zeph stopped to buy crumpets from a street seller and kept on walking, eating as they did.

"At least you don't have to steal these anymore," Zeph said with a full mouth.

"Uh-huh." Drasko studied him with humor. "So, you are a big man now?"

"Third in command."

"That is something." Drasko sized him up. "Little gypsy," he said quieter and broke out in laughter when Zeph elbowed him in the ribs.

"You know," Zeph said, giving the leftover of his pastry to a beggar and smiling to himself, "any other man saying such words would be hanging from a light pole by now, his guts hanging out, his family watching."

Drasko finished his pastry and wiped his hands. "Good thing I used to give up my meals for you when you were seven because your gypsy arse was too little to steal like a true thief king."

They broke out in laughter.

Perhaps it wasn't their long-forgotten friendship that now was bonding them together, but what *sort* of friendship they'd had. Both orphans and nicknamed "little gypsies." Both homeless with no one to turn to for help. They'd shared hundreds of freezing winter nights, sleeping by bonfires on the street. Drasko had brought Zeph many meals when Zeph almost died from pneumonia.

They'd thieved together.

They'd laughed together.

They'd almost died together once.

One especially awful winter night—Drasko, eight, and Zeph, seven—they had made a pact that one day, they would rise above everyone else in this city. It was a silly desperate pact as they trembled from cold in a filthy corner of some dingy alley, sharing an old rag and trying to survive until morning.

Many such hopeful pacts were created in the slums every day. Theirs had come true.

"So, the Wollendorfs," Zeph said after they'd reminisced on the past. "They are after you. Not serious yet, no. But willing to pay a lot to hurt your men. Intimidate you into some deal. We were paid, you understand. We were ready to deliver. So..."

"So, I will pay much more."

"Easy, brother. It's not about money. First things first, you need to speak with Handley."

"And he is...?"

"Inigo Handley. Runs the Bankee Syndicate. He's heard of you, of course. Never cared much. But now that you are under my protection, he'll be interested." Zeph winked.

Drasko laughed through his nose. "Your protection, huh?" He reached for Zeph and fixed his tie, adding, "Little gypsy."

In a second, Zeph's arm was around his neck in a playful headlock, despite Zeph being much shorter. Drasko's hat rolled to the ground. The sound of cocked guns crackled behind them.

Zeph grinned as he ruffled Drasko's hair and whispered in his ear, "I don't care that you are the Diamond King. I will whip that gypsy ass of yours like Mrs. Borgh once did for stealing her stockings."

With a laugh, he let go.

Unable to wipe a wide smile off his face, Drasko fixed his jacket and picked his hat off the ground.

They chatted some more about the old times and Drasko's disappearance, his life in India and Zeph's work for the Bankees.

"Times change. So do fortunes," Drasko said.

Zeph snorted, giving him a side glance. "You don't say."

"I'll see you tomorrow night then," Drasko eventually bid farewell.

"Done deal, brother. I shall talk to Handley." Zeph studied him again, then shook his head in disbelief and gave his hat a tweak. "Lucky bastard."

Drasko only laughed.

But another matter made him flex his fingers in annoyance as soon as the Bankees walked off.

He wasn't a violent man anymore, but—

Ah, there was always that "but."

Competition and dirty tactics were the bittersweet taste of the diamond trade and the Wollendorfs' signature card. So, Drasko would have to be diplomatically persuasive.

An hour later, his carriage pulled up to the lavish building on Park Lane.

"I am here to see Mr. Franz Wollendorf," he said to the doorman. "I am Mr. Hugh, Bank of England. Urgent business," he lied, knowing that the scumbag would not see him otherwise.

A minute later, a butler was leading him through a bright two-story hallway, decorated with Greek statues and luxury figurines encrusted with diamonds. The walls dripped with precious gems.

Drasko rolled his eyes in annoyance as they approached the music room, the banging of some rubbish piano tunes behind it.

"Mr. Wollendorf is entertaining Baroness Greyer and her daughter. And he is happy to see you," the butler said, opening the doors.

Drasko walked in, right away spotting Franz Wollendorf. Despite having a wife somewhere, the coward held another woman's hand to his chest. At the butler's announcement, he stood up with a smile and turned to Drasko, only seconds later realizing who was in front of him.

His face twisted into an expression of horror.

"Mr. Wollendorf," Drasko said, approaching. "A word, please."

"But... How dare you!" Franz backed away, his eyes widening in panic, his face turning red. "No! This man!" His scared eyes darted to the butler. "I want him out!"

He had no choice or chance when Drasko, much bigger and stronger, grabbed him by the front of his vest, dragged him several feet away from the ladies, and only then punched him in the face, sending him flying onto the floor.

A female shriek and a sharp gasp came from behind him, but he didn't turn.

"You don't know how to fight, whether with your fists or your wits," Drasko said calmly, cracking his knuckles and taking leisurely steps toward Franz. The diamond rival was only years older than him but heavy and clumsy, whined in pain, and cowered away from him on the floor. "Only like a coward, behind my back."

The butler was shouting in the hallway for help. The women whispered behind his back.

Drasko bent down and picked up the resisting Wollendorf by the scruff like a rag doll. He brought the man's face closer to him.

"Now, I am not doing worse damage because we wouldn't want to create a bad impression on the women present here, would we? But you listen attentively. The Bankee Syndicate now works for me. If needed, the Smethwick Syndicate will too. So will the Yiddishers. The Metropolitan Police is getting paid by? You guessed it, me. You so much as breathe in my direction, and I will make bullets rain on you. You ever send anyone to hurt my wife? They will find you floating in the Thames. Understood?"

"By God, you are—"

"God does not tell you that you are stupid. He shows you."

Abruptly, Drasko let go of Wollendorf—simply unfolded his fingers, and the petrified man lost his footing, stumbled back, and onto the floor.

Drasko fixed his tie and turned his attention to the women, who held on to each other in shock.

With a smile, he walked up to them and offered his hand to the older one.

"My apologies for the disruption, my lady." He kissed her hand most graciously, then did the same with the younger woman.

While Franz Wollendorf ran out of the room, blurting pathetic threats under his breath, Drasko did what he did best with women. He held his gaze on them a little too long, bowed with utmost grace and a dazzling smile, and complimented the baroness on her dress and her most enchanting smile, which made the non-smiling baroness indeed smile.

Then he turned to her daughter.

"You are wonderful on the piano, miss," he lied blatantly, cringing at his own words. "My wife, Grace Mawr, is an exceptional piano player. It would be her honor to hear you play."

And when he was walking out the door, the two women whispered to each other.

"How truly graceful!"

"They say his wife left an earl for him. No wonder!"

34

DRASKO

"I have never been this high above the city," Zeph said the next day as he smoked, gazing out the window of Drasko's office.

Drasko and Zeph had spent hours talking about the past, the present, and the future. Both amused. Both nostalgic. Both careful around each other but slowly rekindling the bond that had come from the worst times in their lives.

"Literally or metaphorically?" Drasko chuckled, leaning back into his chair behind his desk and studying his friend. He couldn't get enough, was still trying to reconcile the seven-year-old boy with the ruthless Bankee.

Zeph turned around to grin at him. "I don't know about your brain, brother, but you definitely developed a smart mouth."

He walked over to the desk, picked up the blue diamond, the size of a cherry pit that Drasko had gifted him, tossed it in the air, and caught it midway.

"Before we meet the bossman, you need to know a bit about him."

Drasko took a sip of whisky, crossed his feet at the ankles on top of his desk, and got ready for a good story.

"Mr. Inigo Handley, the current head of the Bankee Syndicate"—Zeph lit a cigar and settled in the chair across the desk from Drasko—"was the grandson of the famous Frank Handley, the right-hand man of Rocco. Rocco was the founder of the Syndicate in the first half of the century. Frank Handley was the reason for the war between the Bankees and the Smethwicks. He was an extraordinary man, staged his own death and funeral, escaped to America with his wife, a former courtesan of the Belle House. The story is truly captivating and wild. One day I'll tell you all of it."

A crooked smile tugged at Zeph's lips as he nodded as if he had been there during those times.

"His staged death was the reason for the Bankees and Smethwicks' final alliance. So, Frank and Maude Handley moved to New York, had a son, Aston Handley, who then married the daughter of the Bowery Boys' boss. You see? Two gangs. A marriage that sealed the alliance and established a strong business bond between New York and London. And then Inigo was born. Grew up in the trade, of course. When he was twenty, business with London was shaky. Opium was gaining popularity. The wars over its distribution started. Naturally, Inigo was sent to England to *fix* things."

"At twenty?" Drasko raised his brows in surprise.

"At twenty. He is a bit over forty now and more of a politician, smart and—"

"A criminal."

Zeph cocked a brow. "Oy, he is planning to run for Lord Mayor of London."

"Interesting."

"His grandfather, Frank Handley, had a reputation as a vicious fighter, the most ruthless yet the most loyal and honorable Bankee."

"Uh-huh."

"It is true. He built buildings in St. Giles, schools, hospitals, reformatories. Much like you. Frank Handley was also an orphan and a street thief."

Much like me. "Why are you telling me this, Zeph?"

Zeph took a puff of his cigar and narrowed his eyes at Drasko through a cloud of smoke.

"You have two advantages," he said in a low but sharp voice. "One, Handley values strong character, men who have potential and perseverance."

"So, I used to be a homeless street thief who rose to the top. I see. What is the other one?"

A slow sip of whisky followed as Zeph locked eyes with Drasko over the rim of his glass.

"Me, of course." Zeph clicked his tongue, and his expression softened. "I don't yet know what sort of man you've become, Drasko. But I hope I am not wrong. So, what can be better than the third in command of the Bankees vouching for you?"

Drasko laughed. "Selling yourself, as always."

He was glad to finally get his friend back, still amused by the coincidence, and regarded it as a sign—to never forget where he had come from.

And he was, in his turn, yet to learn what sort of man Zeph had become.

That same afternoon, Drasko found himself in an opulent office of an old gothic-revival mansion, sitting at a redwood desk across from Mr. Inigo Handley.

Handley indeed looked like a politician. He was a heavily built man with a giant beard and mustache, his gaze prying, his lips never letting go of a cigar. He seemed to be permanently shrouded in thick cigar smoke.

And he was quiet, letting Drasko speak for some time as he studied him with a curious glint in his eyes.

"I will put your men on payroll," Drasko said after explaining the problem with the Wollendorfs. "You tell me what you want, and I will get it for you."

The corners of Handley's eyes crinkled as he narrowed them on Drasko. "For protection?" His voice was low but deep and commanding, much like those Parliament men who could suddenly talk in a booming way that drew everyone's attention.

"That's a start." Drasko observed the Bankee boss with attention to every detail, as he always did with the important people he was contemplating striking a deal with. "What I truly want is for your men to shadow the Wollendorfs and their most important men—lawyers, accountants, and such. To ensure they don't make dirty deals against me with someone else or get anywhere near me or my wife again."

Making a deal with a crime syndicate of any type had never been in Drasko's consideration. But dangerous times called for unusual measures.

What concerned him more than anything now was the auction and Grace's safety until Uriah's game came to an end. After that, he entertained the idea of leaving the diamond industry.

They smoked some more, drank whisky, talked. Zeph was mostly silent, closely watching both men.

"Gem business…" Handley finally said with a vague smile.

Only men at the top knew that alliances such as this one started small and grew into much bigger things, often more dangerous but also exciting as the two powerful consortiums were about to share their business ground.

Drasko started from afar, with his most charming card. "Does your wife fancy diamonds, Mr. Handley?"

Handley's smiling eyes shot at him. "What woman doesn't, Mr. Mawr?" It wasn't a question but a statement. "Her birthday is coming up. She asked for—what do you know?—a Mawr diamond necklace."

"How old, may I ask?"

The man's eyes flashed with a hint of irritation. "Thirty-two," he said after a prolonged pause.

"Her favorite color?"

"Pink."

Drasko nodded. Tomorrow, Handley would get a box with thirty-two rare pink diamonds and a note, *For a woman who deserves the best.* Maybe, a bit more elaborate praise.

Handley finally spoke again. "Mr. Mawr, we don't do simple jobs for the wealthy. We do business. What we had with the Wollendorfs was supposed to turn into a business enterprise. Imports, you see? They don't only deal diamonds. But..."

But?

Handley leaned forward and twined his hands in front of him on the desk. "I've heard of the Wollendorfs before. Heinrich does not have much of a business mind. While Franz, how should I put it, is a man guided by greed more than morals. I pride myself on having a good sense about people."

Drasko waited for him to continue.

"Back to what I was saying. We make alliances, Mr. Mawr. Mutually beneficial, of course. More importantly, ones that promise to give both sides more power and open many doors."

Drasko nodded in understanding. That was a universal truth. Brutal men kicked the doors. Smart ones opened them with keys they acquired through partnerships.

"I am here for it, Mr. Handley," Drasko said, realizing it was time they moved past the diamond foreplay. "Are you acquainted with Mr. William Harton?"

Handley's brow lifted in curiosity. "Leader of the House of Commons? No. A powerful man, they say."

"Indeed. I know him and his family quite well. I will introduce you. I heard you are planning on running for Lord Mayor."

And just like that, without saying anything more, the opportunities were already laid out and the alliance made.

Zeph nodded in approval.

Handley lit a candle, set the candle holder in the center of the table, and opened a desk drawer. A small icon of a saint and a razor appeared in his hands. His prying eyes were on Drasko again.

"You don't need to be a religious man, Mr. Mawr. But we sign with blood. No contracts. No witnesses. It's very simple, but make no mistake. You betray us—" His gaze hardened.

"I have no reason, Mr. Handley. You, on the other hand—"

"You won't find more committed people than those who break the law for a living, yet their lives depend on loyalty. Morals and laws are not the same, Mr. Mawr."

Drasko looked at Zeph—they both knew that. Their poor childhoods had ingrained that in their hearts.

In minutes, the little fire hissed from the drops of blood, three shades of it dripping into the flames.

Just like then, Drasko thought of his deal with Uriah.

"And now," said Zeph with a mysterious smile when they left Handley's office, "it's time to learn what sort of man you truly are, brother."

35

DRASKO

Originally a music hall, the Elysium Club was established by two partners from France and was immediately called by *The Gazette, "a place of vice and folly. It has it all—Arabic dancers, Italian singers, Greek musicians, Spanish cigars, French wine, a midnight orgy, a game of cards, betting—choose your vice!"*

Decades later and now owned by the Bankees, it was still a vaudeville venue but private and catering to London's almighty. The owners did extensive research into every member, protected their privacy, and kept away the reporters. More notably, some of the most important deals were made here. Naturally, with an abundance of liquor, beautiful loose women, and superb entertainment.

"Quite an establishment," Drasko said when they were already two-courses and three bottles of whisky deep into the evening.

Twenty-foot-high ceilings, glittering chandeliers, brass railings, leather booths, red curtains, and a wait staff with the precision of trained soldiers—the Bankees, it turned out, had taste and money and owned the most exclusive club in London.

"The best chateaubriand and escargots in the city," Zeph boasted, motioning with a fork in front of him at the table loaded with gourmet dishes. "Also! The most expensive whisky and vintage brandy."

The noise of the loud chatter of the guests clashed with the blare of an orchestra on stage with a giant booming tuba as a centerpiece.

There were over a dozen of Drasko and Zeph's men at the table, shrouded in the scent of liquor and thick cigar smoke. They ate and drank and shared stories as the performance on the stage changed from an opera singer accompanied by satyrs to a poet who entertained the audience with political jokes to a naked contortionist who was booed off the stage.

The air was thick with smoke. The smells of liquor and rich foods were even thicker. The place was loud with singers and can-can dancers.

Grotesque costumes, bare skin, outrageous wigs, and seductive batting of impossibly long lashes—Elysium was known for its exotic performances and most notorious clientele but a strict privacy policy, considering it offered private rooms in the back. It employed thirty guards, inside and outside the establishment. This place, after all, catered to influential men.

Beautiful women strolled between the tables, chatting with the guests.

"Bijoux!" Zeph motioned toward one of them with his cigar.

Bijoux wore a lush skirt or two or three—too many to count, much like those fashionable outfits from the thirties. Her upper body was wrapped in a shortened bodice, some type of brassiere. Her giant wig was red, and so were her lips, stretched in a seductive smile.

"The table trick, Bijoux. Please! We have a guest." Zeph winked at her.

"The table trick?" Drasko mused.

Just then, Bijoux lifted the tablecloth, sank to her knees, and disappeared under the table.

Drasko laughed, realizing what was happening, and shook his head. "That's a no."

"Listen, brother." Zeph leaned over, his whisky-sparkling eyes smiling at Drasko. "Bijoux is a good lay, good company, and a good woman all around."

Under the table, Drasko felt her hands on his knees sliding toward his thighs.

"No." He chuckled and gently pushed her hands away. But they returned to the buttons of his trousers, undoing them so fast, he wondered if that was, indeed, a magic trick. "Sweetie." He fought them off, fumbling under the table, then pushed back, lifted the tablecloth, and scowled at the smiling woman. "Young lady, get out of there. I will pay you anyway, but I am not interested."

"Tsk." Zeph studied him with pity. "You are a boring man, Drasko Mawr."

"I have a wife," Drasko grunted, buttoning up and motioning to one of his men to pay the girl.

"Ah, right! Newlyweds. Are you neck-deep in your wife's pussy? Is that the reason for your hostility toward other women?"

Drasko sucked in his cheeks in irritation.

"No?" Zeph snorted. "What is not working? Your cock or your attitude?"

Drasko scowled, took a gulp of whisky, and lit a cigarette, right away thinking about Grace and the night they had spent together. He should be home, trying to seduce her.

"You see, everyone needs a wife," Zeph explained. "A proper obedient homey wife. A wife is meant to give a man a break."

"A break?"

"Like going on a vacation. Teas. Naps. Dance parties. Dinners with her boring friends and aunties. Silly chats about the latest crochet pattern or hat fashion. All that nonsense. This"—Zeph motioned to the dancers on stage who lifted their legs vigorously to the blasting can-can music—"this is life, mate. Why would you want one woman when you can have a different one every week?"

"A vacation, huh?" Drasko leaned back against the sofa, amused by his friend who was quite the devil's advocate.

There was a time, only recently, in fact, when Drasko indeed indulged in this lifestyle quite freely. Now he looked at the half-naked women in translucent garments and wished that one day he could see Grace like this in his bed, provocative and trying to seduce him.

"A wife is for your peace of mind," Zeph said, tapping him on the shoulder to get his attention. "A mistress is for your soul. And for your dick, of course."

Drasko shook his head with a chuckle.

"It is true," Zeph continued. "What is a man without his dick? A happy dick—a happy man. A happy man—a happy wife. Do you see what I am getting at? The correlation?"

"Why not have your wife take care of it?" Drasko argued, Grace on his mind again. She didn't know even a fraction of bedroom pleasures, yet no woman had ever occupied his mind as much as she did.

"You are joking, aren't you?" Zeph scoffed and turned to one of his men. "Warrington, mate, tell me something. Does your wife's mouth make your dick happy?"

The short red-haired man snorted into his whisky glass. "She doesn't bring her mouth lower than my chest." He roared with laughter as did other men at the table.

"Train her," Drasko suggested.

Warrington shook his head. "That's unorthodox, sir. Sex and family are mutually exclusive."

"Nonsense."

"Fact."

"You have little faith in her."

"She doesn't like that sort of stuff."

"Because she doesn't get anything out of it."

The man frowned at Drasko. "What's that supposed to mean?"

Drasko shrugged. He had understood when he was with

Yamuna that a woman could only make a man happy if he did so in return. In bed, too, among other things.

"You make her happy—she makes you happy," Drasko explained. "It's a barter. Get creative between the sheets, mate."

Zeph motioned drunkenly to stop the discussion. "Listen, listen, listen. Forget all that nonsense." He wrapped his arm around Drasko's shoulders and pointed his two fingers with the cigar between them toward other tables. "Do you see any potential wives there?"

Drasko caught sight of a woman in a modest dress at a table with men and other women. "She is a wife." He tipped his head in her direction. She certainly looked proper.

"Yes. But! She sleeps with her husband's partner."

Drasko pointed at another woman in an elegant evening dress at the nearby table. "Her?"

"She used to work at the Belle House, the luxury brothel on Piccadilly. That was how she captured the banker."

Drasko chuckled. "I can't win, can I?"

"Not with your silly idea about wives. By the way, I am yet to meet yours. Rumor has it, you stole her from an earl. True?"

"Something like that."

"So, what is she doing right now, brother?" Zeph leaned over to bring his cunningly smiling eyes closer to Drasko's.

Drasko rolled his eyes in annoyance. "She is at home."

"My point exactly." Zeph stabbed Drasko's chest with his forefinger then cheered him with his whisky glass and downed it.

Drasko studied him for a moment then stretched his hand and tapped Zeph's chest where his heart was. "That's where the trouble starts. One day, you'll find out."

Zeph snorted and shook his head. "Big words, brother. Big words. Maybe yours." He tapped his heart with his hand. "No woman can heal a heart broken too many times."

The scene on stage was changing. The orchestra went quiet. A dozen or so men in extravagant costumes and giant veiled wigs stepped on stage, lowered themselves, bowing, and stilled.

The lights dimmed.

A woman stepped onto the stage—a pink, two-foot-high extraordinary wig with flowers, a lavish red dress with long sleeves and a low décolletage. A mask on her face. She looked like she owned the stage as she took a seat at the piano.

A man wearing a powdered wig, a vest over his naked torso, old-fashioned breeches and stockings walked out with a violin in his hand. A Venetian mask hid his eyes, only revealing a rouged mouth.

When they started playing, the crowd went dead quiet.

"Watch them." Zeph nodded in the direction of the stage. "I saw them once here. They are phenomenal."

"Who are they?"

"Don't know. But I will find out."

The pianist and the violinist were accompanied by the orchestra. But there was no mistake in who was the highlight of this performance. Not even the lead singer, a woman dressed all in black with a red veil over her face, though her voice, like a devil, seduced with its hoarse yet hypnotizing contralto.

There were exotic notes from the piano, accentuated by the sensual sounds of the violin.

The crowd was quiet, not a whisper in the packed hall.

And Drasko watched, mesmerized. He loved music, and the pianist was certainly not an average vaudeville musician. Her fingers moved in intricate staccato octaves, then in a wild swift scale passage.

Drasko felt the hair on the back of his neck stand on end.

No, not an amateur at all.

Zeph leaned in to say in his ear, "I told you. They are phenomenal. And the pianist is simply outstanding."

With his fingers holding the cigar, Zeph beckoned to the maître d'. "Tell the pianist to come over to our table afterward."

"Not possible, sir," the maître d' apologized. "She has played here several times over the years. But that is the agreement—she doesn't stay or converse with the public."

Zeph grabbed the man's tie and pulled him closer. "Listen, my friend. Some important people here"—he tipped his head toward Drasko—"want to be introduced. So do your best."

He let go of the tie and tossed a golden coin at the man.

"You know what I found out, brother?" Zeph returned his attention to Drasko. "Women who have talents are often great in bed. You see, there's a correlation between—"

Only Drasko didn't listen. He stared at the pianist. Not her lavish costume, or the Baroque pink wig, or the mask that, unlike that of the violinist, hid her entire face. No. He was fixated on her fingers, the way they moved along the keys, the way she performed the *Devil in music*. The fucking tritone! Eden —of all people—had explained it to Drasko once.

His jaw tightened. He had sworn once that he would not let a woman guide his emotions. Yet this woman wasn't like any before.

The singer's voice faded.

The pianist played the last chord and let go of the keys.

The entire restaurant leaped up to their feet with applause and whistles.

Zeph jumped to his feet, clapping his hands.

Drasko rose slowly, still in a stupor.

There was only one woman who could move her fingers so effortlessly on the keyboard, conjuring the most hypnotic tunes. Only one woman could get a room full of men to rise to their feet in admiration.

"Phenomenal!" Zeph exclaimed, whistling at the performers, then shouldered Drasko. "The singer is not bad, but the pianist! Oh, I am going to bed that woman. For her sheer talent."

"No, you won't," Drasko said in a clipped tone, sucking his teeth, his hands applauding as he muttered, "Brava, darling, brava."

YAMUNA

Andhra Pradesh, India
Drasko, 20-21

After little *jaan* passed, Drasko thought his heart would forever be buried in a tomb.

It was Yamuna, the daughter of the local scribe, who made his heart gasp and take in full breaths of life.

Yamuna was older than him by five years, her amber eyes full of kindness, her soft hands capable of healing his scars.

She was everything Drasko wasn't—patient and full of love. Like the river she'd been named after, she filled the gaping hole in his heart, opened him up like a dry flower and breathed life into him.

He was twenty years of age when she first smiled at him during a local wedding.

"You dance so well," she said then, "for a *pardesi*." *A foreigner*.

She laughed so enthusiastically that Drasko, for the first time in a while, grinned and didn't take his eyes off her the whole night.

He wanted to get lost in someone. What he didn't know then was that for the first time, he would feel the need to anchor.

"I don't ask anything of you," Yamuna said when he had

been visiting her by night for a month. "Off you run. To other women."

But he didn't. He came back for more, and she gave it freely.

"I don't need anything in return," she explained, having lost her husband and son to malaria only a year before. "I don't make deals. Nor do I want promises easily broken."

But Drasko never went to another woman and gave himself to her completely.

Only twenty, he felt like an old man. And Yamuna made him young again.

Careless days, full of laughter. Hot nights, spent in lustful fever. Her eyes shone with so much acceptance that when she undressed him the first night they were together, he blushed at the way she kissed his scars, healed them with her caresses, then worshipped his body like he was holy.

He told Elias then that he didn't know what women were until her. Didn't know what sort of man he was in bed until she taught him how to touch her.

Elias grinned at such words. "You know what they say. In this part of the world, they got the Kama Sutra down to a science."

Drasko realized one day that he didn't care much for the Mawr business. Suddenly, the money didn't matter, and diamonds didn't shine as brightly as his lover's eyes. He wanted to stay in a happy world, void of grudges and rivalry and greed.

Then the Wollendorfs happened. That night, he knew everything would change again.

And it did.

The day they found Alfred Mawr's body, Elias told Drasko, "Run."

Drasko had never been afraid. Nor was he now. But he had to be careful because now he had Yamuna to keep safe.

She stayed silent for some time when he told her what he wanted to do. "I don't think we can," she answered.

But of course, they could!

And he didn't listen to her, didn't pay attention to her lingering gazes, a sad smile like she knew what life had in store for them.

He went to talk to Uriah. "We want to travel," he said, starting the conversation from afar.

"*We?*"

"Yamuna and I, we are getting married and we want to travel for some time, see the world."

He knew by the way Uriah cocked his head that he didn't like the idea and suspected that Drasko wasn't planning on coming back.

"Do you now…" Uriah said dryly.

"Maybe Borneo. We will stay with Elias for some time. Then London."

"London, hmm. What about Mawr Industries?"

"I could help out. Perhaps, in London."

"Help out?" Uriah's lack of words always indicated the upcoming storm, yet Drasko still hoped for the better. "So, you are giving up your life for… what exactly?"

"I love her. I want a family."

"Juvenile."

"I am a man!"

"Spare me the drama, Drasko."

"I don't owe you anything anymore. I don't ask anything of you. Not money. Not support. I need a life of my own."

Drasko knew it then, felt that this feeble attempt to break free was pointless. As long as Uriah breathed, Drasko would always be a prisoner. The prior tragedies came to mind, one after another, after another, Uriah's entire life spotted by them and others' blood.

"We need to travel to Delhi tomorrow," Uriah said indifferently. "It's an important meeting, and I need you there. When we come back, do as you please."

Drasko should have known it felt too easy, should have taken Yamuna with him.

"I am staying," she announced the night before he left. "Everything is the way it is supposed to be." So very calm, her hands caressed his body but didn't quite soothe the ache that burned inside him like a premonition.

Only a month passed before Drasko returned to an empty house, not a trace of Yamuna.

"Her body was burned as per tradition," her father said grimly, not meeting Drasko's eyes.

"She was bitten by a venomous snake," his maid explained.

Only Drasko knew that Yamuna was an herbalists, she saved people who were one foot in the grave. She could not have possibly met so senseless a death.

But her existence was merely plucked out of his life.

And again, he didn't get to say goodbye...

Weeks passed of him trying to make sense of the cruel workings of fate. His grief was different this time. Not overwhelming, wanting to break out and destroy the world, but quiet, submissive, the *experienced* kind.

The gaping black hole in his heart came back, growing bigger. The hate in his veins ran deeper.

This time, Drasko suspected it was Uriah who had taken another dear person out of his life.

Drasko still wanted to run from this cursed place that swallowed lives. He wanted to be like Rakshasa, free and feared and alone so as never to know the pain of losing his loved ones again.

He got a giant tattoo of Rakshasa. The vicious tiger with bared fangs took up his entire back. It looked like its claws ripped Drasko's healed scars, the reminder of where he had come from and who he needed to be.

With time, the tattoo healed, yet Drasko always felt the ghost of the beast on his back.

He wanted to leave India again, but Uriah wouldn't let him.

"You need to think reasonably, my boy," Uriah said. "You are just like me, whether you want it or not. When fate takes something away, you take more from others."

Drasko had never thought of it that way. And for the first time, his rage changed course.

No, he wouldn't run. He would roar at his prey and charge forward like a fearless tiger. He would rip anything that stood in his way. And if there was something worthy of keeping—he would do so, by force if needed, and protect it at all costs. He could only do that if he stood at the very top, higher than Uriah ever had.

"I don't have much time left," said Uriah one day, and Drasko's eyes snapped at him in confusion. "I am sick, you see, and I won't last long. But I shall see that you have all of it. That you get your freedom."

The words felt like a lie.

"You shall be the richest man in the world. The most influential too," Uriah said. "But wealth and power require sacrifices. For that, you have to give up everything else."

"I have nothing left." That was the truth. Drasko had nothing but rivers full of diamonds, lifeless things with imaginary value.

"Reputation. Fame. Loved ones." Uriah narrowed his eyes at Drasko.

Drasko chuckled devilishly, bitterness twisting the pieces of his broken heart farther apart. "I have none of that."

"You will." Surprisingly, Uriah smiled. "But the path of a king is a lone one. If you want to be one, you have to sacrifice. If you give up your silly notions, I will give you the world, my boy." And then he said the words Drasko had been waiting for a long time. "And I will give you the biggest treasure, the Crimson Tear."

37

GRACE

"My dear! That was simply outstanding!" Julien said, pacing around the green room of the Elysium in excited agitation. "The way you played tonight! Oh! Divine!"

Julien still wore his Renaissance wig and Venetian mask.

Grace sat on the table, kicking her booted feet, her mask dangling in her hand. One of her fingers curled a strand of her giant pink wig. She was truly happy.

They had done this several times in the past—her sneaking away from the Sommervilles' house, playing at notorious establishments such as this, her face concealed by a mask or elaborate makeup. She loved the thrill of anonymity, the exhilarating sense of freedom and danger.

"You were phenomenal!" Julien went on, gesturing theatrically like he always did. "Oh, I wish we could play that for the ton. It's much too scandalous, I know. But the public here, they were ecstatic. Did you see that?"

Julien walked up to her and cupped her smiling face. "They all applauded standing up. Some important men were there, the owner said. And—"

"So was her husband," a voice behind him said.

Julien turned around and froze.

Slowly, Grace slid off the table and lifted her chin. *God save me.*

Angry? No, her husband didn't look angry. But out of all places and times, how in the world did he happen to be here, the one night a year when she played anonymously?

"Where is Nina and the other guard?" Drasko asked, stepping toward her.

Julien moved aside, smiling apologetically, though this situation was entirely Grace's fault.

"One man is at Julien's house, waiting outside," she explained bravely. "Nina managed to track me here. She is at the back entrance. We…" She nervously licked her lips. "It's not her fault. She's still on guard. But…" She exhaled nervously. "You and I made a deal, too. I can go whenever I want."

Drasko nodded. "And you are at a brothel venue."

"So are you, husband."

His jaw tightened. "I am a man."

"And I am a woman."

"Precisely. Did you have a point?"

She did not give in. He had no right to taunt her. No right! She had her freedom. They had agreed upon it.

"If you are dining with questionable women, then I want to do what I love—play piano."

"For the questionable women and their clients?"

She shrugged. "Men like you?"

A dangerous sparkle flashed in his eyes. Grace had gotten to learn that gaze and understood the rumors that were passed among the women of the ton. Drasko's green eyes mesmerized women, who liked that feeling of being for a brief moment invisibly scandalized by its straightforwardness.

That same gaze now held her hostage. And she realized she enjoyed it. It reminded her of the night they had spent together. The night that had changed everything she ever thought about men and pleasure and bedrooms. But mostly, herself.

Slowly, Drasko walked over and stopped right in front of her. He raised his hand and gently tipped her chin.

His full lips moved in a barely concealed smirk. Just like the morning after the wedding, when he was trying to teach her a lesson.

Except this time, she felt a shiver of delight at his touch.

"You were, as always, phenomenal, darling," he said unexpectedly. "But this time, you pushed it. You tricked your guards. I can't have you running around the city on your own. For your own safety and my peace of mind. Is that understood?"

She pushed his hand away and lifted her chin higher, standing her ground. Or perhaps, wanting to push him farther, past that invisible line that kept them so proper. The last time she did it, she ended up in his bed.

"Oh? That right?" He feigned surprise and brought his hand back to her chin, taking it between his fingers.

She let out a little smile and pushed his hand away again.

He took a tiny step closer, his body against hers so that she had to crane her neck to look at him.

"Interesting," he muttered.

The words burned her with the memory of what he'd done to her the night they'd spent together, his expert kisses and wicked tongue, his big, muscled body on top of hers and the ease with which he handled her, made her shut up, then made her moan like a libertine, all through the night.

Grace had tried for days, tried in vain, to get rid of those images—the way he caressed her and kissed the lines on her skin left by the tight corset. How gentle he was the first time. Then the second. And the third… The way her legs shamelessly hung over his shoulders as he sheathed himself inside her. His grunts as she touched him. Her moans as she lost herself in him. The exquisite mixture of light pain and unimaginable pleasure. The way he murmured, "Close your eyes, Grace. Just feel," and all the shameless things he did to her body afterward.

She felt so much that night. His whisper, "I love your little moans," had scorched her to the core as he slowly thrust inside her, and afterward, when she lay in his arms, breathless and beautifully used, his murmur, "Tell me, wife, did you ever think that marriage could feel so good?" made her wonder how long she would have to wait for their second night together.

She was done lying to herself.

She wanted him to strip her naked and touch her everywhere. Wanted him to bring his mouth to her breasts and kiss them. Wanted him to unbutton his trousers and take her, use her body again. She wanted to know that she made him wild with those same thoughts. She wanted it all. Wanted him. Was wet for him like a wanton woman.

And the worst part wasn't finally accepting it. The worst was that when he looked at her like he did right now, she was sure that he read her every thought.

Oh, he did.

His fingers found their way to her face again and stroked her cheek.

He leaned over and his nose grazed her cheek in that soft caress she'd learned from him.

"You push my hand away," he whispered, "and I will lift your skirt and fuck you right here."

The breath hitched in her throat. His mischievous eyes burned her with a dare.

With her heart in her throat, Grace pushed his hand away again.

Surprised, Drasko cocked a brow. "Is that how it's going to be, wife?" An amused smile started on his lips.

"I suppose it is, husband."

His hand slipped around her waist and yanked her up to her tiptoes, flush against him. He was about to say something when a loud bang at the door stopped him in his tracks.

"To be continued," Drasko said, his gaze dropping to her lips.

The maître d' was at the door. "Mr. Brodia was asking for you, sir. And… Well, he insists on meeting the pianist."

Drasko glanced at Grace's dress, his gaze pausing on her low décolletage.

"Tell Mr. Brodia that I am taking *the pianist* home. Julien!"

He turned to the instructor, who leaned against the wall by the door, his arms crossed at his chest. "Julien, you were marvelous."

"My pleasure, sir," Julien said eagerly but with an awkward smile, biting his nail as he watched Drasko approach.

Drasko put his hand on Julien's shoulder. His fingers tightened as he leaned over and said in a hushed whisper that nevertheless reached Grace. "I see my wife in an establishment like this again, and I will cut off your fingers. I see your hands on my wife again, and she will not have a piano instructor. It would be a pity. I truly do like you."

38

GRACE

"Why are you playing dress up and performing in a questionable establishment?" Drasko asked Grace on their ride home.

"Why are *you* there?" Calmly, she removed her ridiculous wig and tossed her head, shaking her hair that fell onto her shoulders.

Was she embarrassed? Not a bit. Was she afraid of his wrath? She knew there wouldn't be any. She expected him to scorn her, perhaps. But no, her husband was, as usual, calm, and it confused her and secretly delighted her—he was nothing like her guardians.

"I'll rephrase my question," he said without any hint of hostility or bitterness. "I don't forbid you to pay social visits, go to parties, play whenever you want, whatever you want. But by God, Grace, have better judgment. I said you have your freedoms. But a place like that? Why? Is that some sort of rebellion?"

"Soon, places such as that will be the only ones I am allowed to play at. Ristofori won't allow me to play in his orchestra. And the wealthy will not accept me in their houses. They don't say that. They are simply *not available*."

"The Duke and Duchess of Trent?"

"Ha! They will never invite me to any of their gatherings anymore. The marchioness won't see me, though months ago it was agreed that I would play at her Summer Ball. None of them want to associate with me. I suppose. Because…"

"Because of me. To be precise, because of the scandal with the earl."

Grace didn't answer. Drasko was the wealthiest man in Europe, yet rules were rules, and the titled simply had more of them.

"You should understand," Drasko said, "that there is one thing that's more powerful than reputation and can salvage even the worst one."

"Money?" Grace guessed.

"Not just money but its amount. I will make a deal with them," he said. "I will make the duke come and beg you to play."

"Hmm." She stared at the pink wig in her gloved hands. "Because he wants your diamonds? He can get them elsewhere."

"He cannot. You underestimate what the Mawr Auction is about. It's not about art or beauty, though they are obvious. It's about the display of power and competition."

It was the first time Drasko was discussing the auction with her.

"The duchess?" He glanced at the wig on Grace's lap. "She wants to be the Queen, but she can't. And since the Queen will not bid on jewelry that she is gifted anyway, the duchess has only one way to shine—and that's to snatch the crown jewel of the auction."

"So, you want to blackmail her?"

"Simply business, darling. Isn't everything?"

The mischievous glint in his eyes was back. He would want something from Grace, she knew what exactly, and for the first time, she wanted him to say it. That he wanted her, wanted another night. She was growing fond of their bedroom business deal.

Their carriage pulled up to their house. Drasko stepped out and glanced at her outrageous costume yet didn't comment. He offered his arm to her, not a sign of disappointment on his face as if he hadn't just caught her performing at a viper's den accompanied by a half-naked theatrical group.

"And what do you want from me?" she dared him as they walked inside.

"I want you to play for me. Whenever I want." He nodded to the doorman and pulled away from her.

She held back from chuckling in surprise. "That is all?" she inquired as he was already walking away.

He stopped short and turned to meet her gaze. A smile grazed his lips as his eyes swept over her dress again.

"That is all. Have a good night," he said and walked away.

Disappointment washed over her as she returned to her room and cast her gaze at her reflection in the mirror.

Those masked performances at the Elysium used to be a taste of unattainable freedom. It had felt like that tonight, right up until her husband walked into the green room. Any indication of ridicule or disdain on his part, and she would have defied him. But with his calmness, her little act of rebellion had lost its charm. She felt dirty as if she had betrayed her own worth.

Grace listened for the signs of him in his room next door.

Nothing.

She tossed her wig into the corner and threw her earrings onto the bureau.

She simmered with disappointment as she took off layers of makeup, tugged irritatedly at her bodice and skirts as she got rid of her silly dress.

She wanted some sort of punishment from him, expected his bitter remarks, perhaps crude comments, him saying, "I want my night." She wanted him to demand it too, the idea arousing and replaying in her head over and over. She wanted him to take her, forcefully, so that she could get what she wanted—one more night—without having to ask.

The night they had spent together invaded her daily existence. The images, equally disgusting and arousing, had populated her head. Until they didn't stop. Would *not* stop. Infected her mind throughout the day. Until the shame was tucked away, and all that was left were unexplainable erotic visions that chased her everywhere. The memories didn't fade. They only grew more insistent. But in order not to go insane—and Grace was honest with herself—she needed more of her husband.

But—Grace stood by the full-size mirror and studied her naked body—her husband didn't want her.

The thought was hurtful.

Her eyes paused on the edgy scars on her arm.

Did they make her ugly?

She looked at the dark reddish scar under her ribs, the mark of the sickness that she'd had since childhood, the one that Rivka had healed, or so Grace hoped. Her fingertips cautiously patted the scar.

Had Drasko seen it that night? Resented her for that?

She bit her lip, turned away from the mirror, and put on a sleeping gown and a robe over it.

Music played in her head, filling her with joy at how it felt to play on stage.

Then the memory of Drasko's hands flickered in her mind, his crude warning, "I will lift your skirt..." Then his indifferent, "Good night."

She couldn't sleep, couldn't think of anything but him. She had to play. This time, to play out her fantasies.

Grace lit a candle and padded out of the room.

The house was quiet, the second floor dim and empty. So were the stairs. The servants would be asleep. Him? Perhaps, he'd gone back to the Elysium.

The floor was cool under her bare feet as she opened the door to the pitch-black music room and walked to the piano.

Weeks later, and her heart still fluttered at the sheer beauty of it, shimmering in the candlelight that beamed off the gilded ornaments.

Grace set the candle on top of the piano, took a seat, opened the fallboard, and touched the keys.

The sound seemed so loud in the dark, in the emptiness of the sleeping house. Yet, instantly, it seeped into her pores, bringing balance to her disjointed thoughts.

The music burst from under her fingers as she started playing a tune from memory. She hummed until the words broke off her lips.

"The spell of the moonlight, the whisper in the dusk," she sang. *"One glance. One touch. The memories of us."*

Grace sang, forgetting herself and all her worries. When the song was over, her hands slid back onto her lap, and she closed her eyes.

Her heart expanded tenfold, too big for her chest, her feelings too deep for the man she'd once mocked on her wedding day.

A shift in the air made her eyes snap open—she wasn't alone in the room.

There came a soft rustle of clothes behind her, a faint trace of whisky and smoke in the air, instantly making her body come alive at the familiar sensation. *Him.*

Something touched her hair. Her heart boomed.

"I like hearing you sing," he said softly from behind her.

She wanted to turn but was afraid to break this moment and held her breath as she felt his big form move closer. His leg went over the bench on the left side of her. His body shifted down her back. His other leg swung over the bench until he sat behind her, his legs on each side of hers.

She trembled at his closeness, the anticipation of more of it.

His lips tickled her earlobe as his husky voice said, "You are enchanting, do you know that?"

His hands came into the view of the candlelight, gently picked up hers, and brought them to the piano keys.

"Will you play?" he asked against her cheek. "Just for me, darling. Play."

He let go. His one hand rested on her waist. The other gently pulled back her hair on one side, exposing her neck, and a soft kiss in the crook of her neck sent goosebumps along her skin.

If only it was humanly possible to focus while he was touching her!

Her eyes fluttered closed as another little kiss grazed her skin, right behind her ear, her entire body on edge at the touch.

"Play," he whispered.

She opened her eyes and pressed the first keys.

What would she play? What would make this moment last?

"Come dream with me," she sang as her fingers touched the keys.

Both his hands slid to her thighs, the fabric of the gown so thin it felt as if it weren't there, her body completely bare underneath it.

"Sing," he whispered, his big hands moving back and forth along her thighs in unbearably soft caresses.

Arousal swept over her, soaking her between her legs as he planted firefly kisses on her skin, the little fires traveling into her very core.

She tried to think of the words, of the chords she was supposed to play, neither her fingers nor her voice keeping up with the rhythm of his kisses.

"Come dream of what won't be." Her voice trembled.

The light only showed the front of her gown, his legs clad in trousers on each side of her, his hands on her thighs starting to gather up the fabric, the hem of her gown rising to her mid-thighs, exposing her knees.

His hand snuck under it, to her inner thigh.

She faltered on the keys.

"Don't stop," he whispered.

She closed her eyes, kept on playing, trying to keep the tune. She tried thinking of anything but his hand, slowly making its way between her legs. Until his fingers were there—a gentle touch on her tender parts, making her gasp, sending shivers of pleasure from her sex through her body.

Her fingers might be talented. *His* were wicked as they slid deeper, explored her flesh, first carefully opening her up, then moving in rhythmic strokes.

She moaned between the words. Her breathing turned shallow.

His other hand pushed open the robe and cupped her breast, his fingers brushing against her nipple as his other hand stroked her sex.

"Open wider for me," he said huskily.

She was shy and embarrassed, her mind willing her to protest. Yet her body knew exactly what it wanted, how to react, how to take him, asked for more as she bucked into his touch.

His kisses on her neck grew deeper. His tongue swiped at her skin.

She forgot the words, forgot the music. Her hands aimlessly caressed the silent keys, pressing them disjointly, in cue with the little fires that licked her flesh as she dissolved in pleasure.

"Will you write a song about this?" he whispered.

A needy mewl escaped her. "Do you..." His fingers grew more insistent, knowing exactly how to make her body sing. "Do... ah.... do you want me..."

"Yes, I always want you, darling."

"To write a song..." She moaned.

"Yes."

She half-opened her eyes to see her gown hitched up and bunched up at her waist, her legs spread shamelessly for him, his fingers working her sex.

With a grunt, he bucked against her. His fingers continued their wicked game, delved lower, pressed harder, until they eased their way in, burning her flesh with slight pain at the invasion, then pleasure.

Her mind was blank, but her body wanted more. Another finger penetrated her, the two of them slowly thrusting in and out, his thumb rubbing her clit. The outer rim of pain where he stretched her was nothing in comparison with the pleasure deep inside her, the way it grew gradually, like a music piece with its timid start that slowly grew into a climax.

Her hands dropped to his thighs. Her back against him, she was pushing herself into him. She turned her face, captured his mouth in a kiss, and moaned as his tongue parted her lips. His mouth on hers, his hand between her legs, his kiss undid her, funneled the pleasure that spiraled inside her until its crescendo rushed through her body in a powerful wave.

She tore her mouth from his, threw her head back against his shoulder, and moaned into the darkness, repeated cries leaving her as she clamped around his fingers. She forgot about shame, melted under his mouth, playful and gentle on her neck as he worked her through her release.

Until it subsided, and she pushed her legs closed, suddenly aware of what had just happened.

His fingers eased out of her. His hands disappeared. Her nightgown fell to her thighs.

"There." He planted a kiss on her temple. "Your moans when you come are as pretty as your singing."

Without another word, he rose from behind her.

In a moment, he was at the door. He halted and turned around. "Would you like to play for me again sometime?"

Don't leave, she begged. "Yes," she whispered.

In a second, he was gone, leaving her restless and lost.

Suddenly, the room was too empty, the darkness too unwelcoming, the air too cold and lonely. Void of him...

She didn't understand why he did what he did, why he left her wanting more instead of taking everything he could from her. And oh, he could. And she would give herself to him so eagerly.

Unless he knew what he was doing and wanted to torment her.

Why? She didn't know.

But he was already punishing her by leaving her wanting more.

39

DRASKO

As expected, the announcement about the Mawr Auction caused a hurricane of rumors.

Who would be attending?

Who would bid?

The official catalogs were sent out to the attendees. But what were the "mystery" items, yet to be announced? The catalogs were shared, reprinted, quoted, and published in multiple newspapers. The Crimson Tear was, again, at the center of speculations.

And the wealthy were already quarreling over the diamonds.

The German steel heiress was rumored to have claimed her stake on the obsidian raven, the *Guardian of the Night*.

The marchioness was planning to bid on *Cupid's Spear*, but so did her sister, and the two uninvited each other from their birthday parties.

The president of the Bank of London was furious. His daughter refused to marry the wealthy French importer unless he fetched her the *Europa's Abductor* at the auction.

A rumor circulated in the higher circles that anyone who would dare bid on the Crimson Tear would be life-banned from the Duchess of Trent's circles. The rumor was, of course, true. The duchess had her vain heart set on the legendary diamond.

Telegrams flooded the Benham Auction House and the Mawr offices. People from all over the world begged to attend despite the overwhelming number of requests and the restricted capacity of the auction house. The wealthiest offered extraordinary sums of money for the pieces in an attempt to purchase them in advance. Carriages crowded the auction house as some paid personal visits to Mr. Kleinstein in a futile attempt to buy his favors.

The streets around the auction house were blocked off and guarded by armed men day and night.

"It is madness, Mr. Mawr!" the director said in a telegram just this morning.

Madness was the greed with which the wealthy competed for the jewels.

But even the bluest of blood needed a lesson once in a while. And Drasko was determined to teach one as he arrived at the Duke and Duchess of Trent's house at noon.

The most annoying thing about visiting noblemen was the wait. Despite having the most excruciatingly boring lifestyle and an army of servants, the noble houses always greeted the visitors the same way:

"Please, wait."

And there came a half an hour of wait, the intended "expectation" of *Their Graces*.

Except Drasko valued his time, and the Duke and Duchess of Trent were pushing it.

So, when the two appeared in the hallway, condescendence on their faces as they sashayed toward him, Drasko purposefully looked at the clock on the wall and smiled most gracefully, greeting them.

"Mr. Mawr! What a surprise!" the duchess sang.

Eccentric in her tastes, she reminded him of a cockatoo in her bright red dress, a garnet necklace with emerald accents, and a carriage for a hat on her head.

"Indeed," the duke said. He was more like a hippopotamus, calm on the surface but with sharp teeth if needed.

"I am afraid I am pressed for time," Drasko interrupted as the duchess started talking about tea and such nonsense. "Apologies for such short notice. I have come here to let you in on the decision I've made."

"A decision?" the duchess cooed as if the affairs of the mortals were below her. "Does it have to do with the auction?"

She expected anything but what Drasko said next. "Certainly. I am moving the auction to Paris."

"Paris?!" the duchess gasped in alarm. "Oh, my, but that is impossible, Mr. Mawr! What a dreadful idea—"

"You see," Drasko interrupted, smiling again most politely, "my wife is the most brilliant piano player in London. You know that, Your Grace."

"Well, yes—"

"And I would like her to play for the most honorable people who appreciate her talent."

"But of course! Certainly! But—"

"But!" Drasko cut the duchess off again. "It seems that this country is not accepting the certain intricacies of our marriage. Or me. Or perhaps not able to separate our personal matters from her talent. As I remember, when Ristofori, the conductor of the London Orchestra, was scandalized by an affair, high society flooded his concerts like his infidelity was the highlight of his talent. My wife dared to leave a nobleman for what was best for her, and she is being punished by the ton. The artistic status quo in England is a bit too patriarchal for my taste. France, on the other hand, is very much more liberal. The Prime Minister himself wrote to her, inviting her to play for his biannual government ball."

The couple exchanged panicked glances.

"Mr. Mawr," the duke said with extreme politeness. "I assure you, my wife and I are true patrons of music."

"I know that and appreciate it." Drasko bowed gracefully, conjuring the most concerned expression. "But you see, the marchioness will not let my wife play at her ball. And that upsets me deeply. I planned to give this city the most praised jewelry masterpieces, and in return, this city merely..." For deeper effect, Drasko pursed his lips and nodded as if in pained contemplation.

"Oh, that is appalling!" the duchess exclaimed in feigned disdain. "The marchioness? How unlike her!"

Drasko checked the clock. He was getting tired of this little circus.

"Unfortunately, I have to leave," he said. "We have guests for dinner tonight. My wife is performing. So, you see, I have to hurry. I cannot upset her. She is such a sensitive soul."

The duchess glanced between him and the duke. "But Mr. Mawr—"

"Unless..." Drasko cocked his head as if in contemplation.

The duchess froze.

The duke swallowed hard.

"Unless?" they asked at the same time.

"Unless you'd be willing to grace us with your presence for dinner at my house. My wife is dedicated to her craft. And I'm dedicated to her. You are so very welcome to stop by, as patrons of music and all. Considering you might not hear her play in London anymore. Or attend the auction in France," he added quieter. "Perhaps, we can find a way out of this unfortunate circumstance with the marchioness and all..." He trailed off and locked his eyes with the duke.

"I shall not be blackmailed, Mr. Mawr," the duke warned, his chin trembling, and his wife elbowed him not so discreetly.

Drasko bowed just slightly. "Of course not, Your Grace."

If the titled wanted to play games, he'd play along. He had learned a long time ago that everything was a negotiation. And for the first time in centuries, titles weren't the main leverage—wealth and power were.

"You are not like the French," Drasko explained, marveling at his own sugary flattery. "They don't have your dignity. And the French Prime Minister's wife should not be wearing the biggest English treasure, the Crimson Tear. But she probably will. Hmm. Thank you so very much for seeing me, Your Graces."

He turned on his heel and walked out, chased by the shocked stares of the Duke and the Duchess of Trent.

THE GAME

Andhra Pradesh, India
Drasko, 21-27

When a king is born, he is talked about for a lifetime. When he dies, he is forgotten as soon as the new one takes the throne.

For some time, the diamond trade had been buzzing about Drasko Mawr.

He had abandoned the idea of a free-spirited life. Now that he didn't have anything to lose, he seized the reins of Mawr Industries, proving that neither Alfred nor Uriah had ever been as brilliant as him.

He handled negotiations, traveled Europe, went to America. When he ran into the Wollendorf brothers, he was polite and businesslike but saw through their sly friendliness every time.

"Let them think they are smarter," Uriah said, getting weaker by the day, staying by Drasko's side but letting him handle most of the business.

Another trip to London was overdue. This time, Drasko had an agenda. He had "his people" now, many of them. They spread rumors and fed the newspapers the information that Drasko wanted to give them. He posed for pictures with high society, the Duke of Trent, and the like. He visited the most reputable auction houses in Europe and arranged showcases of the wonders of the Mawr jewels.

He commissioned the construction of a tower, adjacent to the Mawr Building, and built a room at the top for himself. The small space with the windows all around was where he occasionally spent his nights, watching the city with murky lights under industrial fog. In his tower of solitude, he smoked, drank, and thought about the future. He would stay there until dawn, watching the rising sun shed the pink hues of its first light, drowning the city in orange-pink haze. *His* city.

He spent his first winter in London, fascinated with the snow. For hours, he stood on his tower's observation deck, smiling under the steel-cold wind, his face lifted to the sky as he let the snowflakes melt on his skin.

He thought of little *jaan*, wished he could've shown her the first snow, just like he had once promised.

The thought painfully tugged at his heart.

Drasko tried to locate the doctor who had treated her and found out that the man had died in a gruesome accident. The last hope to talk to the person who knew what had happened on that night years ago was lost.

He gathered info on everyone he was concerned about, including the Mawrs. He kept files on people of interest, found dirt on the Wollendorfs, and made friends with the members of Parliament. He traveled across the world, did favors and salvaged reputations, made powerful friends, and made notes of who his enemies could be in the future.

And he made sure that the wealthy never forgot whose diamonds adorned their necks and wrists, their wealth trickling into his pockets.

He partied with Elias. He acquired a paramour, then another. Then a house, then several, then invested in land. He acquired steamships and bought a small factory that was going to build vehicles powered by fuel. He donated to schools and built a craftsman building in the East End that trained people for his new businesses.

He smiled and shook hands with the titled but preferred to dine and drink in the dingiest parts of the city. Where people didn't know him and didn't care. Where he didn't have to wear a mask. Where the darker shade of his skin fit better than his immaculate suit. Where once in a while he found incredible characters, cornered by poor circumstances and at the end of their rope, or the brilliant minds drinking their lives away, or those who dreamed of a new life yet couldn't afford the hope.

Just like he had been once.

And Drasko gave them opportunities.

That was how, one night, he found Tripp, an Irish lad in so much gambling debt that he wrote a goodbye note to his impoverished family and stopped at a tavern for one last drink before ending his life. One drink turned into four, bought by Drasko. A year later, Drasko didn't have a more loyal man than his Irish bodyguard.

Not all Drasko's deals were well-calculated.

He bought the Grand Marquis on Baker Street. Bought it on a whim, because some pretty little thing had dared to send a blow to his male pride.

Grace Sommerville.

Ah, she had changed the city for Drasko. In fact, everything changed the first time he met her.

She was a piano virtuoso, sixteen, who, for years, had stunned England with her musical skills.

The first time he heard her play, in 1887, he couldn't take his eyes off her on stage. In a concert hall with hundreds of people, she was a marvel—pretty, talented, and so very arrogant.

The next day, he saw her in a company of adults on Piccadilly. A pretty face. Flowers in her hat. The dress perfectly hugging her doll figure.

Fascinated, he didn't mean to stalk her, only wanted to see

more of her. So he followed the company to the Grand Marquis restaurant on Baker Street and took up a table several feet away.

She noticed him then, peeked from behind her guardian, her pretty eyes sweeping over his face and widening in, yes, horror, Drasko was sure. Her guardian turned her head and cast a condescending look at him.

A minute later, the maître d' was at Drasko's table. "I am afraid I have to ask you to leave, sir."

"To leave?" Drasko scoffed.

"Our important guests would like the company to be more... exclusive."

Exclusive...

Drasko heard the words perfectly well. It was his tanned skin and starkly dark hair that had perhaps confused the maître d'. Drasko didn't know his own roots, though as a street child, he had often been called a gypsy. Such racial sentiments were common in London. Yet, in the city where the newspaper headlines screamed the Mawrs' name, this maître d' had no idea.

Drasko couldn't remember the last time someone had so bluntly insulted him.

"I would like to speak to the owner," he said coldly.

An hour later, he walked out of the restaurant having become the owner of the establishment.

But though triumphant at this little deal, his heart burned with resentment for the young woman who thought low of him.

He started despising London itself, though during every trip, he prolonged his stay. His mind didn't let go of the young woman. It wasn't pride, per se, it was his *male* pride that hurt at the sight of Grace Sommerville despite his admiration for her talent.

Two years later, he was at one of her performances when Elias Bayne introduced them.

"I have heard of you, yes," Grace Sommerville said with a cold smile, her eyes drifting to Drasko's scars. "Please, excuse me," she said hurriedly and moved on to talk to yet another admirer.

And Drasko gritted his teeth.

He was twenty-seven then and knew what women wanted. He stood tall and led with his assertive gestures that made the most conservative women follow along. Something about him made women gaze in trepidation and warily adjust their hair. Women had a flair for scarred men, rich men, and more importantly, powerful ones. If the biggest monster in the world had the biggest wealth, women would line up to try to charm him.

Turned out that his scars—he'd have enough paramours who told him so—were intriguing, like those of old-time warriors. Four straight lines stretched in perfect symmetry from his right brow across his cheek and ended at the side of his face. A dozen more, deeper ones, etched his body, hidden by the fashionable clothes.

"Art," a rejected marchioness commented behind his back. "I bet he had it done on purpose. Like those outrageous tattoos that sailors have on their bodies. So distasteful. They say he has one of those drawings all over his back," she whispered with spite. This didn't keep her from sending him flirty gazes throughout the evening, much like many other women.

The Duchess of Trent approached him with poorly concealed eagerness. "Mr. Mawr, when do we get to enjoy the promised wonders of the Mawr treasures?"

She was, of course, hinting at the legend of the Crimson Tear, but was also wondering about the slowly curated through the newspapers rumors that Mawr Diamond Industries was collaborating with the world's best jewelers to create outstanding examples of jewelry artistry. Such an exhibition auction was in the making, indeed, and the wealthy were itching to get their hands on the most prized jewels in the world.

Yet, with all this attention, that haughty Grace Sommerville walked away from him every time, without as much as a polite smile.

And Rakshasa on his back hissed in disapproval.

So, Drasko prolonged every stay in London, telling himself that the beautiful pianist had nothing to do with it. *Nothing at all.*

Uriah preferred to stay back home, in India. And that suited Drasko just fine, for he'd developed strong resentment for the man who'd once been his idol.

The one thing Drasko didn't understand were the words Uriah had said that one night. "A quest, a diamond game, so to speak. And at the center of it all—the Crimson Tear. It's worth a fortune, and that fortune will be yours, my boy."

The diamond hadn't surfaced yet. They rumored it was a legend, perhaps a clever lie created by the Mawrs themselves. The craftsmen of Golconda, who handled a vast majority of Mawr supplies, had their own tales going on—that the ones in possession of the Crimson Tear always died a gruesome death. First Alfred's wife, who had received it as a wedding present. Then his daughter, who had had it around her neck. Then Alfred Mawr himself, who had kept in on him. The next victim was soon to come.

The rumors went on and on.

No one had seen the rare diamond yet. But Drasko had. He knew it was real, mused that after years of trusting him with everything, Uriah still hid it, refusing to show it to a single soul.

"That quest, the Crimson Tear business..." Uriah finally said one day when Drasko was back in India.

It was December 1890, and Drasko was planning to go back to Europe right away. He resisted his Indian home, the empty walls and rooms, the solemn reminder of the losses he'd taken to be where he was now. Only by night did he feel free. He shed his expensive suit, his tailored shirt, and jewel-encrusted rings. He put on the *kurta pajama* and walked barefoot to the village nearby. Asha had her own children, but always smiled softly and made tea for him and Rupesh. She served them simple *biryani* and cold mangos that cooled during the summer heat, while he and Rupesh sat under the banyan tree in front of their bungalow and talked about life, sometimes all through the night.

Drasko often stayed there until morning, slept on the straw mattress, listening to the echoes of Rakshasa from the past. He woke up by sunrise, walked back to his house, and changed into a suit. Then spent a day lost in work in the office or went to Golconda for business—anything not to be where everything reminded him of his past.

One day, Uriah, unusually agile, announced that he would take a tour of the river delta and revisit the mining sites, specifically, the Priya Corridor.

Uriah hadn't paid attention to the laborers, nor did he know what was happening in the valley.

Drasko did.

Just the other day, he saw a report stating that the Priya Corridor was highly unstable.

Drasko wasn't sure what made him keep silent about it, or perhaps, he knew, yet didn't admit, that he would be a culprit.

He didn't meet Uriah's eyes when he heard the words. But an uncanny feeling saturated his entire existence, like a premonition. Rakshasa silently growled behind him.

For the rest of the day, Drasko sat in the office, deep in his thoughts. He smoked one cigarette after another as Rakshasa simmered in revenge.

The grim news came later that evening: a part of the Priya Corridor had collapsed, burying Uriah Mawr.

Even then, Drasko didn't believe it. He ordered the corridor to be cleared, had the body dug out from under the rubble and brought up to the village. He studied the mangled remains of a white man with a caved-in face that was unrecognizable and, to his own surprise, didn't feel a thing.

Finally, he walked up to the body, searched in the dead man's bloodied suit pocket, and found the one thing Uriah had never parted with—his diamond watch.

At last, if only for a short while, the dark tidal wave of hate inside Drasko subsided. But it never quite went away. His business with Uriah wasn't over yet.

With Uriah's death came Drasko's invisible coronation, all assets and shares of Mawr Diamond Industries now in his name.

At last, Drasko Mawr was the Diamond King.

Did the news bring him joy? Not a bit.

Every night, when business was over, Drasko did what had become a habit. He took off his expensive suit and jewelry, put on his simple attire, and, barefoot, walked to the village to have dinner with the only people he called family.

Only Rupesh understood what Uriah's death meant. "Do you think you are finally free?" he asked.

Drasko shook his head. "Not yet."

In the past years, Drasko had understood that Uriah was a hateful man, void of affection or compassion, a heartless executioner who often spent years stalking his prey. He did things quietly, expertly, played God, just like he had done fifteen years prior at the Ol' Days tavern in the Port of London when Drasko accidentally crossed his path.

Drasko had one last game to play, perhaps the most important one. Its true prize? A mystery.

Sometime before the accident, Uriah had sat Drasko down.

"I am sick and shall not last long. When I'm gone, you will inherit the Mawr business. But only if you agree to the game. I have important people overlooking it all."

Uriah was wicked, indeed.

Drasko should have refused the offer. But he had nothing to lose and secretly sensed that Uriah would find a way to shackle him anyway.

"What sort of game is that?" Drasko had asked suspiciously.

"The Crimson Tear is worth more than any other jewel in the world. You are worth everything I've bet on. To be a great man, you have to make sacrifices. Then you are truly a king. I call it the Diamond Game. In the course of several years, you shall receive letters, six of them in total. Certain people will be involved. Certain tasks will have to be accomplished. If you don't comply, you will lose everything I've given you. When it is time to reveal the Crimson Tear and put it up for auction, if you fail to do so, you will pay with your life. Rules can't be broken."

Completely perplexed, Drasko stared at him. "That is—"

"A high price to pay, yes. But in exchange for grand power? Not so much."

"Why wouldn't I want to put the Crimson Tear up for auction? Unless I don't have it."

"Oh, you shall have it." Uriah's eyes sparkled with mischief. "That is the deal. When you know you have it, if you decide to keep it, you will trade your life for it. The Crimson Tear is meant to be auctioned. That is my will, and my people will see to that."

Was it worth it? Drasko had a number of his own businesses going on. Mawr Industries? If he lost it, he wouldn't regret it. And with as much hate as he had for the man, he wanted to prove him wrong, win this silly game, and finally be free.

Perhaps, in that moment, he didn't realize that this was baiting, that the Mawr brothers were good at challenging others and knew Drasko too well—he had never backed away from a good challenge in the past. Not the Thuggees. Not Rakshasa. Not this.

Uriah smoothed a contract on the table in front of Drasko and picked up a quill and a razor. "We shall seal it with blood."

Without hesitation, Drasko made an incision on his palm and watched the crimson tears drop onto the cream paper and mix with Uriah's. Just like the day of Rakshasa's attack.

"Deal," Drasko said, sealing his fate.

Now that Uriah was dead, the game was about to begin.

41

GRACE

Grace couldn't hold back her smile as she rushed from the dining room to the kitchen, giving orders, and checking the table arrangement for the dozenth time.

The guests were arriving for dinner one by one.

Mr. Brodia and his right-hand man came first.

"The Bankees," Drasko had informed her beforehand, to her shock, though the gangsters, to her delight, were dressed with utmost style.

He had told Grace he had grown up with Zeph Brodia on the streets, and Grace instantly took to the man who had known her husband the way no other person in the world did.

Rivka came, donning one of her beautiful handmade dresses, Mr. Brodia right away weaving his charms around her.

Julien was dazzling and elegant in a blue three-piece suit.

"Am I allowed to kiss your wife's hand?" he addressed Drasko with feigned trepidation, making both Grace and Drasko chuckle.

Elias Bayne arrived with another couple.

"His cousin, who married a banker from America. They are visiting," Drasko explained to Grace in a concealed mutter.

"Elias!" She had liked the man instantly when she met him at the Mawr building.

"Grace." He beamed at her with a grin that was like sunshine on a cold day.

Elias was tall and muscled, just like Drasko. He did not come across as a man of leisure. Nevertheless, his immaculate three-piece suit indicated a man of wealth. While Drasko was reserved but powerful in his silence, his mere presence in the room drawing inquisitive stares, Elias was free and open in his manners, generous with laughter, and was in a true sense a man of the world. It was no wonder that only minutes later, Julien's blue eyes were on him, wide with admiration.

"My lawyer, Mr. Lennard," Drasko introduced another arrival to Grace.

One of his managers came. An architect, "the genius behind the Mawr Building." A jeweler from Asia attended.

Drasko introduced her to them one by one, a company so mismatched, yet when Grace stepped into the drawing room to check on them, they all looked at ease, smoking, drinking, laughing.

Among them were Julien and Rivka, her favorite people. Tears sprung to her eyes at the sight, and she flitted out of the room to calm herself.

"Darling?" Drasko caught up with her in the hallway and took her hands in his, his worried eyes on her. "What is the matter?"

"Nothing." She smiled through tears. "I... I simply want it to be perfect. I..."

She tried to walk away, but he wouldn't let her go. "Darling?"

"This is the first dinner at our house and..."

A lump in her throat swallowed her words. She tried to turn, but Drasko caught her by her shoulders.

"Grace, look at me, please." She lifted her eyes to meet his, worried and caring. "What is it?"

"I have never had a dinner party with my friends. At the Sommervilles', my friends were never allowed. Julien was never invited. Never have I..." She sucked in a breath, willing herself not to cry. That would be embarrassing to say the least.

His fingers tipped her chin, the green abyss of his eyes taking her in.

"It's already quite perfect with you here." He smiled that calming smile that made her worries wash off that very instant. "Now, leave everything to the servants and, please, join me with the guests."

She nodded, her heart suddenly too big for her chest. "Yes."

"Grace?" She lifted her eyes to his again. "You can have whoever you want for dinner any time. And your friends are always welcome."

She nodded again. "Thank you," she whispered.

He kissed her on the forehead, and her heart hummed happily as she stepped into the drawing room by his side.

"What is this contraption, Mr. Mawr?" the lawyer inquired, pointing at a device that stood like a monstrous machine on a small, wooden table. "You always have the most peculiar things in your house."

"A phonograph," Drasko said. "Invented by Mr. Thomas Edison."

"Explain?"

"I will show you!"

He walked up to the device, cranked the handle that started rotating a peculiar cylinder attached to a needle, and music poured out of it.

"I have seen this machine at the science exposition!" the jeweler exclaimed as the guests gathered around the device.

"Indeed. They can record too," Drasko said.

"Oh, do we get to hear your voice?"

"You get to hear my wife playing."

The guests exploded in a heated discussion.

If there was one truth Grace was willing to accept tonight, it was that she felt more alive than ever when Drasko was around. His smile at her was often seductive, his rare laughter contagious. His voice floated above all others. His gaze found her amidst a dozen people, even when they were in different parts of the room. It made her heart flutter.

And when he was out of the room if only for a moment, her heart was already calling for him to come back as if an invisible thread connected them.

She was feeling so much for him and was finally accepting it.

"You look beautiful, Mrs. Mawr," Zeph Brodia complimented as he came over to chat with her.

"It is so very nice to meet you," Grace said, omitting *what* she'd heard about him.

"Your friend…" Mr. Brodia cleared his throat, glancing at Rivka, who talked to the lawyer. "Who is she?"

"Are you interested in my friend, Mr. Brodia?"

"Why, simply inquiring. I think I have heard of her before."

"She is a healer."

"Ah! So I was right."

"Is that so?"

"Yes. Your husband told me about her."

"Oh?" So Drasko discussed her with his friends—Grace swelled with pride.

"I know several people who are familiar with her healing practices and one who…"

"Who?"

Mr. Brodia leaned in as if he was sharing a secret. "Who had a fortune read by her."

"Do you believe in such things, Mr. Brodia?" Grace smiled broadly, not knowing if it was judgment or curiosity in his inquiry.

"I am intrigued. I gathered by her name that it was her. But when I heard the stories before, I imagined… well, I suppose when you hear the word "healer," childhood tales about witches and old unattractive recluses come to mind."

Grace laughed. "I see. And Miss Rebecca doesn't fit the description. Why don't you ask her yourself?"

Mr. Brodia was distracted by Elias. But Grace noticed Mr. Brodia following Rivka with his gaze as she made her way to Grace.

"How are you, my lovely?" Rivka asked as she and Grace observed the guests. "It's a wonderful company."

Indeed. This was the humblest party Grace had attended. There was no doubt that Drasko somehow managed to put everyone at ease. Or perhaps, the people he kept close were worldly and open-minded while Grace was used to circles with strict etiquette, rigid formalities, and outdated ideas about power.

"I am happy, Rivka. So truly happy."

Grace's chest tightened as she remembered her fears about her husband's nature only months ago. The ache at being so unjust about him resonated with the dull pain in her abdomen. On instinct, she pressed her hand to it.

"The pain is coming back," she said quietly.

Rivka's worried eyes snapped to Grace. "When?"

"Just a day or two. It is mild, very minimal. I hope it doesn't grow into a monster." She flinched at the words.

"The last healing session was hard on you, Gracie. It will take time, perhaps several more years for the pain to go away completely. It will, my lovely."

Grace nodded. She caught Rivka's cautious glances at Mr. Brodia. "What is it? Do you know him?" Grace whispered.

"It's nothing." Rivka waved her off.

"Liar. He said he had heard of you. Mr. Brodia!" Grace called out to him, beckoning him to approach. "Will you tell us more about what sort of work you do?"

And she was puzzled by how Rivka, always confident, seemed uneasy next to him, her posture rigid in his presence.

He didn't look at Grace this time, only at Rivka. "Miss

Rebecca, what does a beautiful woman such as yourself occupy herself with?"

"You know what I do, Mr. Brodia. My grandfather and I own a drug store," she replied.

"And you do healings," he probed.

"Yes."

Mr. Brodia smiled charmingly, his eyes never leaving Rivka. "I might be in need of healing myself."

"Hmm." Rivka visibly stiffened. "For what, may I ask?"

"My heart, you see. Broken, lonely, and in need of being in good hands."

Grace stifled a chuckle. That was certainly a very direct, if not inappropriate, comment.

But Rivka's smile faded as she locked her eyes with the man. "In a different part of town, certain establishments cure that very quickly. Overnight, in fact. And the good thing is that you can do it every night, Mr. Brodia, with a different healer, if you know what I mean."

Grace inhaled sharply at this brazen remark.

Mr. Brodia didn't respond.

Rivka excused herself.

Grace touched his shoulder. "I apologize, Mr. Brodia. Miss Rebecca is never—"

"She is right, Mrs. Mawr," he cut her off and gulped the rest of his brandy. "She is absolutely right. Except, many of us, after years of searching, find the one healer we stick to."

He winked at Grace and excused himself.

42

GRACE

The party soon moved to the dining room. The first several courses brought in the smell of exotic spices.

"Our chefs are at war, you see," Drasko explained the mix of traditional dishes and the Indian ones, though Grace's mind stuck to the word "our." "One cook is a master of South Indian cuisine. The other chef is English and is on the brink of quitting because he cannot learn the dozens of spices that our other cook has on the shelves." The guests laughed. "Everything in this life is a negotiation, a war at the start until the peace treaty is made." His smiling eyes met Grace's.

A month ago, she would have laughed about it or come back with a bitter answer.

But now… now it was different.

Peace treaty. Was that what this was? She had never been at war with him. He had never explained why they were supposed to be. Yet she sensed that when he'd married her, his knowledge of her was much greater than she had first thought. His wasn't a peace treaty, but rather a swift invasion—of her thoughts, her feelings, her… heart.

The butler came in. "Mr. Mawr, the guests have arrived."

"More guests?" Grace turned to Drasko in surprise.

"The Duke and Duchess of Trent," the butler explained.

Raised eyebrows and glances were exchanged around the table.

Drasko nodded, rose from his seat, and helped Grace up.

"What is this, Drasko?" she whispered in shock.

"A business deal." He winked.

Grace had only been to the duke's house once, during a ball, when she had performed for a New Year's celebration several years ago. She had always been and still thought she was but an exotic creature to the public. With her talent, she was treated like a rare pet. The wealthy didn't necessarily have a taste for music but simply strove to surround themselves with the best. And if the newspapers and the Music Academy said Grace Sommerville was, then she was.

Never had Grace expected to see them in her own house. Granted, Drasko's mansion was more lavish and tasteful than the duke's.

Yet at the sight of the noble couple walking through the marble hall toward them, she felt unexplainable trepidation.

This was, indeed, some sort of game Drasko played. Grace saw clearly through their forced politeness and insincere smiles, the way they sashayed into the dining room, how they nodded at the guests, their eyes sweeping across the table.

"What a surprise!" Elias said without much enthusiasm.

The duchess flicked her hand fan. "Oh, we saw Mr. Mawr only this morning. He was so persuasive about us coming for dinner, and we are such admirers of Mrs. Mawr's work, that when we were passing by, we simply had to pay our respect."

They didn't want to be here—that was obvious. Yet they smiled politely and eventually studied the exotic dishes with curiosity, gawked at the servants dressed in traditional Indian clothes, perked their ears at the conversations about America and the Orient, and as if on cue, when Drasko set his utensils down during a conversation, did the same.

To Grace's surprise, the rest of the guests seemed not to care for their presence. The lawyer and the architect talked loudly to Drasko—they all owned wealth greater than the duke. Mr. Brodia, Elias, and the banker discussed the business in New York —they knew more about the world than the duke with his dusty ideas of power.

And soon, the duke and duchess looked around as if lost. The people who surrounded them were bigger than the noblemen. The world was changing. New money poured in. The new rich disregarded the titles and blue blood. Power had shifted, and now it was in the hands of the brilliant minds and daredevils who worshipped science and new ideas.

When Elias's relation, the American banker, mentioned the President of America, the duke entered the conversation. "How do you know the man, may I ask?"

"Family friends, for years," the banker replied with a careless shrug and resumed his conversation with Elias, while the duke nodded humbly, and his puffed-up chest deflated a notch.

Julien entertained the duchess with a discussion about the newest performance at the Royal Opera.

And Drasko observed it all, quiet satisfaction in his gaze that now and then met Grace's and spoke the silent, "Everything is perfect."

"Mr. Brodia! What do you do? I don't believe we have met," she heard the duke say.

Elias smiled into his glass.

Grace worriedly looked at Drasko.

"Imports, Your Grace," Mr. Brodia answered most gracefully. "All sorts of imports. All across the world. America, Italy, France. France, yes. Wonderful country!"

Drasko's lips curled, hiding a smile, and Grace held back a chuckle.

The duchess stiffened. "France? Ah, Mrs. Mawr!" She abruptly turned to Grace. "I just so happened to run into the marchioness earlier today."

"Is that so?" Grace met her husband's smiling eyes.

"Indeed. She informed me that you didn't respond to the invitation to her Summer Ball. She seemed quite upset. Arrangements have been made for you to perform."

Lies. "I did not receive the invitation," Grace said.

"How odd! Perhaps it got lost with the courier. Well, she said that she was going to visit you, if that is all right with you. You can discuss the details. She is most excited about you being there. So is the rest of London. Your talent is unprecedented."

Grace felt Drasko's gaze with her every pore. It was all his doing. He was a brilliant businessman, truly. His reputation was warranted.

When the party moved to the music room, Grace sat down at the piano and played a part of the "Danse Macabre"—the piece she loved yet knew was too daring for conservative minds like the duke and duchess's.

And all through her performance, she felt *his* eyes on her, felt proud to be in this room with him, and despite a dozen people, played only for her husband.

She finished the piece to loud applause, the loudest from the duchess.

"Drasko, your wife is simply perfection," Mr. Brodia said.

"Indeed," her husband replied, and she pursed her lips to hide a smile.

Drasko, Drasko, Drasko, she repeated his name in her mind, the syllables that tasted like potent whisky. Laughter and chatter spread across the room. She marveled at how carefree it was. Happy at finally hosting such a wonderful dinner, minus the duke and the duchess, she nevertheless looked forward to it being over so she could be alone with her husband—a thought she right away shamed herself for.

Though that wouldn't happen tonight, she realized a bit later. Mr. Brodia would stay late into the evening. Elias was quite drunk, and she offered to let him stay the night.

But that was all right. For once, Grace was happy. At last, she got to meet her husband's friends.

The duke and duchess were the first ones to leave. The duke was quite drunk, his arm wrapped around Mr. Brodia's shoulder as they had a heated discussion, not a clue that he had just made friends with the Bankee Syndicate. The duchess melted under Julien's compliments. Their visit was Drasko's business deal, one he had made for Grace, and she wondered why he made an effort at all, why he did all those things for her despite telling her their marriage was yet another deal.

There was a lot Drasko wasn't telling her. She still ached to know it, know more of him, nurtured an unusual fantasy of what the two of them could be. In the future. The future she was frequently envisioning lately. The two of them. Perhaps, their children.

His children…

She couldn't ignore anymore how her heart softened in his presence, how cheerfulness swept over her when she heard him talk about her.

She felt a foot taller by his side as they walked the duke and duchess out and were about to bid farewell to them.

"Mr. Mawr," the duchess said with unusual ease in her gestures, "perhaps we could borrow your Indian chef sometime. I would love to have my chefs learn those wonderful recipes of yours."

"Absolutely, Your Grace," Drasko answered with a familiarity that would be noticed if the duke and duchess weren't so obviously drunk. "Oh, and, Your Grace!" Drasko wrapped his arm around Grace's waist. "As to the auction, I will ensure that the duchess has the first look at all that we intend to display."

"Ah!" The duke drunkenly raised his forefinger in the air. "So, the auction is in London? Do I hear you right, Mr. Mawr?"

"Yes. I decided that the Mawr treasures truly belong to the best of England."

"You have it, dear," the duke reassured his wife, patting her on the back, as they stumbled out.

Grace met Drasko's eyes. A moment of silence passed between them, like this was a language of their own.

She still didn't know what he wanted, why he had done all that for her. It was not the game of power—he'd played many, and she wasn't part of it.

Then what?

The only thing she was sure of was that her husband had many secrets, and she didn't know a single one of them.

THE
FIRST LETTER

London, England
Drasko, 29
(Three months before the wedding)

Drasko was in London when the wheels of the game started turning—he received the first letter from the dead man.

Cream paper. Uriah's personal seal on it. A diamond in the center.

Standing by the window in his office, Drasko stared at the letter for some time and couldn't bring himself to open it.

The city behind the glass lay under a thick blanket of smog. The clock loudly struck noon.

He finally took a deep breath and tore the brown seal open.

> *Charles Hatchet, the Earl of Weltingdon, is to receive the document attached to this letter. He is to sign it as an acknowledgment and agreement to fulfill the stipulations on a day in the near future yet to be determined.*

Completely perplexed, Drasko turned the paper back and

forth, searching for something else, another clue, or more information.

That was it?

He had expected a more sinister task. Instead, it looked like he was sorting out late Uriah's affairs.

So be it.

He requested his assistant to gather all he could on Charles Hatchet.

Turned out, that the earl's late father owed a debt to Mawr Diamond Industries. The documents that came with the letter held the deeds to multiple properties as well as bank shares, collateral for the late earl's debt that Charles Hatchet was to receive back when the stipulation was fulfilled.

So, Uriah is dismissing the debt and giving the property back to Charles Hatchet?

It was unlike Uriah Mawr to forgive the debts. So, Drasko dug deeper.

Charles Hatchet wasn't poor but by no means wealthy, spending more than he could afford, raking up more debts as he drank and partied his way through London high society. He had a paramour, an opera singer. He had a secret child he'd fathered with her. But nothing else indicated his importance to Uriah Mawr.

Drasko was reluctant to visit the man next day. But such was the agreement—he was to fulfill the tasks himself.

Charles Hatchet was an amiable short man in his mid-twenties. His expression was slightly hostile when he received Drasko, undoubtedly, on account of his late father's debt with the company.

"You are not..." He frowned, then his eyes widened at Drasko. "Wait, but you are! You are most definitely *the* Drasko Mawr!"

His flat smelled of wine and cheap cigars. The drawing room chair housed someone's dress and stockings, a bottle of wine, and two empty glasses on the table. *So much for a titled man.*

Charles's expression fell. "This must be something truly important if a man such as yourself shows up instead of sending an attorney." Realization rendered his face with an ugly scowl. "If you came to collect, I have nothing to offer you," he said too sharply. "If you came to blackmail or threaten, I assure you—"

"I do not handle those sorts of things. Quite the opposite," said Drasko indifferently and produced the documents sent in the letter.

Oh, the glee on the earl's face when he read the agreement, the way his money-hungry eyes searched Drasko's when he asked, "Do you have an idea of when I am to receive back the rights to my father's estate?"

"No," Drasko answered, not bothering to add the courteous "my lord." "I suppose, I will see you soon."

Drasko left, and for once, he, too, was utterly confused.

44

DRASKO

There was one rule about privacy at Mawr Diamond Industries
—no one was allowed to talk to the reporters.

Those who broke the rule were either told to do so by
Drasko's clever public manager or they simply lost their jobs.
And no one wanted to lose a job at Mawr Industries.

The reporters caught a whiff of juicy stories quickly but often
had to resort to the most doubtful sources. Only a few stuck to
the facts. And only one man wrote about the Wollendorf deal
gone wrong, yet didn't speculate. Instead, he wrote a clever
projection of the future of the diamond trade.

The man's name was John Papadakis, and he just so
happened to be standing outside the house gates when Drasko's
entourage was leaving.

"Mr. Mawr! Your comment on the Duke and Duchess of
Trent! Their special interest in the auction and the French
involvement?"

Drasko chuckled—more at the ingenuity of how fast the
rumors traveled.

He motioned for his carriage to stop, got out, and started
walking on.

"I am John Papadakis, with the *Tribune*," the short slender man in his twenties introduced himself, walking step in step with Drasko.

Coincidentally, Drasko had read the articles by Papadakis. The reporter was young yet didn't resort to dirty tactics. *Fresh blood*, Drasko assumed. *And honorable at that.*

"I know who you are," Drasko replied, lighting a cigarette and offering one to the reporter.

He studied the man, his shabby but neat suit, cheap but clean glasses, and inquiring and eager gaze.

Everyone deserved an opportunity. Once upon a time, Drasko was a bet. And ever since, he had had a habit of giving others a chance.

Papadakis was hungry for any information. Drasko was willing to share it. With his own agenda, of course.

"Your connection with the Duke and Duchess of Trent, sir?" the man repeated, nervously smoking as he tried to keep up with Drasko's wide stride.

"What connection?"

"They were having dinner at your house last night, were they not?"

"Yes. They enjoyed my chefs' fine cuisine."

"That is all?"

"And music. They are patrons of the arts, and my wife is a brilliant pianist."

"Rumor has it, the ton was not too accepting of the situation with the duped earl."

"Duped? Is that what the rumor is?"

"That is what the talk is, Mr. Mawr."

"I can tell you that she was about to marry the wrong man. If you ask the earl, his lordship will explain."

"I did, sir. He said you got what was meant to be yours. While he was a gentleman and simply walked away from a woman who deserves to be happy with the man she loves."

Drasko snorted. "Oh, my! He said that?"

"Highly intoxicated, but yes. He is married as of yesterday."

"To the woman who deserves to be happy with the man she loves?"

Papadakis chuckled, his admiring eyes on Drasko. "Highly unlikely that was the case, Mr. Mawr. But I am here because of a different matter."

"More rumors?"

"No, not rumors, just fact-checking."

"Mr. Papadakis." Drasko tossed his cigarette away and fixed his tie as he walked. "I am pressed for time, but I have an offer. Does your wife like diamonds?" He had noticed the wedding band on his finger.

The man's eyes snapped at him in surprise. "We come from a small town up north, Mr. Mawr. We live modestly."

"Would she like to have diamonds?" One of Drasko's favorite things was to gift diamonds to others, since he couldn't stand them in his own home.

"This sounds like a bribe, Mr. Mawr. And I do not—"

"Considering what I am about to offer, it would be a welcoming gift. This is what I need. Number one, I need you to write in your newspaper that I am madly in love with my wife, and that is my actual statement."

"Noted. Good to finally confirm it."

"Number two. The auction is to be held at the Benham Auction House, but you already know that. What you don't know is that the Duke and Duchess of Trent indeed will have the first viewing of the auction items."

"How coincidental that the Duchess of Trent is on good terms with Mr. Kleinstein of the Benham Auction House."

"Yes. Coincidences are all over the place. Omit that part. The initial idea was to host the auction in France. But the duchess is a big admirer of Grace Mawr's talent. In appreciation of her support, Mawr Diamond Industries, indeed, decided to keep the auction on English soil."

"Noted."

"Number three. The Duchess of Trent is absolutely worthy of

such a masterpiece as the Crimson Tear."

"What about the Queen?"

"Mawr Diamond Industries is crafting a special piece for Her Majesty."

"Is that true?"

"I have just decided it is. And you are the first to know. The duchess is the one woman *besides* the Queen, who deserves the likes of the legendary Crimson Tear. And those will be *your* words in the article, not mine."

"I see."

Drasko was playing in her favor. So be it. Noblemen needed a pat on the shoulder, much like pampered little dogs that strove for attention.

"I will give you the first exclusive breakdown of the guests and the pieces at the auction, Mr. Papadakis."

"In exchange?"

"In exchange for you printing exactly what I tell you. And after the auction, I am offering you to be the official public relations representative of Mawr Diamond Industries."

"Sir?" The man's eyes grew large.

Drasko met his shocked stare. "Do I need to repeat myself?"

"No, no, sir."

"Is that a yes or a no?"

"A no to not repeating. A yes to the public relations job. Absolutely!"

"Good."

"And the Crimson Tear?"

"What about it?"

"No one has yet seen the legendary diamond. And I mean, *no one.*"

"I have."

"But do you have it?"

Drasko hated lies. But this was a game, and for the sake of the game, he uttered, "Yes."

"Oh, that is a sensational confirmation, Mr. Mawr. And your connection to the Bankee Syndicate?"

Drasko smiled at the young man's audacity. He definitely liked him.

The reporter shrugged with an apologetic look. "I had to ask. It's my job."

"What about it?"

"Do you confirm?"

"Confirm what?"

"Your connection?"

"What sort of connection are we talking about?"

"The illegal trade, sir."

"I only trade diamonds, Mr. Papadakis. *My* diamonds. Legally."

"So there is no other connection?"

"Mr. Papdakis, was it you who did the article last year on the Bankees' whisky exports?"

"Indeed."

"And you talked to the Bankees, am I correct?"

"Yes, sir."

"What is your connection to them?"

"Business."

"Illegal trade?'

"What? No!" A laugh escaped him, then ceased abruptly. "I see," he muttered.

Drasko motioned for his carriage, then turned to Papadakis. "I would like the draft of your article on my desk tomorrow," he told the man. "Now, have a blessed day, Mr. Papadakis."

He thought about what he'd said to the reporter throughout the day. Pushing the story that he and his wife were in love was a cheap trick. But he was doing it for her reputation more than anything else. The marchioness's ball would be filled with lords and ladies studying him and Grace under a magnifying glass, asking questions, smiling politely and exchanging all sort of garbage rumors behind their backs. So, naturally, he did not

leave much option for the Duke and Duchess of Trent either—
they would have to play along and sing their praises about
Grace.

Drasko was used to large posh events but in recent years
preferred smaller companies with people he trusted.

But this was Grace's opportunity to shine, and lately, he had
a hard time denying her anything.

Only now her behavior back when she was a Sommerville
made sense. How her dresses were of poorer quality than those
of her guardians, how closely they curated her life, how little
freedom she had, how self-aware and intimidated she was
around them.

If he needed to play the game of pleasantries to make high
society kiss the ground his wife walked on—he would do it. If he
needed to step over his pride to make her feel safe and cherished
—he would do it. Even more so, he would tell the world he was
madly in love with her, so that she didn't feel ashamed of their
marriage. Would he be lying?

He was thinking about her far too much. But he had known
that would happen as soon as their lives collided. Known it the
day he stepped into the church. Or perhaps the first time he
heard her play. Or—

It didn't matter. Elias was right. Once Drasko set his sights on
her, she had drawn him into her world. And he didn't fight.
Didn't want to. She was his destiny, and he felt it the way one
felt the sun on a cloudy day or a dark night—it was there and
always would be. That was the nature of the universe.

"Finally," he heard Elias's voice in his mind.

"I envy you," Zeph had said when he found out that Grace
Mawr was the pianist from the Elysium. "She is fierce, brother.
Talented. Is she good in bed?"

Drasko had only rolled his eyes.

Could he tell his friend that he had only bedded her once,
fucked her with his fingers once, and kissed her fewer times than
any other woman he had ever had?

Yet the raging want for her was driving him insane. And wanting to bed her was only a small part of it. Away from her, that need was manageable. But as soon as she was around, it grew like a monster.

Like it did only that very evening, when he was returning home and the carriage rolled through the house gates.

Lately, Drasko had gotten to love coming home and walking into the house as piano tunes seeped from the music room. When Grace played one of the epic concert pieces, the entire ground floor seemed to breathe in rhythm with it. The servants straightened their shoulders and walked more elegantly. The guards looked graceful, like lords. There was a thick air of celebration. Drasko's house had a sound—her music.

Except, today, when he walked into the house, it was quiet.

Too quiet.

Samira met him in the hallway, a worried look on her face. "Sir, the missus is unwell."

"Unwell?"

"She was in pain all day. She has a fever, Eden said. She looks so pale."

"Did she have supper already?" Drasko tossed his jacket to the doorman and started for the stairs when Samira answered, "She left."

He stopped short. "Left?"

"Eden helped her into the carriage, and they both left. An hour or so ago."

Blood started pounding in his head. "Where?"

"She's had those pains since childhood, Eden said. And when it gets so bad that the missus can't move, they go to Miss Rebecca. Miss Rebecca has been helping her—"

"Tripp!" Drasko barked, ripping his jacket out of the doorman's hands. "Carriage! Now!"

He had carefully collected the information about every person in Grace's life, what they did and where they lived, including Miss Rebecca. And it just so happened that he didn't know anything about his wife's illness.

At this point, he was done lying to himself—that this was an arrangement, that he was acting civil for the masquerade's sake.

He cared. In fact, so bloody much that his heart was booming louder than a war drum as he darted out of the house and jumped into the carriage.

Samira ran out after him. "Sir!"

"What is it?" he asked impatiently.

She clasped her hands in front of her, her pleading gaze on him. "Sir, you will bring the missus home, won't you?"

45

DRASKO

Grace's carriage was parked at the corner drug store on 8th Street. Miss Rebecca's flat was behind it.

Nina stood by the entrance.

"She could barely walk, sir," she tried to explain as Drasko approached. "I was about to send you a message—"

He did not let her finish, just rushed through the door, into a dim hallway, then the drawing room, to one small parlor, then another.

"Grace!"

A maid tried to stop him, but he pushed past her, then past Eden who stood outside the door to a small room.

All these bloody doors, the rooms, the servants...

"Grace!" Drasko stepped into a small room like nothing else he had ever seen in London. But in India, they were so common —thick curtains, handmade rugs, low divans, vibrant colors, incense and candles, the smells so familiar he inhaled deeply, taking it all in.

"Mr. Mawr." Rivka's voice brought him back to reality as she stepped into his sight of vision. Her gaze was as always calm and kind. "Gracie is all right. But she needs some time to recover."

He stepped around her, and there she was, his wife, the sight of her so small and fragile that it made his heart clench.

Grace lay on one of the divans, curled into herself, both hands under her cheek. Her eyes closed, her parted lips opened now and then with labored breaths.

"Grace?" he asked softly as he walked up and sank to his knees.

Momentary panic rushed through him, then subsided—she didn't seem to be in danger, though visibly in pain and so very, very beautiful, even at her worst.

Drasko stroked her hair and studied the sweaty strands sticking to her forehead, her chapped lips, her eyelashes against her pale cheeks.

Her eyes fluttered open.

She saw him but didn't show surprise, seemed disoriented.

"I will be all right," her voice struggled through the silence between them.

"I want to take you home," he whispered, stroking her hair. "Is that all right?"

"I need a little…"—her eyes fluttered closed—"a little time… so I can walk," she said barely audibly.

Her feeble voice scared him. So did her ghostly mutter. The sight of her brought the memories of his past, people lost, time spent on things trivial instead of next to those who mattered.

Grace looked like a flower plucked from the ground and left for too long without water. She was wilting, still so beautiful but so weak.

His chest tightened at the sight.

Rivka's scrupulous gaze was on him as if she could see through him. Knowing the stories about her, he was sure she could. He was grateful Grace had a friend like this, giving her comfort when no one else could. When he, Drasko, wasn't there for her.

He grew angry at himself in seconds, at his own lies, his deceit, the games he played with her, teaching her those little lessons, one at a time, coaxing her out of her timid shell, provoking her. Whereas he should have told her how he felt and how much he cared.

"I am taking her home," he said, rising to his feet.

Rivka nodded. "Please take the medicine and tea. She will need them tonight and perhaps tomorrow."

"Tell me. Tell me what she needs."

"She will be all right by morning, Mr. Mawr," Rivka said. "She just needs care."

"Care?"

"Yes. Eden has done that for years. She knows what to do." That inquiring gaze of hers was on him again.

"Eden?" Why in the world did a maid know how to serve his wife and he didn't?

A flash of anger came and went as he looked at Grace again.

"The Sommervilles never told me about these pains of hers," he said bitterly.

"Of course not. Grace was a mere job for them. A contract," Rivka explained.

A contract—the word cut into him like a razor. That was what Drasko had called Grace right after their wedding.

"Do you know why her maid knows more about her than her guardians, Mr. Mawr? Not because the Sommervilles didn't care. But because her servants did. They loved her. Worshipped her. She played for them, you know."

"For the servants?"

"The Sommervilles did not much care for her or her talent. They were cold people, almost soulless, if I may. They only let her practice at a certain time. It was the saddest thing! They raised a piano prodigy and could not tolerate piano music!"

Now it made sense, Grace sneaking around, so protective of her music.

"Whenever the Sommervilles were away, Gracie played for the servants. I was there once, when she was twelve or so. A rare occasion, for I wasn't allowed there. She ordered all of the service staff into the music room and had chairs lined up in a row like at a real concert. Only twelve, she was so excited about it, polite and attentive. She put on her best dress, asked the staff to remove their caps and aprons—to make them feel like they were at a concert, you see. She stood by the piano and bowed to them." With a kind smile Rivka absently looked around as if remembering that night. "Then she announced the music piece she was about to perform."

Rivka's gaze drifted to Grace on the bed, so much endearment in it that Drasko felt envious of their friendship.

"She took a seat at the piano and played... Played... Played... And in the end, she got up and bowed again. The staff flung to their feet and applauded, Mr. Mawr. With tears and smiles. Oh, how they applauded! For some of them, that was the only concert they had been to or ever would. It made them feel important. And so for years, this was their little secret, Grace and the servants. For them, those performances were special. For Grace, that was how she learned to play from the heart. The prodigy of London was born out of playing for the servants. They were her most valuable audience. Until someone spilled the secret to the Sommervilles. And it all came to an end. And they started locking the music room..."

Drasko's heart throbbed.

Eden had once mentioned that Grace had had to follow strict rules at the Sommervilles'. But locking up the music room so she couldn't play when she wanted? What monsters would do that?

And here he was, making more rules for the woman he, of all people, should give the world to on a golden platter. The woman his heart was beating so hard for.

Drasko had tiptoed around the edges of his feelings for so long, clinging to the cliff of sanity. One wrong step, and he would fall headfirst. And the time had come, had come in fact a while ago.

He couldn't pinpoint when exactly he'd started free-falling. When Rivka's story began? Or when he'd heard the words,

"Grace is hurting"? Or when he stepped into his silent house hours ago? The house that, without Grace's music, was full of ghosts? When he'd first heard her play, years ago? Or perhaps when he'd stepped with her to the altar on their wedding day and finally felt her in his grasp?

No matter.

He had tried so many things to win Grace over. Bribing her, lying to himself that he enjoyed the game.

There was no bloody game. Not with her. What he wanted, all along, besides winning her heart, was knowing that she was safe and happy.

Not Eden or Rivka or Julien or God knows who would ever care more than him. They couldn't. They hadn't learned to fight monsters to do so.

Grace was his.

With her music and her pain and laughter and sadness. He wanted it all, all of her, suddenly envious that someone had a bigger past with her than him, greedy to know more, the things she'd never told others. For that would make him "the only one."

Drasko picked Grace up in his arms and cradled her against his chest. Her head lolled onto his shoulder. She whispered, "Home," or something of the sort. And he carried her out of the house like the biggest treasure he'd ever held.

The memories came back—how it felt to care for someone, love fiercely, without shame, and know what it was like to be loved back.

This woman in his life was his everything. And yet, he hid behind sarcasm and bitter jabs, played with the words and her feelings, acted like a peacock, spread his bushy tail so she could see what sort of man he was, what he had, how much he could offer, and how fast he could conquer her.

He was ashamed of himself.

He held Grace in his arms the entire ride to their house, thinking and thinking and feeling—her body against his, her hands resting on his chest, her breathing growing even, worried to death when she whimpered just slightly but weak with tenderness when she rubbed her cheek on his shoulder.

And he shamed himself for striking deals with her, whereas he could just gift his affection and hope that one day, it would make its way into her heart and perhaps bloom with something in response.

At the house, the guards stood silent as if in mourning at the sight of them arriving.

He carried Grace to his bedroom and lay her on his bed. She murmured something in her delirium, and he whispered words of comfort. His chest tightened at the sight of her fragile body, curled up, and he caught himself in a moment of desperation, for the first time in years, not knowing what to do.

Eden came in with a tray of hot tea and vials of medicine that she kept around for these episodes.

"I will take care of her," she said, pouring the contents of one vial into a hot cup of tea. She sat down on the edge of the bed, gently shook Grace awake, and made her drink it all.

All the while Drasko watched in a stupor. How did he not know any of this?

Eden nodded. "I will stay here, if I may. I shall see that she doesn't dwell in her nightmares too long."

"Nightmares?" he asked, surprised.

"She's had those since childhood, yes, sir. Especially when she had these pains. Quite awful. But I need to undress her and—"

"You may go," he cut her off.

"Sir, I—"

"You. May. Go," he insisted, nodding toward the door.

When the maid was gone, he gently shook Grace awake.

"Grace, I need you to get up for a moment."

She murmured something but let him help her up, gazed at him half-asleep and confused but didn't argue when he undressed her with the care of a doctor.

When she was only in her undergarments and camisole, he pulled a blanket over her. With only a faint light by the bedside, Drasko took a seat in the chair in front of the bed.

He didn't want a drink or a cigarette. There wasn't an ounce of sleep in him. He would sit and guard her sleep until dawn, until she opened her beautiful eyes, free of pain. He studied Grace and wondered how he had gotten so far in his denial about his feelings.

Drasko didn't know how much time had passed when her whimpers came, low at first, then growing louder as she curled into herself. Her hands crumpled the sheets.

He frowned, studying her face marred with invisible agony.

Another whimper came from her, her breathing suddenly heavy.

"Grace?" he called out, leaned over, and stroked her hair.

"Monster..." she murmured in her sleep.

His heart answered with a hurtful thud at the word. "What is it?"

"Nightmare," she whispered, sleepily rubbing her eyes. "Will you stay?"

The sound of her voice curled around his heart. He'd never leave even if she asked him to.

Drasko took off his shoes and his vest and crawled onto the bed behind her. His arms around her, he drew her into him, her back against his front.

"Sleep," he ordered gently.

"The monster will come," she said in her sleep. "With blood and screams..." She trailed off.

An ache saturated his heart as he kissed the top of her head. "He won't," he whispered. "Not when I am here."

He thought of the scars she tried to hide, the one below her ribcage, an atrocious mark of something from her childhood, something she never talked about and even her maid didn't know—he had asked.

He would protect her. From his business, from the Wollendorfs, from the diamond game. From more scars, if he could help it.

"I am right here," he whispered, watching her fall asleep and making a silent vow.

And she took his big hand in both of hers and cradled it to her chest.

46

GRACE

Her husband had seen her in her vulnerable tears, in her angry fits and mocking laughter.

And now, he had seen her at her worst.

Days had passed since her pains had gone away like they always had. Grace didn't discuss the episode with Drasko save for a soft, "Thank you," the morning she woke up in his bed.

Drasko didn't mention it, though his gaze on her became more attentive.

Grace was grateful for the days without pain, for the friends she now could freely have by her side, and for her husband who woke in her the most profound gratitude.

She spent her spare time learning anything she could about him. If his answers were elusive, she talked to the servants, *his* people, the ones who had been brought from overseas.

Grace was a musician, and if she'd learned anything throughout the years of practice was that persistence paid off.

And, oh, was she determined to know her husband better.

She had never been allowed anywhere around the servants' quarters at the Sommervilles. Now, she let her curiosity out. She freely walked into the kitchen, the size of a drawing room, the air thick with steam and spices. So many unusual scents assaulted her at once that for a second, she felt dizzy, exotic images fluttering in her mind like a colorful kaleidoscope.

There was a lot more Indian staff than she'd assumed, their vibrant loose garments in contrast with the strict English uniforms.

She smiled at the group of kitchen staff who flashed toothy grins, awkwardly bowing and wiping their hands on their aprons.

Narayan, one of the chefs, greeted her with a gracious smile, proudly showed her around, the tandoor oven and the rows of spice jars, and explained the intricacies of Indian cuisine.

She asked Samira to give her a lesson on Indian fashion.

Grace asked, asked, and asked so many questions that finally, the servants started telling stories without a prompt. How Drasko found immense joy in riding an elephant as a boy. How he fought with the Thuggees when he was a young master. How one summer, when he was with the work crew in the river delta, shirtless and tanned, a visiting Englishman mistook him for a worker. Drasko obeyed his every order and kept silent through every insult only to tell the Englishman at the end of the day that he didn't do business with men who didn't appreciate those who worked hard to make him a fortune.

Grace was falling in love with her husband. She cherished every minute with him, though he spent most days preparing for the auction. She craved him and wanted their second night, way overdue. But he wouldn't even mention it. Was there shame in asking him? But then he might say that he had been right.

Ah, the devil. This was indeed tricky.

She asked him about their wedding day. "You never told me why you married me."

He stiffened, though he didn't show emotion. "Several reasons."

"And they are?"

"One will offend you. Another will scare you. There is one more, but I am not yet ready to admit it."

She was intrigued. "All right then. Offend me. It wouldn't be the first time," she said with a smile.

"It's part of a deal I made some time ago."

"A deal," she echoed. "Why me?"

"Not sure."

Disappointment swept through her. "All right. The other reason—scare me, husband."

"No." His gaze hardened. "Not yet."

Two answers. Both mysteries. "Will you admit the third one?"

"All in good time."

And she was left with nothing again.

He cared for her, she knew it now, the only person who rightly did, besides Rivka and Julien. He started staying at breakfast longer and exchanged stories with Samira, mostly in English. And though those were stories from his years in India, they were meant for Grace.

So, she listened and asked questions and played piano in the evenings, leaving the door open, hoping that he would hear, and stiffened when he walked in yet continued to play but never sang.

She thought the infatuation with her husband was growing inside her. But no, this was deeper. She couldn't explain the overwhelming feeling of being next to him, the need to be closer when he already was, the flutter in her stomach when he gazed at her, the way she craved to know every bit about him, was hurt that she didn't, wanted the world to know he was hers.

Several days were left before the Summer Ball. It would be their first public appearance. She would perform, and she practiced day and night on the piano. It had to be perfect.

One day, she rode down Piccadilly with Nina. Grace had started enjoying having the woman by her side, a fighter at that. She constantly asked her all sorts of questions.

"When you fought men back home, during the matches, did you wear—"

"A one-piece, yes, and pants."

"No corset, huh?"

Nina gave her a side glance.

"Of course not." Grace laughed at her silliness.

Nina fascinated her, like any woman who was willing to step out of her comfortable life and do what pleased her. Especially something as extraordinary as martial arts. Grace secretly wished there was an opportunity when Nina had to fight. No, not to see her hurt, but to see her in action. The only action she'd seen until now was on the streets, Nina twisting big men's arms who dared to come close to Grace for no reason and once knocking out a man who followed her and Rivka at the City Square.

Riding down the street, Grace was about to suggest taking a walk when she spotted a familiar figure in the crowd—Zeph Brodia. He was walking by himself, seemingly not in a hurry.

Grace ordered the carriage to stop.

"Mr. Brodia!" she called out, fighting her way through the busy street toward him. "Mr. Brodia! Good afternoon!"

He smiled, shaking her hand. "What a surprise, Mrs. Mawr. Business? Pleasure? A sunny day out?"

"Too sunny for my taste." She fanned herself, the sun so bright that her summer hat felt like a hot bulky furnace on her head.

The street was indeed steaming with summer heat, the smoke from the factories too dense, the street hawkers too loud.

"I saw you in the crowd and wanted to chat," she admitted. "If you have a minute, of course."

"For you? Always! Anything in particular?"

She shrugged as they walked in an unknown to her direction. "Drasko said you knew each other before... Before he left for India. Is that true?"

"Absolutely. We lived together."

"Oh?"

"On the streets." Mr. Brodia smiled.

Her own smile fell. "Was he really a thief?" she asked carefully.

"Did Drasko tell you that?"

"No." She shook her head. "He doesn't tell me much. Doesn't want to, I suppose, but I..."

"But you?"

"I would like to know more about him. Where he came from. What he was like a long time ago, when he was little, perhaps."

"We lived in the slums, Mrs. Mawr." Mr. Brodia nodded, his hands clasped behind him as they walked. "We stole for a living, yes. If living was what we had. Most children that age don't survive for long. Did you know that?"

She bit her lip at the words.

"Then he disappeared," he continued. "I didn't see him until weeks ago. I thought he was long dead. It never occurred to me that Drasko Mawr, the Diamond King, was the boy I shared stolen bread and sleepless winter nights with in the East End."

"I am sorry."

"No need. We all have stories. Some people start well and end up in a ditch." He chuckled. "I like my story better. And Drasko's especially."

"What sort of business do you have with my husband now?"

"Are you worried?"

"Should I be?"

"Not with Bankees' protection. No, you should not." He grinned. "But there is a lot Drasko won't tell me. So, there is that."

"Protection, you say."

"Any man with such fortune needs protection, Mrs. Mawr. Though I have a feeling that the protection is more for you than him."

"Me?"

"You don't know your husband. A lot of what he does has to

do with you. Trust me, men like him would give their lives for their loved ones."

Loved ones.

"Women, Mrs. Mawr, make us do beautiful things. Also reckless ones. They make us lose our minds."

She laughed. "You are not talking about my husband."

That was, indeed, too much—loved ones, reckless, losing one's mind—too many words at once that didn't make sense in her and Drasko's arrangement.

"Your friend, Miss Rebecca," Mr. Brodia said suddenly.

"What about her?"

"A beautiful woman. Unmarried. Intelligent. Mysterious. A healer and a fortune-teller. What did I miss?"

"Oh, a dozen other things that you would know if you knew her better." Grace's heart warmed at the thought of her friend.

"How do I get to know her better? She seems a bit... hostile with me."

"It didn't seem so. Not at dinner."

"But she refused to dine with me again."

"Oh?"

"When I invited her a week ago."

"Did you?"

"And yesterday."

"I see..."

"In fact, today, I stopped by her shop to ask her again. She wouldn't give me a minute of her time."

"Mr. Brodia!" Grace bit back laughter. "You are a persistent man."

"Sometimes, you meet a person, and you feel... Hmm..."

"You were saying?"

"That she is like no other."

Grace nodded. She had felt the same way the first time she'd been introduced to Drasko.

"And I've known many women," Mr. Brodia said with melancholy. "But this is quite peculiar," he added as if to himself.

"Perhaps, the women in the establishments you frequent are of a different kind."

He turned to her as they walked, a humorous flash in his eyes. "That's a clever stab, Mrs. Mawr. I shall never forget that the first time I saw my friend's wife, she wore a pink wig, a Venetian mask, and was accompanied by a half-naked orchestra."

Grace blushed.

"I didn't mean to offend you, Mrs. Mawr. Please forgive me!" He pressed his palm to his heart. "I am used to talking to your husband in a very informal way, you see. Please—"

"No offense taken, Mr. Brodia. You are right. But I would like you to tell me more about my husband. And why he is nice to me now when he doesn't have to be."

"Why, men are absolutely illogical creatures when it comes to women they fancy. Unlike women."

"Women are not?"

"Women love men for their money, fame, confidence. No woman loves a man for the sheer beauty of him."

"Interesting."

"It is, isn't it?"

"If you assume that I want to get along with my husband because of his wealth, I do not. I was supposed to marry someone who didn't have anything but a title."

A newspaper boy ran up to Mr. Brodia and passed him a folded piece of paper. "A message, sir."

Intrigued, Grace studied the boy and Mr. Brodia, who read the message, then produced a pen from inside his jacket, scribbled something on the paper, and gave it back to the boy, who disappeared in the crowd in seconds.

"You know him?" Grace mused as they resumed walking.

"He is part of the Bankees' street runners."

She creased her brows in confusion.

"Nothing is quicker and more efficient than children," he explained.

"You employ children?"

"We give them work, yes, but also a home and protection. Why, you seem surprised. Don't be. Drasko and I grew up on the streets. We had neither. We used to steal, sleep in the gutters, and burn fires in the winter to keep warm. It was a matter of luck that we were *adopted*, if you may, by those who had more resources. Most homeless children don't get lucky. They die young. Or, if they grow up, they don't value things and others' lives."

"Do you?"

"Absolutely. And so does Drasko."

Elias's words came to mind, something he had said to her during the dinner at their house. "Drasko is the sort of man you ask for a thousand and he offers a million. He can get to know you and then cut your throat, metaphorically speaking. But only one look at someone, and he will offer his hand to pull that person out of the gutter. He has a unique sense about people."

The words had fascinated Grace then. But of course, her husband had unlimited resources.

"He values diamonds, I assume," Grace said in contemplation. "And what he owns."

"Diamonds are simply a product of trade, Mrs. Mawr. As to what Drasko owns, he doesn't own *you*, despite you being his wife. And yet..."

She turned to meet his smiling gaze. "And yet?"

"The way he talks about you..."

Her heart fluttered. "What does he say?"

"It's not what he says but *how* he says it. Like he has no other business in the world besides making you happy. Though he doesn't notice it himself. You are a woman. Women have a notion for those things, do they not?"

"What things?"

"Assessing men and their inclinations. Women are good at that. Unless, of course..." Mr. Brodia trailed off with a smile, making her even more intrigued. The way he talked left so much unsaid.

"Unless?" she pressed on.

"Unless a woman is blinded by her own feelings. Feelings make one lose perspective."

"My husband never loses perspective."

"Perhaps, you don't know your husband well enough."

"I wish I did, Mr. Brodia."

He chuckled. "Tell me something, Mrs. Mawr. Do you suppose your life would be different if you married that earl?"

It stunned her—the question so brazen, yet the one that in all the time spent with her husband had never crossed her mind.

She absently scanned the crowded street, searching out couples, some seemingly happy, others with blank expressions as if they were mere strangers to each other.

"I never thought of it." Embarrassment, mixed with repulsion, washed over her. "Nor do I want to think of it. And..."

"And?"

"And it petrifies me to think that I could've married that man."

"Why?"

"Because he is not even a fraction of the man I thought he was. And my husband is... Well, perhaps you were right about losing perspective."

Perhaps, she didn't need to have this conversation with a man she barely knew. But she was greedy for any bit of information about her husband. Feelings bubbled up inside her when she talked about him.

A whistle came from the other side of the street, then a closer one. Another boy ran up to Mr. Brodia and whispered something in his ear.

"I shall be there," Mr. Brodia said with a nod, and the boy took off down the street.

"Would you care to explain all this business with children?" Grace inquired. "You have me curious."

"You see, when one of the Bankees is in trouble, we have code words to send a message around."

"Code words?"

"So strikingly blue."

"Pardon me?"

"The code phrase—'so strikingly blue'—is for a kidnapping threat. 'So strikingly yellow' is for enemies infiltrating our establishments. 'So strikingly red' is for a blood fight or ambush. 'So strikingly dark' is for a life threat. We have a number of them and change them every season."

"How does that work?"

"If you ever see street children salute with a flick of their fingers on their hat or blinder—they are ours, they work for us. And the code is a request for attention or help."

"How unusual!"

"Helpful, I should say. When we are in public and surrounded by enemies but unable to speak clearly or give a sign, that's when the code comes in."

"And then?"

"And then"—Mr. Brodia grinned at her—"the fastest message system in the city goes in motion—Bankees' street runners. Newspaper boys, flower girls, fruit sellers, shoe cleaners—there is always someone watching. Because there is always an enemy at your heels."

The grim words made Grace shiver in unease.

Her gaze immediately swept across the streets, noticing children here and there, one of them, a crossing sweeper about ten years of age, nodded to her and flicked the underside of his blinder with his fingers.

"Huh." Grace looked around, amused. "Do you have enemies, Mr. Brodia?"

"Not currently. The last one ended up on the bottom of the Thames."

Her head snapped in his direction.

Mr. Brodia winked. "Don't take it to heart, Mrs. Mawr."

But the dangerous sparkle in his eyes did not escape her.

"Does my husband?" she inquired.

The humor in his face faded. He sucked in his cheeks.

"Mrs. Mawr," he said, avoiding her eyes, "I am afraid I have urgent business to attend to. It was my pleasure."

He bowed and, within seconds, was walking away, never having answered her question.

THE
SECOND LETTER

London, England
Drasko, 29
(A month before the wedding)

As head of Mawr Diamond Industries, Drasko finally made perhaps the most important decision of the past decade.

The cut-throat business didn't bring its former satisfaction. The South African diamond mining was growing, the competition cutting the Mawr trade at every corner. And though Mawr Industries was still the biggest and most reputable diamond company in the world, Drasko didn't need to prove anything to anyone. He had a better idea.

He would make a deal with the Wollendorf brothers, he decided. An alliance with the second-largest diamond mining company would make both stronger than ever before.

Uriah's pride had kept him from seeing more opportunities. Drasko's pride shifted his attention to more exciting areas—science and technology.

And so on a warm April day, only two months after the first letter, Franz and Heinrich Wollendorf, Drasko, and a dozen associates, sat at an outside restaurant on Willingberg Street.

The day was sunny. Their guards stood smoking at a

distance. The waiters were gracious. And the wine to celebrate such an occasion was aged two hundred years.

Too bitter, thought Drasko, wondering why this decision only years ago had brought the death of Alfred Mawr and now was the matter of a stroke of a pen.

Well, not that simple.

This was only the initial discussion of the terms, one Drasko had purposefully arranged in a public place.

There would be many such meetings in the next several months, with lawyers and accountants, international dealers, board members, and stenographers.

The Wollendorfs and Drasko knew the importance of what was about to transpire. The brothers were beset with poorly concealed gloating, for this had been a small victory but a victory, nevertheless. Drasko simply couldn't wait to let some of his responsibilities go away, giving him more time to tunnel his interest elsewhere.

And he couldn't stand looking at Franz Wollendorf. Something about the man reminded him of Uriah in his thirties, the similarity making him wish he was done with this deal already.

"We are very pleased with the decision you have made," Franz Wollendorf said, stroking the diamond ring on his middle finger.

He was the oldest brother and the main negotiator, his brother Heinrich much like Alfred Mawr had once been. *A long time ago.*

"I am pleased to think that the merger will make us indestructible in the international trade," the older Wollendorf continued, no doubt already contemplating how to eventually have Mawr Diamond Industries to himself.

Drasko didn't care much.

There was something odd about this sunny day. The street was empty, void of carriages or pedestrians. Eerily quiet, too.

The associates on both sides were exchanging whispers as they studied the business proposal documents.

Drasko narrowed his eyes on the figures in the distance—men smoked at every corner, their heads low, bowler hats concealing their eyes. Not *his* men, he knew that much.

He turned around searching the opposite side of the street—more men stood at the far end.

Drasko tensed with unease. The Wollendorfs didn't have an interest in intimidation tactics, not when they were getting what they'd wanted for years, or at least part of it.

At that precise moment, the clock on the Tower of London struck three somewhere in the distance, and the waiter approached with a tray.

"This was brought for you, sir," he said, lowering the tray that contained a letter to Drasko.

"Brought by whom?" Drasko inquired, a chill running through him as he stared at the cream letter, the brown seal, and a diamond in its center. *Letter number two.*

"No one among the staff knows exactly who brought it in."

Drasko's jaw clenched as he picked up the letter and tore the seal open.

> *You are not to sell Mawr Diamond Industries. Nor are you to make any sort of deal with the Wollendorf Consortium.*

The two lines made him suck his teeth in bitterness.

Franz Wollendorf fixed his tie as he flicked his eyes at the letter. "Is everything all right, Mr. Mawr?"

Drasko remained calm, slowly picked up his wine glass, and took a sip. *Too bitter.*

Suddenly, he was too hot, his expensive suit of the thinnest wool too bulky, his shirt sticking to his skin.

Rakshasa hissed behind him, bringing him to full alert.

He was being played again. Uriah, even dead, still held the

reins. This time, he was about to make Drasko look like a whimsical man.

That shall not do.

This very second, Drasko decided to go against the grain. How far did Uriah's dead hands reach, after all?

"Everything is all right, gentlemen," Drasko said, crumbling the letter and tossing it onto the table. "Let us continue."

Heinrich and Franz smiled so insincerely that Drasko felt the urge to rip those smiles off their faces.

The chatter resumed.

The documents were exchanged.

Suddenly, there came a strange shift in the air, not a breeze but something more profound, as if the air was being pushed by a giant wall.

The ground trembled.

Drasko, used to living in the country, not yet deafened by the noise of the city and attuned to such changes, set his wine glass down. His eyes darted around, the streets suddenly clear of anyone, even the smoking men, only the Mawr and Wollendorfs' guards standing around.

The shaking of the ground grew heavier. And though no one yet noticed, the wine glass in front of Drasko started trembling on the table surface, inching away from him. The flowers in the vases shivered. The heavy sound of something being trampled grew louder.

"Sir?" someone inquired worriedly as the rumbling from the distance turned into roaring with astonishing speed.

"Sir!"

"Mister Mawr!"

"Franz!"

"Heinrich!"

"Watch out!"

There were no hills in London, but the horse tram appeared out of nowhere, at full speed, heading directly at them.

"Move!" the shouts came, and Drasko pushed off the table, diving away, right as the horses and the tram they carried crashed with full force into their sitting area.

Tables and chairs burst out of the way, much like people.

Drasko was slammed onto the ground, Tripp on top of him, covering him.

The carriage slammed into the front of the restaurant, sending the glass from the window in sparkling fireworks.

When the crashing sounds stilled, Drasko slowly rose from the ground and shook the shards off his suit. His eyes searched for his partners, who were rising from the ground in shock.

People, suddenly many of them, ran toward the restaurant. A crowd was already gathering where there had been no one just a minute ago.

The tram sat mangled, sideways, halfway into the shop. Both horses lay on the ground, legs broken, bones pushing ghastly at their skin from within. Blood painted the ground red. But the driver was nowhere in sight.

Drasko glared around.

The crowd was gaping, growing by the second, and behind the people stood a man, smoking, a bowler hat low over his forehead, his eyes unmistakably on Drasko.

Another man stood a distance away.

Two more stood across the street.

Uriah's men. Drasko gritted his teeth. *Very well, warning received.*

He knew that the decision he had just made would make the Wollendorfs his enemies. But he'd learned to respect his enemies and their success. The more powerful the enemies were, the greater the sign it was that they chose you for your power, too.

A bitter smirk formed on Drasko's lips as he took his hat from one of his men and put it on.

"Gentlemen," Drasko said coldly, "I am not a superstitious man, but I am afraid we have to postpone our deal."

"Wait... What?" Franz grimaced. "This is uncalled for!"

But Drasko was already walking away.

Rakshasa burned on his back with the too-quickly-forgotten hate that was coming back, growling at Franz Wollendorf's words behind him, "You shall regret it, you gypsy."

48

DRASKO

"I searched the house," Grace said one day, "and I couldn't find a single diamond. Will you tell me why?"

"I don't mix business with my personal life," Drasko answered.

He didn't lie. Until the diamond game, that was true. True until the Crimson Tear had become part of it, and so had Grace.

Tonight was an exception. But then, there were so many lately.

Drasko knocked on the door to Grace's room.

"Come in!"

Grace stood in front of the mirror, Eden fixing her skirt, and Drasko came to a halt, mesmerized by the sight of her.

Grace turned, giving him a full view of the luscious emerald gown adorning her slender figure. Her hair was elegantly pinned at the back of her head and cascaded down her back. The dress opened her shoulders but left her arms covered.

She studied him too, his tuxedo and bowtie. Every day seemed to be enhancing her confidence. Her gaze had gotten hotter lately. Flirtier? Perhaps, it was all in Drasko's head. *Wishful thinking.*

She was breathtaking, though she was rightfully so even in a simple sleeping gown. *Or without it.*

"Gorgeous," Drasko complimented, taken by her beauty. "I have something for you."

Already dazzling, Grace didn't need diamonds, and the jewelry box in Drasko's hand was already burning his fingers. But today was important for Grace, and consequently, for the upcoming Mawr auction.

He opened the jewelry box and took out a necklace. *The* necklace—because of its cost, he'd had to hire an army of Bankees to escort them to the ball later.

Eden clasped her hand over her mouth.

Grace only dropped her gaze to the necklace, then lifted her eyes to Drasko.

"It consists of 9,235 diamonds weighing 320 carats," he explained as he stepped behind her. "A ninety-two-carat centerpiece." He wrapped the necklace around Grace's slender neck. "Seven hues of diamonds. Five jewelers. It took them ninety-six hours to complete the piece."

When he clasped the necklace closed, he stepped behind Grace and looked at her in the mirror.

Two layers of diamonds encircled her neck. The centerpiece was a rose made out of pink diamonds. Smaller yellow diamonds formed little butterflies. Dangling from the lower level were dozens of teardrops.

Grace put on the matching earrings he offered.

"The necklace is called *Arcadia*, after a Greek myth about Utopia," Drasko said. "It's supposed to be displayed at the auction. The fifteen pink diamonds in its center were cut from the same rough stone of the highest purity. Do you like it?"

She met his gaze in the mirror. "I do. I suppose it is worth—"

"A Buckingham Palace," he finished, then flinched at the words once said in a dingy tavern at the port. His memories were still infected by Uriah's words, but he shook them away.

"Don't go pawning it and running away to America or something." He winked at her.

She chuckled, the sound of it traveling through his entire body.

He met her playful eyes again. Her every glance was like a zap of electricity, every lingering gaze like warm candlelight in the dark.

There was a giant gap between only months ago and today. Her gestures were laced with a determination that puzzled him. Perhaps, she was growing used to him. This might be a good time to tell her what this marriage was all about. And everything else, everything meaning the bet, the way he had grown up in India, Rakshasa, the Wollendorfs, the game.

Grace turned to face him, her delicious lips so close that his previous thoughts vanished.

She stepped closer and lifted her face to him, her beautiful hazel eyes smiling. "Will you run away with me? Before the auction?"

How was it possible that she sensed something was coming, something painful that even Drasko didn't know about?

"You can keep the necklace," he said softly, shifting to the safer topic as they studied each other's faces.

She smiled a little. "You want me to wear it to the ball."

"Yes. But it is yours if you want it."

"I will wear it if *you* want."

Her smile became flirty as she raised her hands and fixed his bowtie, the gesture so simple but making his every cell come alive. Her fingers brushed gently against his chin, playfully but intentionally, a flirty butterfly touch. With a wicked little smile on her lips, she took his chin between her fingers only for a moment, mimicking his gesture, as she said, "But I don't mix business with my personal life, husband."

Touché.

Her touch was gone right away. In a second, she turned away. But his body flared up at the image of her in his head—

naked, with no diamonds or clothes, panting underneath him in the explanation of what that *personal life* was.

He studied her in the mirror, that delicious little smile he wanted to taste, and stifled a lustful grunt. Oh, he would have made her elaborate, but they were already pressed for time.

And so it was that one of the most expensive pieces for the Mawr auction adorned his wife's neck as an hour later they entered the marchioness's ballroom.

Heads turned in their direction.

The dancers stopped.

Hundreds of lights seemed bleak in comparison to the shine of the *Arcadia* diamonds.

Whispers swept across the large, crowded hall decorated with pompous statues and exotic plants, serving the finest wines and exquisite dishes that no one would talk about afterward because everyone would talk about the Mawrs.

Drasko knew it. So did Grace. An army of Bankees had followed their carriage and now guarded the entire block outside —the necklace was worth a fortune.

But the necklace didn't matter. *She* was Drasko's crown jewel, indeed, yet he'd never told her so.

The marchioness hurried toward them. "Ah! Mr. and Mrs. Mawr! I am so honored!"

Snake, he thought, noticing her hungry eyes on the necklace.

"Tonight's performance—we are so grateful!"

Of course, they were.

The Duke and Duchess of Trent were next to them, singing praises. Others already speculated about the price of *Arcadia*. The marchioness glowed with pride—it was her event that revealed one of the most talked-about pieces of the upcoming auction. The wealthiest of the city ah-ed and oh-ed in envious admiration. The more champagne and brandy they drank, the more open their stares were on Drasko and Grace.

Elias Bayne materialized out of nowhere, insistently hooked

his arms with Grace and Drasko's, and led them away from the insincere greeters.

"Drasko, mate, see to it that your beautiful wife does not get eaten alive by the local piranhas," he said discreetly. "You should know that's all the entire ballroom is talking about."

"The necklace?" Grace asked with a smile.

"You and Drasko."

"Oh."

"If you need to be saved, I am here for it. In fact, I should find my cousin and task her with keeping you company this evening."

Grace laughed. "That's all right. I am soon to perform. But, Elias!"

"Yes?"

She touched his shoulder. "You are my favorite person in this entire ballroom. Did you know that?"

Elias broke out in laughter, bowed to her then cocked his brow at Drasko. "You see?"

Drasko shifted his gaze to Grace, who cast hers down, yet he knew, could tell by the way she smiled to herself and bit her lip that this was a sweet provocation.

"Is that so?" he asked.

"I should go," Grace said, smiling. "Julien is waiting for me. I need to get ready and change."

"Grace?" Drasko called out to her and met her inquiring eyes. "I hope you destroy their little vain hearts with your music tonight."

She didn't answer but lifted her chin and walked off, leaving him with Elias.

"You are doing something right," Elias said, taking a gulp of champagne.

Drasko met his eyes. "How so?"

"There is a glow about her. This… When she looks at you… Or better, when she doesn't. Like she avoids it."

"And you suppose that's a good thing?"

"She is smiling when she doesn't. She is always smiling. Even when she's not."

"You don't make sense."

"She is glowing. You are blind, that's all. In love, of course. But whatever you are doing, keep doing it. Are you done playing games with her? Did you tell her yet?"

"About?"

Elias released a frustrated puff. "Why she is with you."

The truth would break her, Drasko knew. In the worst-case scenario, she would deem him a liar or insane. Perhaps, she would not forgive him—what he had done in the past and why she had been dragged into his present. And if that were the case, he wanted just a little more time with her. One more night, two, three, a kiss, a dozen, a hundred, however much he could get before the dreadful day of the auction.

So, Drasko waited.

Right now, he waited for his wife to perform. The necklace was a nice touch, but Drasko had come for the performance. For the first time, Grace would play with him in the crowd as her husband, and he stood tall like never before, his heart pounding in anticipation.

He spotted Heinrich Wollendorf in the crowd. The man nodded at him and hurriedly looked away. His brother, Franz, was too cowardly to show up at any event Drasko did.

"Ladies and gentlemen!" announced the concierge on the stage in the center of the hall, making the room full of people go still. "We are proud to present the jewel of music, Mrs. Grace Mawr."

Grace was performing a piece by Vivaldi, fierce and intricate —Drasko had heard it many times, knew it by heart, and anticipated the sound of it in a hall so grand.

The crowd surged toward the stage. Those behind it parted, letting the musicians walk to the stage.

Once again, the sight of his wife left him gaping, just like everyone else.

Grace walked up the steps, into the light of the stage, and the shocked gasps surged through the crowd.

She had changed indeed into a dress made entirely of pink feathers. A low décolletage exposed the upper slopes of her breasts, her shoulders completely bare. Her skirt flared into an intricate bell-shaped feathered contraption. A crown of feathers was in her hair.

Her dress would cause outrage for being too scandalous. But Grace looked like a goddess.

Poorly concealed gawking, envious stares, admiring leers from the elite—this was Grace's revenge against the staples of high society.

Drasko couldn't hold back a broad smile.

Her eyes found him in the crowd. She lifted her chin—she was taking the reins of who and what she wanted to be, and he was so bloody proud of her.

Elias nudged him with his shoulder. "If I didn't know better, I would have said that she was born a Bayne."

Drasko took a sip of whisky, watching her over the rim of his glass.

"Thaaaat's my wife... Brilliant," he muttered, pride swelling in his chest.

The small orchestra on stage looked like a mere prop compared to her. The violins, cellos, flutes, and a harp could not take away from the pure magic of the piano under her fingertips.

For half an hour, the crowd was frozen on their feet.

Men licked their lips and smoothed their mustaches, feeling fooled by the fate that would never let them have a woman like her.

Women's faces fell as they realized they'd never *be* her.

Drasko couldn't look away, smiling at how flawlessly Grace performed, though he knew the everyday grueling practice that went into it. His body hummed at the sight of her expert fingers racing up and down the piano keys, the same fingers that were fluttery and hesitant against his body the night they spent together.

And when the last piano notes echoed in the air, the ballroom erupted with applause.

Grace rose to her feet and slowly turned toward the audience.

Drasko greedily took in every detail—her graceful smile, the elegant nod and bow, the way her chin lifted just slightly as she dragged her gaze over the crowd as if it were her domain. There was a new confidence about her, a regal calmness. If these people were the cream of the crop of London's high society, she was undoubtedly their queen.

As if she knew exactly where Drasko stood among hundreds of others, her eyes found his. Across the sea of people and applause and conversations and clinking of champagne flutes, their gazes locked.

And there it was again—a fleeting shift in her gaze, a second-long vulnerability as if she were waiting for approval, like she had done so often in the past with her guardians.

Drasko applauded louder, and mouthed, "Brava."

The applause would not stop.

The marchioness walked on stage. "Dear guests," she said, her elaborate dress fading next to Grace's beauty, "may we ask Mrs. Mawr to perform an encore?"

The cheers were deafening.

Grace curtsied.

"An encore it is." The marchioness nodded. "And Mrs. Mawr is singing one of the songs she composed herself! How wonderful!"

Grace took a seat at the piano again, a smile on her lips. And when she touched the keys, Drasko knew the song, perhaps not the lyrics, but the sounds that had echoed through the hallway of his own house so many times, the sounds he'd learned by heart on the nights he listened to her music from behind the closed doors.

"*Silver burning in the heat,*" she started singing, a sensual tune so stark in comparison with the orchestral piece she had just played. "*Hazel drowning in the green.*"

"What is the song about?" Elias inquired. "I cannot quite grasp the meaning."

Neither could Drasko. At first. Until her next words.

"*Two shall whisper in the night. Two shall make the sun too bright. Two shall sing and make me wild and the lonely night alive.*"

A wave of shock washed over him as he started realizing the meaning.

"Is she singing about lovers?" Elias kept guessing. "That would definitely cause more rumors."

No, she wasn't singing about people, or at least that wasn't what "two" meant. Drasko's silver rings. His green eyes. His fingers...

When the song was over and Grace stood on stage, smiling graciously at the applause, Drasko pursed his lips in quiet astonishment—his wife was more daring than he'd ever believed she could be.

"Mr. Mawr, but how are you so lucky?" someone cooed next to him.

"Your wife is so mysterious."

"What is the song about?"

"Life, the past and the future," he answered vaguely. "Excuse me."

He walked toward the stage and waited for the others to make small talk with his wife, for the first time impatient and not wanting to share her with others.

"You were, as always, outstanding." He gave her a peck on her cheek.

"Thank you," she said, her cheeks flushed with that pretty pink he loved so much.

"You slayed them, darling. Your song was so sensual."

"Was it?" She looked away with a nervous smile.

"The newspapers will print the lyrics tomorrow."

She bit her lip.

"Do you mind telling me what the song is about?"

She was silent, avoiding meeting his eyes. "Where is Julien?" she asked.

Drasko stepped into her line of vision and dipped his head to meet her eyes.

"It's all right if you don't want to tell me," he said with a smile, placing his hand on her waist and drawing her closer. "I will tell you myself, and you tell me if I am wrong. Because your song"—he leaned over to whisper in her ear so no one could hear—"reminds me of my fingers pleasuring you one night in the music room."

A scarlet blush enflamed her cheeks.

Two young women danced by, singing, *"Two shall sing and make me wild."*

He chuckled. "So, you not only performed a vague song about your husband pleasuring you, but you got the ton to sing along."

"It's art. My songs... They are art."

"They are," he said low in her ear. "Will there be a song about my tongue between your legs? Called, perhaps, let's see, *Eloquent Prelude?*"

"Oh, God. Stop it!" She took a step away from him, her face flaming red when he laughed loudly. "You are insufferable, truly," she muttered.

He motioned to a waiter. "There, darling." He passed her a glass of champagne. "To cool off your pretty, burning cheeks. Let me know if you need help writing those lyrics."

She took a gulp of champagne, and he leaned over to whisper, "Perhaps, I can add my own. About you. The way your toes dig into the mattress when you forget yourself in pleasure."

She bit her lip, staring at her champagne flute.

"Or how your lips part and your head tilts back, your pretty eyes widening as if you have seen God."

Even the tips of her ears turned red, and he wanted to kiss

them, kiss that blush away until a new one came—her being undone under him.

"Or the way you arch your back when I touch your nipples."

"It is... I do not..." Her eyes were anywhere but on him.

"Another night, darling, and you will write so many songs."

"You were absolutely marvelous!" a female voice came from behind them, turning them around.

Dammit.

The brunette was as always gorgeous in her lavish blue gown and diamond pendant—why, the one he had given her years ago. Her smiling eyes were on Grace.

"Mrs. Mawr. I am in awe of your talent."

Grace nodded. "Thank you."

"My lady." Drasko smiled courteously. "What a surprise."

Surprise it was indeed.

His former paramour, Madeline Andreu, a wealthy titled widow only in her thirties looked, as always, dazzling. Memories flickered in his mind—her sharp tongue, exquisite taste in jewelry, an inquisitive mind, the witchery she did in bed.

Drasko needed to walk away. He wasn't interested and didn't want Grace to feel uncomfortable.

"Excuse me." Grace glanced between them, gave him a cold knowing smile, and walked away.

49

DRASKO

Madeline was a smart woman, and her approaching him and his wife was certainly with purpose.

"She is beautiful," Madeline said, her eyes on Grace in the crowd, who, in turn, chatted with other guests but glanced in Drasko's direction and was now downing her third glass of champagne.

Drasko never dwelled on his past relationships, never promised women what he couldn't give. Those in the past were fair exchanges. Madeline knew it well, and several years ago, they had had quite a grand time together.

What surprised him was the unusual nostalgia in Madeline's voice when she was telling him about her trip to Russia, yet her gaze leisurely swept over Drasko's form.

What he enjoyed was Grace's hostility as she studied Madeline from a distance.

"You are not interested," Madeline reproached, noticing his eyes on Grace.

"Pardon me?"

Madeline was an admirable woman of intellect and beauty, the qualities he'd once appreciated in her, yet they didn't affect him anymore.

"You cannot stop looking at your wife, Drasko dear." Madeline gave him a sad smile. "She is indeed lucky. And judging by the way you look at her, so are you."

He didn't know what to say to this, to the woman who had once occupied his thoughts quite a bit.

His eyes shifted to where Grace had just been, but she wasn't there.

"Please, forgive me, Madeline, but I do need to go."

She nodded, the light in her eyes fading.

"You deserve to be happy, Drasko," she said, trying to hold on to him for longer. Her gaze was etched with melancholy. "I hope you finally realize that letting someone in your life is not a weakness."

She had always understood him, accepted what little of himself he had to offer, and wanted more. Every woman always had. And at last, Drasko had a woman he wanted to give all of himself to, but his dear wife was nowhere in sight.

He pushed past the people, searched all around the ballroom until he saw her and Julien walk toward the entrance doors.

"Grace?" He caught up and blocked her path.

She smiled one of those smiles that didn't reach her eyes. "Julien and I are leaving."

"Julien and you." He cocked his head.

Julien cleared his throat. "I was merely escorting Grace, Mr. Mawr."

"What is the matter?"

"Nothing." Grace tried to walk around Drasko.

He blocked her path again. "Grace?"

"You are humiliating me," she whispered and tried to bypass him, but he stepped in front of her.

"How so?"

Julien stepped aside, awkwardly studying some Greek sculpture.

Grace looked down at her hands. "The way she looked at you, that woman, the way others looked at both of you, talking."

She met Drasko's gaze. "Tell me there was nothing between you two in the past."

That anger in her eyes made them the prettiest shade of burned honey. Her nostrils flared. Her rouged lips were pursed. His wife was jealous of another woman, upset, delightfully so.

"I cannot say that," he admitted.

"Ah!" That bitter flash in her eyes was back. "Go on then. Maybe the headlines tomorrow will wonder why Drasko Mawr needed a wife at all when there are plenty of women to keep him company."

She pushed past him.

Julien shrugged. "Is Elias Bayne here?" he inquired.

"Yes. Somewhere. Do be mindful."

"Of what, Mr. Mawr?"

"Of Elias. I don't want to lose my wife's instructor to wild sea adventures."

Drasko motioned a hurried goodbye to amused Julien and caught up with Grace.

"So, we are going home. Fine," he told her. "I would love a private performance."

He flashed smiles to the passing guests and caught sight of Grace's little glares in his direction. Rakshasa on his back sang at the fact that his wife acted like a possessive lover. Finally!

The hurried clicking of heels behind them and a loud voice stopped them in their tracks.

"Leaving?" The marchioness caught up with them. "So soon?"

"Newlyweds," Drasko explained with a smile. "My wife is very protective of our evenings together. If you know what I mean."

"Liar," Grace whispered as they were walking out into the courtyard a minute later. "You should have stayed with your little paramour."

"She is not."

"But she was."

"A lot of things happened in the past. Or did you think I was saving myself for an arranged marriage all my life?"

She glared at him as they approached their carriage, reluctantly took his hand as he helped her inside and held her impossibly lavish feather skirt. She pushed his hand away, that pretty scorn on her face making him grin.

"Mr. Mawr?" A figure approached, right away blocked by Tripp—Papadakis.

Drasko motioned his guard to step aside.

"I heard Mrs. Mawr's performance at the ball was divine," said Papadakis.

The press, of course, was not allowed inside, but the man's presence here was quite timely.

"One of the songs my wife performed was composed by her," Drasko said to the man. "*Two Chances of Bliss*, a truly poetic piece. Print it tomorrow."

Papadakis nodded, scribbling in his notepad.

"Heinrich Wollendorf attended," Drasko added. "*The biggest diamond rivals came together for a night of beautiful music. Mrs. Grace Mawr might have tamed the diamond war, if only for an evening.* Print that too. Don't mention the marchioness."

He hopped inside the carriage and shut the door.

"Enticing newspaper rumors?" Grace asked with bitterness.

"Is something I said not true?"

"You didn't need to mention my song."

"Do I hear regret? If you don't want your private life known, you don't sing about it to hundreds of people. But you did. Will you at last admit to yourself that you are very much infatuated with your husband? Because your jealousy was a clear sign."

"What am I to do when my husband openly converses with his former paramour?"

He understood her bitterness now.

The frequent thought in the last weeks that she could've ended up with Charles had angered him, disgusted him, and infected his mind with horrible visions. If even a fraction of such feelings coated her words right now, then he was done torturing her.

His playfulness deflated in an instant.

The carriage started moving, and they sank into the dimness of the small space, so very intimate, just like everything when they were alone.

"You still don't see it, Grace," he said quietly.

"See what?"

He exhaled loudly in tension.

They had danced around each other for weeks, and he was about done waltzing through this marriage business. He had never been afraid of his feelings.

With her? Well, she had changed that. Pride was the answer. But also that same silent dread at the thought that she would be punished for his affection. And yet, he so desperately wanted to take a chance.

"My problem is that I have a wife who I cannot stop thinking about," he said finally, tense as a rod, confessing for the first time. "This two-nights-a-month business is nonsense. The only reason I can keep myself sane is because I have the memories of the night in the music room, and the night you stayed in my bedroom. It's hell, for I go in circles through those memories. And yes, I can serve myself with my hand. But I shall never go to another woman, nor can I look at any other woman, because my wife takes up my entire bloody mind."

He had always been truthful with women he courted and bedded. And yet, Grace was the only one he hid his feelings from.

"You are lucky we have an agreement," he continued. "Because I wouldn't have let you out of my bedroom for weeks otherwise. I have to change my sheets every day because they are soaked with my need for you. I have to excuse myself at meetings because I think of you and it makes my body react in a way that's inappropriate in public. So, other women, Grace? They don't exist. There."

Grace stared at her hands, and he couldn't make out if she was shocked by the explanation or happy. This was a confession on his part, however small, and he clenched his teeth, waiting for her reaction.

"So..." she whispered. "You haven't been with other women since... since we married?"

That was some accusation! "No, I have not. And I don't intend to."

Silence followed, testing his patience.

"Tell me you are jealous, Grace, and I will never talk to any woman I was close with."

"How many?" She gave him a side glance.

He stifled a relieved chuckle. "*That* I won't tell you." His wife was curious, and that was a good sign already. "Tell me you were jealous, and I will never so much as say a word in their company."

"I am," she said softly and pursed her lips but turned to meet his gaze.

"Good. I am your husband. Only you get to touch me."

"And I don't get to very often."

Stunned, Drasko cocked a brow. "Do I hear a complaint?" he inquired carefully.

"I am merely stating a fact."

"Perhaps you should tell me more often what you want, darling."

"Perhaps..." She leaned into him, and her hand glided to his thigh, the gesture so surprising that he instantly felt himself grow hard. Her champagne-sparkly eyes flicked to his lips, a wicked smile on hers. "Perhaps, my husband is incapable of fulfilling his marital duties."

In-bloody-capable?

He had to repeat the words in his mind again, had to do a double take, to make sure it was, in fact, his wife, leaning so close to him, touching him in a way that only happened in his bedroom. One time. One night.

"Say that again?" he dared her.

Her hand didn't move. She had had quite a bit of champagne, enough to loosen her mouth, and that mouth was undoubtedly asking for attention.

She didn't repeat herself and didn't look away when her hand on his thigh shifted, making his body come alive under her touch.

He dropped his eyes to her lips again. "If you so much as move your hand an inch closer to my privates, I will abandon the silly notion of being a gentleman and show you right here and now how dedicated I am to marital duties."

Her gaze burned with that hesitation again. The desperation of wanting it and yet being afraid—so obvious despite how much she tried to hide it.

A part of Drasko wanted her to move away, just so she burned with her need for longer, until they got home, because he was not letting her go tonight. *Absolutely fucking not.*

But the bigger part of him dared her.

And then her hand moved. Just an inch. An inch in the direction of no return, burning Drasko with prickling heat.

And he was done playing this game.

A single thought ran through his head, *"I'll wreck her tonight,"* before he pulled her flush against him and kissed her.

50

DRASKO

She parted her lips for him so willingly that Drasko knew the moment he kissed her it would be the other way around.

She would wreck him. It was only a matter of time. Days, perhaps, or mere minutes.

Minutes, yes, because as soon as he pulled her against him, she quickly straddled his lap, as if she'd done it before, as if the expensive dress crumpling over his lap didn't matter.

He was already losing his mind to her, to her scent that raced into his nostrils, the messy kiss and their lips greedily fusing together. Her fluttery breaths against his lips when she protested, "My dress," though she was the one who'd straddled him, disregarding the delicate feathers coming apart at the seams. Her, "Drasko," when his hands fought her skirts to find their way under them, to her legs clad in stockings, then higher, where he found her bare skin and gripped her thighs, hoisting her closer to him.

He wanted to fuck away every tortured second of being unable to touch her. It had been too long. He'd only had one night with her. Two—two per month—that was the agreement.

Fuck agreements! He would fuck her into next week.

Whisky's bitterness and champagne's sweetness mixed on

their lips. Low moans, soft mouths, rough touches—he couldn't hold back.

Everything was too much and too intense. The hunger with which Grace kissed him as he fought his belt and the buttons of his trousers. The desire that spiked in him when her hand touched his privates, if only through the fabric. Her gasps when he yanked at the feathers, trying to find his way to her breasts. Her whimpers when he did, unveiling more and more of her bare skin, tearing the garments at the seams.

She moaned when his other hand snuck under her skirt again, fought through the silk ruffle of her undergarments, and his fingers found their way into her soaking wet warmth.

"Fuck," he muttered.

He wanted more. More of her. More of them touching each other. Less of the annoying feathers that obstructed his access to her. He tried to maneuver among them, all that bird nonsense that hid her body.

She panted. He grunted. She moaned. He kissed her harder.

"I want my night," he muttered as her fingers unbuttoned his vest, though he wanted them where his undergarments were about to be ripped by his erection. "Turns out, I am not such a patient man. Not with you, Grace."

A grunt escaped him, then a quiet curse.

He tried to find more of her hot flesh beneath her undergarments, then gave up and ripped the fabric apart.

"There," he said impatiently.

He just needed enough of her bare to get inside her.

But no, no, no, he could not do it in a hurry. He wanted her to crave this, so much that she abandoned this nonsense about two nights per month that he, in fact, had come up with. He should have said every week. Should have said twice a week. That would make the wait bearable.

Her closeness right now was anything but.

Drasko thought he was an expert in bed. But she—she was weaving her woman's charms on him with her innocent whispers and hurried touches. Her hands so unskilled in the art of pleasing were lighting his every cell, leaving a trail of little fires in their wake as they trailed down his body.

One little moan of hers made his hardness twitch in anticipation.

One little whisper, an absent, "Yes," to his touch sent his heartbeat racing.

One touch—just a brush of her fingers against his bare cock— would be the death of him. Good thing her lips hadn't touched it yet, for he would perish in ecstasy.

Dammit!

He was kissing and touching his wife, meanwhile falling apart like an adolescent boy at the first sight of a naked woman.

"Up," he ordered and hoisted her off him, then sank onto the floor between her legs.

He yanked her to the edge of the seat, pushed her legs open and her skirt up.

And there she was, his wife and all her charms right in front of him, peeking from behind the ripped undergarments.

She tried to close her legs, but he kept them apart.

"There." He took her hand and brought it to the junction between her thighs. "Show me how you touch yourself."

"I don't," she panted, her bewildered gaze on him.

She was so undone and beautiful. The top of her dress was pushed down, exposing her breasts. Her pink feathers gathered around her thighs, her long legs clad in stockings open for him.

She looked like a woman seduced by her lover—a sight that made Drasko grunt with want.

"Liar." With a smile, he pushed her legs open wider. "Do it. Slowly. Touch yourself for me, and I'll watch."

He leaned over and kissed her, coaxing the bravery out of her, until he felt her hand move. He sat back on his heels and watched as she pleasured herself, first timidly, with a look of utmost shame on her face, though her eyes were blazing.

"Did you think of our night together when you did it alone?" His eyes were on her hand moving in slow delicious strokes. He pushed his trousers down, freeing himself, and fisted his erection.

Grace was quiet, for the first time openly studying his manhood as he leisurely stroked himself.

"Darling? I need an answer."

"Yes," she exhaled, not looking up, breathing heavily as her eyes bore into his hand wrapped around his hardness.

He covered her hand with his, for a short while following her movements, then gently pushed her hand away and replaced it with his.

He stroked himself. His other hand stroked her.

"Look at you," he whispered. "So beautiful."

He leaned over. His lips replaced his fingers.

She threw her head back and whimpered, swaying just a little, letting herself be pleasured.

She moaned loudly as his tongue licked her throbbing flesh. She threaded her fingers into his hair, guided him this time, moved her hips to get him where she wanted.

He stroked himself, craved to be inside her but wanted to see her fall apart first. He grunted and cursed, slowed his strokes so as not to come, and gave her soft orders.

She did as she was told, opened wider when he asked, used her fingers to open herself for him, mewled as he licked at her wetness, and moaned loudly when she came on his tongue, her moans like a song that belonged only to him.

And then Drasko, the great lover he thought he was, lost his patience.

He found himself on top of her, thrusting in her as gently as he could at first, though he wanted to spear her through.

"Jesus," he grunted.

Had it ever felt so good? No. Had any woman ever looked so beautiful half-naked? Never.

Her extravagant dress made her look like an angel, her body

splayed among the feathers as he rummaged through the silly mess to find more of her skin.

His movements grew hurried and greedy as he thrust into her. The feeling was different than ever before. His blood was sizzling. His cock was hard and needy. He didn't want to climax. He wanted to be inside his wife, wanted to infinitely feel her closeness.

"Tell me if I am too rough or if it's too much," he told her and smiled when she whispered, "More," though she was too inexperienced yet to tell him what *more* meant. It was so hard to hold back, but he tried, wanting to see her fall apart around him one more time.

"Do you like the way your husband feels inside you?" he asked and grunted at her eager, "Yes," at the way she whispered, "Drasko." The way her lips sought out his. The way her hands in his hair became frenzied. The way she gently bit his neck, whimpered, and buckled under his thrusts.

She came again, seized around him, gasped, and he wished he could see her face, that expression of awe as if nothing had ever felt so good—him, inside her, on top of her, licking at her neck as her moans echoed through the dim space.

And then his mind switched off and gave in to the sensations of being inside her.

A few more thrusts and Drasko came so powerfully that he couldn't get enough, still thrusting inside her afterward, still hard and wanting to come again, but eventually forced himself to stop.

He helped her dress in the shambles of feathers that still clung to her body.

When the carriage pulled up to the house, he wrapped his jacket over her shoulders and helped her outside.

He had completely forgotten about the army of Bankees, the most dangerous gangsters in London, who had escorted their carriage home while he was making love to his wife. He had forgotten about Tripp and Nina, who suddenly appeared behind them as they walked to the house entrance, Grace's dress leaving a trail of little pink feathers behind.

Holding his hand on the small of Grace's back, Drasko ordered, "My bedroom," and she obeyed, walked silently by his side until they were upstairs.

His eyes dropped to her diamond necklace as he shut the bedroom door behind them.

"That has to go." He took the necklace off her and tossed it carelessly onto the bureau.

He licked his lips and noticed her eyes dropping to his mouth right away.

"I like when you look at me like that," he said, taking off his bowtie.

"Like what?"

"Like you want me to lay you on my bed, kiss you head to toe, and do obscene things to you that take you to your peak and make you moan so beautifully, but you are afraid to say it out loud and instead, dance around, waiting for me to take the first step." He started unbuttoning his vest while she stood motionless and watched him with a dare in her beautiful hazel eyes. "Sort of like that." He took a step closer. "It's all right, because I like being first. First steps. First night. First *chance of bliss*." He chuckled. "I will have so many of your firsts, Grace," he murmured, stepped into her, and kissed her. His arms wrapped around her delicate waist and drew her flush against him.

"You want more tonight?" she asked absently, her fingers already twisting in his hair.

Her question was so untimely that he pulled back to catch her eyes. Was that hesitation in them?

"I do," he said. "We both know how this night might carry on. But only I know all the things I can do to you. Say yes, Grace. Let go of your silly modesty."

"Things?" she whispered against his mouth.

"And if you leave my bed before I tell you that you can do so, I will fuck you into next year. Understood?"

Her lips parted in a response, then closed.

"Grace, make up your mind. I am not demanding anything from you. Nor am I forcing you. I am simply asking—"

"Yes," she cut him off. "Will you stop talking?"

She kissed him greedily. Her hands snuck under his shirt.

But he didn't stop talking. And as he ripped the pieces of the feather mess off her body, he whispered obscenities, the things he would do to her, which part he would invade first, something about *Two Chances of Bliss*, and *An Eloquent Prelude*, how many times she would reach her peak, how many times he would take her before sunrise, that she would not be allowed to wear clothes in his bedroom anymore, that he wanted her in his bedroom during the day.

And he followed up. He laid her down on the bed, spread her wide like an eagle, and started with *An Eloquent Prelude*.

51

GRACE

Drasko avoided her for two days. Two days and no sight of her husband!

Grace tried to fight the bitterness as she sat alone at lunch and read the latest *Tribune* article:

Grace Mawr's Hidden Talent:
Her Song "Two Chances of Bliss" Is Truly a Poetic Work of Art,
Quickly Becoming the Public's Favorite.

Irritated, Grace tossed the paper aside.

Stupid.

This was all stupid. Her songs. Her pathetic attempts to seduce her husband. She was too caught up in her feelings while he was simply treating her as... the deal, right. They had agreed upon it. So now, after their night together, he was avoiding her.

Another newspaper headline drew her attention:

The Diamond King Hires an Army to Guard the Summer Ball As
His Wife Wears the Most Expensive Necklace in London.

Was that his ploy to advertise the auction? Dressing her like a doll, decorating her with diamonds, the stones he himself never touched?

A seedier newspaper—and Grace had requested a servant to buy as many as he could find—was much bolder.

If Wealth Defines This Country, Then Who Are the True King and Queen?

Of course, the article was about her and Drasko.

To others, he was the Diamond King. But Grace had known him for a while now. And behind the powerful Drasko was a different one. Quiet. Withdrawn. Sometimes playful. Most of the time gentle.

She had learned to observe him secretly, noticing a frown on his forehead, the way he got quiet when no one was looking, deep in his thoughts. In rare moments like this, his gaze lost its coldness and acquired almost nostalgic warmth. Those weren't happy thoughts.

Could she ask him what bothered him? He would dismiss her, with his forced humor, like he always did.

That was why she never asked him about the *two nights*. The desire to be with him made her weak. She shamed herself for that and tried to act cold.

And she found the release—in her music, the notes that carried with them all her feelings, the lyrics that told her story.

The auction was in a few days, and she knew, rather felt, that it was important to Drasko for a different reason than to prove the grandeur of the Mawr treasures. But Drasko would not tell her.

Grace met Rivka in the botanical garden.

"Why, you are all bright-eyed today!" Grace exclaimed as she embraced her friend. Her own mood had been sulky the last several days. "Is there something happening with you I am not aware of?"

"Nothing," Rivka dismissed her too quickly.

"Liar. You are such a lovely liar!" Grace laughed. "Tell me at once!"

"There is nothing to tell!"

"Very well then. I shall not tell you what Mr. Brodia said about you the other week."

"Zeph? What did he say?"

Grace narrowed her eyes on her friend. "Since when do you call Mr. Brodia by his first name?"

Rivka huffed in annoyance and pretended to study the magnolia tree they were passing.

Grace cocked her head, observing her friend with curiosity. "I have never seen you like this, Rivka."

"Like what, my lovely?"

"Hesitant."

Rivka, always so confident and wise, was suddenly quiet, her gaze roaming around, her smile ghostly.

"Very well, don't tell me," Grace said, disheartened.

They walked in silence for a while before Rivka spoke again. "Mr. Brodia and I went to the theatre yesterday."

"I see. Zeph, you mean."

Rivka blushed.

"Why is that a secret?" Grace asked.

"It's not."

"Why are you coy about it?"

"I don't know."

"You refused him many times. He told me so. What made you change your mind?"

Rivka's prolonged silence was unlike her. "There is a brief accident in the future..." She went quiet again. "Did you know that some have pre-set paths in their lives? Others have variations. I don't know how to explain it..."

"You never told me that before. Did you see something?"

"Something... grave, I suppose. And if it's avoided, he and I..." She shrugged nervously. "I don't want to have a choice or blame myself for someone's life if it were to happen."

"Can you not see it?"

"Not my own path. Not clearly, no."

Despite the sadness in Rivka's voice, Grace was intrigued, never having been able to pry anything about her own future out of Rivka.

"But you did not seek me out today to talk about me, Grace," Rivka said knowingly with a much more cheerful smile. "What is bothering you, my lovely?"

"You won't tell me anything. What's the point?"

"Why do you want to know?"

"Why wouldn't I?"

"Do you care?"

"Of course, I care what happens to me!"

"To you? Or to the two of you?"

"This is a deal, Rivka. Drasko and I are a deal. He said so. We decided so."

"He is a great businessman. Seems as though you are learning to make deals too, Gracie." Rivka laughed. "I told you to be patient, and you listened. Everything should be fine. I am happy that you finally don't resent the man and can peacefully live by his side."

"But that's not what true marriages are!"

Rivka raised her eyebrows. "Plenty of them are. So is yours. Yours is a good deal, Gracie."

"But marriages... He is not... I am..." Gah! She couldn't find the right words.

"Gracie, I think you got the best deal of all of them. This deal is working out. And the deal is only as good as the parties fulfilling them."

If Grace heard the word "deal" one more time, she would jump in front of a carriage.

But Rivka only laughed. Laughed! While Grace wanted to cry!

"I see what you are doing," Grace said with hurt.

"Your deal—"

"Quit it!" Grace shouted and right away was ashamed of her own reaction. She took Rivka's hands in hers and met her eyes. "I am sorry, Rivka, I didn't mean to yell."

Rivka pulled her hands away and started walking, Grace following her.

"You need to ask yourself one question, Gracie," Rivka said, suddenly no smile on her face. "If it came down to the worst scenario, if something threatened your marriage, perhaps threatened Drasko, if he sacrificed himself for you—despite what you think he feels, and you are probably wrong—but if he did, would you be able to carry on without him with no regrets?"

Grace frowned at her. "What are you saying?"

"Would you?" Rivka pressed on grimly. "And if it came down to it, what would you be willing to sacrifice for this *deal* of yours? Because when you think about it, truly think about it, you will realize how much you are not telling yourself or him. And perhaps you should. Truth, however hard, is a weapon."

Grace halted, watched Rivka carry on until her friend noticed her absence, turned around, and met her gaze.

"Rivka," Grace said, her stomach twisting with unease. "What are you not telling me? What do you see?"

Rivka walked back to her. "Humans are incredible creatures, Grace. There are little people with the hearts of warriors. And there are brutal warriors with tender hearts. Most people are not what they seem. What *you* need to do is look inside yourself. The biggest strength is not wearing a mask for others and putting on a show. The biggest strength is having the courage to see oneself for who one is, show it to others, and be able to carry on with one's chin lifted high."

The words haunted Grace for the rest of the day.

She sat alone at dinner, the empty seat of her husband gaping at her with scorn. She barely ate and sat in the dining room until the darkness fell.

Samira turned on the lights and asked her softly if she wanted tea.

"Did he send any messages?" Grace asked.

"No, madam."

"Did he come home at all while I was gone?"

"No, madam."

Grace nodded, rose from her chair, and walked to his office.

The heavy doors opened into a large room with a giant cherry wooden desk, black leather furniture, and floor-to-ceiling bookshelves. Plush carpet, palm trees, Indian avatars on the walls—this was so Drasko, exotic and mysterious.

In all the months that Grace had lived here, she had never made it to his office. Perhaps she should have, but he had never invited her.

Grace inhaled deeply, absorbing the scent of sandalwood and frangipani, laced with whisky and tobacco, all of it such a bizarre combination, yet so Drasko.

She brushed her fingers along the cold wood of his desk, then went around it and took a seat in the leather chair, so big it swallowed her.

She looked around, trying to see things through Drasko's eyes. This was what he was accustomed to seeing from his throne, day after day, yet not even once had she walked through these doors.

Her gaze swept across the paintings from exotic lands and the sculptures of Indian deities, the art so unique and not the usual collection of lifeless masterpieces that many of the rich liked to hoard.

And then her eyes dropped to the desk in front of her with neat stacks of papers on both sides, pens, and quills, and—

She took in a sharp inhale.

A small painting drew her attention. She picked it up and studied it up close.

There it was—the scene that had nagged at her for years, that awoke the dark feelings as she first met him.

A flash of memory.

A scene from her nightmares.

No, it can't be...

Goosebumps covered her skin at the sight. His biggest secret was right there, in front of her eyes. The story he had never told her. The story that none of his servants ever talked about, no matter how much she asked.

She needed to see him!

It was close to midnight when she rushed out of the house.

Nina followed. "Ma'am, it is much too late."

Grace only shrugged, summoning the carriage. "If it's any consolation to you, we are going to look for my husband. Do you know where Mr. Mawr is? Perhaps he is in a questionable establishment."

"I think not, ma'am."

"And you would know?"

"He is not that sort of man."

"Again, you wouldn't know."

But Grace knew it too.

She was afraid of her feelings, so intense and taking her by storm. Was afraid of that unexplainable connection she'd felt the very first time she saw him in the crowd. And she was afraid to lose it.

She had been wrong all along. Drasko Mawr wasn't cold. He had a beautiful soul that he hid in the deepest corners of his heart, afraid to let others see it. Powerful men had that fault. They shared compassion and wits, keeping their best parts to themselves, as if they were the biggest treasure.

Grace had found out where he had spent the first nights after their wedding—his place of solitude, the tower. If he wasn't still working or wasn't at the tower, then she was wrong about him, but it was worth trying.

Determined, she rode to the Mawr Building, the ride gloomy, her heartbeat racing ahead in hopes of finding him there.

The night guard at the Mawr Building greeted her with a deep bow. "Mrs. Mawr, welcome."

"Is my husband here?"

"I believe so. His guard is upstairs."

"Wait here," she told Nina and took the elevator upstairs.

Tripp sat in the chair at the office door.

"I need to see my husband," Grace declared.

He rose, protecting the doorway. "He is at the tower. He is not to be disturbed when he is there, ma'am," he said apologetically.

"I need to see him," she stated simply, already relieved at the news.

"I am not allowed to go up there, but you can leave a message."

"By God, Tripp! Step away from the door!" she snapped, having lost her patience. "I *will* see my husband. And if you don't let me through, I will not talk to you for the rest of my days. It's not a threat, but a promise. Step. Aside."

Casting his gaze down, Tripp opened the door for her.

She walked through Drasko's dark empty office and paused at the door that led to the tower.

Her bravery died right there, but there were things she wanted to know—from him, not from the newspapers or silly gossip.

Determined, she pushed the door open.

The tower was just as dark. The little windows along its walls shed the dim moonlight inside. Grace held her breath as she set her foot on the first step of the windy metal staircase, then another, and slowly made her way up, every step making a bell-like ring.

She reached the top, a small platform surrounded by a cylindrical wall and a door. What would wait for her there?

Her heart galloped as she knocked and, without waiting for a reply, pushed the door open.

A lone lantern illuminated the small room with windows all around it. A mattress lay on the floor, a pillow and a sheet over it.

Her eyes fell on the figure across the room.

Drasko sat with his back against the wall, his forearms resting on his raised knees. Smoke curled around him from a cigarette burning in an ashtray on the floor. A bottle dangled from his fingers. He was barefoot, his trousers rolled up, his shirt half-unbuttoned and untucked.

He was again so very... humble.

Their eyes locked across the dimly lit space. He didn't look angry, but his gaze burned through her.

His voice was unusually quiet but with a hint of a dare when he blinked slowly and finally said, "So, you are here, Grace."

52

DRASKO

No one was allowed at the tower. It was truly his. This place was built to remind him of *the lone path of the king*, the words spoken once by a man who had taught him everything and indeed made Drasko's path lonely.

The words were truly sad. Perhaps not to those great men who lived to serve others. But to those who built a fortune for themselves, made allies and enemies, but didn't have a single person by their side to share their success with.

Drasko had gotten to understand it. Hence his need to build other businesses. Hence his aversion to diamonds. Hence him seeking out brilliant minds and investing in their visions of the future, a future for the people. He understood that once he reached the top, there was nowhere to go. He couldn't build higher, but he could build wider, making room for those who would stand by his side.

And now Grace was here, the only other person ever having set foot in this room.

Drasko had tried to avoid her for several days. It was easier to be away from her. Easier to pretend those nights together were a simple deal. It was easier to tell himself that she wouldn't be hurt in this wicked diamond game. That she wouldn't be like those others, who'd lost their lives because of him.

Lies, of course. Nothing was ever easy with her.

His heart was heavy, his mind a mess. Two days were left until the auction, and two more letters were yet to arrive. As fearless as Drasko thought he was, he dreaded them, was going mad, hoping that somehow, the game would spare her.

"What is the matter, darling?" he asked with intentional indifference and took a swig from the bottle in his hand.

Whisky was supposed to dull the growing need to be close to her. Instead, it made him acutely aware of her standing in the doorway as if the air between them was made out of invisible wires that connected her every move to his.

She had sought him out, here of all places, with the intent to —what exactly?

"Why are you here?" she asked.

Because the night they had spent together was still fresh in his memory, he wanted to say. The thought of sleeping in his room with her sleeping in the next one was unbearable. Because he wanted more. Because she was his madness. It grew day by day and tore him apart. Because he was afraid that whatever this game was, he would lose her. And that thought was devastating.

He could tell her all that. What would she say?

"Why are *you* here?" he asked instead.

Her gaze shifted to his mattress, then to his bare feet, to the bottle.

"Did you get scared that something happened to me?" he asked. "If anything had, you would have all the freedom you once told me you wanted. And all my money."

He wasn't sure why he wanted to hurt her with his words. Or perhaps, he wanted her to argue.

"Is it easy to lie to yourself?" she asked. He cocked a brow. "Because when you told me on our wedding day that you despised our arrangement no less than I did, you lied. Lied to me. Did you lie to yourself, too?"

He wondered if she finally understood where he had come from, why this was happening. So, he let her talk.

"You coming to my performances in the last years was no coincidence, was it? But you won't tell me about your past."

"And you want to know about my past?"

"Why can't I?" she snapped, much louder this time. "Tell me, Drasko, why? Why?" She bit her lip and frowned a little. "Elias has a past with you. So does Brodia. Men and women at your company do. Women at the balls smile knowingly. And I... Of all people, Drasko, I..."

If only she knew...

"I am your wife, am I not?" She went silent, studying her gloved hands.

She was so pretty in her burgundy dress, with flowers pinned to her hat. So vulnerable, making Drasko's heart ache. So oblivious to many things in his life. But would she accept the truth if he told her?

"Why does everyone get to know you while I only get little pieces like a homeless dog?" she inquired quietly. "A bit here. A night there. You use me to teach me your lessons, to prove me wrong. 'Here, Grace, a piano, be happy,'"—her bitter words made him flinch—"'here, darling, two fingers, be grateful,'"—she mocked him in his voice—"'smile, darling, play for me, while I live my life with other people.'" Her voice grew louder and turned shaky as she continued. "'There, Grace, a necklace, so you can look like a doll and make me proud.'"

It wasn't what she said but how she said it, for the first time so vocal, not an ounce of haughtiness, just hurt in her eyes that gazed straight into his heart.

Her chest shook as she continued in a voice that broke slightly. "Your servants know about your scars, Drasko. But Grace—oh, Grace doesn't need to know." She smirked. "'Here, Grace, talk to the duke and duchess, tell them how well you play, tell the reporters how grand your husband is.'" A soft sob interrupted her speech. "It's been months and I still don't know a single bloody thing about your past."

Her eyes, misted with tears, met his, and his body wanted to turn inside out at the need to comfort her.

Drasko could tell her a lot of things. But all of it led back to when he was a boy, to the awful events, to the enormous pain that he would not share with her—she'd had enough of her own. He simply couldn't tell a little without telling the entire story. And the story... Well, it would hurt her.

The silence lasted for a long minute. Disappointment swept across her face. She looked away, widening her eyes to keep her tears from spilling.

What would he tell her? That she lived inside him, in his heart, growing bigger every day? And the only time he was at peace was when she was next to him?

Drasko couldn't bear seeing her so upset, but he wanted her to say it—that things were changing between them, and she wasn't just accepting them but wanted them that way.

"I see," she whispered and turned on her heel.

Her hand had just grabbed the doorknob when he called her name.

"Don't walk away," he warned in a low voice. "Not now, Grace."

She paused, her back to him, her head low.

She didn't move.

He didn't breathe.

The stillness was tangible. The silence ate at his heart.

Finally, he rose to his feet. "Tell me what you want, Grace."

"I want you to tell me why this had to be this way," she said quietly without turning. "Why you have the scars. Why you can show me your secret tunnels but won't tell me where those scars come from."

He flinched at her words.

She slowly turned around, tears streaming down her cheeks.

"Why I don't deserve to know you like others. Why, Drasko, can't I have a part of you?"

"You already do, Grace. More than you think."

He was all hers, if she wanted. His past was hers, too, if she cared. So was his present and, he hoped, his future. And he so desperately wanted to have a future together.

"With time, I can give you the answers, Grace, I promise." When the auction was over. When he knew she was safe.

He took slow steps toward her.

"Is that what you are here for?" he asked. "In the middle of the night? Because you are jealous of others and want to know more than them?"

"You."

"Me?"

"I am here because of you, Drasko. Because I want you."

He took another step closer. "You want me to take you home and to my bed?"

She shook her head.

"No?" His heart fell. "You don't want another night? A new month is due," he said, hating himself for baiting her.

She shook her head. "No, Drasko. I don't want those anymore."

He stopped short.

Couldn't be. She didn't mean it, did she?

She wiped her tears with the back of her hand, quickly and with determination, not taking her eyes off his.

"I don't want that agreement. I don't want *agreements*, Drasko. I want to have what lucky people have."

He didn't respond.

"Be able to tell each other how they feel and what they want."

"So, tell me."

She smiled through tears.

"But you know it, Drasko. You know it just as well as why you sit behind the music room doors and listen to me play when you think I don't know it. Why you come to my room and touch my things, your scent lingering there long after you are gone. Why you bought me the pianos in the first place. No, not as a bargain. Don't lie. Rich men like you have others do work for them. They don't spend days making deals with people so they can buy rare pianos for their wives."

Her lips parted in a little sob. For the first time, she seemed unafraid of her emotions. Her beautiful eyes held him hostage.

"My reasons are the same ones as why you watch me sleep," she said. "Why you carry me home when I am in pain. Why you went to my performances for years." Tears spilled down her cheeks, falling freely, and she didn't hide them. "For years, Drasko! Don't underestimate me. I remember every one of them, you in the crowd. I knew from the very first time we met that, at some point, life would bring us together. And I remember your stares, intense and intimidating. I wondered why, though I didn't know you then and was afraid to ask, afraid of such blunt attention from a stranger."

He took the last step that covered the distance between them. The slowest step, the most careful one. He raised his hand to her face and stroked her cheek with the back of his fingers.

She blinked away her tears but didn't look away.

"So, you tell me, Drasko. You are so brave, so important, flaunting your knowledge and power. I will be wherever you are. In the tower, in the tunnels, on your ship. Anywhere! You made me marry you. You made me yours. And no matter what you say—that we will have our freedoms and part ways when this deal is over, or whatever game you are playing. No, Drasko. We won't. Tell me we won't! Because I want to be with my husband as long as my husband tells me that we are not playing games anymore."

"We are not." He mustered all his courage to start this conversation. "But there is something you need to understand, Grace. You can't be mine unless your heart makes that choice."

"It did," she said so quietly, yet he heard it, the silence between them so loud, it sent a shockwave through him.

His heart thudded in disbelief.

He bowed his head to hers. "I will tell you about my past, I promise. There are things you might not accept. But right now, you have to accept one lie."

"Tell me," she demanded, her hot whisper grazing his lips.

"I lied on our wedding day. I lied when I said that I despised this arrangement. And I never intended to let you go," he said and searched her eyes for the reaction.

There were more lies that he had tried to cover up by simply not talking about his past. What he needed to do first was to talk about how he felt.

"Will I scare you if I tell you that when I first saw you, Grace, I hoped that one day, you would be mine?" She flinched at the words. "I was angry that you didn't try to charm me like other women. I was jealous that the bloody earl attracted you more than me. I was already the wealthiest man in London, yet you never expressed any interest in me. It drove me insane, Grace. It wounded my pride. Yes, it did. And I gloated on our wedding day that you were trapped with me by the cruel deal. I told myself that I would make you pay. But it was short-lived anger. Because right away, I promised that I would do anything to make you change your mind about me."

He brought his hands to her face and gently wiped her tears that didn't cease.

"I am sorry for all I made you go through," he said. "But I wanted to pry your heart open. I wanted you to see that what you thought you felt for Charles was a tiny drop of what your heart was capable of. And I wanted it to be mine. Someday. Even if it took years." He inhaled, trying to suppress the feelings that burned his chest. "I always wanted you for myself, Grace. So badly it hurt. But there is an ocean between you being my wife and you being mine. You might think I am delusional or a cruel man—"

He didn't get to finish the sentence.

"I've never crossed an ocean until now," she cut him off, rose on her tiptoes, and kissed him.

53

DRASKO

She kissed him first...

Demanding—there was no other word for what her kiss was. She ached for him, and no power in the world could make Drasko pretend that he didn't crave her more than air.

He'd once known a love calm and accepting. What he felt for Grace was turbulent, challenging everything he knew about patience and himself.

This wasn't a calm love. It was like a stream, little and playful, that grew into a wide river, determined in its course, then rushed to the cliff where it fell off, from high above, and crashed into the whirling mass beyond, then resumed its course, stronger than ever.

If only there was more time...

Drasko had no patience like before. In seconds, the kiss turned ravenous, his body on edge, answering to hers.

She wanted him in her life—the thought was burning him with desire so deep that he swept her into his arms and held her so tightly that she whimpered.

He forgot that she was part of a twisted game, that he was putting her in danger by simply loving her. He lost himself to his feelings. The most powerful man in the city gave in, so brilliantly and to a woman.

Letting himself show all his love was so overwhelming, it made his head spin.

And she matched his passion. Her tongue sought out his, her desire obvious as she tore off her gloves and cupped his face.

It was a confession, and it unhinged him.

Drasko didn't ask her permission, wasn't careful like he had been before. He pulled her bodice off and undid her corset. She fumbled with the buttons of his shirt, then tore it off him. He undid her skirt. She tugged down his trousers.

He was burning from the need to attack her like a savage. He wanted to ask her how she would like it this time—rough, sweet, hard, or gentle. But she wouldn't know. He was supposed to take charge, show her, *teach* her.

"Tell me what feels good," he muttered as he tried to kiss her everywhere, her face, her neck, her shoulders. "I want to hear it, Grace," he whispered against her skin as his hands cupped her breasts, and she arched into his touch. "I want to hear you. Just like the music you play. Every tune. Every note."

"Yes," she whispered, already naked in his arms, only in her stockings, a heap of clothes at their feet.

And then his patience was gone.

He took her on the bare wooden floor, his arms around her back, holding her off the floor in a feeble attempt to save her from its coldness. His own knees scraped at its roughness as he thrust inside her deeply, pausing as he filled her up, wanting to prolong the pleasure of being inside her.

And then she was against the window, her front and cheek against the cool glass as he took her from behind, the city buried under the smog and dotted lights, watching calmly as their bodies, feverish with need, ground against each other.

In a minute, he whipped her around, hooked his arm under her thigh, opening her, and rubbed his tip against the center of her aching flesh.

She moaned at the contact, her core seeking his invasion. He entered her in one deep thrust. She cried out, and he silenced her with a ravishing kiss, thrusting into her warmth, penetrating her with an increasing urgency.

He kissed her hard, his lips swollen, hers so eager. They were messy and greedy as they took mouthfuls of flesh, with lips and teeth, gripping, pulling, matching each other's panting.

A gust of wind blew through an open window. The city smoke saturated the air. A distant ship bell rang the time. A train rumbled in the distance.

Yet they were alone in their fever, bonded like never before, two in one, moan against moan.

Rupesh had once told him that lust was desperate but love was patient.

Oh, but Rupesh didn't know this kind of love. Drasko did, dissolved in it as he held Grace in his arms. It gushed like water through a broken dam.

The feelings that had been locked away for too long suddenly were set free. The words that had been kept silent were silent still but finding their way through the impatient thrusts and careless moans.

Abruptly, he picked her up, and in seconds, she was on the mattress, his giant body kneeling before her as he finally rolled down her stockings.

Then he was on top of her, inside her again.

Love was in her cries when she came hard, trembling under him, her limbs clinging to him as she pleaded for him not to stop though she could barely handle any more.

Love was in his primal grunt that broke out loudly as he thrust in her one last time and came too, proudly sinking into her heat.

It was in the final kiss he gave her, lying on top of her—not on her lips but on her shoulder, a tiny peck. He rested his forehead on the spot he had just kissed, thinking this was madness, smiling as her fingers weaved into his hair.

Love was in the soft panting, two in one, as their hearts beat against each other's. The city below them was loud, but their feelings were finally the loudest.

Drasko shifted off her, lay on his stomach, arms folded to cushion his head as his gaze slowly traveled along her naked body next to him.

"Did I hurt you?" he asked, wanting to wrap around her right away but giving her room.

Come here, he willed her, and she did as if she'd read his thoughts.

She shifted to her side, facing him, propped her head with her hand, and brought her fingers to his back.

"No," she said simply and ran her fingers along his back.

Rakshasa purred. It fucking purred, powerless under her touch that could quiet a monster!

Her fingers tapped against his skin.

"Staccato?" Drasko guessed.

Grace laughed a little, the sweet sound trickling into his soul.

"Staccato is articulation. You can't feel it without a sound," she explained.

"What do I feel, then?"

You, he answered for her.

"A tempo," she said. "This one is *presto*."

She moved her fingers quickly, like a dozen little mice running across his back, and laughed.

"And then there is *allegro*." She did the same, but slower, more rhythmically.

"And then a gentler tempo, calm and thoughtful"—she glided her fingers against his skin in soothing strokes—"*adagio*, slow and more sensual. And then there is *largo*"—her fingers slowed even more—"a tired one, contemplative."

"A contemplative tempo, huh?" he mused quietly, didn't want her to stop.

They lay in silence for some time, her fingers aimlessly touching his scars. He knew the exact spots she stroked—

Rakshasa's claws, then its fangs, then the deepest scars that ran across his back, top to bottom, starting at Rakshasa's lifted paw as if it was the one that had done the damage.

Drasko trembled at her touch, how close she was to the monster.

He shouldn't have let her touch him like that, not without her knowing what it all meant. But then he heard her humming. Softly first, absently, then a little louder, her voice calming the storm inside him.

Her fingers joined in, matching the tune in her head, and he inhaled deeply, his back rising, pushing against her fingers that didn't stop moving.

"What are you playing?"

Her fingertips tapped against his back in the familiar rhythmic practice.

She chuckled through her nose. "A song."

"About me?" he asked without thinking.

Her fingers stilled, then splayed flat over his back, moving in a soft caress.

"All my songs are about you, Drasko," she whispered.

He rose on his elbow, cupped her face, and kissed her, claiming what once had seemed impossible.

"Tell me, Grace," he demanded, pulling her under him, her warm breath colliding with his. "Tell me I am not alone in this madness," he finished barely audibly, the most courageous thing he'd ever said—asking his woman to stand by his side, wanting to know that she was his.

He could feel her deep breathing, a too-swift brush of her fingers against the scars on his face, her soft whisper, "I am here."

Her lips came back to his for more kisses as her hands weaved into his hair.

The words sealed the black hole that had been growing in his heart for years.

Three simple words. A promise. An acknowledged feeling.

His were years in the making. Hers only months. But if that was a tiny speck of hope, he would take it, cherish it, tend to it as if it were a seedling, raising that tiny little hope into a beautiful bloom.

He could. Oh, Drasko could! He could do anything—he knew how. With her by his side, he felt invincible. If the woman he loved with all his heart was there for him, there was nothing in this world that could break him.

He kissed her passionately, unwrapped her, like a gift, from the sheet, positioned himself between her legs, and thrust inside her, slowly this time, consummating this confession.

She whispered something else, something about her being "his," or him being hers, the words broken by gasps and more kisses. He thrust into her as she urged in whispers, "Deeper," "Faster," and between those, demanded a promise that he would be by her side.

How could she not know that he'd wanted her all along? That when he hid behind his spite and feigned coldness, the mocking and the threats, the bargains and the deals, he was trying to stitch together their lives like he did his business? And he was failing. It wasn't working. He despised himself for that, for all those years he'd watched her play, hiding in the shadows like a thief, wondering if he could make her one of the precious diamonds in his display.

Until the third letter.

That fucking letter!

A dead man had a say after all, making him and her another business deal. And if there was anything he'd learned from the past, it was that he, Drasko, did not deserve loved ones, because they all became collateral.

And so he took her slowly this time, asking her without words to forgive him, knowing it was too late to build the walls between them.

Afterward, they lay threaded together. Grace nestled in the

crook of his arm. Her eyelashes fluttered closed, brushing her cheeks. Her graceful hand rested just beneath his ribs.

Drasko tucked her closer to him, stroked her shoulder, and stared at the dark wooden beams of the ceiling and the skylight window in the center that revealed the starry sky.

The beauty of the stars was often deceiving. He had learned that a long time ago, when he laughed under the starry skies, only to find out much later that the very moment of happiness would one day bring him pain.

Her body molded with his as if sensing and wanting to comfort him.

How easily she fit into him!

How easy it was to just be.

How easy it was to exist in this one moment, not thinking about the auction or two more letters from *him* and hope, hope, hope that this moment would last and the stars above him weren't liars.

54

GRACE

Grace woke up alone on the cool mattress. The room sank in the early dawn. Her eyes searched for Drasko until they paused on his tall form out on the observation deck.

She slipped into her chemise and tiptoed outside.

The city was waking up, cloudy, pink on the horizon. The tower gave an eagle's eye view of the buildings beneath.

Drasko stood like the king of the world. Hers. Broad shoulders, strong build, barefoot, only in his trousers.

The tiger, ripping his skin with its claws, was on full display.

Rakshasa, she mouthed. The more she repeated the name, the smoother it rolled off her tongue, as if she were taming the dangerous beast.

Her heart ached at the sight of Drasko, so breathtakingly handsome.

She'd been talking to herself for days, coming to terms with her feelings.

Intimidating? Of course, he was. Dangerous? Undoubtedly. But undeniably, irresistibly magnificent.

The sheer power in his gaze made others steel their spines in a feeble attempt to match his, in vain. She had realized that the men of the ton might have blue blood, but they were exotic birds with inflated vanity.

Her Drasko? Oh, but he was a tiger, free and dangerous and so majestically powerful. And she would rather be next to a tiger in the wild than with a pack of pretty birdies in a gilded cage.

Good morning, husband.

Grace smiled at how much she could read him, the way his head cocked just a bit to the side, sensing her behind him, his shoulders tensing by an invisible fraction of an inch that didn't escape her.

He moved, and the muscles rippled across his back, bringing the tiger to life.

She reached for it, wanting to hush the beautiful beast, but then pulled her hand away.

Drasko turned. His gaze met hers. His hand reached out for her. "Come here."

She hesitated, only now realizing how high they were, only the metal railing separating them from the lethal drop.

"I've got you," Drasko murmured reassuringly, and she slid her hand in his.

He pulled her closer and stepped behind her, his big hands gently settling on her waist, holding her against him, for the first time so open and intimate in the daylight.

"Do you see that?" he asked.

"See what?" She only *felt*. Him, his touch, his strength, seeping into her every pore when they were this close.

He brought his lips to her ear. "Your city, Grace. You wanted to shine? You already do. You'll play in the most beautiful places, the most magical music. Your music already is."

She thought it over, wondering why he thought that was what she wanted.

So, she asked him in return, "You already have it all, Drasko. You want your wife to be famous? Is that what it is?"

His hands left her waist. Cold seeped through the fabric where they had just been.

"The world only has the value we give it." He stepped to stand next to her, his gaze on the city, the breeze throwing a strand of his black hair over his brow. "The same goes for money, pretty things, and fame, yes."

He slid his hand in his pocket. "You see these?" He pulled it out and opened it—dozens of melee diamonds glistened like specks of glass on his palm.

He stretched his arm in front of him and wiggled his fingers, the pool of glitter catching the light.

"These were simple stones, from the ground, until we gave them meaning and value."

Grace's eyes widened, her stomach tightening, as he tilted his hand, and the tiny diamonds started spilling, dropping from the tower into the morning air.

"The more we tell people that these are precious"—the diamonds trickled, one by one, off his palm and down, down, down—"the more people want them. As if these stones are a symbol of happiness. As if they increase a person's self-worth. But diamonds don't shine." He smiled sadly. "They only reflect light."

The last diamonds dropped off. Drasko lowered his hand to his side and gazed at the city.

"Most people down there wouldn't care if they found a diamond," Drasko said with sadness in his voice. "They wouldn't know what it was or what to do with it. If they wanted food, they would trade the biggest wealth for a crumb of bread. Because the stones can't fill you up. Not with food. Not with happiness. But there are two things that can. Two things that, throughout history, people were willing to sacrifice their lives for."

"And they are...?"

"Talent and love."

The two words made her feel strong and vulnerable at once.

"It's not the fame I want for you, Grace, though you have it already. I want your talent to affect others like it does me. Your music inspires people. It makes them aspire for more."

She nodded, grateful for the words.

"It took two decades," he spoke again, "a cruel man for a father, deep scars, fractured hopes, and a heart full of hate to realize that I don't need this city to bow to me, though it already does. I don't need tunnels and grottos filled with precious stones to feel powerful, or the rarest one worthy of a kingdom to feel important. I could flood the Thames with diamonds... A river full of diamonds... Can you imagine?"

His voice was deep and low but so vulnerable.

"I have it all. If I lose it, I will have it again. I rose to the top, and if I get knocked off my feet, I shall rise again, higher yet. Power is a skill that can be learned. Those who achieved it the hard way know it too well. And yet... I am willing to trade it all for one more night of you telling me that you want me, truly want me, in your life. For the hope that you might feel a fraction of what I do. A river of diamonds—I would give it all for you, Grace."

His words made her breath catch. He had never given her a reason to think that he might feel that way.

"I would throw it all to the wind," he said, "stand bare, with nothing at all, ready to do it all over again and rise to the top if you agreed to stand next to me in life, hand in hand, and accept anything that was to come." His voice grew low, his eyes still on the city. "I would give it all to you, make the world bow to you if you gave me so much as a tiny hope that your heart could one day be mine."

Her heart was already begging to be his, thudded hard at the words. She didn't know what made him speak like this. This confession was so much deeper than the one last night. She sensed that something was happening or was soon to happen, something important and dangerous that made his words urgent.

She spoke then, trying to choose the right words like she did in her songs, thinking every one of them over.

"You are finally telling me how you feel, but you won't look at me, Drasko," she said softly.

He turned to face her, his jaw clenched—the strongest man she knew with the most vulnerable green gaze she'd ever seen.

"Why?" she asked simply. There were so many whys, and she still didn't have a single answer.

Why now. Why her. Why the marriage. Why she sensed the day he walked into the church that they would end up like this, facing each other and baring their souls. Why that very day it made her scared, like a premonition.

She felt like she was on top of the world and so afraid to fall, afraid they would both fall. It was easy to fly, until the winds changed. And they *were* changing. Ever since he stepped into her life, she could sense it like never before.

"I don't need this city to bow, Drasko." She took a moment to think. She needed to be calm, though the overwhelming feelings inside her were rising like a tide. "You must have mistaken my desire to share my talent with people for vanity." She smiled. "I don't need your diamonds either. Nor the approval of others, though only recently I thought I did."

He flinched, barely, though she noticed. She noticed so much in him lately, as if they were tuned to the same pitch, like the instruments she played.

Grace thought of every occasion in the past when Drasko had showed up in her life, bringing a strange sense of déjà vu.

"Women say…" she went on quietly, not breaking the eye contact. "Women say, that if they are lucky, they will have one man in their life who will make them feel like a storm is coming. And the first time I saw you, I felt it… I didn't know you, yet I felt like I did. You must think I'm silly."

She inhaled and held her breath to keep the emotions down.

Finally the clouds broke above the horizon, revealing the first rays of sunshine.

Grace met Drasko's gaze again and marveled at the golden

light cast onto his face by the rising sun, making him so achingly handsome.

"I am not afraid of storms, Drasko. I grew up alone. With barely any friends. In constant pain that I thought was a curse. With a talent that I thought was a blessing. With a family that wasn't my own. Was I happy? No. One man who I thought loved me stood me up on my wedding day." She chuckled. "Burned down like that old clavichord. You were right."

He always was, though she had a hard time admitting it.

"You changed it, Drasko." She inhaled with her whole chest, trying to hide a sob. "You… You make me feel alive. You make me sing. And you make me play the best music I've ever played."

A sob finally shook her. She'd never felt like this before, vulnerable and yet ready to walk to the end of the earth for the man she was falling in love with.

"I don't know how and when it happened, but I thought of you as mine." She bit her lip, ashamed of her words. "And I wanted—silly, I know—for you to tell me that I was yours. I realized it hurt to think this marriage is still an unwanted arrangement."

"It's not."

"I know that," she whispered, the air burning between them as they gazed at each other. "I will stand by your side if you let me. I will keep your secrets if you trust me." The painting in his office came to mind. "I want you to look at your scars and know they were worth it. And I will look at mine and bear the pain, because eventually, it all led me to you. Or so I'd like to think."

Darkness swept across his face, a trace of panic as if she had found out his secret.

His expression was pained. "Do my scars scare you?"

She shook her head.

"Do you think I am a monster?"

How could he ask that?

"No," she answered. "But you are mine, Drasko." Her heart

bloomed with hope. "Perhaps, one day you will deem me worthy of your secrets." She smiled weakly.

"My scars were left by a monster. Though he is long dead. Because when he went for something I loved, I was ready to give my life for it."

An ache seized her heart—at the monstrous visions that had chased her in her nightmares, the same as in the picture in his office.

He took her hand and brought it to his face, letting her fingers feel the texture of his scarred skin, the texture that she knew so well.

Slowly, he turned her hand to expose the inside of her forearm—the scarred lines, faded with years and not nearly as deep as his.

"We are so alike," he said, his thumb brushing along her scarred skin. "Because my scars are the same as yours, Grace. Haven't you realized that yet?"

She flinched as the sick feeling grew inside her. The wind suddenly stilled, making his next words so vivid.

"That monster from your nightmares, he was real."

THE
THIRD LETTER

London, England
Drasko, 29
May, 1892

The third letter reached Drasko on a sunny May day in his Mawr office.

At the sight of it, tentacles of hate wrapped around his neck, choking him. This could be a single mindless task or another dagger into his independence.

This time, Drasko disregarded the sinister sparkle of the precious diamond centered in the brown seal and opened the letter swiftly.

On May 28th, precisely fifteen minutes after three in the afternoon, you are to walk into St. John's Church and present Charles Hatchet, the Earl of Weltingdon, with the document that is enclosed with this letter. The bride's guardians are to sign another paper.

If everything goes smoothly, the bride is yours.

Drasko stared at the words with a sense of utmost shock.

So, he was to marry. Some innocent soul had unknowingly crossed Uriah's path. Or was that another debt to collect?

Did it bother Drasko? He had agreed to it.

Was he hoping it wasn't Charles Hatchet's paramour, the opera singer? The idea disgusted him.

But he needed to know *who*, for the simple reason of preparing himself for the least amount of surprise and to make proper arrangements. He would marry, yes, he had no choice, but it didn't mean he would accept her as his wife, whoever the poor creature was.

Drasko sent his men out on the task and spent the rest of the day in his office.

Waiting, waiting, waiting.

But nothing could prepare him for the name of the bride brought to him that very evening.

Grace Sommerville.

She was to marry the earl?

Stunned, he repeated her name again and again, telling himself this wasn't possible.

No, Uriah wouldn't do it, not out of spite, and definitely not out of good intentions. But he had planned it all along, known what would happen. Of course, Uriah had. It was coming—the circle of repeated mistakes, unfulfilled hopes, broken expectations. Just like Uriah had warned him.

Drasko was utterly at a loss. He had always been certain that with the research he'd done for years, he'd have his own say in what *she* would be to him.

Nothing, he'd promised himself the first time he saw her play.

Nothing at all, he had told himself for years, wanting to get closer yet knowing what consequences that would have.

And now…

He didn't sleep that night. He paced around his house, then took a carriage to the tower and from the top of it, watched London wake up, the dawn creeping up to the blanket of heavy clouds that hung over the city.

This is nothing, nothing at all, he repeated like a mantra as he gathered his men later that day, arranged for the guns in case there was pandemonium among the guests, and waited in the building not far from the church, obsessively checking his watch.

Two o'clock.

He tried to stay calm. It was just a task.

Fifteen past two.

He would handle it with utmost professionalism.

Thirty past two.

He didn't have to get involved with her, despite the supposed marital vows.

Forty-five past two.

He was angry, at Uriah, at fate, at himself, at *her*.

Three o'clock.

After all, the Earl of Weltingdon might refuse to sign in favor of a grand vow of love.

But that, of course, was a joke. Drasko knew it as soon as, fifteen minutes later, he stepped into the church and saw the earl, whose shock at recognizing him soon changed into poorly concealed anticipation. No broke man ever sacrificed a great amount of wealth for love, and Charles Hatchet proved it.

Drasko still hoped that something would miraculously put an end to this farce.

Until his eyes met *hers*.

Hope bloomed in his chest for a minuscule fraction of time, but right away was dismissed by her sharp gaze. He couldn't deny that out of all twists of fate, this was the cruelest yet. In a matter of minutes, she was to be his wife.

Drasko clenched his teeth. Rakshasa burned on his back.

He couldn't help the memories, both their blood mixed on the bungalow floor the night of the attack. Not when he stood at the altar face to face with Grace Sommerville and for a tiny second was whipped back in time, her mesmerizing gaze swallowing him whole and spitting him back out.

Grace Sommerville was twenty years of age. Drasko was

twenty-nine. And no human soul resented her as much as he did.

Though once upon a time, it was quite different.

They used to call her *choti*, a little one.

And once upon a time, he simply called her little *jaan*.

But that was in another life.

56

DRASKO

The past had the power to heal. But it also had the power to rip one's heart into shreds.

Drasko sat on the floor, his back against the wall as he told Grace everything from the very beginning. How he'd been a street thief, the encounter at Ol' Days at the port with the two men who changed his fortune. He told her about her mother who had made a choice that ruined many lives.

He told her the stories slowly, gauging her reaction.

Knees raised to her chest, her arms hugging them, Grace sat next to him and listened, first without interrupting, then asking questions, hesitant at first, as if doubting the truth.

Soon, the words poured out of him easily, at last undoing the lies and tragedies that he'd carried with him for years.

"I rode an elephant?" she asked in quiet amusement.

"Yes, on my lap," he said with a smile.

There was so much hurt in her gaze that it pained him. But what was he to do? She deserved the truth. Before, he'd thought that it would devastate her. But he simply couldn't hide it anymore. The past was their present. And who knew if they had a future and what the auction would bring.

"How did you find me?" she asked.

"Lawyers, bankers, a paper trail. Uriah was still alive, and I was careful not to let anyone know about my findings."

"So, when you came to my concerts, you knew already?"

"Yes."

"Why didn't you tell me?"

He smirked. "Because you'd think it was a cheap trick to get you to like me. Would you have believed me if I told you that on our wedding day?"

She shook her head, understanding.

Of course not.

He told her about Rakshasa, and there were tears in her eyes as she openly studied his scarred face while her fingers aimlessly rubbed her own scars.

He wiped her tears, and she held his hand to her cheek, leaned into it, and closed her eyes, coming to terms with their past.

"I saw the painting of Rakshasa on your desk," she whispered as if she was afraid to summon the demon.

Drasko nodded.

He had commissioned the piece from an Indian artist. It was the scene from their past. A giant tiger with clawed paws and bared fangs took up most of the picture, just like Rakshasa on his back. In the center of the picture, in a tiny space, as if inside the tiger itself, stood a boy with a poker, protecting the little girl who cowered behind his back.

The picture was a reminder to Drasko of what he had to do to protect what was his. The true king was not the one who possessed the most treasures, but the one who took care of the people he loved.

He told her about her childhood.

At last, she smiled. "I used to wear diamonds?"

"A diamond on your bangle that you fearlessly threw at Rakshasa. A diamond on your anklet, yes. I made them myself."

He hoped that she now understood the scents that had haunted her all her life, the foreign notes that trickled through her songs that she could not make sense of. Why the vibrant colors in his house affected her so, and the sound of Hindi perked her ears.

But Drasko had noticed it, hoped it would wake up the memories buried for the longest time deep inside her.

He told her about her own death.

"Died..." she whispered in quiet horror. "That was a terrible lie to tell."

He nodded but didn't tell her how the day he got the news, for the first and only time in his life, he had cried uncontrollably on the street and punched the man who could destroy him for that.

"We had *The Gazette* sent to India, you know," he said, aimlessly studying his hands. "Just like many others, from all parts of the world. Business, you see. I saw Uriah keep the same *Gazette* issue for days, reading the same article. *January, 1885*," Drasko read from memory with a smile, "*Grace Sommerville debuts at the Christmas Ball with an intricate piano piece that stuns the Duke and Duchess of Trent, the biggest patrons of music.* I wondered why Uriah held on to that article until a suspicion crawled into me. And the next time I was in London, I started investigating."

"That was how you found me?"

"Yes. In March of 1886, you performed with the famous Ceritelli. In June of 1886, your name was involved in the London Orchestra scandal. The cellists refused to play under the lead of a girl."

She cast her eyes down.

"July, 1887. You collapsed on stage right after your performance."

Her smile waned. "I had those pains again."

"I wish I was there for you, Grace. So that you knew that one person cared. Because your guardians never did."

"Rivka was there," she said grimly.

"I will build Rivka a palace for all she has done for you." He took a small pause. "August 1887, *fifteen-year-old Grace Sommerville stuns the audience with the most intricate piece yet*," he continued. "I was there, Grace. That was the first time I met you, heard you play, hoped you'd recognize me. Silly, of course. I can go on and on. I know them all. I followed your every step once I finally found you. And despite the bitterness of noticing how self-conceited you'd become—"

"I didn't think I was—"

"I admired you," he cut her off. "The next time I saw you, only a few years later, you were already a young woman, beautiful yet... still vain. Or so I thought. I wanted to despise that person who had once given me utmost comfort and hope and then forgotten all about it."

"But I didn't know!"

"I know, Grace, I know. I used to be a hateful man. I am willing to admit my faults. My thinking wasn't rational. It stemmed from pain, having lived through many heartaches. I once thought I lost you. And when I found you, I imagined a happy reunion, only to find out that you would talk to anyone but me, as if I were an undesirable."

Her eyes misted with tears, she shook her head. "No, Drasko," she whispered. "No."

This talk was crowding his heart with feelings that were hard to control. For what could be more courageous than laying out his entire life in front of her, with all its scars and torments, and hope that she would accept it with grace and understanding?

He was telling her who she was, who she had once been, their lives finally weaving the separate threads together.

"In the last months, I realized that I was wrong about you," he said quietly, reaching for her face and cradling it between his hands. "That you were simply lonely and hiding your vulnerable self under the mask of confidence. That your guardians were cruel people. Years of resentment and the lies I was telling myself about my own feelings... And only several months with you to realize that I never hated you, not for a second. I hated that I still cared. I despised myself for being drawn to you like a hopeless opium addict to an opium den. I was falling for you. Thought you hated me. And that was the worst feeling in the world."

Her sob drew him closer. He bowed his forehead to hers.

"I did *not* hate you," she whispered, her shoulders shaking as she tried to hold back another sob.

She took his hand in both of hers, just like she used to back then, years ago, when she was little and didn't yet know the meaning of its comfort.

"We are bound by our past, aren't we?" She smiled through tears. "Rivka calls it destiny. Though I grew up desperately wanting to know more about my past and trying to remember. And you lived, trying to forget. I didn't mean to cause you so much pain, Drasko. Please forgive me, will you?"

Her eyes searched his for forgiveness, her fingers still stroking his hand.

"There is nothing to forgive, Grace."

"I never meant for you to hurt so much," she said in a trembling whisper.

"It wasn't because of you." He leaned over and brushed his lips against hers, finally saying the truth. "It was because you weren't there."

Tears streamed down her face—because of him. And he kissed them away, whispered the promises until her beautiful smile was back—also, because of him.

He told her about the Crimson Tear, the diamond game, and the letters, omitting the dreadful terms.

"What is going to happen, Drasko? Uriah was an awful man."

"I don't know, Grace. But I will do everything to make sure you are safe."

"What about you?"

He smiled, confident he would sort it out. "He wants the Crimson Tear. He shall get it. I promised."

There was only one day left. One day until the auction. Two letters to receive.

"Promise me that you will," she pleaded. "No matter what, he shall get his bloody diamond. Because I... I don't want to lose you. It would be"—she wiped her tears—"quite awfully boring without you around."

He laughed and kissed her forehead. She tilted her head onto his shoulder and rested her hand on his chest.

The journey in the carriage was filled with stories, the decades they'd spent without each other. What was one more day to wait until the dead man's mystery was unveiled?

When they reached home, they held hands and walked into their house different people.

There were smiles. There was hope. There was love.

The future suddenly looked so bright!

"Well," Grace said as they walked into the main hall. "I suppose Narayan's cooking is quite fitting for the occasion." She chuckled as Drasko pulled her into his arms. "Should I make a menu request?"

He grinned, his heart too big in his chest as he buried his face in her hair, happily inhaling her scent.

The butler cleared his throat and bowed. "There is a letter for you, Mr. Mawr. Urgent. It arrived this morning."

He held a tray out for Drasko, one single letter on it.

Cream paper.

Brown seal.

A diamond in the center, shining with a sinister wink.

Eerie silence stood in the air as Drasko raised his eyes to meet Grace's.

Her smile fell.

57

DRASKO

Drasko's heart boomed as their carriage approached the East End.

Puzzled, Grace turned the letter back and forth in her hands as if there was supposed to be some hidden clue in it.

> *Today.*
> *Five in the afternoon.*
> *45 Frying Pan Alley.*
> *Mr. Cuttler will be awaiting you with further instructions.*
> *Both Drasko and Grace Mawr are to be present.*

Grace slid her hand into his. It made his heart beat even harder with the eerie expectation of what was to come.

Why did Grace need to be there? But of course, she had been part of the game since the day they married. Or, most probably, since the day she was born.

Drasko kept his eyes on the window so she didn't see the worry in them.

"It will be all right," she said. "After all, he can't hurt you anymore, can he? You will get the diamond and put it up for auction. How can you not? What could possibly stop you from it?"

Uriah was cunning. Drasko knew it and he hated himself for the fact that Grace, of all people, was the one reassuring him, whereas he had sworn a long time ago to protect her.

Mr. Cuttler lived alone in a small flat on the second floor of an obscure building in the East End.

Drasko and Grace stood in the middle of the drawing room as the man in a pince-nez, with a balding head but bushy beard studied them, his eyes mostly on Grace.

"I received a letter only yesterday, instructing me about today," he said, clearing his throat several times. "You see, I was told before that this day would come. I abandoned my practice several years ago."

"Your practice?" Drasko frowned.

"Ah, yes. I was a doctor, yes, yes. I thought you were aware."

A doctor?

Drasko's stomach twisted at the word. Grace winced.

The man pushed his pince-nez up his nose. "To be honest, I am as perplexed as you. Let me explain. Some time ago, years, in fact, a man did me a very big favor. If it weren't for him, I would have been ruined financially, and so would my family and, naturally, my children."

"What man?"

"Mister Edmund Bach, a very wealthy man, though I had never heard of him then."

Uriah, no doubt.

"In that moment of despair, when my life was about to crash into tiny pieces, and the lives of many with it, I gave a promise to him that, one day, I would return the favor."

Of course. Who if not Uriah would bribe or blackmail?

Mr. Cuttler nervously smoothed his beard. "Two years ago, that man came to me with very specific instructions." He shifted uneasily. "You see, my life was a success after I was spared the ruin. And when the man asked me to perform surgery, naturally I agreed. Without thinking twice! This is my vocation, sir, do you understand? Was, to be correct. I'd retired only a year prior. But of course, I would do as I was asked, even if it was close to a miracle—which the man made very clear right there and then. But I promised. Yes, I did. He saved my life, and I would save his. Or someone's."

A surgeon, then? Drasko still did not understand.

"The man, Mr. Bach, paid me nevertheless, upfront, a sum of money that I was hesitant to accept, you see, considering how much he'd done for me already. *'The surgery will be performed on a young woman,'* he explained. *'She has a condition, a pain she's had since childhood. And that pain only grows worse."*

Drasko's jaw tightened. He felt Grace shift.

The doctor gave her a meaningful look, then turned his worried gaze to Drasko.

"The man explained that the chance of that woman dying from her condition increased with age. Whereas if the surgery was a success, she would live a long and healthy life."

The words punched the air out of Drasko. He remembered the night Grace was brought from Rivka's, her pains that she had dismissed the next day as some chronic condition.

The chance of dying…

Sick at the thought, Drasko kept his gaze on the doctor. "But…?" He saw it coming, knew there was something else.

"But here is the complication," the doctor said, glancing up at Grace again, then fumbled with his pince-nez and cleared his throat. "The chances that the surgery will go well and without complications are very small."

The room started swimming around Drasko. But he clenched his jaw and tried to focus on the doctor's words.

"In fact," the man droned on, "there is a significant chance that she might not survive. And I… I would never perform such a surgery unless I observed the patient myself. But, I promised. I promised. I would do my best," the doctor finished quickly and exhaled heavily, his eyes darting between Drasko and Grace.

"That can't be," Grace gasped.

A nasty feeling gathered in Drasko's stomach. "It can't," he said. "No. That—"

"This is nonsense!" Grace interrupted. "Rivka wouldn't agree. She said I was getting better. And I trust her! Drasko! What is this?"

His heart pulsed in a nasty, awful beat. He met her panicked gaze. "Grace, it's not happening. I will sort it out."

For the first time since getting the letters, Drasko was at a loss.

He turned to the doctor. "You are not doing a surgery," he declared. "Absolutely not. Not until I get an expert opinion elsewhere."

His mind reeled. How was it possible that his wife's condition was so bad, yet he didn't know about it? How was it possible that this man did, though he had never met Grace before?

Mr. Cuttler spoke again without raising his eyes. "You see, when I was given the instructions, I was told that when the lady in question comes"—he gave Grace a quick nervous smile—"the surgery was to be performed that very same day."

"No," Drasko snapped at the same time Grace whispered, "This can't be."

"Out of the question," Drasko gritted out. He took Grace's hands in his. "Grace, nothing will happen. This is some trick, and it won't do. Will you please wait outside? Please. I need to clear something up with Mr. Cuttler."

She nodded, her frightened eyes on him, and rushed out of the room, leaving Drasko alone with the doctor.

"I need you to tell me what you know and what my wife has to do with Edmund Bach."

The doctor cleared his throat. "When I received the letter several days ago, informing me of your visit, the date and time and the name of the young lady, I did my own investigation, Mr. Mawr. I tried. Very hard, yes. It's not a trivial matter, you understand. A person's life... And I located the person who knew about the original doctor—Dr. Chescu was his name—who performed the surgery on the little girl"—he motioned toward the other room—"the young lady in question. You see, the doctor is long dead."

"Go on?"

"I didn't get much information. But from what I understand, a decade or so ago, the young lady, then a little girl, had some type of defect in her that made her sick. The surgery was necessary, but the pains continued. So, another surgery is needed to rid her of the cause of it. I... Sir..." The doctor rubbed his forehead, then pinched the bridge of his nose. "This is all very strange, but you see, I cannot *not* do it. I promised. In fact, well, I suppose I should tell you that there is a possibility that I might be stripped of the funds that I accumulated if I refuse to do it. Yes, yes. And considering the circumstances and the defect that might kill the young lady soon, I feel I am obliged to perform my duties."

No. No. The diamond game was supposed to be without a sacrifice. A human sacrifice, that is.

Reputation. Fame. Loved ones...

Uriah's words infected Drasko's mind again as he frantically tried to find clues, something he had missed, something that would tell him what this all meant. He would not agree to this surgery, no matter the letter and the warning.

"I don't have anything."

"You will. But if you want to be a king, you have to sacrifice."

Drasko's mind tried to work its way around the puzzle until it was impossible to push away a thought so atrocious that he felt dizzy, had to walk up to the table and lean on it with both hands to give himself a moment to recover.

No, not her.

Blood pumped between his ears.

This is wrong, so very wrong.

"What sort of defect?" Drasko croaked, bile rising to the back of his throat.

The doctor shook his head in confusion. "Not sure, sir. I have never heard of this sort of thing before. Supposedly, it's a stone."

THE DOCTOR

London, England
Fifteen years prior

Dr. Chescu, the sign said under the dim gas light next to a door into a shabby brick house.

Uriah had found out the random name from the sailors on his ship. Mihai Chescu was an older man in his fifties, a widow, with a little daughter. He was a trusted surgeon in precisely the part of London Uriah needed—impoverished, ridden with immigrants, where brilliant professionals were willing to do for a large sum of money what no reputable men in their profession would anywhere else.

It was deep at night when Uriah brought—carried—his little niece into the doctor's house.

The place was dim but warm, with the overpowering smell of antiseptic and medicine. Bright carpets decorated the walls. Old portraits hung among them.

But the doctor's room was void of any decoration except a table, a bench, a couple of chairs, and a cabinet with medical tools.

After a short inspection of the girl, Dr. Chescu raised his confused eyes at Uriah.

"But... sir, it is some sort of poisoning. The fever can be

brought down. Her pain can be stopped. I shall give you the medication—"

"That is not why I am here," Uriah cut him off.

He put a pouch, heavy with gold, onto the desk, and in a chilling voice explained what he needed.

"But a surgery! What mad idea is that?" Dr. Chescu exclaimed, staring in shock at the money pouch, then wiped his sweaty forehead, removed his glasses, and rubbed his eyes.

"Yes. A surgery. And I need you to put this"—at that, Uriah reached into his inside pocket and produced a red stone— "inside her."

Dr. Chescu had done many things in his life. He had patched up criminals, cut off infected limbs, he'd ventured into brain surgery, a successful one at that, and had done procedures that made grown men vomit. Called "a gypsy doctor" and a brilliant one, he had saved lives, but he hadn't taken any.

And now this…

"She is a child," he said, dizzy from this vile offer. "I need you to leave. I don't know what this sick plan of yours is. Nor do I know who referred you to me. Nor do I care about that." He motioned to the pouch. "Leave at once."

The door behind him squeaked, and a little shadow appeared in the crack. A pair of curious eyes stared at Uriah.

"Sweetheart, please, close the door," Dr. Chescu said.

"Oh, what do we have here?" Uriah's eyes suddenly came alive with a malevolent glint at the sight of the girl. He walked to the front door and invited one of his men in. "Take her"—he nodded toward the doctor's daughter—"and keep her in that room."

"You have no right to—" The doctor's protest was silenced with a blow to his head so harsh that he sank to his knees. When he raised his eyes, the barrel of a gun was pointed at his face. The tall guard motioned the gun toward the door where the little girl's shadow had disappeared.

"No-no-no-no-no! Please! Sir!" The doctor threw himself at

the guard, who only shoved him away and walked into the adjoining room. "Stay quiet," his voice echoed from there, followed by his daughter's meek response.

Uriah motioned at little Grace. "You have an hour. And no choice. I'd hate to punish your little girl for this one."

No begging helped. No rationalizing worked. The darkest night was when one had to hurt an innocent soul to save another.

Mihai Chescu didn't know that Uriah always got what he wanted, and this was no exception.

"It will kill her," the doctor said grimly, succumbing to the monstrous task.

"Then see to it that it does not," Uriah answered coldly.

He leaned against the wall, his arms crossed at his chest. He watched with some sick curiosity as Dr. Chescu gave the girl a sedative mix, talked to her softly until her body became limp on the surgical table, then closed his eyes and recited what looked like a prayer before he undid part of her dress and prepped her abdomen for the task.

And Uriah watched, watched, watched... His eyes bore into the girl as the scalpel cut into her tender flesh. They shone with malice as blood pooled at the wound. They narrowed with sick curiosity as the stone he'd been hiding for years took a wash in carbolic acid.

For a brief moment, perhaps for the first time in years, the need for vengeance eased the claws around his neck as he watched the stone disappear in the freshly cut flesh.

What was ruining the truly catalytic event were the doctor's pathetic sniffles.

But the doctor couldn't help himself.

Never had he done surgery with tears dripping down his cheeks, his glasses smudged with them. His stomach was twisting, but his hands were as always steady.

When all was said and done, the little girl on his surgery table lay peaceful in her drugged sleep, her doll-like face pale like that of an angel. The fresh scar on the right side of her abdomen, just below the ribcage, was neatly sewn. The spot was the safest with the highest chance of her being healthy for years to come. Yet Mihai Chescu felt like Frankenstein, the bile clogging his chest from what he had just performed.

"Well done," said Uriah as he pushed off the wall and approached the table.

"She needs rest," Dr. Chescu muttered, "and she needs medication and—"

His voice trailed off as Uriah roughly picked up the girl and, calling for his guard, walked out of the room.

"A monster," Mihai Chescu whispered.

And when his little daughter ran out of her room and wrapped her little arms around him, he broke down in tears and sank to the floor by her feet.

His daughter was only nine. She lowered herself to the floor next to him and stroked his balding head.

"She will be all right," she said.

"She won't," the doctor sobbed.

"She will, dada. She will."

"A stone sewn into a child. It's... It's monstrous! I am a monster!" sobbed Dr. Chescu, then grabbed his daughter's little hand and kissed it. "I need to report it. I have to tell. I will be back, my sweets, I need to do something. You will be all right?"

She nodded and stood without moving, barefoot on the cold floor, watching her father dash out of the house, listening to the front door slamming shut and his hurried footsteps.

For some time, she stood motionless, clinging to the last traces of him, for she knew, sensed at that moment, that he would never come back.

That night, Dr. Mihai Chescu hurried toward the police station. Angry thoughts roared in his head. Bile was gathering in his throat. Tears kept coming.

He stopped on a poorly lit street, waiting for the approaching horse carriage to pass, when he was pushed from behind.

The horse screamed. The driver shouted. But Dr. Mihai Chescu didn't make a sound as the churning wheels cracked his bones and split his skull, his death instant, while the mysterious stranger, who had pushed him, hurried into the darkness, away from the crime scene.

59

GRACE

"Something is terribly wrong, isn't it?" Grace asked during the carriage ride home.

"It will all get sorted," Drasko answered in an eerie voice.

"Drasko, look at me, please," she insisted.

He had not met her eyes since they left Mr. Cuttler's house.

The news had stunned her. This was some charlatan's trick. She had lived with pain for years and gotten used to it. With Rivka's healing, she was getting better. So much better! During the last year, the pain had only come back once.

"They will finally go away," Rivka had promised, and there was no other person Grace trusted more.

The visit to the doctor had scared her. Whatever was said behind the door left Drasko unsettled, and she wanted an explanation.

He took her hand in his but still didn't look at her. "It is all part of the plan," was his answer.

"Drasko!"

He finally turned to meet her eyes and smiled—oh, so insincere.

She cocked her head, searching his face for the truth. "At last, you tell me everything. At last, things between us are changing. At last I know who I am, and you still hide the truth."

The cold Drasko was back, with his patronizing gaze and careless dismissal. "I told you a lot of things. And there is more you'll find out when the time comes. What I promised is that you will be safe, darling."

That *darling* was back. There were many variations of how he said it, and this time it was the shade that he used to keep his distance.

"It's not my safety I am concerned about," she murmured, disheartened.

"I need to think, Grace. Please... I need to figure some things out."

And she shook her head, scared by the hint of desperation in his voice.

Dinner passed in silence. The confessions had stitched together her past and her feelings for him. Yet she felt things were falling apart again, and there was no way to get to him, the stubborn man that he was.

Drasko drank more than usual, barely touched his food, and after dinner, studied her in silence for the longest time until he asked, "Will you play for me?"

He sat on the sofa in the music room, a glass of whisky in his hand, his tie and vest off, his shirt unbuttoned at the neck.

Grace cherished the sight of him—at home, undone, in her musical citadel.

"Will you play one of yours?" he requested.

Grace switched off the main light, leaving on the sconces that cast a dim light around the room. She lit a candle and set it on the piano.

"I have had a recurring nightmare since I was a child," she said, brushing the piano keys with her fingertips but not playing yet. "It's always so real. A monster attacking. Claws. Fangs. Roars. He is about to take the thing I love the most." Tears burned her eyes. How could she have known that her nightmare was a memory? "So, I yell at the monster. Terrified, I scream and scream." Her voice shook. "And scream..." she whispered.

"Is that how it ends?" Drasko asked softly.

"Right before I wake up, the monster is always yanked away from me. I never know the force that does it. Never see it." *Until now.*

She finally looked at him, drowned in his luminous green eyes, so sad tonight.

There he was—the husband she'd never wanted, the man she'd feared for years, the person who had haunted her with memories she had so desperately tried to bring back.

What a difference a few weeks could make!

She studied his weary face, his green eyes searching hers. He was the same husband she was now deeply, irrevocably in love with. That same man who now made her feel cared for and loved.

The two of them were bound by the pain of the past. He was her past and present and future. He put the broken pieces of her together. In return, she wanted to heal his scars. What good was the music that she played for thousands if it couldn't heal the person she loved?

"*In the darkness of my dreams,*" she sang quietly and pressed the first chord of the keys, her eyes still on him.

Something shifted in his gaze. His chest rose with a deep inhale.

"*In the lightness of your eyes.*" She smiled and played another chord. "*Whispers drifted from the past.*"

The words started floating out of her, in sync with the music, the gentle sounds of D Minor, soothing and sad but also full of hope, the nightmare story laced with a fairytale of the daylight.

She played about Rakshasa, the song she had written when she first learned about it, then changed it later, when she got to know the beast better.

She sang for Drasko. She always had. But this time, he knew

it. This time, she wasn't hiding. This time, her voice and music filled the room, scaring away the shadows into the corners.

When the song was over, Grace slid her hands off the keyboard and looked at her husband.

He stared down at the empty glass in his hand, chewing on the inside of his cheek, the look so haunted that it scared her.

She rose slowly and walked up to him. "I want you to forget." She took a seat next to him and leaned into him. "Tell me how. I want you to stop thinking, at least for tonight."

She started undressing him. He started undoing her garments. His eyes lingered on her body, no lust in them, just some vague sadness. As if he was trying to memorize this moment. As if it was the first and the last time they were together.

Grace wondered what made him so quiet tonight, so patient. Puzzled, she studied his face, searching for the cause of his sorrows.

"When I first saw you, I was swept away," he said quietly, bringing his hand to her face and tracing the contours of it with the tip of his forefinger. "When I first heard you play, I was mesmerized. When I first heard you laugh, I was envious it wasn't me who made you happy, because once upon a time, I could. Once upon a time, I was your favorite person, and then, a decade later, you wouldn't speak to me. And then I married you, Grace. I was scared senseless that day, I can admit it now. I dreaded the minute you'd tell me you hated me. And you did."

I didn't mean it, she wanted to say but stayed silent.

"When I first had you," he continued, "I knew two nights would never be enough. I made a promise to myself to make you happy so that you always wanted more. I won't chase you, won't force you into anything, Grace. I will always love you and hope that one day, you forget that perhaps you don't feel the same."

The words stung her. How could he? After what they had

said last night and this morning, he dared to assume that she didn't feel the same.

"You are so smart, Drasko," she said, wanting to be harsh yet sensing there was a reason behind his somber smile. "And such a fool. So blind in your assumption that my feelings are any less than yours."

"Grace, I am—"

"Shh," she quieted him. "You need to stop talking."

She kissed him, knowing that before, their intimacy was what stitched together the feigned resentment and the growing desire. Perhaps, now she could show him how much she needed him, wanted him, craved him.

He wasn't in a hurry to take her. And she let her hands explore him, studying the sensation of the scars under her palm when she cupped his face. His hands on her body moved without purpose, not chasing the high. His lips hovered above her skin between the prolonged kisses, as if tasting her. His fingertips skated across it as if trying out a new tune.

Like a musician.

When Grace practiced her concert pieces, she did so with deliberate stubborn intention. And that was how Drasko navigated his life.

When she composed her songs, she let the tune lead her, replayed the same parts with variations, listening to the right notes, tasting them.

That was how Drasko was tonight, mindlessly following some inner tune.

"I want to take my time with you," he said. "And not here."

He picked her up in his arms and carried her out of the music room.

And in his bedroom, he laid her down and bathed her with kisses again, so expertly sliding off her stockings and undergarments that she didn't notice when she was bare in his arms. His lips found the scars on the inside of her arm, kissed the traces of

Rakshasa, then kissed her belly, the skin around the scar that hid the source of her pain.

Grace tried to keep up, wanted to soothe his scars too, but he was in charge tonight, on some quest to learn every inch of her. She had intended to make love to him. Instead, he was loving her body so fiercely, it left no room for anything else.

She let go, let him open her in shameless positions, caress her where it ached with need, kiss her where it burned for him, invade the parts of her that now belonged to him only.

The night morphed into hours of passion.

Drasko took her again and again, invading her with his fingers and tongue, then taking her again as she was already smeared in his spend, the two of them a hot needy mess. His movements lost rhythm and became sporadic. And she drowned in him.

After hours of love-making, they still longed for more. And as they lay entangled on the sheets damp with their desire, they couldn't stop kissing and nipping at every inch of each other, their skin raw, lips swollen, muscles aching.

Her scars pressed against his. They were puzzle pieces of time that had finally snapped together.

Grace was happy. She rested her head on his shoulder. Her fingers stroked the dusting of hair on his chest. She did not speak. Neither did Drasko, now and then kissing the top of her head.

But through this happiness, there poked a sense of unease. His tenderness felt like the last wish of a condemned man.

60

DRASKO

Oh, the wickedness of it all, the menace with which Uriah had crafted the game!

As a veil of moonlight draped the bedroom through the open curtains, the thoughts swirled like thick black tar in Drasko's mind.

Grace was asleep, tucked under his arm. Reluctantly, he untangled himself from her. He needed time to think clearly, to come to terms with what was about to unfold in the next few days. Perhaps, tomorrow, at the auction.

The bloody auction!

Naked, Drasko padded to the open window and lit a cigarette. Drag after drag, the smoke scorched his lungs, for seconds at a time overshadowing the ache in his bruised heart.

He tried to figure out where it had all gone wrong. But there was no reasoning the actions of a ruthless man. When it came down to the night Drasko had agreed to this deal, he should have known that Uriah would take the most precious thing Drasko had.

But then, years ago, Drasko had nothing to lose.

Uriah had thought he had taught Drasko that everything was perishable, and power was the only thing worth fighting for. But

Drasko always remembered what Rupesh had once said. "You can't escape your heart. No matter how far you run."

Would Drasko have agreed if he knew the gruesome secret behind the Crimson Tear? If he hadn't, would Uriah carve it out regardless? Then Drasko would have no say. While now, he could save her.

A life for a life.

He heard Grace move and saw her sit up. The moonlight cast a perfect haunting glow on her naked body.

She was half-asleep, a mythical creature, her skin porcelain-like in the moonlight. Her luscious hair spilled down her breasts.

The ache inside him grew tenfold.

"Drasko?" she called out.

He walked up to the bed, then kneeled before her, and buried his face in her lap.

Her gentle hands sank into his hair. "Drasko, what is it?" she asked with worry.

He stayed silent, inhaled her scent, drowning in grief for their future, the grief that already was taking root deep inside him.

Was this the last time they would be together?

The time before the last?

How many more would they have, if any?

"Drasko? Talk to me? Please?" she begged in a whisper, her fingers stroking his head.

He was on his knees and wanted to weep at her touch, grieving it already. He didn't answer, didn't dare take away *her* hope. Those who lived in the fear of dying were already dead. And by God, did he want to live! With her!

"Talk," she whispered again.

He couldn't. How could he? What would he say? *It's either me or you, meri jaan?* That wasn't an option. Never was. Never could be. Not in a thousand years! He'd rather die than take a minuscule chance of losing her.

A coward? Yes, he was, selfish in his love for her. He would have given it all up, promised anything to the devil if he could only stay by her side for longer.

But death was a trading card. The devil was dead, too. Yet his plans were in full swing.

Drasko lifted his head and met her eyes, thankful for the dark that concealed his pain.

"It will be all right, Grace," he said. He would protect her like he always had.

She cupped his face and shook her head, not believing a word. "It will not, will it? I can sense it. But you won't tell me."

His scars tingled with the memories of the past. The bets. The deals. The bargains. There was always a price for everything that he had ever cherished.

And his fearless Rakshasa gave out a tiny helpless whine.

"I shall always stay by your side," she said. "Just promise me... That you will stay by mine."

He should have said yes, one word, so short, so hard to say.

I wish.

He smiled. "I am yours, darling, remember?"

"And I am yours," she promised, tracing his scars with her gentle fingers.

And he lied again. "Everything will be all right."

Rakshasa roared, burning his back with the same despair he had felt the night he had killed the beast.

Except this nightmare was invisible. And Drasko didn't have a weapon, except his own life.

61

DRASKO

Sleepless until dawn, Drasko slipped out of bed before Grace awoke.

He got dressed like he usually did for a special occasion.

For a moment, he debated whether he should write her a letter or not. Finally, he scribbled several lines on a piece of paper and slid it under his pillow. If he came back to his room tonight, that meant he would be alive, and he would get rid of it. If not...

Drasko had his coffee. Read the newspaper. The headlines screamed with the reminders of what day it was and how it would unfold.

Wild Crowds Surround the Benham Auction House!
Greet the World's Richest Families That Attend the Most
Exclusive Auction!

If only they knew.

The drawing room was cast in early sunlight, too sharp for his gloomy thoughts.

His butler came with a letter. "A boy just brought this."

Cream paper, brown seal, and a diamond in the center—
Drasko knew what it would say.

I should burn it, he thought with indifference but finally
ripped it open to see the fateful words.

The Crimson Tear is to be up for auction at the
Benham Auction House by six o'clock.
You remember the terms...

Drasko thought of Grace again.

A roar broke out of him, loud, savage, like that of a tiger. He
punched the wall, again and again, his knuckles bursting with
blood and pain.

Right away, he went still, his forehead against the wall, palms
above it, the cold marble calming the rage inside him.

For the longest time, he stood by the open window, pressing
a white handkerchief against his bruised knuckles, and watched
the restless sparrows jump from branch to branch.

There had to be a way out of this. He would give it all up.
Every penny. Every diamond. His own businesses. He would
walk away from her, yes, he would, if only he could live in her
shadow, in a world where she existed, watching over her,
knowing that she was safe.

He heard the click of her heels against the floor in the
hallway and mustered all his confidence to face her.

"Good morning," he said as she walked in, in a beige
summer dress and hat, her intense eyes on him right away as if
she were trying to read him.

"I have to meet Mr. Kleinstein, the director of the auction
house, at noon," he said. *With the Crimson Tear.* "But I was thinking... I need to sort out some business, and then... Then, well... I
thought maybe we should skip the auction and stay home."

This could be their last day together.

"Home?" She scrunched up her eyebrows in surprise. "But... The diamond, Drasko. Where is the Crimson Tear?"

He didn't know how to lift himself up and smile so she didn't suspect anything. He had told her some watered-down story about Uriah's game. Not the terms, of course.

So, now he talked about the auction, avoided looking at her, tried to sound cheerful though his chest felt like a lifetime of sobs had collected there and waited to burst.

He was still talking, trying to come up with the right words, something cohesive, without giving away the storm raging inside him.

It happened within seconds, the succession of actions—the sound of her quick steps, her dress momentarily brushing against him, her body suddenly pressed against his, her hands cupping his face. For a heated moment, their eyes met. Her quick whisper, "I love you," grazed his lips. And before he had a chance to say anything else, she shut him up with a kiss, passionate and insistent.

His entire body wanted to burst into pieces. He wanted to carry her away from everything that threatened this happy moment. He wished for many more to come yet knew—fucking knew—that he'd run out of time.

She withdrew abruptly, little fast breaths escaping her.

"Well," she said, gently pushing away from him. She started fixing her dress, her gaze everywhere but him. "I suppose I should leave you to your business." She turned around to walk away.

And the ache in his heart came back. Drasko felt the prickle of it.

This is it.

Finally, he had it all, *her*, she *was* his all, and these were the last bits of it.

"Grace," he called out, halting her to a stop, her back to him as if she were a thief running away.

He walked up to her, willing himself to be patient. Control—that seemed to be his enemy around her.

He placed his hands on her delicate waist, her body right away responding with a little tremor.

Drasko closed his eyes and inhaled her scent, flowers and powder and love, wishing he could trap it so it was the last scent he knew at the end, whatever that "end" meant.

He bowed his head, resting his forehead against the top of her head. These were their last moments together, the most precious and so powerful in their helpless finitude.

Soon, he'd be gone, having never told her enough times how much she meant to him.

"I love you," he whispered, then opened his eyes, and straightened up. "Come here," he said too swiftly, knowing that if she repeated the words back again, he'd break down.

He nudged her to turn around. His heart skipped a beat as he met her eyes misted with tears. He could drown in them. If he could, he would have, for that was how he'd prefer to die. He *would* die for them. And would kill for them, too. He would gather all the diamonds in the world and throw them high into the sky on a sunny day, so that they rained like fireworks in the sunlight and he could see her eyes light up in awe instead of hurt.

"I hate this," Grace said softly. "These moments. They only last seconds, and I hate them."

"What moments, darling?"

"When we are about to part for the day. It… It has always been like this, since day one."

He smiled. "I shall see you soon."

Was that a lie?

He reached for her face. "There"—he tucked a loose strand of her hair behind a ruby pin—"you look beautiful, darling."

He kissed her forehead and took a step back, letting go of her, trying to ignore the devastating thought that this was goodbye.

He took a ride to the Bankees' headquarters.

"Zeph, I need to talk to you and Mr. Handley."

Zeph studied him suspiciously. "What is happening, mate? Besides the auction and all. The city is buzzing."

Mr. Handley met them in his office.

"What can I help you with, Mr. Mawr?" inquired the man, shrouded in the finest suit and thick cigar smoke, his gaze heavy and probing. "By the way, my wife is delighted with her gift. She sends her warmest regards. But I assume there is pressing business since you came to see me on a day like this. Shouldn't you be at the Benham Auction House?"

"How much do you care for this city?" Drasko asked, taking a seat across the desk from him, Zeph by his side.

Handley raised his eyebrows. "Mr. Mawr, that's a heavy question. This is our home. Our turf. Our place of business."

"I am not talking about your business. How much do you care for the wealthy?"

"With all the influence that the Bankees have, we cannot, nor *will* we, jeopardize our ties with the city. Perhaps, you'd care to elaborate?"

Drasko chose his words carefully. "What if you had Mawr capital at your disposal?"

If Handley had fewer manners, he would have whistled or laughed, at the least.

He cocked his head just a bit, studying Drasko as if he could read his thoughts.

Zeph seemed amused, rolling a cigarette between his fingers and looking between the two men.

"What are we talking about, Mr. Mawr?" Handley finally asked, a businessman after all.

"If something happens to me, and it might, and it probably *will*," Drasko said, slowly taking a cigarette case out of his jacket's pocket, "I want my wife to be safe." He pulled a cigarette out. "If there is ever a chance of her being harmed, a complaint from her, any unfair treatment by the mighty, a mere rumor that might jeopardize her career, the tiniest threat to it—I want you to give this city hell. Pull the funds out when needed, make those accountable bankrupt, and cut them off from their gold mines. In short, do your worst."

Zeph leaned over to offer the light. "Harsh."

"Not quite. Just business. I want your word that no one in this lifetime will dare cross Grace Mawr. And on top of the services you already handle for me, in my will, I shall leave you and your men shares of Mawr Industries. You will, it is a promise, be richer than the royals."

"Oy, a will?" Zeph shifted uneasily in his seat. "What's this nonsense about a will?"

Handley narrowed his eyes at Drasko. "What is it that you think is about to happen, Mr. Mawr?"

"If I told you I knew, I'd be lying. It's a precaution."

"Hmm." Handley took a moment to think. "You know what they say, 'You put your trust in the gangsters and all...'"

Drasko's gaze shifted to Zeph. "I've found that gangsters are more loyal and trustworthy than noblemen."

Zeph flicked his cigarette, shaking the ashes off, and sucked his teeth. "I don't like this sort of talk, brother. I worry."

"There is no need to worry. What I need right now is a deal. *If*"—Drasko took a meaningful pause—"I am gone and anything ever threatens my wife, I want you to wage war on this city."

Handley sat in silence for some time, then lit a candle, opened a drawer, and took out a small icon of a saint and a razor.

62

DRASKO

He should've known that there would be no grand fight, no unnecessary display of cruelty—no, Uriah had always done things smoothly.

So, Drasko was deep in his thoughts when his carriage got stopped at Pimbrone Street.

"A horse tram is stuck in the middle of the intersection," Tripp said, peeking out the window.

Even when his carriage was directed into a smaller street, Drasko didn't suspect anything.

"The other men are stuck behind," Tripp said.

Only when his carriage was suddenly at a stop and Tripp pulled his gun out of the holster did Rakshasa stir.

A cold shudder crept over Drasko.

This is it.

Five horsemen surrounded their carriage. One stuck his head inside. A derby hat over his bushy brows, his eyes flashed at Tripp who stuck the barrel of his gun into the man's face.

"Wrong move and I blow you into pieces," Tripp ground out.

The man's cold eyes shifted to Drasko. "If you value your wife's safety, you will come with us, Mr. Mawr. Nothing funny. You are aware of the terms."

Drasko put his hand on top of Tripp's gun, lowering it. He had expected it to be different. More men? More blood? A shootout?

"He stays here." The man nodded toward Tripp as Drasko stepped out of the carriage and buttoned up his jacket.

People walked down the street, carriages and bicycles passed by. Gray clouds weighed onto the buildings, threatening to break out into a summer downpour, just like back then, when it had all started months ago.

The musty air was suffocating. Blood pounded in Drasko's ears. Yet, tense as an iron rod, he obeyed the commands with calculated calmness. He had always been aware of *the terms*. And now, no matter what happened, Grace's safety was his priority. He had broken the rules, and he had to pay.

Five horsemen studied Drasko. No guns on display. No unnecessary violence. Yet, he knew that one wrong move, and they would do their worst.

Grace was supposed to be home and safe. And yet, he had a feeling she wasn't.

"Where is my wife?" he inquired.

The man motioned toward the carriage parked behind the horsemen. "They are waiting for you. Please, come."

This was the hierarchy of brutality. Thugs were violent. Gangs dealt with a bang. Police thrived on absolute authority. But the cruelest deals were bloodless. Those who turned fortunes around, often did so in silence, with a small nod, one word, or a snap of their fingers. When the most powerful men were taken down, the grim fate usually snuck up on them.

But Drasko had known it would come down to this.

So, he stepped into an empty carriage and took a seat, willing himself not to fight, no matter what.

The man joined him. In a split second, a black bag was over Drasko's head. The low words, "Do not make a sound," followed.

The carriage was on the move. Drasko tried to listen to the

sounds on the street, counted the time, and paid attention to the turns. But his heart was louder than his logic, beating to the dreadful thoughts of Grace in danger.

The ride was short. He was guided out of the carriage and into a building, with the heavy bang of a metal door closing behind him. The echoes of the machinery behind the walls were a clear sign they were in some warehouse, a factory, perhaps.

He was pushed at the same time as the bag was yanked off his head, the light in the room too blinding, making him squint.

He whipped around and found *her*.

"Grace," he whispered but wanted to roar at the unfairness of it all.

She wasn't supposed to be here.

The guards shall be fired, he thought angrily, then rushed toward her.

"Drasko," she whispered, her pretty eyes full of panic, and ran into his arms.

He stroked her hair, calming her, as he studied their surroundings.

The room was large and empty, a warehouse of sorts—high stone ceiling, moldy walls, crates of all sizes lining the perimeter.

A dozen men stood around, none of them his, several guns casually pointing at him and Grace.

He couldn't fight, not with Grace at his side. This was the deal. *Fuck.*

A heavy silence hung in the air, save for the echo of the footsteps as several men shifted and the hiss of the matches as they lit their cigarettes.

"It will be all right," Drasko whispered to Grace, who clung to him. "Did they hurt you?"

"No."

He glared around at the men who simply stood in a circle around them, watching them indifferently.

"What is happening?" Drasko demanded.

No one answered, but the door at the far end of the room opened.

Two men walked in. A cane clacked against the stone floor, the sound of it mixed with a heavy shuffle—the limp of the third man behind them.

Drasko squinted, trying to make out the person behind the guards, until they were only twenty feet away and parted, revealing what they'd hidden.

For years, Drasko had thought this could be possible.

For years, he had hoped it wasn't.

Yet, the cold smirk under the gray mustache was unmistakable. So was the cunning sort of squint, under the gray brows, the deep wrinkles marring the pockmarked face so familiar but belonging to a ghost.

His beady eyes lingered on Drasko. The devil himself was back from the dead, right in front of him, with that familiar cold raspy voice, giving Drasko chills, when he said, "There you are, my boy. Look. At. You."

63

DRASKO

An expensive suit over a skinny hunched body. A bowler hat over the gray hair. Small vulture eyes. An ivory cane with a gold eagle head, the diamonds for the eyes sparkling maliciously.

The memories assaulted Drasko.

Uriah's hatred had infected his life a long time ago. That hatred was contagious, now taking over Drasko's entire mind in this single moment of facing the man he had once admired and then hated with all his heart. The man who was supposed to be dead.

The guns were lowered.

The men stepped back, widening the circle.

Grace pulled away from Drasko and lifted her chin at the man.

"Who are you?" she asked so bravely it made Drasko's blood boil at the way Uriah's eyes sharply snapped at her.

"Your relation, dear, your uncle by blood. I am Uriah Mawr," he said.

Disgust coiled inside Drasko at the sound of his voice.

Grace gasped and looked at Drasko. "But..."

"But you thought I was dead." Uriah chuckled, the wheezy nasty chuckle of a sickly man. "I must admit, I quite enjoyed living incognito. Watching you, my boy"—Uriah shifted his gaze to Drasko—"as you had a grand time with your wife."

"You are a monster," Grace whispered, and Drasko put his hand on her waist, holding her in place.

"You enjoyed my little present, did you not?" Uriah nodded toward her. "You see, she was going to marry that title. For money. Just like her mother once did. But I had to gift her to you, Drasko. You deserved to use her for as long as you did."

As long as you did...

Drasko ground his teeth, though harsh words from Uriah were nothing new.

Uriah leaned heavily onto his cane, wincing, seemingly in pain, and walked up to Grace.

"She turned out quite splendid, did she not?" He flicked his hand toward Grace, but his spiteful stare was on Drasko. "Did you tell her everything?"

Drasko kept silent.

"But of course, you did!" Uriah chuckled. "I bet you could not keep your mouth shut. You have been following her like a loyal dog for years, kissing the ground where she walked. And now she'd started sinking her claws into you, hey?" He laughed, the sound sharp, followed by a coughing fit. That ugly smile was back on Uriah's face. "Did you not learn anything, Drasko?"

"This is between you and me," Drasko finally said, letting go of Grace and taking a half-step to shield her, as if he could.

"You are fooling yourself, and you know it, my dear boy."

Drasko hated the words, hated the fact that he owed his success to this man who still had the upper hand.

"Let her go, and we can sort it out," Drasko said.

Uriah clicked his tongue. "No can do. You see, despite me being alive and well"—he chuckled again—"I knew you would have your goons with you. Which, I have to admit, were quite difficult to get rid of. But not impossible! Not impossible... Keep that in mind for the future. As for her"—he nodded toward Grace—"you already gathered that she would be crucial to our little game." His chapped lips widened in a smile that did not reach his eyes. "So, I made arrangements with a third party. It is all done. There is no way to turn things back. No way out of the deal, my dear boy. A deal is a deal. We have agreed, signed with blood, remember? And, yes, yes, the men I hired will finish this game one way"—his eyes shifted to Grace then back to Drasko—"or another. If anything were to happen to me, you know what I mean?"

Drasko knew this, was prepared for this, and the confirmation only made him madder.

"What is he talking about?" Grace muttered.

"A deal is a deal." Drasko nodded, keeping his eyes on Uriah. "Though it will not end the way you wanted it to."

"No?" Uriah raised his brows. "I know you failed the previous task. But there is still time."

"What way?" Grace asked in a shaky voice.

Surprise flickered on Uriah's face. "She doesn't know?"

"Know what, Drasko?" Grace demanded.

"That the Crimson Tear has to appear at the auction, or else…"

"But you said that you would have it, Drasko," Grace insisted. "You *said* that. Where is the diamond?"

Uriah's eyebrows rose slowly. An amused chuckle escaped him. "You did *not* tell her… Oh, my… What a gentleman. I am impressed, Drasko."

"Tell me what?" Grace shouted and turned to Uriah. "Tell me what!"

Drasko saw the dangerous glint in Uriah's eyes, wanted to stop the words, but they'd already left the man's mouth. "That if the diamond is not at the auction, Drasko forfeits his life."

Drasko grunted. "Uriah, let her go, and we will—"

"But the diamond," Uriah said loudly, turning his eyes to Grace, "is inside you, dear."

Grace gasped. "But…" She covered her mouth with her palm, her eyes wide with shock. "But… The doctor…"

Drasko took a step toward her. "Grace, don't listen to him. He is—"

"It's true," Uriah cut him off. "Fifteen years ago, it happened, yes. That scar you have, dear, have you wondered where it came from? Have you imagined that you might be the biggest treasure in London? And not because of your silly talent, but because you are carrying the rarest stone in your body. That's something, hey?"

Drasko's insides turned at the words.

Uriah shifted toward him, his chapped lips curled into an ugly contempt. "You were supposed to get the diamond at the doctor's."

"Let her go. It's between you and me," Drasko said through his teeth.

"But we need the diamond, my boy."

"No."

"But that was the agreement. Or else... Six o'clock at the auction. It's out of my hands." Uriah raised his one palm in the air with an innocent expression on his sinister face.

"You are a spiteful man. You truly think that you can win?"

"But I will. Do you see what we have going on? An auction. Six o'clock. The Crimson Tear."

"The Crimson Tear won't be there."

"Pardon me?"

"It won't be."

"Or else."

"So be it," Drasko stated.

Confusion etched Uriah's stare. "Don't be a fool, Drasko. I raised you well. I taught you that a man of power—"

"Always has a choice. I'm making mine. That was the deal."

Uriah shifted his stare to Grace. "Your mother was a whore," he said sharply. "Your father a drunk. And your husband is a fool in love. A life for a diamond, the deal was. And you still have a chance—"

"No!" Drasko said loudly, contemplating strangling the man

or beating the life out of him, though that would not change much.

"You have a chance," Uriah continued, stepping toward Grace. "We can retrieve the diamond, and your husband will be spared."

"Madman," Drasko spat out when Grace suddenly stepped toward him and fisted the lapels of his jacket.

"Drasko," she pleaded with quiet despair, "I will do what he wants—"

"No," Drasko said sharply.

"But you cannot—"

"No!"

"There has to be a way!" she shouted, pushing away from him and turning to Uriah.

"No!" Drasko roared and drew her into his arms.

Her eyes were misted with tears, lips trembling.

"Listen to me, Grace," he said urgently. "I made a deal. You are not part of it. And you are not going to do anything reckless." He brought his lips to her ear and whispered a lie, "I shall sort it out."

He kept consoling her, tried to talk sense into her, promised that it would be all right, though he knew it would not.

She cried and argued and thrashed in his arms, trying to push away, but he held her tightly against him.

"It will be all right, Grace. It will be all right. Let me do what I need to."

"But—"

"It's the way it is."

He kissed her forehead, his heart breaking into pieces. He murmured another promise, words of consolation, disregarding the men around them, the hostile stares, and the sharp impatient tapping of Uriah's cane against the floor.

Until she went quiet in his arms, sobbing.

Finally, he looked at Uriah and took him in—his cruel smirk, the triumphant glint in his eyes, the noticeable anticipation of this tragic ending. This was the last lesson from a man who had no compassion.

And yet, in this last silent standoff, Drasko met Uriah's eyes and did the one thing he never thought he would.

He didn't say it out loud but pleaded with his gaze.

Please, don't.

Please.

Please...

The man had given Drasko everything and was now robbing him of the most precious thing.

But it was too late to reason with him. Others' pain was Uriah's lifeline.

So, Drasko averted his eyes.

In the end, it wasn't between him and Uriah. In the end, it was between him and Grace.

He took her face between his palms and gazed for the last time into the beautiful hazel eyes that had made him feel so alive in the last months. They were full of tears, and he prayed that she would never have a man who would cause any more.

"I love you," he whispered. "I should have told you from the start that I always loved you, that everything I did in the last years was with the hopes of one day sharing it with you."

"No, Drasko," she sobbed. Tears rolled down her cheeks. "Don't you dare..."

He smiled, despite the weight that was crumbling his heart. The tragedy wasn't in him giving himself up. The biggest tragedy was that he was madly, deeply in love with his wife. And he didn't have any more time left.

"No, no, no," she whispered, grabbing his hands and holding them tight against her as if she had a say in what would happen next.

"I talked to Zeph," he said. "He knows what to do."

Uriah signaled to his men, and the three of them stepped up to Drasko and motioned toward the door.

"No-no-no. Drasko!" she shouted.

But Drasko couldn't prolong this. If he did, he would break down in front of her or beg Uriah to change things. But this was the deal, the fucking deal.

"The months with you were the best months of my life," he said in a shaky voice.

"Don't you dare," she sobbed, shaking her head.

"It was a privilege to hear you play for me."

With a deep breath, he smiled softly, let go of her, and followed the men to the door.

He heard Grace's desperate shout. "Drasko!"

Her heels clicked fast against the stone, suddenly cut off by the sound of a struggle. "Let me go!" she screamed. "Let him go! Drasko!"

Her voice cut into his heart, making it bleed.

But he didn't turn.

Grace was the beginning and—he always knew—would be the end. But he'd hoped that she would fill many happy years in between.

Now that they'd run out of time, he was glad that he was the first one to go. For the first time, he wouldn't bear the pain of living in a lonely world. He couldn't, *would not* live in a world void of her. Not again.

Grace's screams followed him to the door. He fought an urge to rush back, to break the arms of the men who dared touch her, break Uriah's face at that, make him cry, and turn him into a bloodied mess with his punches.

He wanted to tell Grace the last words, but there were so many. Touch her one more time, but it would never be enough. Promise her again that it would be all right though it certainly was the biggest lie he had ever told.

Rakshasa roared, trying to break out of its invisible prison.

But Drasko didn't fight.

For *her* sake, he wouldn't.

He had made a deal. And a man was only as good as the promises he kept.

Drasko knew what was to come. He closed his eyes as he stepped through the doorway and thought of Grace, his heart silently screaming for her.

And she answered, her loud voice echoing behind him, "I agree!"

His eyes snapped open.

He made a move to protest, but a rope suddenly snaked around his neck, choking him. A hand pressed a cloth over his face, and the nauseating stink of chloroform suffocated him into darkness.

64

GRACE

"I agree!" Grace shouted, seeing Drasko being led away.

Her heart pounded. Bile rose to her throat. She was dizzy and sick with the thought of what was inside her body, with the realization of what this dreadful deal was.

She rushed after Drasko, but a man caught her by her waist and held her back as she tried to fight him. She kicked and thrashed but to no avail.

The man finally let go, Drasko already gone, the absence of him making her dizzy with horrible realization.

She whipped around toward the elder man who calmly watched.

"You are a monster!" she shouted at him.

His lips curled in an ugly smirk.

Tears streaming down her face, Grace stared him down.

Uriah Mawr—she had hated the man before she knew him, felt the spite the same way as Drasko when he had told her the stories of the past. Uriah Mawr was her relation, the *only* relation she had in this world. Yet, she wanted him gone, was disgusted that the same blood ran in her body.

"What is going to happen to Drasko?" she asked, afraid of the answer though she already knew it.

"He. Dies," Uriah said, accentuating every word, and studied their effect on her. "I put years into this bet with my brother. I won. I put years into making Drasko what he is, showing him what it means to be a true king. And he didn't learn."

"You can stop this... this... this game. You make the rules."

"I cannot. I made sure the rules couldn't be changed. It's out of my hands. Men who were paid a hefty sum will wait for the Crimson Tear at the auction until six o'clock sharp and execute the terms accordingly. I removed myself from such decisions for the precise reason that someone might try to manipulate the events."

Panic wrapped around her, making nausea rise to her throat. She knew what the man was capable of.

She remembered Drasko's stoic expression, the pained one at the doctor's the day before, him kneeling naked before her last night while she demanded answers but he wouldn't give her any.

Tears streamed down her face—he knew all along the gruesome truth and was bidding farewell to her this morning.

Blood thrummed in her ears. Drasko wasn't supposed to forfeit his life, not according to Uriah's plan. She knew it, and she knew the man waited for her answer.

"You know what makes men weak, my dear girl? What turns the strongest of them into mopping rags?" he asked. "Women. Yes. The gender that is only good for breeding. That silly notion called love? It ruins men's grand plans. When you were little, I already knew you were growing up just like your whore mother. So, I got rid of you the night we arrived in London. You were only five then but already a menace. Yes. Hmm... A wonderful year. A year when Drasko dedicated himself to his true path. Well, not quite. There would be others. That Indian girl who tried to turn him into a commoner. She didn't deserve him."

Grace flinched. She knew the story. Yamuna was her name. Grace felt her hair stand on end at the thought that her death was Uriah's doing.

"You killed my mother," Grace said. "You killed my father. Your brother. Drasko's lover. You killed"—she held the words back, still not quite at terms with the truth—"me," she said quieter, "in a way."

She spat at him, angrily, her spit landing on his shoes.

Uriah smirked. "You give me too much credit, dear. I *should* have killed you, indeed, but the story wouldn't be the same. Look at us!"

"You are a pathetic man," she gritted out, her hands balled into fists at her sides.

"I knew you'd become useful one day to teach our dear Drasko a lesson. I saved you. Yes. Be grateful. I cut off all communications so you'd never know where you came from or who you were. No correspondence. I made arrangements with a family who were decent enough to raise you with the utmost attention and greedy enough not to care about what happened to you afterward. They were paid well. And look at you—the perfect example that a woman would do anything for money. Including marrying a stranger. A wealthy one, of course!"

"I didn't have a choice," she argued.

"But you did. You could walk out of that church and spend the rest of your life sweeping floors and playing at taverns. But that wasn't to your liking, was it, my dear?"

The man was right, and she didn't like that.

"So, you chose a wealthy stranger."

She didn't answer.

"You know what amuses me?" Uriah said. "My instructions did not say anything about marriage."

She frowned, confused.

"Drasko was following my instructions, you see. He had to. But those particular ones were simply to present the earl with the documents, and once the earl walked away from you"—Uriah smiled crookedly—"they said, *'The bride is yours.'* Nowhere did it say that Drasko had to marry you. He could make you his mistress. He could lock you up. He could set you up in a house and wait for what came next. But Drasko! Oh… As much as he is brilliant and determined, everything that had to do with you always made him sentimental and reckless. He got carried away. I knew then that this game would be perfect. So more the reason to show him that it's all for nothing."

Elias's words came back to her, the words she'd disregarded during the dinner at their house. She didn't know a fraction then of how she and Drasko were connected through decades and continents.

"What you see in him is a powerful man," Elias had said. "But beneath this strength is a wounded heart. The biggest heartbreak of his life is what makes him carry on. What gives him meaning. I hope you get to know about it one day. That heartbreak might just save him. What he wants is for you to see past what everyone else sees."

She was Drasko's heartbreak, she now knew. Her death, her absence for years, her not-so-amiable reappearance—all at the hands of the cruel man who stood in front of her, his eyes piercing her to the core. Uriah had separated them for years yet didn't understand what he had truly done—he had made their bond so much stronger.

Grace had never had anything to fight for. Her talent was a gift. Charles—perhaps a souvenir. But Drasko… Drasko was worth living for. Dying? She thought of the night before, thought of her life before him, and nothing in it ever was worth much. She simply would not live if he weren't by her side.

"I agree," she said quietly. "I agree to give you the diamond. Take it. Bring Drasko back."

A sinister sparkle flickered in Uriah's eyes. "You do know the consequences."

"You will let him go and all this is over."

"I meant for you, dear. You will not survive this."

"But I might."

"But you won't."

She flinched. Her heart galloped at the words. "But *he* will," she said quietly. "If the diamond gets to the auction? He will. Those are the rules, am I right? You promised?"

The victorious glint in his eyes didn't escape her. Yet she wasn't scared. What scared her was that she might not see Drasko again. But there was no way around it. She would never accept Drasko's sacrifice. And this vile man would never grasp the reason for her decision.

Perhaps, there was a chance she would live. And that minuscule chance, the hope to be with Drasko again, was worth a savage surgery, the sharp knives, and a thousand more pains. Years of it. Those pains had taught her how to fight. They had led her to Drasko. What was one more?

Grace took a step toward the man, her chin lifted high.

"You have a deal," she said quietly.

Uriah's eyes narrowed on her. "I figured this might work out one way or the other."

He nodded to his men. They nudged Grace to move—toward that same door where Drasko had disappeared.

Her chest tightened. Perhaps, she would see him. Perhaps, she would get to kiss him, hold his hand while this awful thing would be taken out of her.

There was another giant space behind the door, another room, filled with equipment, a factory of sorts, suddenly loud with banging sounds and the motors working. Men in soiled work robes gawked in their direction but didn't stop working. Young boys in dirtied clothes sat on crates, smoked pipes, and stared.

Grace moved on reflex, humming a song in her head, trying to calm her raging heart. And when she slowed, Uriah's cane tapped the back of her skirt.

She was escorted toward another door at the end of the giant room. Only as they were approaching it, did she feel dizzy, stepped aside, and rested her hand on a barrel, catching her breath.

"I need a moment," she whispered, closed her eyes, and tried to calm the shakes in her body.

Fate was cruel. But life was a miracle. Hers was, now that she knew what had happened to her, where she had come from, and how it had reunited her with Drasko.

For him, she would cross oceans. And for him, she would risk it all, including her own life.

The cane tapped her skirt. "If you intend to trick me, it won't work," Uriah rasped behind her.

She opened her eyes and right away saw two boys only several feet away, who sat on the crates and polished tin jars.

One of them smiled and nodded in greeting, his hand reaching for his blinder and flicking it with his fingers.

A sudden memory jerked her upright.

The blinder. The fingers. The Bankee salute.

She sifted through her memories and blurted quietly, not believing that it would ever work, out of sheer desperation, "So strikingly blue…"

The boy's expression changed, his smile gone.

"Get going!" Uriah pushed her with a poke of his cane into her back, ushering her toward the door as she heard a whistle behind her, then another one echoing on the opposite side of the warehouse.

65

GRACE

Grace was led to a small room, empty, with only a filing cabinet, a couple of chairs, and a long table in the center.

Dazed and confused, her body exhausted from fear, she looked around.

A gas lamp sat in the corner, its shine sharp. yet leaving the other corners dark.

"Let's make it quick," Uriah said, setting his cane against the cabinet.

Three men were in the room with them. Others had been left outside the door.

Grace looked around in panic. "But... A doctor, a surgeon. I need a surgeon for this."

Uriah shook his head. He checked his pocket watch which glistened like a giant diamond. "Forty-five minutes past three. We don't have much time if you indeed want to save Drasko. Men will be waiting at the auction until six. And then—"

The razor-sharp glint in his eyes made her swallow hard.

"There." He produced a vial out of his pocket and passed it to her.

She frowned. "What is that?"

"Opium. That shall do."

"I need proper anesthetic. And a doctor who will fix the wound. And—"

"I don't have time!" Uriah barked, making her wince. "You are being difficult. You don't have a choice. Nor can you make demands. Either you do what I tell you or we wait here until six. And then, well… I suppose, you will be relieved of your wifely duties for good."

"Don't—"

The words died on her lips.

She popped the stopper and took a bitter sip from the bottle.

"What do I do now?" she asked.

His eyes slithered along her torso. "Undress."

One word, like a stab. Her breath hitched in her throat. The men coldly stared at her.

Uriah saw her hesitation. "No one needs your petty modesty. Drasko definitely doesn't." His voice acquired cruel sharpness. "We are here for one reason and one reason only."

With trembling hands, Grace took off her hat, then unbuttoned her bodice and pulled it off.

Hands in his suit pockets, Uriah stared her down with sardonic amusement.

Grace trembled, feeling violated. She undid her corset, slipped it off, left only in her skirt and the camisole, the thin fabric the only thing that covered the top of her body.

Shame washed over her at the men's eyes on her. She felt assaulted without being touched and tried to hug herself.

"On the table," Uriah ordered.

"But the anesthetic…" Grace argued as she took a seat on the table.

The stone was inside her, where the scar was. Somewhere *deep* inside her. If it had been there since her childhood, it was—

The gruesome image made her sick, bile rising to her throat. She was going to throw up, she was sure. Weakening horror washed over her as she pressed her hand to her stomach.

Uriah shifted, his features suddenly sharp and sinister in the light of the gas lamp. He produced a small case out of his pocket. His eyes met hers. That same crooked smile reappeared as he opened it.

A shiny scalpel lay there, so small yet so dangerous, sending her heartbeat racing.

Tears stung her eyes. It was hard to breathe. Her mind created a sequence of sickening events that would follow—him slicing her skin, digging into her flesh, ripping out—*oh, God*—something buried inside her for years.

Her chest shook with suppressed gagging. As if hypnotized, Grace watched him take the tiny instrument out of the case.

"We need a professional to do this," she insisted weakly. "Otherwise, I will—"

"Yes, you will. That is the plan, dear. Can't you see?" His vulture eyes flashed with hate as he took a step toward her. "It *was* the plan all along. Do you think I would let Drasko have it all? No great man is made without sacrifice. And you will have pain. Oh, yes. Love is pain. You will bleed. So much—a river of blood."

"You need a disinfectant. And anesthetic. And—"

His raspy laughter made her flinch. "This is not a surgery, dear. This is a sacrifice. Was supposed to be one from the start. But your stupid brain still doesn't see it for what it is."

His words tore deep, yet Grace tried to shake away the grisly thoughts.

"Are you willing to go through with this?" Uriah teased her, enjoying this sadistic game.

"For him?" Grace blinked away tears. "Anything," she whispered, terrified at her decision.

Uriah's gaze darkened. "I have to admit you are not quite like your whorish mother."

"And you are a monster."

"No anesthetic, then," he said crassly. "This shall be quick. And I shall do it myself."

The gas lamp in the corner hissed. Its light shifted, morphing the shadows on the man's face into a satanic mask.

He nodded to the men. They walked up, grabbed Grace by the shoulders, and pushed her to lie down on the table.

She tried to fight, tried to get their nasty hands off her, but they held her down, by her bare shoulders, her wrists, and her feet, their touch outrageously brutal and invasive.

"You can't just cut me open!" she protested.

But Uriah's scowl appeared above her. "Oh, but I will. And I will enjoy it, too."

In one, quick movement, he cut open her camisole through the center, exposing her abdomen.

She took in a sharp breath.

"Please," she begged. For anesthetic. For a proper doctor. For a chance to survive this. For something to quiet her panic or give her strength to go through the inevitable pain, already tangible in the evil shine of the sharp scalpel in Uriah's hand.

She could do it, she told herself. Yes, she could.

She shut her eyes tightly and thought of her Drasko, praying to see him, and if not, asking for God or whoever ruled this mad world to give him another chance, let him come out of this nightmare unharmed.

A loud bang suddenly rattled the door behind them.

"Are you ready?" Uriah's voice rasped above her.

His cold hand touched her abdomen, and she sucked in her breath, repulsed by his touch, not wanting to open her eyes so as not to see his gloating leer.

"This shall hurt, I promise," he said with a sick kind of glee.

Again, she thought of Drasko.

I love you.

Her heart beat madly. Her nerves were on edge. No amount of opium would keep her dread at bay. And she conjured the memories of him. Prayed. Held her breath when the sharp scalpel grazed her skin, the spot she knew so well, the spot that had given her so much pain and promised a lot more of it.

A shout echoed behind the door. The men's grip on her loosened.

"Hold her!" Uriah snapped.

Another shout came, then a succession of loud gunshots.

A vortex of shouts suddenly followed, the walls trembling at the heavy assault on the building somewhere outside the room.

Then a bang at the door shook the room.

The scalpel's jerk against her skin pinched her with the pain of a tiny incision.

"What in the hell," Uriah murmured.

Another loud bang shook the room and the table Grace lay on.

Her eyes snapped open. The three men above her glared at the door. So did Uriah.

At another deafening bang, the door burst open, and the men let go of her.

One gunshot boomed in the silent room, another deafened her, and a third followed in quick succession.

The men above her collapsed, and there came the thuds of their heavy bodies hitting the floor.

Uriah's face contorted in shock, the scalpel in his hand frozen in midair.

"Get your fucking hands off her," a familiar voice barked. "Move away! Step the fuck away, I said!"

And suddenly, two dear-to-her faces were above her. Mr. Brodia, his eyes widening in shock on her bare abdomen. And Rivka, her lovely Rivka, who stroked her hair, murmured something, and helped her get up.

More shouts followed from the open door.

"Boss! All clear!"

"Fourteen men outside and inside the building."

"All apprehended!"

"Three are down!"

Mr. Brodia pointed his gun at Uriah against the wall.

It worked—the brief thought flickered in Grace's mind as Rivka assisted her from the table, then helped her put her corset on.

Suddenly, Grace stopped short.

"No!" she snapped.

"Grace, it's over. You are safe," Rivka reassured her.

"No! No-no-no-no-no," Grace repeated, caught Rivka's hands, and squeezed them. "I need a doctor. Rivka, perhaps you can do it."

Rivka shook her head, a little frown on her face. "Do what?"

Grace started talking fast. "I have... It's awful, Rivka. Drasko's life depends on it. I have... Those pains. You were right. Something was inside me. A diamond, Rivka. A diamond is inside me. The pain, the cures, the healings. Remember?"

Tears burned her eyes at the realization that she wasn't saved, that she had to go through with it, for *him*, for herself, for both of them.

"That was the cause. This man, this monster... There is a stone in me, Rivka. Please, help," she whispered, bringing her hands to Rivka's face and stroking it. "I need to save him. He can't go. I won't let him." A sob escaped her.

"Grace, no. You don't need to," Rivka argued.

But tears already streamed down Grace's face. "You can do it. I know you can. You shall do it properly. Quickly. I trust you. I only trust you, my lovely. I will survive, I know. For him. But you have to. I beg you—"

"Grace, listen to me."

But Grace wouldn't, she couldn't. This was her chance to show Drasko how much she loved him.

So she cupped Rivka's face and begged through tears, "Please, my lovely. I need you to do this. You are the only one who can. Please, save him," she whispered in broken sobs.

With a smile, Rivka wiped Grace's tears. "You have little faith in me, Gracie."

She dug into her skirt pocket and pulled something out in her fist. When she opened it, a gem the size of a walnut lay in her palm, reflecting the light with its bloody red shine.

THE HEALER

London, England
Years ago

She was rumored to have the "sight of the devil." Many outsiders called her the spawn of a witch, on account of her late mother's healing gift. Yet the ones who believed in the old practices came asking for her help.

Pain wasn't a burden. It was a beast. And Rivka was a beast-whisperer, her healing powers growing stronger year after year. So did her visions. Those, alas, she couldn't tame.

The night her father died, Rivka knew it would happen long before it did.

She *knew* in her own way. Just like she knew about the births and deaths before they came, people's sorrows and blessings before they happened. Some called it a gift. She thought of it as Pandora's Box, with all things haunting and dark.

She also knew that the girl brought to their house for surgery one night brought death with her. She had seen it for a while. Rivka knew her father's death wasn't an accident. But *that* she couldn't change. She wasn't a magician. She was just a girl with the *sight*.

The night she lost her father, she knocked on her grandfather's door, who took one look at her and understood.

"It's all meant to be, Rivka," he said to an orphan who would grow up by his side and help him in his drug store.

Five years later, on a day like many, a woman with a girl walked into their store. The woman looked around thievishly when she spoke.

"My mistress's daughter, she has pains now and then. Occasionally, so terrible that she doesn't leave the bed for a week until it passes. My mistress, you see, would not consider anything but the best doctors. But they are helpless. Perhaps, there is something else... Not conventional... Perhaps, another method. A *way.* I heard—"

The rumors about Rivka's healing methods were known across the city. And though she helped her grandfather at the drug store, its substantial income came from the people who came asking—for help, for advice, for healing, or about the future.

But right now, Rivka studied the girl brought by the maid, the girl with dark hair and pretty eyes who waved her hand in shy greeting.

She saw it all over again—her father, a child's body on the surgery table, a red stone. She saw far-far back—a monstrous beast with fangs, a young boy at the girl's side, the seas and the distant lands. And she saw far ahead—that same boy, now a man, that same stone the color of blood, and a blazing fire, a fire of destiny that would destroy so many.

The girl in front of her was so full of light. Beautiful tunes filled Rivka's head as she approached. But also pain. There was so much pain.

Rivka took the girl's hand in both of hers, the tune in her head growing louder at the touch.

"My name is Rebecca," she said. "You can call me Rivka. I shall help you."

The girl threw a surprised glance at the hands holding hers, then lifted her hopeful eyes to meet the pitch-black ones.

"I am Grace," she answered with a shy smile. "You can call me Gracie."

Rivka didn't blame her for her father's death. Fate simply worked the way it did, occasionally with a warning that so many blindly ignored.

What Rivka didn't expect was to grow so close to the girl.

Years went by, and Grace was brought again and again by her maid for the healing sessions that often lasted all day. As Grace grew older, she started escaping her chaperons to come see Rivka and go to a theatre, an exhibition, or for long walks, finding comfort in the only friend she had.

Rivka loved her dearly. She came to Grace's house once, but the Sommervilles were pretentious people. "The likes of her," they said in mutters to each other, and Rivka was never welcomed back.

That didn't stop Grace, who was fierce in her love and loyal to her best friend.

Rivka saw *him* once, the boy from Grace's past, the man from her future. At one of Grace's performances, he stood in the back of the crowd, his eyes on Grace. And Rivka's mind got possessed by the visions of what had been and what would be, so powerful that she could sense the man's presence for days.

"Who is that man? The one with the scars? You know him," Rivka confronted Grace once.

Grace only scoffed. "He is a rich man, a diamond miner from India. I've been introduced but he is …" Grace's air of hostility was suddenly gone. "There is something about him that I can't explain, nor can I tell how it makes me feel," she said, absently brushing her fingers over the scars on her forearm. "Scared, I think."

Rivka studied her in silence.

"Oh, don't look at me like that." Grace broke out in laughter, then blushed. "He is not a suitor. Nothing like that."

"You like him?"

"By God, no! I don't even know him. But his eyes have this

strange intensity. As if he is looking *through* me. I can't explain it. Do you ever meet people and feel like you know them, from far-far in the past, perhaps a previous life? But of course, you do!" She looked at Rivka with hope. "Do you see something?"

Rivka only smiled, never once having told her friend anything she saw or sensed, trying to make sense of her vision, Grace and the man and the red stone and the blazing fire.

And now and then, Grace succumbed to the agonizing pain.

"Rivka, take it out of me, whatever it is. Please, help," Grace would beg, curling in her bed in agony.

"Not yet," Rivka replied year after year, doing everything to ease her suffering.

"Not yet," she repeated, not once having told Grace what was wrong with her, but waiting and waiting for a sign.

One night, when Grace turned fifteen, she came to see Rivka. Cheeks sunken, eyes bright with fever, pain folded her in half.

"I need help, Rivka," she whispered, collapsing in Rivka's arms.

That night, Rivka called on the spirits. She murmured prayers. She lit the candles.

And finally, the spirits spoke.

There was a time and place for everything, and if in several years, a procedure such as this would have killed Grace, the pain and infection would have killed her sooner. But now—

Now Rivka stood gazing down at her friend as her grandfather stood by her side.

Silent tears rolled down Grace's cheeks as she withered in pain.

"Drink this," Rivka ordered calmly, pushing a sedative tea into her hand, and waited until Grace's eyelids fluttered closed in a deep sleep.

Rivka saw it clearly now—what she had to do.

"I need my medical bag from the attic. It's time," she finally said to her grandfather. "Let us get the surgery table ready."

67

GRACE

Grace stared at the stone on Rivka's palm. "But that is... Is it...?"

It was, no doubt, the Crimson Tear.

"Jesus..." escaped Mr. Brodia's lips as he, too, gawked at the stone.

But one pair of eyes bore into the red diamond in more shock than anyone's.

Uriah Mawr clenched his jaw in disbelief.

"It's a scam," he rasped, breaking the silence that was laced with the smell of the dead men's blood on the floor.

"It's not," Rivka said, smiling at Grace. "You have it, lovely. Do what you need to do."

Grace still stared in disbelief when a roar broke out behind her. Something pushed her out of the way, and Uriah's hunched figure lunged at Rivka and snatched the diamond out of her hand.

"Mine!" he snarled and rushed toward the door, limping and skipping.

"Hold still!" Mr. Brodia barked as he pointed his gun at Uriah scurrying out of the room.

If Drasko's fate was in that vile man's hands, Grace would end him.

She didn't hesitate, didn't think twice when she snatched the gun out of Mr. Brodia's hand and fired at Uriah limping away.

One shot.

One man.

No regrets.

No more cruelty.

Uriah's body jerked mid-air, then collapsed onto the floor with a dull thud.

She started trembling at what she had done, staring at the body on the floor that seemed so much smaller now. But she had never despised someone so much, and Drasko didn't deserve any more cruelty.

Still alive, Uriah slowly rolled onto his back, a crimson puddle growing underneath him on the floor. Blood gathered in the corners of his mouth. His hand still clutched the diamond.

"Too late," he wheezed with a bloodied smirk. "You are too late. The diamond is not at the auction. Drasko is going to die."

Grace felt the movement next to her. Mr. Brodia pried the gun out of her hand. He raised the pistol, cocked it, and fired at Uriah.

In an instant, Uriah's head jerked. Blood trickled from the bullet hole in the center of his forehead, and the sinister light in his eyes extinguished.

"Bastard," Mr. Brodia blurted out, then turned around. "Miss Rebecca, you need to help Mrs. Mawr. And fast. I will find Drasko."

"They have him. This man's guards, they have him," Grace murmured, still fixated on the bony figure on the floor.

"Mrs. Mawr! You need to get to the auction. Elias is waiting there."

"Yes," she murmured, absently.

"Now!"

"Yes, yes!" Grace turned around, dizzy from the tincture and the smell of blood, nodding as Rivka helped her dress.

Mr. Brodia gave orders to his men, then passed her the red diamond.

"My men will take you to the auction as fast as possible. I will sort things out here, and Miss Rebecca and I will find Drasko. Perhaps, she can *see* where he is, considering she can pull two-decade mysteries out of her pocket." He flashed Rivka a smile.

"Twenty minutes to five," one of the Bankees said as Grace stormed out of the building with six of them by her side. "Do you ride?"

"Pardon me?"

"Do you ride horseback?"

Her confused look told him that was a no.

"The fastest way to get around these days," he said as he helped her on one of the horses tied outside and mounted it behind her.

"Faster! Please, faster!" she pleaded as they trotted through the city, carriages and trams left behind, passersby parting to let them through.

"Here!" Grace commanded as they approached the crowded police cordon around the Benham Auction House.

She fought through the crowd and toward the entrance.

Five minutes after five.

She rushed through the crowded main hall.

"Grace!" She saw Julien in the crowd, but she had no time for him.

She rushed up the grand stairwell, to the upper floor, and the main auction hallway.

It was even more crowded, its walls lined with the Mawr marvels, guests dripping in wealth, sipping champagne to the pleasant tunes of an orchestra.

The seats before the stage were occupied. The rest crowded around.

The grandeur and beauty exceeded any such exhibition before. The art pieces were illuminated by soft lights. The room glowed in the shine of thousands of diamonds of various hues and sizes.

But Grace didn't stop.

Ten past five, the clock on the wall said.

"Grace! Grace!" Elias was pushing through the crowd toward her. "Where is Drasko?"

"I don't know. But I have the stone. I do, Elias! It has to be displayed by six. By six! You hear me? And they still need to do the authentication!"

"Come!" he ordered.

They ran to the director's office.

A dozen or so men turned their heads to Grace and Elias as they entered, Mr. Kleinstein, the director, among them.

She took the red diamond out of her reticule.

"The Crimson Tear," she said as the men stared at the red stone in her palm.

Someone cleared his throat. Several men rose from their seats.

Another man chuckled. "Is this some sort of joke?"

Mr. Kleinstein slowly approached, his eyes on the diamond.

"This is Mrs. Mawr," he explained, his eyes glued to her palm and the gem.

He reached for the diamond then paused, then finally took it between his thumb and middle finger, his hand shaking.

The rest of the gentlemen rose to their feet, their eyes, too, on the Crimson Tear.

"I understand that Mr. Mawr did not condescend to attend his own auction," that same appraiser said bitterly. "And you, ma'am, whip a stone out of your reticule and want us to believe it is *the* diamond in question?"

Grace lifted her chin, her gracious smile on the director as she spoke. "I will spare you the grizzly details of where it came from."

Elias stepped forward. "I believe the jewelry experts will be better able to determine what this is. Mr. Kleinstein," he said, "please, conduct the authenticity check. As per Mr. Mawr, this diamond has to be on display no later than six o'clock."

Five-thirty, the clock said.

The appraiser and experts got to work. They set up their contraptions and took turns inspecting the stone. They exchanged whispers and murmurs, and one of the appraisers blew his nose in a handkerchief and wiped his teary eyes.

"By God, it is so pure," he muttered in a shaky voice.

"And the rarest hue of red!" another exclaimed.

"Truly, a wonder."

"Excellent grade, ideal cut."

"Gentlemen," said the bitter appraiser, his eyes now bright with diamond fever. "The authentication is complete. It is a privilege."

Five-forty-five.

Grace watched with a pounding heart as the men signed the authentication papers. The opening bid was agreed upon. A special glass case with a black velvet cushion was brought for the display.

Five-fifty-five.

Her mind screamed. She tapped her foot, checking the clock every minute.

At last, Mr. Kleinstein gave a sign.

They walked out into the auction hall, packed with lords and ladies. The crowd quieted. Necks craned in the direction of the man who wheeled out the podium with the glass case.

The Duke and Duchess of Trent sat in the front row, the duchess's eyes boring into the cloth that covered the glass case.

"Ladies and gentlemen," the director announced with an air of utmost importance. "The auction is starting."

Grace stood behind him at a distance and thought of the small stone in the room full of people, a stone, so insignificant, yet that had caused so much pain.

"The Benham Auction House is proud to present the Wonders of the Mawr Diamonds!"

Her gaze swept across the room, searching for Drasko or some indication that the message had been received.

"We believe our main prize is here. We present to you the Crimson Tear."

He stepped to the glass case and theatrically whisked the drape off it.

The crowd gasped in awe.

The duchess flung from her chair, her eyes on the glass display. Someone in the front row fainted. The crowd rose to their feet to take a better look at the legendary diamond and exploded in deafening applause.

Only Grace exchanged bitter glances with Elias.

The small insignificant-looking red gem had ruined many lives. It had almost ruined hers and Drasko's. Yet, it was now cheered to by the world's elite.

The clock struck six.

68

DRASKO

Pushing through the nausea, Drasko opened his eyes.

The hard light of an unshaded lamp blinded him. He was in some type of a windowless cellar. Five armed men were in the room with him.

His movements attracted attention.

"Why am I still here?" He sat up on the cold floor. "Where is Uriah Mawr?"

One man lit a cigarette with an air of superiority.

"You are rich *and* lucky," he said, exhaling the smoke and inspecting the tip of his cigarette like it was the most curious thing. "That pretty lady of yours, she is a fighta'."

The other men chuckled, seemingly at ease.

Anger started taking root in Drasko at the words. The drug's effect was wearing off. He needed to fight. These men, no matter how many of them were here, didn't stand a chance.

As long as he didn't get shot, that is.

And then?

He'd made a deal. Uriah was cruel but a man of his word. He wouldn't touch Grace, not when Drasko had agreed to—

"Your lady agreed to the surgery."

The room spun in front of him again.

No. He shook off the dizziness in his head and stood up. *No, she can't.*

The men instantly straightened up. A few of them pushed off the wall and touched the guns tucked under their belts.

"She did," the man said. "For you. You are lucky. She saved you."

"No, no..." Drasko stared around, horror twisting his stomach.

He'd expected to be dead by now, beat up at the least, Uriah taunting him.

But not this, not the nauseating news about Grace.

"Where is she?" he asked quietly, meeting the men's intense stares, one by one.

"Don't know, mate. Sit the fuck down."

"I want to talk to Uriah Mawr," Drasko gritted out.

"He is with the lady," the man said indifferently, the others observing Drasko with curiosity.

"How much time has passed?"

They only smirked.

"I will pay you," Drasko insisted, conjuring the most confident expression and fixing his vest and jacket. "I will pay you more than him."

"We already got paid."

Drasko shoved his hands in his pockets. "I have more. I will make you rich."

The men chuckled but exchanged meaningful glances.

He took slow steps toward the man in charge. "So rich, you will not know what to do with the money. You know who I am?"

The men's chuckles subsided. Money always worked. The little wheels in their brains were turning, and Drasko had counted on it.

"We are waiting for the orders," one of them said with hesitation, looking at the one in charge.

"How much are you getting for this?" Drasko asked.

He was a businessman. These men knew it. What they didn't know was that he never left the house unarmed. And though his gun was gone, while he talked, his hand in his pocket undid the clasp on his leather bracelet, releasing a razor. "I will give you ten times more. Each of you."

The man in charge cleared his throat and turned with his side to him as he looked at his men, trying to figure out by their expressions what to do.

"That is what businessmen do. They negotiate," Drasko continued, taking another step toward the man. His blood was pumping away the remains of the sedative, giving him back his strength. "But you are not businessmen. You are soldiers. And the unfortunate thing about soldiers—"

His hand flew out of his pocket as he lunged at the man in charge.

This was not businessman-like. But Drasko was many things. And one of them was a ruthless fighter.

He attacked the man so quickly that by the time the others collected themselves, only in seconds, the man in charge was sinking onto the floor, his hand pressed to the gaping wound on his neck, gushing with blood.

Before the first gun was drawn, Drasko had already head-butted one man, twisted him, and used him as a shield.

A gunshot rang through the room, deafening and piercing the man Drasko was holding. The body was pushed into another man while Drasko lunged for the next one.

Not one of them would be able to tell precisely what happened, how it was humanly possible for a man to move so fast, like a tiger in the jungle, a predator, always a step ahead of them. The ones who survived would not remember clearly how in less than a minute, all of them were disarmed, broken, and incapacitated, and Drasko calmly went about the room, collected the guns, and, murmuring under his breath, "The negotiation is over," walked out.

There were no men outside the dingy cellar. The staircase led straight out onto the street.

As soon as the light hit Drasko's eyes, he squinted, and the urgency spiked his heartbeat—he had to find Grace.

"Time!" he shouted at a passerby. "What time is it?"

"Twenty minutes after six."

He'd been out for more than an hour!

Disoriented, he darted in one direction, then in another. He had no idea where to look for her.

He rushed to a crossing sweeper boy, catching him by the shoulder. "So strikingly blue!" he blurted, but the boy only frowned at him.

Fuck!

He saw the boy who sold matches across the street, ran up to him, and repeated the words.

And there it was, the Bankees' ingenious system—the boy whistled loudly, and another whistle echoed from down the street.

"Find Brodia!" he barked.

He glanced around at the street signs, assessing his location, and ran in the direction of the auction house, the match-seller following on his heels.

Not her. Just not her, Drasko's feverish mind repeated.

He was hoping that the Crimson Tear was not at the auction. No humiliation or public scorn mattered. What mattered was that Grace did not go through the gruesome procedure that could ruin her life and break Drasko. He would never forgive himself.

Another whistle sounded from the distance.

The boy behind him answered.

In a matter of seconds, the ground shook with the horse's hooves. Atop the horse—a man Drasko had never looked forward to seeing more than now.

"Grace! He's got Grace!" He rushed to Zeph, who

dismounted and met him mid-way. "He's got Grace. She is in danger!" He fisted Zeph's suit jacket and shook him. "I fucking asked you, Zeph—"

"She is safe!" Zeph grabbed him by his shoulders. "She is fine! Brother, you have no idea what happened!"

"Where?"

"Safe!" Zeph fisted the front of Drasko's vest and shook him to calm him. "That guy? Your uncle? Whoever that sick pig is—"

"Where is Grace?" Drasko repeated, his wild eyes on Zeph.

"At the auction. She rushed there because of the deal. The stone. And you. Fuck, brother, you could've told me, no?"

The world that was wildly spinning around Drasko at last slowed down.

He let go of Zeph's jacket and put both hands on top of his head, closing his eyes as relief pulsed through his veins.

Safe.

Safe.

Safe.

His eyes darted to Zeph again. "And Uriah?"

"Dead." Zeph shrugged his shoulders.

Safe.

Safe.

Grace was safe.

A gust of wind ruffled his hair. Thunder broke out above them, just like that day he'd walked to St. John's Church.

Drasko lifted his face to the sky, feeling the cool breeze graze his hot skin.

"Wait…" He turned to Zeph. "But the diamond. How…?" He met Zeph's cunning smile. "How did the diamond…?" He frowned and stepped into Zeph in a warning. "Don't fucking tell me—"

Zeph pushed him in his chest. "Oy, calm, my man. Stay calm. He did not touch her."

"Then how—"

"If you'd fucking told anyone what was happening and what the deal was, it could have all been avoided, you know." Slowly, as if there was no worry in the world, Zeph lit a cigarette. A boy ran up to him, bringing a message. "To the auction house," Zeph ordered the boy. "I want several dozen of you there. Now."

"How?" Drasko barked impatiently.

"Rivka had the bloody stone all along."

"Rebecca?"

"Yes. Miss Rebecca, Rivka, that beautiful witch. Some magic. That woman, I tell you. I was visiting her at her shop when the news came about Grace. The story is as wild as everything that has to do with the Mawrs. Crazy uncles, cursed diamonds, forced marriages, fucking tigers." He loudly exhaled a cloud of cigarette smoke into the air.

"We need to go to the auction," Drasko said impatiently, an eerie sense of unease still in him.

He needed to see Grace and make sure she was indeed safe. His mind was already racing toward her, a new hope taking root in it that they had survived the worst.

Suddenly, a siren rang in the distance.

"The city siren," a passerby said, everyone on the street halting to a stop, their heads turned in the direction of the emergency sound.

Where the Benham Auction is, Drasko thought, his heart skipping a beat.

A hansom cab flew by. Then another carriage.

"Disaster!" someone shouted.

The newsboys started running in that direction.

Without the knowledge of what was going on, Drasko's heart started pounding, an uncanny feeling gathering inside him.

Rakshasa clawed at his back. His scars started to burn. Something was wrong.

His eyes widened at the smoke rising in the air, a dark cloud of it thickening above the buildings in the distance.

Policemen on horseback trotted by barking orders, "Move out of the way! Out of the way!"

Curious gawkers followed them.

A man halted next to Drasko and Zeph and shook his head.

"Another blow to the wealthy," he muttered grudgingly. "The Benham Auction House is on fire. Dozens are trapped inside."

69

DRASKO

"Grace!" Drasko roared, his heart thundering, as he rushed through the smoky crowded street in front of the auction house.

The building was ablaze. The orange monstrosity of the fire clawed at the sky.

The street was crowded chaos.

The Metropolitan fire brigade was busy with hand pumps, blasting water at the entrance. A crowd of gawkers gathered to watch, but only a few helped the lords and ladies standing and sitting on the curb, charred, muddied, coughing and crying.

"Grace!" Drasko darted between them, shouldering the bystanders, frantically whipping around in search of the familiar silhouette. "Graaaace!" he roared.

"Everyone is out of the building, they say," someone commented.

"There might be a few still trapped in the auction room," another speculated.

Drasko's heart pumped with anxiety as he shouted Grace's name and grabbed the women who looked like her only to find unfamiliar faces.

Cries and wailing echoed amidst the shouting of the fire brigade workers and the policemen trying to control the crowd.

And no sight of Grace.

"Graaaaaace!" he roared, panic taking over him.

"Mr. Mawr!" a voice turned him around.

Julien looked like a coal miner, jacket off, his usually pristine shirt smudged with ashes. He sat on the ground and cradled a man in his arms as a doctor hovered above them.

"Elias?" Drasko recognized the familiar face on Julien's lap.

"I need to—" Elias, seemingly in a daze, his clothes partially burned, pushed away the doctor and tried to rise from the ground but collapsed.

"Where is Grace?" Drasko demanded.

"I..." Elias groaned, his eyes fluttering closed. "I was helping others to exit. I was calling for her. She was there. It was smoky. And..."

He coughed into his arm, tried to get up again but collapsed into Julien's arms.

"Oh, dear." Julien touched Elias with trembling hands, then looked up at Drasko. "He was helping people to get out of the building. And then a beam collapsed on top of him. We dragged him out. But Grace... Mr. Mawr, I am not sure where she is. I—"

Another crack of thunder spilt the night sky, and heavy rain-drops started coming down.

"Get a line of people to pass the buckets!" a fireman shouted.

A whistle came. Then another. And another. Young boys and men started pouring from everywhere as Drasko's gaze wildly scanned the crowd for the familiar face.

"She is not here. She is not here," he repeated, searching the street. "I am going in."

He rushed toward the entrance.

"Mr. Mawr!" Julien called out.

"Sir!" a fireman shouted at him as Drasko shielded his face from the billowing smoke rolling out of the entrance. "You cannot go in! It's not safe! It's about to collapse! Sir!"

But Drasko didn't pay attention. *She must be there.* If she was, he would find her, even if it cost him his life.

"Mr. Mawr! Wait! Wait!" Julien caught up with him and yanked him back. "You'll need this."

Coughing, he snatched a bucket of water from one of the boys and poured it over Drasko, then did the same with one more. "Go!"

In a second, Drasko was at the entrance, wrapping his cravat over his nose and mouth.

In another, he darted inside, smoke burning his eyes.

The sudden heat, like a wall, assaulted him as he fought through the flames at the entrance.

The grand hall was thick with smoke. The curtains, the beams, and the artworks on the walls were in flames. So was the grand staircase that he took three steps at a time, shielding his face from the flames darting at him.

The second floor was worse.

He weaved among the smoldering furniture. It was hard to see, hard to breathe. But he'd been here before, knew the floor plan, and he veered among the collapsed debris into the main auction room.

"Grace!" he shouted as he ducked away from the falling flames that, like rockets, shot down from the ceiling. "Grace!"

The auction room was ablaze. The flames were everywhere. The displays were melting. The smoke suffocated him. His lungs wheezed, and his damp shirt hissed as the fires licked at it.

But there was no fire, no flames, no calamity that would stop him as he fought his way among the exploding jewelry displays and flaming rubble.

Rakshasa growled in determination.

For her.

For them.

For the only chance they had.

He wildly looked around.

Another charred beam crashed down, missing him only by an inch.

The Mawrs' grandest display of wealth was up in flames that

warped all around Drasko, yet the most precious thing was somewhere among it.

A blast of fire roared toward him, and he ducked and lunged to the side.

He saw her then, her motionless body on the floor, flames creeping up to her feet, her skirt already melting at the hem.

"Grace!" He rushed toward her and took her motionless body into his arms. "Grace, Grace, look at me!"

He wiped her ashy face and stroked her hair, willing her to wake up as his lungs screamed from the smoky assault.

She moved then. A tiny cough escaped her. Her eyes fluttered open as she tried to say something, but her head lolled onto his arm.

"Grace, I'm here," he murmured, the sudden hope giving him wings.

He took off his soaked cravat and wrapped it around her mouth and nose. A cough was suffocating him. The air sizzled in his nostrils and throat. Sweat dripped down his face. Unbearable heat enveloped him.

But he disregarded the pain, lifted Grace into his arms, and marched through the flames that licked at his feet, scorching his skin and roaring at him, threatening to swallow them whole.

The blaze didn't have a chance. Not when Drasko had gone through worse to protect what he loved.

He marched on, whispering love words to her, disregarding the smell of burned hair and the feeling of the clothes singing against his skin that sizzled with blisters.

"Stay with me, Grace," he murmured, holding her tightly against him and shielding her from the roaring flames, as he stomped through the debris and walls of fire around him, down the stairs. "We need to go. We have to," he kept saying like the prayer that Rupesh had tried to teach him once.

When he walked out of the auction house, he thought he was half-dead, half-blind, and burned to the bones. His lungs were shot, his skin scorched. He was dizzy, but his heart pounded with a relief that even the night he fought Rakshasa for little Grace could not compare to.

He had her.

"Another survivor!" someone shouted.

A fireman doused him with water, putting out the little flames that Drasko didn't notice, his shirt smoldering off his body.

He carried Grace across the street and sank onto his knees.

"They are safe!" someone yelled.

A line of dozens of young boys and men snaked toward the building with buckets in their hands, working faster than the fire brigade.

Sirens, shouts, cries, and whimpers. Doctors, firemen, onlookers, and reporters.

Madness whirled around! Blankets were passed around. Water was brought from everywhere.

Rain drizzled, but it wouldn't save the auction house.

"You are safe, you are safe, you are safe," Drasko repeated, cradling Grace in his arms, and smiled when she stirred and coughed. "There you are, *meri jaan*. You are safe."

He looked around at the gawking crowd, saw Rivka and Zeph, rushing in his direction.

Julien, looking like Prince Charming who had gone through an epic war battle, rushed up to Drasko. "How is she?"

"She should be fine," Drasko said, stroking her hair. "Elias?"

"He is recovering. A lot of people would have been trapped inside if it weren't for him. And so would I. I owe him my life."

"Careful," Drasko warned with a soft chuckle. "He might just take it too seriously."

Mr. Kleinstein stood in the middle of the street, clutching his hair in alarm as he stared at the crumbling glory of his establishment.

The street was illuminated orange. The hypnotized faces, some horrified, some in awe, were lifted to the giant blaze that lit up the night sky, swallowing the sparkles and the whirls of smoke.

"There are no people inside! Everyone is safe!" a fireman shouted.

Zeph whistled to his boys. The whistles echoed through the crowd. In seconds, the line of boys and young men dropped the buckets, as if on cue, and started walking away.

The building director ran up to him. "Wh-what are you doing?" He waved at the empty place where the line of helpers had just been. "Those boys? I need them."

"Well, they are mine, and they are not getting paid. Nor am I jeopardizing them for the sake of your enterprise."

"But the fire!"

Zeph nodded at the lords and ladies, who gathered around like charred peacocks with their tails down. "Get them to put it out. This is their party."

The Duke of Trent wobbled over. "Mr. Mawr, they got it! They got it! The Crimson Tear! The duchess got it! It is safe! Oh, the miracle! Mr. Mawr, the doctors are coming. They are—"

Drasko wanted to throw the duke in the fire.

But the sound of his voice floated away as Drasko looked at Grace in his arms.

Ashes were falling heavily, getting caught in Grace's hair like snowflakes.

"Grace, love, look at me." He stroked her face, smudged with ashes, her hair singed at the edges. "Wake up, darling. You have to. We have plans, remember? Children, America. So much music to play. You hear me?"

Her eyelashes fluttered. She finally opened her eyes, blinking slowly, and coughed.

"I brought the diamond, Drasko. I had it," she murmured.

He smiled, tears welling up at the sight of her coming to.

"I was on time," she whispered as another little cough broke out of her. "But you weren't there... And I didn't want to leave...

457

Because you weren't there... I waited and waited... and waited..."

Her voice faded, and he kissed her face, a kiss for every word.

A deafening crash shook the street—the roof of the auction house collapsed and sent flames and sparkles like thousands of fireflies high into the smoky sky.

Another deafening crack followed—that of thunder, splitting the sky—and the rain came down in a merciless downpour.

It cooled Drasko's wounds and soothed his aching heart. He grunted into the sky, thanking the universe for saving *her*.

Grace stirred, blinking away the rain, her eyes meeting his.

He tucked her in closer to him and leaned over her to shield her face from the rain. He kissed the raindrops off her lips, then kissed her fingers, one by one, making sure they weren't damaged. Those beautiful fingers played the most wonderful music for his heart.

Her hand cupped his face. "I waited for you," she said weakly.

Drasko wanted to roar at the horrific thought of what could've happened to her.

Her ashy fingers brushed against his lips. "And you came."

He kissed her fingertips and cradled her in his arms.

Again, he was on his knees, but this time, grateful.

He buried his face in her hair.

"I did, love," he whispered. "I did."

70

DRASKO

"It was a bad idea not to go to a hospital or call for a doctor," Grace said as she cleaned Drasko's wounds that very night.

Her hair was still a mess. Her singed dress and the rest of her clothes were in a heap on the floor. Wearing only her undergarments and camisole with a little bloodstain on the fabric from where Uriah's scalpel had grazed her, she looked every bit like an angel who had fought her way through hell.

She had told Drasko what had happened.

He had sworn he would find Uriah in hell when he died.

"I'd rather you stay with me for a while," she cut off his threats.

Their bedroom was dim and smelled of ashes. Drasko's own clothes were in the same pile on the floor. He sat in his undergarments on the chair as Grace stood between his legs and carefully inspected his burn wounds.

She had insisted on doing it herself. And now he watched her with silent admiration, unable to look away. The worst was behind them, and she was his, so very his, for so very long, he hoped.

The diamond game seemed a distant affair. So did the fire. Only its pungent scent that saturated the air was a reminder of what it had taken for them to be here, with no threats to their future.

"Did you know that Nina finally pulled off her skirt?" Grace said with a smile.

"She did what?"

Grace chuckled. "When you left this morning, Nina and I were on our way to Rivka's. We didn't take more men. We thought we'd come back to the house right away. Then three of Uriah's men surrounded us. I don't think they expected Nina to fight back. And she pulled off her skirt—poof!—like those vaudeville performers." Grace laughed. "She'd told me so before, but I didn't believe her. She does, indeed, wear those long black bloomers under her skirt. And her hat never fell off her head when she fought the men. Can you imagine? She looked like some sort of fantasy hero when she kicked the men around like they were tin soldiers. She made truly bizarre sounds, too, like forced gasps. And then..."

"Then?"

"Then more men came," she said sadly. "They drew guns on her. While I just stood there..."

"That's why you have her. She is meant to guard you, Grace."

"She does. Thank you for that."

He nuzzled the thin strap of her camisole over her shoulder.

Grace smiled, not stopping what she was doing. "Hold still, please."

He didn't listen, kissed her collarbone, and rubbed his nose against it.

"Patience," she said, chuckling, and added, "husband."

Slowly, he slid his hands to her ribs, tracing her delicate silhouette. "I can't."

He kept placing little kisses over any bare skin he could find, as she laughed through her nose.

"I've decided on the names," she said.

"What names, darling?" He tilted his head at her.

"Our children. Eva and Bron." She bit her lip, carefully cleaning his wounds. "Do you like the names?"

Was there anything he didn't like about her? Was anything better than a promised future with her? A whole life!

He couldn't stop looking at her, remembering. All those years of angst, of grieving her loss, then finding her again and protecting her from her past. Falling in love with her, despite trying not to. Keeping their past a secret, despite knowing that she deserved the truth.

And now she was telling him she wanted a future, had thought about it, dreamed about it...

"Do you like them?" she asked quietly.

His eyes misted with tears. He pressed his forehead to her shoulder. "Yes, darling. Anything you want."

Her slender fingers weaved into his hair, the gentlest touch yet. She kissed the top of his head.

"You saved my life," he said. "No getting rid of me now. You are stuck with me for life."

"Well, I can be resourceful when I am set on an idea."

"Of us?"

"Of Eva and Bron."

He laughed, lifting his head and meeting the most beautiful smile he'd ever seen.

But her laughter died out. Her chest rose as she took a deep breath, her gaze on him luminous with love.

"When I first saw you, years ago, I was scared," she said, resting her hands on his shoulders. Her eyes roamed his face. "When I married you, I was furious that you didn't give me a choice or let me pretend I had one."

His heart answered with a knowing beat—she was repeating his words from yesterday.

"When I first called you a tyrant, I lied. When you first had me, I was ashamed. Ashamed that I wanted more and was afraid to admit it. And I resisted you for as long as I could, because the day you said, 'the road from hate to love is a dark one' you were right. I thought the day I married you was the darkest in my life. Though I never hated you. Never! But I cannot remember the moment when I fell in love with you. Until the road with you by my side was blinding, with so much light. And I wanted to dissolve in it. Was scared that it would burn me, for I didn't know if you felt the same or if I was just a tool for some wicked revenge."

He shook his head. "No…"

"I know." She nodded. "I love you, Drasko."

She was love. She always had been and would continue to teach him what true love was.

"No matter what happens, Grace, and where life takes us, every minute with you is the biggest privilege and blessing, worth going through the worst pains."

She sniffled. "You will make me cry."

"I will shut up."

She kissed him. "Please, do. No more tears."

He smiled, his heart ready to burst. "No more tears," he whispered.

And for the first time, Drasko did not feel hate for the man who had put them through so much pain. Drasko felt like mourning him. With all his power and wealth, Uriah had been the poorest man alive. He had never known the biggest blessing —love.

Love was true power.

Love was patient, surviving decades.

And love was hurried, demanding it all in one night.

Love was pain at the brief thought of what could've happened to Grace.

And it was happiness when she cupped Drasko's face, ever so gently, and kissed his worries away.

Those who lived through it all understood that love was their soul, woven into the core of who they were. Perhaps, it grew old and quiet with age, but it echoed on the lips of their children who carried it on.

Shyly, Grace bit her lip. "I want every night with you, husband," she said, caressing his shoulders. "And mornings. And days. And—"

"You can have every minute of my every day," he breathed against her lips, "and I will still feel like I don't have enough."

"I love you," she whispered and kissed him. "I love you." She kissed him again. "I love you. I love you. I love you."

And he drowned in her love.

Between her kisses, he studied her face, every inch of it familiar yet new. Once, he'd promised her that he would show her the world and surround her with love. He had promised her she would be a queen. And now she was, *his* queen.

He brushed his fingers over the ashes on her camisole.

She looked down at the dirty fabric that he touched. "I look awful, don't I?"

"You do." He nodded.

"Huh?" She gave him a shocked stare.

"This thing covers too much," he explained, grinning, and slid the straps off her shoulder, letting the garment fall to the floor. "You look so much better without it."

The blush on her cheeks deepened. And then, keeping his hands off her became impossible.

He kissed her, pulling her flush against him.

"I am afraid I will hurt you," she murmured, trying not to touch his burn wounds.

"Then you shall have to do the work, darling."

He carried her to the bed, already eager to give her instructions, show her what to do, and see how far she would go this time.

She smiled between his kisses, that shy smile that made him weak with desire.

"Teach me how to leave you wanting more," she whispered. "So you never get tired of me."

He loved her—how naive she was about his feelings, even

more so about his patience with her. He had none. Not anymore. Not when she was so naked, so eager, so his.

"I don't need to teach you, Grace." He stroked her shoulder. "I want more all the time."

"I will not let you out of this bedroom for days, Mr. Mawr," she said softly, for the first time threatening him with a good time, her hands already more daring than they had ever been.

"Don't mistake me being injured for being weak." He grinned. "I will wreck you, Mrs. Mawr."

"I'd like that."

Rakshasa roared in triumph as Grace straddled him, taking charge, so unbelievably confident that it took his breath away.

And then it took away his sanity as she shifted lower, kissing down his body, her hand bravely stroking his hardness. And his dignity as her mouth took over where her hand had just been, and he moaned loudly under her lips, certain that he would walk through another fire and jeopardize his life if that was what turned his shy wife into a passionate lover.

She was making love to him. And he let her do what she wanted, instructing and guiding her, so aroused by his little lessons that he reached the intended destination in record time.

And then, despite the burns that stung his skin, he showed his wife his own idea of a symphony, with all its movements, allegros and andantes, trills and glissandos, until her body sang for him.

He kissed and worshiped and cherished her.

Breathless afterward, they lay in each other's arms, not bothering to cover themselves. Grace stretched her arm under his pillow, resting her head on it when she suddenly crinkled her brows.

She pulled her hand from under the pillow, a letter in it, the one he'd left there this morning.

"Another secret?" She gave it a curious glance and handed it to Drasko.

He shook his head. "It was for you. When I didn't know how the day would end."

Her smile waned, but she opened the letter.

"*It is you, Grace. It has always been you,*" she read out loud and paused, her eyes on the letter, her chest rising slowly in a deep inhale. "*The threads of time brought us together. We were bound by destiny. I never told you enough times how much I ached for you.*" She paused again and pursed her lips. "*But I hope this leaves you knowing that I was always yours, in love, in hate, in sickness. Even in death,*" she read in a voice that grew shaky. "*There is a beautiful word in Sanskrit—Samsara. It means rebirth. In another life, I will find you again. I will always find you,* meri jaan."

Tears pooled in her eyes when she met his gaze.

"Was that supposed to be a goodbye, Drasko?" she whispered. "This morning? You knew?"

He wanted to kneel before her, realizing the power of being capable of doing so for love, the one thing that the dead man had never understood and hadn't counted on.

"Don't you dare," Grace whispered, a tear sliding down her cheek. "Don't you dare ever say goodbye to me."

"Come here," he beckoned her and kissed the tear off her cheek, then planted little kisses on her forehead and eyelids. "I've got you, and I'm never letting you go."

She cupped his face. "You are a magnificent man, Drasko. With a beautiful heart. It's mine because my own heart will simply not survive without yours."

He stroked her hair. "You are my heart's keeper, Grace. My heart's Maestra."

There were a hundred ways he could phrase it, and it wouldn't be enough to explain what she meant to him.

She settled in his arms and drew invisible patterns on his chest, humming something barely audibly. She was happy— Drasko knew that hum.

"I am sorry it took me so long to tell you all the truths, Grace.

With time, you will know them all. Soon, I'd like to take you to the beautiful land that raised me."

"The country that gave birth to me, too."

"Yes. And I'd like you to meet my family, Asha and Rupesh. The man who made me think differently than Uriah and the woman who, a long time ago, was the only mother you ever knew."

"I would love to. I want to see the world with your eyes."

She smiled mischievously.

"What is it?" He nudged her.

"It's no wonder you were a thief, Drasko darling. A shameless thief." Her smile widened. "You stole my heart, and I didn't even notice."

He laughed and drew her into him for another kiss.

He was yet to spend a whole day in bed with his wife. That was a gift, indeed.

He closed his eyes and listened to her peaceful breathing, catching her little sighs and tiny movements.

And he listened to Rakshasa, then smiled and hummed one of Grace's songs.

For the first time in years, Rakshasa was quiet.

THE AUCTION

The newspaper headlines exploded the next day:

Up in Smoke!

Diamonds on Fire!

Benham Auction House in Ruins!

Diamond Tears: What Caused the Fire at the Most Dazzling Auction of the Decade.

What the public talked the most about in regards to the famous Mawr Auction wasn't the tragic loss of the world's most exquisite jewelry craftsmanship. Not even how the wealthy trampled each other to save their skins while Elias Bayne, the dashing captain, and the cleaning help at the auction house risked their own lives, guiding the mad crowd to safety.

Most talked about how several wealthy people jeopardized their well-being in attempts to claim their prizes in the fire.

Miraculously, there were no casualties.

Everything was, of course, insured by the auction.

But it wasn't a matter of money but the vanity with which the wealthy quarreled about the trophies and embarrassment when they lost them to a fire.

The word *diamond* was derived from the Greek word *adámas*, meaning unbreakable. Not many knew that fire was its biggest enemy.

Those present at the auction, the last ones to leave the burning building, told stories of the brilliant flashes of colors and the hypnotic blue flames flickering here and there through the blaze—as the thousands of diamonds seared under the high temperatures.

Most of the purest diamonds combusted, turning into carbon dioxide, disappearing like they'd never existed at all. Many turned into white, caked ugly stones, later re-polished, for which the rare art pieces had to be dismantled, turning into handfuls of much bleaker loose gems.

None of the art pieces survived in their glorious forms.

They said the marchioness wept at the street curb over her *Cupid's Spear*.

The banker's daughter refused to marry the French importer on account of losing her *Europa's Abductor* in the fire, and he came begging to Drasko Mawr to recreate it.

Many vowed to never wear diamonds again, a vow soon to be broken.

But the biggest story was that of the Duchess of Trent.

When the auction room burst into flames, she gaped, mesmerized, at the Crimson Tear, the flames reflected in its blood-shaded glow. While everyone rushed out of the room, the Duchess of Trent ran against the crowd, toward her treasure. Her dress caught on fire. So did her wig. The duke only yelled at her but hurriedly left the room, pushing past the others to safety.

The auction clerk who witnessed it all reported that the Duchess of Trent stepped into the flames as she made her way to the Crimson Tear. She clutched the diamond, finally, in her gloved hand that suddenly caught on fire. She screamed but did not let go. Tears of joy burst from her eyes at the sight of her prize. She stood among the flames, her skirt ablaze, a ghastly smile on her face as she held the Crimson Tear, oblivious of being burned alive.

The clerk dragged her out of the room, and she stood on a smoky street outside the collapsing building, still smiling, her charred wig and dress smoking, her eyes on the bloody sparkle of the Crimson Tear as if she were hypnotized by its sinister shine.

For the rest of her life, the Duchess of Trent would wear gloves to cover her fire-crippled hands. She would wear wigs to hide her singed scalp. But she would proudly tell the story of how the Crimson Tear had withstood the biggest fire of the nineties to be with its proud owner.

And of course, they talked about the Diamond King rushing into the blazing building.

For his diamonds, they first thought.

Until he reemerged among the flames like a majestic Phoenix, his partially burned clothes smoking, as he carried his wife in his arms. They said it was some Hindu magic that made him immortal and as strong as a diamond.

Franz Wollendorf gloated about the epic failure of the Mawr Auction, never speaking a word about his own part in the arson.

But not for long.

Since the Mawr artworks ceased to exist, the wealthy from all over the world started requesting custom orders of the pieces from the Mawr catalog, making the Mawr diamonds more in demand than ever.

Shortly, Drasko would agree to a business merger, not with the Wollendorfs but with his long-term partners in India, keeping his ownership in the land that was the start of it all.

And Grace?

Grace would keep on playing. For Drasko, for their friends, for her servants. And of course, for Eva and Bron.

EPILOGUE
LONDON, ENGLAND

Four years later...

"This is magnificent!" Grace exclaimed to Drasko, her face lifted to the façade of the building in front of them as they stood on its steps.

The Grace Music Academy had opened its doors a year earlier and was once again mobbed with reporters on account of it being issued a royal charter.

Drasko owned a jewelry gallery, a casino, several restaurants, an automobile factory, multiple science labs, and a pharmaceutical company. He was everywhere. Except one place. The music world, his wife's favorite.

Until now.

Several dozen boys and girls, the first students of the academy, offered their beaming smiles as they stood shoulder to shoulder next to Julien d'Auvergne, the academy's director.

John Papadakis, Drasko's main public representative and assistant, gave the reporters the official statement.

"The program is the first such music program implemented

in England," Papadakis said proudly. "For talented children, including the ones from underprivileged families. Boys and girls alike. Please, note that. Yes, thank you. We have agents who look for such individuals all across England. We run auditions. As for the expenses, please, write this down, yes, the expenses are all covered. Including the accommodation and instruments. The program is supported by numerous benefactors, including the Duke and Duchess of Trent." The Bankee Syndicate was, of course, omitted. "And today we are celebrating the Grace Music Academy being issued a royal charter by the Queen. It is absolutely wonderful—"

"This is a great use of diamonds, I suppose," Drasko murmured to Grace as they stood back, avoiding being mobbed with questions.

"Absolutely the best!" Grace beamed at him, her hand wrapping tighter around his forearm.

The revenue from the astonishing number of commissions for the Mawr jewelry art after the infamous Benham Auction had covered the construction of the building a year prior. The number of benefactors who wanted to associate themselves with the Mawrs was staggeringly high.

"Education is becoming a trend. And that is, my dears, the most wonderful change in history," commented the Duchess of Trent during the academy opening.

It had been four years since the wedding, and it had completely changed Drasko's life. He was spending more time with his scientists and made frequent trips to America for industrial research. He had sponsored the brightest minds and lured the biggest talents in the fields of physics and engineering to London. The city finally felt like home. It was home to his favorite people and the woman who, four years into their marriage, still caused his heart to flutter in awe.

"You are getting old," Elias often joked during such conversations.

"I am happy," Drasko countered with a broad smile.

The Chicago's World's Fair in America three years prior had been the most extraordinary trip Drasko had ever taken. Besides being a remarkable example of architectural design, arts, music, and industrial innovations, it was the first time Grace had gone overseas, the first time they had traveled together since their childhoods.

On their way back, Grace was nauseous on account of being with child. *Children,* to be exact. Bron and Eva, just like she wanted, two at once. Grace had gotten her way. Conveniently, her ways always aligned with Drasko's. And when his children turned one, he took them to the tower, stood proudly on the observation deck, both of them in his arms, and studied London beneath them.

"Look," he said proudly. "This is your city."

The Mawrs had continued to make headlines. This time, with Mawr technological innovations, their first automobile, the electric street cars, and an ambitious promise to build the first powered aircraft in the future.

Of course, Grace hadn't ceased to amaze the public with her music.

Just like today as the city gathered in front of the steps of the Grace Music Academy.

Rupesh, Asha, and their daughter had arrived in London several months prior. They now stood by Drasko's side, studying the façade with admiration, never ceasing to be amazed by all things Western.

Rivka was here, of course, pursing her lips to hide a smile as she observed her husband talking to some of the reporters.

Zeph was cordial and reserved as he gave the prepared speech, puffing on his cigarette and occasionally fixing his bowtie. "As the representative of the Lord Mayor of London, I want to pass on his words that the mission of this city is to educate those who cannot afford it and give opportunities to those who are less privileged. Talent is a key that should be able to open many doors. Beauty finds itself in many forms.

And it should find its way into every person's life, regardless of rank or status. Beauty is a gift, and those who have the means should share it with those who don't. We are here for it."

When he was done, he walked to his wife, his eyes searching hers for approval. "How did I do?"

Rivka smiled. "To think that a man like you is a patron of the arts."

"My love, we men of the darker trade have a soft heart for all things beautiful," said Zeph with a grin and kissed her hand, then proudly puffed his chest as he met Drasko's eyes.

Drasko only snorted, thinking that he should tease his friend about the talk they had once had in the Elysium.

Zeph's ideas about marriage and family had changed drastically since Rivka had declined his marriage proposal twice. But then there was Zeph's several-month binge, singing drunk serenades outside Rivka's house, and an attack on her life by a jealous stalker who had stabbed Zeph, and Zeph had almost died. He had claimed that Rivka's healing hands had brought him back to life and announced celibacy for the rest of his life if she didn't marry him, which had become a joke among the Bankees.

And then Rivka had given in. During their wedding, she had secretly shared with Drasko the content of the numerous letters Zeph had written to her.

To this day, Drasko didn't believe his friend had indeed written about "the light of my eyes," and "the healing touch that unraveled my hardened heart and brought the strings of affection to life."

But love had done stranger things to men.

Now, Zeph advocated for the arts.

Indeed, one of the first students in the academy was an eight-year-old boy from a tavern in St. Giles that Zeph had brought to Drasko's house one day.

"I tell you, brother, I listened to him for months. He is like that—what do you call him, that fella, the devil's violinist? Ah, Paganini. Right."

And Zeph was right. Because when the boy performed on his scruffy violin at the Mawrs' house, even the guards crossed themselves in awe. When he was given Julien's violin and performed again, Julien muttered under his breath, "The devil, indeed."

That same boy now stood among the students of the academy.

The press conference over, Grace was preoccupied with the arrangements for the gala.

In the evening, a concert was held to celebrate the royal charter.

The orchestra of the world-famous Winslow Tuck was led by Grace Mawr on the piano.

The Queen attended. So did the Duke and Duchess of Trent, the duchess donning the necklace with the infamous Crimson Tear.

The Brodias sat in the private loge next to the royal one, with Inigo Handley and his wife next to them. Handley was now the Lord Mayor Of London, while Zeph was in charge of the Bankee Syndicate. Outside the music loges, the royal guards stood shoulder-to-shoulder with the Bankee ones. These were, indeed, interesting times.

In the loge next to theirs sat Drasko with a flower bouquet on his lap. Rupesh and Asha sat to his right. Elias and Julien were to his left.

Julien nervously fixed his purple bowtie, then tapped his fingers on his knee, his eyes on the empty stage. It was the first time the American conductor had performed with the female lead.

Glancing at Julien's fingers, Elias covered them with his palm.

"You sure are more anxious about the upcoming performance than the performer herself," Elias said with a soft smile.

Julien exhaled heavily through his puffed lips.

Elias tipped his head toward him as he talked to Drasko. "The man is more nervous about his protégé performing than he was being trapped during the fire at the World's Columbian Exposition."

Elias and Julien had indeed joined Drasko and Grace on the trip to America, and then briefly, Grace had lost her instructor to Borneo, where Elias took him for a two-month trip around the Orient.

Drasko only glanced at Julien with a smile, his eyes returning to the stage.

When the members of the orchestra stepped on the stage and to their respective seats, the public broke out in loud applause.

Winslow Tuck's appearance caused another round of applause. The man with a thick mane of hair and bushy side-burns bowed with a knowing smile. He studied the audience over his glasses, then simply gestured toward one of the stage entrances.

And when Grace Mawr walked out, in a simple beige dress, with a soft modest smile, the entire music hall rose to their feet and the applause reverberated against the marble walls.

She was, as always, magnificent, performing Tchaikovsky's Concerto No. 1, haunting, sensual, and epic. It was an homage to Julien's idol, the Russian musical genius who had passed recently, leaving the music world grieving.

One would think the lead performer, the orchestra, and the conductor were all it took to perfect a musical masterpiece.

Drasko knew differently.

Besides many months and hundreds of hours?

It took sixteen of their personal service staff, twenty-five guards, and dozens of Bankees, for whom Grace had performed the solo part several times.

Bron and Eva, of course—Grace had performed for them separately, and Drasko concluded after the crying fit that Bron had thrown in the middle of the second movement that Bron was definitely an Albéniz lover.

Asha had spent numerous evenings sitting at the back of the music room and listening to Grace play, brushing off occasional happy tears.

"Do you think you have it all now?" Rupesh had asked Drasko one night.

"I have all I need, *bhaiya*," Drasko had replied, "all I need. And now you are here, too."

Drasko had lost count of how many times he had listened to Tchaikovsky's Concerto No. 1. In the music room, out in the grand hall, even outside, standing by the windows to the music room, for Grace was convinced that he had to hear it from afar and tell her if there were faults in her movement transitions.

She didn't have any faults. She was simply perfect.

It was peculiar how much Drasko had gotten used to her music in the last years, yet, every time he heard her perform on stage, it was riveting, taking his breath away, transporting him across the years of his life, making him relive the memories and feelings, happy and sad, exhilarating and devastating. The orchestra, its sounds and chords, were almost tangible like a living creature, that took the audience for a breathtaking emotional ride.

When the performance was over, the audience demanded an encore.

Grace obliged. She always did.

But this time, the orchestra members rose to their feet and left the stage. Instead, twenty-two boys and girls walked out and proudly took their respective seats at the instruments.

They played one of Albéniz's pieces under Grace's lead, not nearly as intricate, but when they finished performing, the hall erupted in applause.

Someone in Zeph's loge whistled loudly.

On stage, Grace and Maestro Winslow Tuck stepped back,

motioning for the children to step to the front, and the entire music hall leapt up to their feet.

Zeph and Rebecca were already outside their loge as Drasko stepped out of his.

"Phew! What a ride," Elias said. "And the children! Can you imagine what they will achieve in another year? In five!"

Zeph's lips curled in a little smirk as his eyes met Drasko's. "It's amazing what street children can learn given a chance."

"Indeed." Drasko chuckled.

"Grace was magnificent," Rivka said.

"As always," Julien agreed proudly.

"Congratulations," said Elias to Drasko.

"It has nothing to do with me. My wife, on the other hand, is a gift."

"She has gotten me to fall in love with music," Zeph said, lighting a cigar. "Tchaikovsky is not bad, but too heavy for my taste. Albéniz, on the other hand…"

Drasko nodded. "Terrific, agreed. *Rapsodia Cuban* in G major especially. My wife can do G major like no one else."

Zeph broke out in laughter. "Nothing like a wife with skillful hands." He kissed Rivka's hand and winked at her.

"Pardon me." Drasko adjusted the bouquet in his hands. "I have to go see my wife."

Downstairs, he heard a little girl talking to her family. "Mother, I want to be like Grace Mawr."

"But you are beautiful, too," her mother said.

"No! I want to play for the world. She is so much better than Ceritelli!"

"She is not," a boy next to her argued.

"She is too! And all those men play under her lead. And she is a woman." She stuck her tongue out at the boy. "One day, I shall be like her. And people shall cry."

"In agony, perhaps," the boy answered bitterly, making Drasko smile to himself.

Emotions, indeed, ran high among the audience. Some sang

praises to the establishment that had inspired several others to be opened across England. Others, mostly women, pressed handkerchiefs to their teary eyes at the joy of seeing a woman being praised by the greatest men, though they didn't quite understand the significance of it.

The admirers crowded the aisles and the access to the stage, exchanged whispers, and craned their necks trying to catch a glimpse of Grace.

Drasko's heart warmed at the sight of her. Even after the blinding success, she was humble. She always took time to talk to the public before she retreated backstage.

And Drasko was already there, in her dressing room.

This was where they had parted before her performance. They had talked, and then Grace had sat in silence for some time, not touching the upright piano but replaying parts of the concert piece in her mind. Then she had kissed him goodbye and left. And Drasko had gone to his private loge, for he preferred to hear her play with the rest of the audience.

This was their little ritual.

And Drasko was in her dressing room again.

Soon, Grace hurried through the door, her eyes burning like stars, her smile so big it made his heart clench with pride.

"How was it?" she asked, stepping into his arms.

For a moment, just like every time, he closed his eyes and inhaled her scent, flowers and perfume and love and happiness and that peculiar yet by now familiar scent of other people and instruments, leather and polished wood and metal. He drowned in the so-beloved sounds trickling through the dressing room door—the little pecks in the air, the percussions and drums, the holsters being buttoned up, and heavy cases set down as the orchestra packed their instruments.

And then there was the taste of her lips when she kissed him, the second kiss of the night, the first being the "good luck" one before the performance. Drasko was always the first and the last one on her music journey on stage.

"How are the children?" she inquired, not stepping away but wrapping her hand around his neck and studying him. Her other hand stroked his hair in gentle rhythmical movements, as if by inertia continuing to play.

"They caused quite a racket when I was leaving the house," Drasko said. "They always do. So vocal. By god, I hope they have your melodic voice when they grow up."

Grace laughed, and he couldn't hold back a grin.

This woman was a fighter, a heart-whisperer, a mother, a wife, a friend, and now a teacher. And though her music belonged to everyone, she belonged to him. If someone asked him what was the biggest treasure in the world, he would smile and motion to his wife.

The assistant director popped his head in to let her know that the reporters were waiting for the interview, and she had an audience with the Queen.

She nodded but didn't move away from Drasko.

"Did you like it?" she asked quietly as if there was a chance he ever *not* liked her performances.

"Absolutely, darling."

"Truly?"

"It was approved by Bron and Eva before. So…"

She broke out in laughter again.

"Guess who approached me before the performance?"

She raised her brows in question. "Tell me?"

"Signore Baldeschi."

Grace scrunched up her brows in annoyance.

Drasko smiled mysteriously. "He asked me if you would fancy playing at the Rome Symphony Orchestra."

"Asked *you*, not *me*."

"Perhaps, he is afraid of you. Or ashamed."

"And I have a feeling it has something to do with you."

"Me?"

She narrowed her eyes at Drasko in suspicion. "He had refused me before, you know it. Multiple times."

"Well, he is thrilled now. Yes, I had a chat with him." Drasko smiled, rubbing his nose against hers.

She pulled away and ducked her head to meet his eyes. "What did you do now, Drasko?"

"I simply talked to him."

"Drasko?" she warned.

"Yes, darling?" He gave her the most innocent look.

"You bribed him!"

"No."

"Blackmailed?"

"No. I might have accidentally pulled too hard on one of those talented fingers of his. You know pianists and their fingers. So sensitive."

"Drasko!" she whined. "You can't just harass people left and right."

"Darling, it's called politics. I was very, very amiable. And it is not all about you."

"Oh!"

"A woman with the grand master. On stage. An equal. You already conquered England. It's time to move forward. You underestimate yourself. Baldeschi approached *me*. He did. He knows he is losing an opportunity with the most celebrated musician in London. And he is too slow catching up with the latest trends. He might be old, but he is not stupid. So there. No bribing. No blackmailing. It was entirely his game. And yes, he would love to meet with you."

"Hmm," she hummed hesitantly.

"You are setting an example, Grace. For other women to pursue their passions," Drasko said, swelling with adoration that quickly changed into mischief. "And I am not talking about the bedroom."

A smile broke out on her lips. "Ooooh, you—"

"Though I know it's your favorite place."

"Drasko Mawr!" she warned.

"I am surprised you don't play any wind instruments."

"Pardon me?"

"Considering how talented your mouth is, it would do wonders—"

"Drasko!"

Laughing, she tried to push him away, but he pulled her into him and gave her a soft kiss on her cheek.

Grace was always a little wound up after she performed, still nervous though she never showed it. Often, she would take her time in the dressing room after the performance, sit in silence by herself, and recap, worrying about the mistakes she'd made, the missed keys, the little hiccups, though no one had ever noticed those except her.

And Drasko had found the ways to ease her self-doubt. With jokes and flirting and random news—anything to soothe her troubled mind. The public didn't know that even the biggest talents occasionally felt like imposters.

Drasko cherished these moments the most. When her smiling eyes studied him, her hands on his chest as she took a moment of silence before flitting away to the reporters and important guests and the benefactors.

Later, there would be an audience with the Queen, then a gala with the Americans and the students, the Brodias and the Baynes, and dozens of people who had become dear friends over the years.

And late into the night, Drasko and Grace would return home, tiptoe to their children's room and watch them like thieves for several minutes, then kiss them goodnight and retreat to their bedroom.

Drasko would tell Grace all about who said what during the event, and the gossips, and she would talk about the next day, perhaps, the ride they would take into the country, or a visit they would pay. They would discuss trivial things as she would slowly undress before him, and so would he, until her hands would be on him and she would silence him with her insistent kisses, and then he wouldn't be able to talk at all, the two of them making each other's bodies hum with the melodies only they could understand.

There would be passionate love-making, intense and occasionally rough as it often was after her performances, as if she tried to ease the tension that had accumulated for days before it.

She would fall asleep in his arms.

Drasko? He would lay for some time staring at the shadows playing on the ceiling, the moon glow casting dim light onto her face. And he would send praises to the universe that had gifted him *her*.

But right now, in the dressing room, he was too aware of dozens of people backstage, hundreds waiting outside to catch a glimpse of her.

Tonight, he had to share her with the rest.

"It is the fate of great women," a man once said. "They have the power to change the world. Their duty is with the people. And so they can't truly belong to one man."

The man was no other than Zeph Brodia, the most sentimental Bankee and the most sensual gangster Drasko knew. But what man in love wasn't? Zeph, of course, referred to his gifted wife he worshiped.

And so Drasko studied Grace for another long moment, making sure her post-performance worries were gone.

"You should go," he said. "They need you."

"Yes." She smiled. "I shall meet you outside."

She was about to take a step away when he pulled her toward him again. "You were perfect, darling. Absolutely perfect."

And she smiled and cupped his face and rose on her tiptoes to kiss him. "So are you," she said, then added in a whisper, "Thank you."

BONUS CONTENT

Subscribe to Kahany's newsletter to receive the **BONUS CHAPTER** from *THE DIAMOND KING*:
www.vladkahany.com

AUTHOR'S NOTE:

Thank you for reading *THE DIAMOND KING*.

Even bigger thanks to those who have patiently waited for this book for almost two years.

If you are curious about some of the characters mentioned in the book, please, read the following:

THE TENDER TOUCH OF NIGHT (a standalone romance and book #2 in *The Belle House* series) is the story about the Bankees, how they started and gained power in London, as well as the story about Frank "Lucky" Handley, one of their leaders, and Maude "Ginger" Daly, a courtesan he falls madly in love with.

Elias Bayne is the son of Ivor Bayne, one of the Bayne brothers from my *Rebels of Gracewyck* series.

Thanks to the readers who spread the word about my books and message me with kind words. Your support means the world to me!

Thanks to Tracy, my editor, and to Linda, for proofreading.

Big thanks to Meghna H. Baba, if it weren't for you, I would

AUTHOR'S NOTE:

have never found out what India truly is, and this book would have not turned out the way it did.

Thanks to my mom, who made me go to a music school when I was a child and encouraged me to travel to India. Look where it got the readers, mom...

And, most of all, thanks to K for spending hours listening to my ramblings about diamonds and for having to look at dozens of book cover versions. Love, your patience with me is astounding.

Kahany,
February 25, 2024

ALSO BY THIS AUTHOR: